FLAME OUT

ALSO BY M. P. COOLEY

Ice Shear

FLAME
OUT

M. P. COOLEY

WM
WILLIAM MORROW
An Imprint of HarperCollins*Publishers*

Excerpt from "Fancy" by Jehanne Dubrow reproduced from *Prairie Schooner* 84.4 (Winter 2010) by permission of the University of Nebraska Press. Copyright © 2010 by the University of Nebraska Press.

HarperCollins books may be purchased for educational, business, or sales promotional use. For information please e-mail the Special Markets Department at SPsales@harpercollins.com.

FIRST EDITION

Designed by Jamie Lynn Kerner

Art on title page © by Trifonenko Ivan. Orsk

Library of Congress Cataloging-in-Publication Data has been applied for.

ISBN 978-0-06-230073-7

15 16 17 18 19 OV/RRD 10 9 8 7 6 5 4 3 2 1

For Bridget and Mary

A stranger drowned on the Black Sea alone,
with no one to hear his prayers for forgiveness.

—"STORM ON THE BLACK SEA,"
UKRAINIAN TRADITIONAL SONG

Each morning my mother's velvet purse
wilted on a chair, empty of midnight contents:
ruby lipstick, tiny lake of a pocket mirror.

—"FANCY," JEHANNE DUBROW

CHAPTER 1

THE RAIN WAS UNFORGIVING.

Dave was doing a lousy job of holding up his half of the house. My arms strained under the weight of his niece's birthday gift—a large backyard playhouse—and it was slow going back to my car. The spring rain had soaked through the layers of cardboard, and my knuckles scraped against the hard red plastic panels where the box disintegrated.

"You know," I said, "that spin-art kit would've fit in the back seat with room to spare." I hefted the playhouse, shoving it hard, but it jammed against my trunk's lockbox, which held my service revolver. "And I bet Tara would've had a lot of fun with the costume trunk."

"My niece isn't a princess dress kind of girl."

I stopped short as a red Subaru sped past, spraying the back of my legs with water. "The kit includes fake mustaches and Groucho eyebrows. She could wear those with the glittery pink sandals."

"Until she trips and breaks her skull. Blood. Everywhere." He reversed, backing the box into the trunk. "Can you lift your left side a little higher?" I raised it up to my shoulders.

"That's the trick," he said.

It wasn't the trick, and the edge slipped out of my hand and dropped to the ground.

"You. Out of my way," I said. He stepped aside, defeated. The steady rain flattened his black curls, and the wet white box smeared the arms of his Jets windbreaker with saturated cardboard. I balanced one side of the box on the edge of the trunk, and using leverage, shoved most of it in. The trunk wouldn't close, so I bungeed the top to protect it from the rain, not that it mattered at this point. I ran around front and climbed into my dry car, starting the engine to get the heat going, and unlocked the door for Dave, who made a distinct squelching sound as he dropped into the passenger seat.

"I hate to tell you," I said as I backed the car out of the spot, "but Tara won't be very impressed with a big soggy box."

"She'll be *very* impressed with a big soggy box because she and her dad will have a project," Dave said. "Is it too late to go back to get the kiddie tool set?"

"Yes." I pulled out, bouncing through a pothole. My thirteen-year-old Saturn was close to the end of its life. "Yes, it is."

"Yeah, and she wouldn't go for the kiddie version anyway. I should remember to buy her gift at Home Depot next year."

I drove slowly out of the packed lot and negotiated the traffic circle, passing the exits for Colonie, Latham, and Cohoes. I missed the Hopewell Falls exit and was forced to loop around a second time. Dave snorted.

On the outskirts of town we passed St. Agnes Cemetery, where my husband lay buried. In the first year after he died I would've insisted we stop. In the second year, I would've taken the drive through the cemetery so I could see his grave. This year, I thought a message to him: "Miss you, babe. See you on Thursday. Wait until you hear Lucy's theory on where babies come from. She's definitely your daughter." I would never cut the thread to Kevin.

The landscape crested, dropping into the city below. Hopewell Falls was all downhill. The Mohawk River bounded the city on the east and the Hudson on the south, the waterfall that formed where the two rivers met giving the town its name. Through newly sprouting trees and mist from the rain, I could make out my own house in the distance. Dad was babysitting Lucy while I helped Dave and worked the three to eleven p.m. patrol. In this weather, I wished I were at home. There would be plenty of car accidents tonight, but the bigger threat were those people trapped inside on a Saturday with their "loved ones," drunk, and if I was very unlucky, armed.

The streets got twisty the closer we got to the river. We stopped at a light, waiting to cross Interstate 787 and beyond that, the short bridge that spanned a small waterway, the last remains of the Mohawk River before it joined the mighty Hudson.

Dave was frowning, his eyes on the Ukrainian church, its gold and sky-blue dome bright against the gloomy afternoon sky.

I touched his arm. "You OK?"

"Never better, Lyons." He shook off my hand. Something must be wrong—I spent most of my time extricating myself from the hugs, pats, and leans Dave used with everyone, but especially me.

"You sure? It's only a birthday party. You're too late to be forced into pin the tail on the donkey. And if you really wanted to escape, you could take my shift for me . . . put on the blues, drive around for eight hours."

"Uh, huh."

"And your brother's doing better." His brother, Lucas, had been unemployed for a while and had divorced again for the fourth time last year, leading to a drunk-and-disorderly charge outside his most recent ex-wife's house. Thankfully, the arrest scared Lucas straight.

"Lucas is doing great, although his plan is to score points off his ex today. I guess Felicia threw a roller-skating extravaganza for Tara's school friends, and Lucas insisted on throwing a second party for all the kids from the church. I'm expecting balloon animals."

"So?"

"So what?"

"So why are you tense?"

He didn't answer. The light changed to green, and in less than ten seconds we had crossed the highway and the bridge from the mainland to the Island.

"It's just, the Island's so closed off," Dave said finally. I stifled a laugh. Annexed by the same Dutch settler who farmed Hopewell Falls back in the sixteenth century, DeWulf Island was hardly some isolated outpost. The channel separating the mainland from the Island was narrow enough that I could probably cross it with a running jump, and if I followed the main thoroughfare we'd be in Troy in another half mile. Instead of taking the straight shot across the Hudson, I veered right, passing a series of side-by-sides, apartments built by the Ukrainian and Polish immigrants who had fled first the Soviets, then the Nazis, and then the Soviets again. The remains of the Golden Wheat bakery, burned down two years ago, lay on our left, and we passed a small Polish grocery that sold Cheetos, Cokes, frozen pierogies, and pickled beets.

"Left here," Dave said, and we turned onto a street populated with more trees than houses, plants lush with the recent spring rains. The street dead-ended at a modest home surrounded by several acres of land. The home's façade was brick with a white porch and black shutters. Purple balloons swung wildly in the breeze, and four cars were parked out front. The bench on the front porch was freshly painted, and a lilac bush sprang up on the lawn, trimmed and blooming. We were at Lucas's house. Or rather, his Aunt Natalya's.

Dave and I wrestled the playhouse up the narrow walk to the front door and rang the bell. Lucas greeted us, beer in hand.

"Jesus, Davey. Did you have to be so late?" he said. "And Aunt Natalya'll kill you if you sprinkle dirty cardboard through the house. Oh, hi, June." He stepped outside and dropped his beer on the arm of the bench, picking up my end of the box. He got a good look at the contents for the first time and grimaced.

"Oh, wonderful. A construction project of my very own."

Matching Dave's 6'4", Lucas was fairer than his brother, his light brown hair sporting some gray, straight, and almost fine. He'd worked construction for over twenty years until suffering a vague injury involving a lot of Vicodin. His new work as a bartender agreed with him. Dave and Lucas bickered about the gift as they walked around the house to the backyard where the party was in full swing.

Backyard was perhaps an understatement. Dave jokingly called it the back forty, and it wasn't a complete exaggeration, the lot extending north three acres. The lawn had room for a two-tiered bouncy house and a swing set. Beyond that was a garden that could produce enough fruits and vegetables to feed everyone on the Island, with sunflowers sprouting along the border between the cultivated plot and the meadow near the property's far border.

Despite all the wide-open space, the adults were grilling and eating on the porch, clustered under the small green tin awning to stay out of the rain. The bouncy castle's turret listed to the left, the weight of the water pooling on the roof about to send the structure sideways. A bunch of kids flinging themselves against the sides didn't help. I was pretty sure this birthday party was going to end in tears, either with the puffed-up monstrosity tipping sideways or the kids being told no, really, they needed to come in.

"Dad!" the birthday girl shouted, "the roof's caving in!"

Lucas Batko handed the box back to me. "This is going to be a disaster," he said as he jogged across the lawn to the castle that was wiggling like a basket of puppies. On the way he picked up a toy axe lying on the ground outside the door. Squeals sounded as he entered the inflatable structure, and the castle surged and rolled as Lucas trudged across the inflated floor, designed for a 50-pound child, not a 200-pound man. He took the axe handle and pressed up on the roof, sending the water from the first turret splashing over the side. Dave and I maneuvered up the steps to the porch.

Dave's Aunt Natalya intercepted us. She moved rapidly despite her pronounced limp, twisting her left hip forward before propelling the right foot in front.

"David, how could you! Forcing June to march through muddy grass with a heavy box." Dave told me she had been in the US since the late 1940s but her Ukrainian accent hung heavy on the edge of her words, her *g*'s lapsing into *h*'s, dropping articles left and right. Small and sharp eyed, her black hair laced with gray, Natalya rested her hands on her uneven hips, the left a few inches higher than the right. "You are no gentleman."

Dave had to fold in half to give his aunt a kiss. "That's not news to Lyons, *teta*."

Dave and I dropped the house on the ground in front of the gift table, and Dave took a green polka-dotted bow out of his pocket and slapped it on the corner. Natalya frowned, but it wasn't at the gift-wrapping.

"Showing up your brother with your big gift?"

Dave held up his hands in surrender. "Can't compete with a bike, *teta*."

Despite being almost eighty, Natalya yanked me toward her, pulling me into a hug. I could smell hairspray and powder, the two things that kept her fresh and presentable in the damp weather.

"Food now," she said. "The children stuff themselves with junk Lucas purchased"—she eyed the pizza rolls with distaste—"but I grilled sausage and have salad from greens I picked myself."

Dave hooked Natalya's hand through his arm. "Good idea. Lyons starts busting stuff up if you don't feed her."

Dave prepared our lunches under Natalya's careful direction. He came back with two plates piled with perfectly grilled kielbasa, dumplings, and salad, a pizza roll balanced on top, with a beer in his hand and a bottle of water tucked in his elbow. We settled in a few chairs near the edge of the porch.

"Hail the conquering hero," Dave said to his brother as he returned, tipping his beer at him. Lucas reached out and grabbed it, taking a swig. Dave's protests were hard to make out with the dumpling shoved in his mouth.

"Good, right?" Dave said. It was delicious. The pierogies were homemade, and the sausage, grilled perfectly, came from a local butcher who made his own. Heavy fare, but delicious.

Dave said between mouthfuls of dumpling, "Aunt Natalya picked out the best food on the table for you."

"Yeah," Lucas said. "She's always trying to butter up Dave's girlfriends."

Dave choked on his pierogi. "I have no idea where she got that idea."

"Wishful thinking on her part." Lucas pulled out a lighter. "I'd better go. We were holding the cake until Tara's favorite uncle got here"—Dave saluted as Lucas continued—"and since he's deigned to grace us with his presence, I better try to get the candles lit before her next birthday."

"Get me another beer, will ya?" Dave called to his brother, but Lucas was already inside. Dave knocked his knuckles against mine. "You're going on shift, but you want one?"

At my no, Dave went to grab one for himself. I dug into my meal.

I was almost done when Dave broke my food reverie. "Me and Special Agent Bascom grabbed a beer last night."

"You and Hale?" I said.

"Yep. I invited the G-man over today. Once I told him about the bouncy house, he signed right up."

I wiped my mouth, preparing to escape before Hale arrived.

"What's your hurry? You two buried the hatchet."

"Mostly." I collected my trash and stood to go. "He's still a shark, but a friendly one." What I didn't want to tell Dave was that I was avoiding Hale because he was chasing me for an answer: Was I or was I not going to consult with the FBI? It had been almost four years since I left, and I wasn't sure if I wanted to rejoin. What's more, I couldn't figure out why they would want me. Why Hale might want me.

As I was about to say my good-byes, Lucas came out with the biggest cake I'd seen this side of my wedding. Scratch that, it was bigger. A princess sat on top, the highest tier making up her skirt, pink and detailed with icing and candy, surrounded by four birthday candles. Below lay her kingdom, the tiers decorated with characters from the *Dora the Explorer* TV show.

"Tara, come up and blow out your candles!" Lucas called. The kids were slow to leave the bouncy house, and Lucas started to pace, beer in hand, checking to see that the candles were still lit while yelling for Tara to hurry.

"Calm down a little," Dave said to his brother. "Let me get her."

Dave pretended to be a giant and said he was going to eat slow children, and the kids came running up the steps and were corralled into singing. At first deliriously happy, the birthday girl began to cry when they went to cut the cake.

"But it's pretty!" Tara said. I worried that Lucas would get upset by the tears but instead he scooped her into his arms, kissing her on both cheeks, and promised to cut *around* the toys dotting the top.

Natalya intercepted me as I was leaving. "You must take leftovers to your friends at police station."

She wasn't kidding about leftovers. By the time I got the four trays loaded into my trunk, I only had forty-five minutes until my shift. Between changing into my uniform, getting a shift report, spreading out the food in the break room, and fighting my way past the crush of people who heard that Dave's aunt had sent some of her homemade dumplings, time ended up being tight. Once I got people started on their food coma, I hit the road.

There were no calls, and I kept my eyes on the sidewalk as much as the roads as I drove, watching for irregularities. In the past, I'd caught a fair number of criminals at or leaving the scene—I'd stopped someone trying to haul two meat slicers and a peppered ham from the butcher shop on Thursday of last week. Paying attention was my business.

As I turned onto Reed Way, the cruiser skidded gently on the pebbled road. I smelled the problem first, an odor of gasoline dampening out the scent of spring grass. As I approached the long-dormant Sleep-Tite Factory, it got worse. Unfortunately, arson was a too-common occurrence in this area. There's nothing to steal—the companies went bankrupt or moved to China decades ago—but bored teenagers or professional firebugs chasing an insurance payment regularly set them on fire. No private industry had replaced the factories, and cities razed them for public safety, paving over the land. I called it in as a fire, because if it wasn't one, it would be soon. I sped up and pulled into the parking lot, far enough away that any fire wouldn't destroy the cruiser if this thing got big.

I ran toward the factory through a Day-Glo blue-green slick of gasoline that trailed over the lawn and the sidewalk, across the street, and toward the river, fire extinguisher in hand. Smoke was light, bare wisps lacing the air, but the air was heavy with fuel, and I adjusted my breathing so I wouldn't get lightheaded. My cruiser became obscure—the gasoline fumes warping the late-afternoon light. Even the sirens, hazy in the distance, sounded distorted, their rise and fall hiccuping, half caught behind the veil of gasoline fumes. From my radio, I could hear Lorraine, the dispatcher, calling out for emergency responders: police, ambulances, fire trucks, everyone.

"10-50," Lorraine said, steady and insistent, giving the code for fire. "10-50."

The factory had closed twenty-five years before, long enough that the boards used to cover the holes in the windows had holes themselves. One of the regular places on my beat, it was usually locked. Today the chain hung loose from a door handle, the padlock cut. There were two fifteen-foot sliding metal doors. I pushed them wide, and they slid easily, opening up onto the factory floor.

The room was empty except for a still-running van, which had "CAR F" stenciled across its door in what looked like primer paint. The vehicle's back door flung wide, a path of gasoline splashed from the back of the truck, across the floor, to the far door. Fire engulfed the far side of the building, a burning mattress now blazing, fed by the oxygen coming from the holes in the ceiling and the roof beyond. The blaze followed a distinct route where a trail of gasoline wound across a floor white with pigeon droppings, the path sparking and then dying swiftly without any kindling. Gasoline fires burn fast and bright, dying almost as soon as they spark, but the flames advanced toward the van and beyond that, a pile of textiles, fabric discarded by the last tenants. It was beyond me and my fire extinguisher.

Based on the volume of the sirens, the fire trucks were a few blocks away, and I backed up toward the entrance. The flames darted under the van, scorching the edge but otherwise leaving it untouched. The fire reached the fabric pile. I could see the edges spark before the whole thing caught fire, flames shooting straight up twenty feet, hitting the wooden ceiling beams. It sent out a painful blast of heat, singeing my hair even thirty feet away. A *whooshing* sound blew through, the fire consuming the oxygen, followed almost immediately by a scream.

Out of the flames rose a woman.

She stepped out of the heart of the blaze and spun frantically left and then right, trying to get free of the fire encircling her, the bright light mapping her thrashing in the air. I ran toward her. The smoke got heavy. I ducked low and pulled off my coat, ready to extinguish the flames. I needn't have bothered—by the time I reached her, her clothes had almost completely burned away, and she stood in front of me tiny and exposed, red skin blackened with soot, hair burned off. Through the smoke, the factory's doors appeared distant and almost unreachable, and I picked her up and moved toward the faint light shining from the exit. She screamed, loud and long.

"I'm sorry, I'm sorry, ma'am," I said. No question she weighed less than a hundred pounds, but my knees strained, and I had to break left as the fire broke right. Under the crackle of the flames I could make out the drip of gasoline down through the wood floors below us, the steady trickle counting off every second I stayed in the building. I gave a heave and went faster.

With the smoke and her screaming I'd missed the firefighters' arrival. Four were dragging a hose into the building. Two broke away and came to me, lifting the woman off my shoulder and running toward two trucks of waiting paramedics, gently placing her on a gurney.

"Make it stop!" the woman cried before breaking down in a coughing spell. After seeing her go up in flames, it seemed impossible that she was alive, let alone talking. Even out here, out of the fire, I couldn't tell how much damage had been done, but underneath the soot I could make out her bright red skin and the beginning of blisters running across her face. The paramedic cut off the string of elastic, the last remains of her clothes, and tried to run an IV.

"It hurts," she said weakly, going silent as one of the paramedics threaded a cannula under her nose, force-feeding her oxygen.

"I can't get a vein," the second paramedic said in a low voice, a bad sign: the more dangerous the situation, the quieter the paramedics, their calmness balancing the hysteria around them. "The burns, I can't get a vein. Let's get her to Memorial."

They secured the woman and lifted her into the van, and I watched them pull away, sirens blaring.

A hand clasped my arm.

"Hey, Lyons," said Greg, a paramedic I'd worked with on countless calls. "Come with us."

After listening to my lungs and checking my exposed skin, Greg diagnosed me as "singed," telling me I'd be coughing for a while and that my hair needed the ends trimmed. I refused to go to the hospital so they insisted on oxygenating me there. From the back of their truck I watched as a half-dozen firefighters pushed farther into the fire, dark smoke engulfing them. The smell of acrid burning filled the air, and flames licked up, heavenward, leaping and grabbing for oxygen, tinder—whatever it could take.

It would take everything.

CHAPTER 2

THE FIRE BURNED FAST, FIREFIGHTERS RETREATING AS THE building lost the first floor. By this time, responders had arrived from Waterford, Colonie, Half Moon, and Troy, and backup was speeding our way from Menands and Albany. Hoses doused the main level, and firefighters on ladders rained water on the second floor. A helicopter from the New York Bureau of State Land Management sped toward us, filled with flame retardant. Two trucks of firefighters soaked the Harmony Mill across the street, keeping any sparks from sending that mill up, too. With all the buildings so close together, putting out the blaze took an enormous amount of effort.

The sun had set, and the fire appeared even more hellish, casting red, orange, and yellow shadows against the hills rising up behind it, making it look like the whole town was ablaze. Working traffic control over a block away, the heat sent sweat streaming down my back.

Lisa Jones, the fire chief from Menands who was supervising the flames along the western perimeter, filled me in: "A lot of these old mills, they're like a lumberyard surrounded by four walls. You know, Type III construction." I had no idea what Type III construction was and said so.

"The old wood frame construction. Wood floors, wood ceilings, wood beams, wood everything except the walls. With all the industrial chemical buildup soaked into the walls, the structures burn fast."

"And with the gasoline?"

"Unstoppable."

Not that the firefighters stopped trying. For almost an hour they poured everything they had onto it. I worked crowd and traffic control, stopping to slide on a pair of boots lent to me by one of the fire companies, so big I could fit my foot with the shoe still on into the boot. They were awkward but necessary, as my gasoline-soaked shoes would create a pyre for me if any sparks hit. Dave arrived on the scene, waving before running up to reroute traffic two streets above. The flames stretched higher, and we had to secure the whole hill.

Chief Donnelly pulled up next to me in one of our squad cars.

"The burned woman our firebug?" he asked.

"Didn't see anyone else on scene, and no one"—I scanned the mob of people, as arsonists often liked to watch their own handiwork—"who's taking exceptional interest in the fire."

"This fire brought out the crowd," the chief said. "Probably imagining it's the ghost of Luisa Lawler."

Most people thought the Sleep-Tite factory was cursed. It had been owned by Bernie Lawler, a name especially important in my house. Back in 1983, Bernie Lawler had killed his wife, Luisa, and three-year-old son, Teddy. They never found the bodies but there was loads of circumstantial evidence: reports of abuse, blood spatter across the basement walls, and worst of all, bloody handprints along the underside of Bernie's trunk where Luisa had tried and failed to escape. Thanks to my dad, they caught Bernie, and he was sent to prison. He was still there.

From a few miles away I watched as a helicopter landed on the roof of Memorial Hospital, ready to take my victim on a ten-minute ride to the regional burn center in Albany. From reports, Memorial had gotten a line into her and pumped her full of fluids. They diagnosed her with "second- and third-degree burns" but beyond that were vague, leaving the thorough diagnosis to the experts in Albany.

As I watched the sky, I saw a spotlight shining over the Hudson, approaching fast, a helicopter sent by the Bureau of State Land Management. The fire-retardant chemicals in the helicopter represented our best hope for relief. There'd be red foam over the building, the whole block, and the crowd if I didn't back them up.

I'd moved them about fifteen feet—a couple hundred people watching a large-scale disaster were hard to motivate. The fire shot up, a roman candle shining bright, before disappearing from view. The building groaned, a dying dinosaur, and the roof came down, followed by a crash as the roof and the second floor piled into the first, and then a boom echoing like thunder as all three crashed into the basement below. Ash coated my mouth. I spat and watched as the walls of the building, with no support, wavered and then collapsed inward, the two walls closest to the hill going first, and the street-facing walls falling a minute later.

And the fire was dead. Not completely out, but manageable. The helicopter dropped its load, the red foam splatting dead center, and all the fire companies moved in on it, dousing spots where flames poked through the field of bricks, the fire reduced to a slow smoldering.

IT ENDED WITH A BANG AND A WHIMPER.

Once we got the bulk of the crowd dispersed, troopers arrived to take over traffic duty, and Dave and I took the opportunity to go over to the regional burn center in Albany to try to talk to our victim.

"I should call my brother. Lucas'll lead the parade," Dave said, exiting off 787 toward St. Peter's Hospital.

"Parade?"

"He worked at Sleep-Tite and did everything he could to get out of it. Indoor jobs make him nuts."

"So he must love being a bartender."

"Well, he loves booze more than he loves being outside." He smiled. "He worked the early shift at Sleep-Tite, and I can't tell you how many times I woke up to my dad knocking on his door, telling Lucas to get his lazy ass out of bed. Of course, my dad would never use that kind of language. He swore in Ukrainian."

We stopped at an intersection, the faux-gothic cathedral on our left, the too-modern state towers on our right. "Was your dad trying to teach him a good work ethic?"

"Yes, but also . . . Mom worked the nights at Sleep-Tite, and my Dad didn't like to leave her waiting after her shift. He was worried she'd get bored, and when that happened, she'd wreck her life just to watch it crash. He was right. That last time she took off, she left from work. Went on a bender somewhere, stole Aunt Natalya's car, and hit the road." He pulled into the parking lot of St. Peter's Hospital, rolled down his window, and punched a button. A ticket popped out. Dave tucked it in his visor. "I guess I hate Sleep-Tite a little, too."

I tensed up as we walked through the halls of St. Peter's. I'd managed to avoid hospitals during the end stages of Kevin's illness. Before things became hopeless, my husband's days were filled with a constant array of doctor's appointments: oncologists, pulmonary specialists, pain specialists, and all of the diagnostic machinery, MRI's, X-rays, blood tests—the list was endless.

We arrived at the burn unit, a sign on the door instructing us to report to the nurses' station. Once there, we explained to a nurse in all-white scrubs who we were and why we were visiting.

"I paged Gayle. That's her patient," he said. "I assume you'll want to see the patient?"

"For a few questions."

He handed us paper scrubs, shoe guards, and a cap. "Go on. Put these on."

A nurse in her mid–fifties rushed out of one of the rooms. She too wore the white scrubs of the rest of the nurses on the floor, and her crocs squeaked with every step.

"Here about our mystery patient?" she asked.

I reached under my scrubs to pull out my badge.

"Like I couldn't tell you were cops from down the hall," she said. "How can we help you?"

"The burn victim's in a lot of pain. We know that," I said. "But we need to ask her a few questions."

"We've barely gotten her stabilized. Her blood pressure's still all over the place—"

"One question," Dave said. "Her name."

"She's unconscious," Gayle said. "Has been since she got here."

"Compromising her health is the last thing we want," I said. "But could you maybe roll back some of the meds? We need to wake her up for one minute, get her name, maybe who to contact."

A light went on over one of the patient's doors, followed by a low ping.

"Dan, can you answer that call?" Gayle said.

The young man agreed, pulling on a cap and tying on a face mask as he hurried to the patient.

"Look," Gayle says, "this isn't some sort of medically induced coma. Yes, she's on pain meds, but the deal is, her body decided to shut down all nonessential functions. Burn shock. All of her skin, including the surface of her lungs, is struggling to heal right now, and we're pumping her with fluids without swamping her lungs and drowning her. She might wake up—"

"A picture," I say. "Can we take a picture of her in case we get any missing persons reports?"

Gayle considered. "That'd be OK, I guess."

The victim lay on the single bed, her lips pale under the ventilator, her hair gone. The visible skin glistened, slathered in lotion meant to replace some of the moisture she was losing. She lay naked under a tent, a gauzy fabric draped a foot off her body. That said, she looked surprisingly good, the injuries no worse than a bad sunburn, blisters streaking across her face.

"You get them out of crisis and clean off soot and ash, they start looking a little healthier. Systemically, though . . . skin's one of our biggest organs, and burns like this, it's like she got stabbed in the kidneys," Gayle said.

Dave pulled out a camera. "OK?" Gayle agreed.

"So what's her prognosis?" I asked.

Gayle explained how the woman had burns of different severity over parts of her body. A few areas remained untouched, or the burns were first degree—"Her feet, oddly enough"—but most of her body had second-degree burns, where the top layer of skin burned away.

"Gasoline burns fast," she said. "Her clothes, slower, which is where we see the third-degree burns."

I tried to figure out where the woman was severely burned. "How much of this is third degree?"

"Twenty percent. Around her shoulders, and across her lower torso. Thank God for natural fibers, which burn faster than synthetic or, God forbid, plastic." A grim look passed over her face. "Plastic can be a mess."

"So twenty percent," Dave said, putting his camera away. "That's not too bad, right?"

"Oh, it's bad. Especially for a person her age."

"Her age?" I asked. "Do you know how old she is?"

"Well, based on the osteoporosis we detected when we did X-rays, I'd put her in her mid-fifties, possibly her mid-sixties. While it's not hard and fast, a rule of thumb is that if you add a person's age to the amount of their body burned to the third degree, you get the percent chance someone might die: If she's in her fifties, it might be a seventy-five percent chance of death, and if she's in her sixties, closer to eight-five." Dave's face fell. Gayle plowed on. "And any comorbidities—diabetes, heart disease, asthma—might mean worse odds."

The woman's breathing got heavy. I didn't see any blips on the monitors, but Gayle picked up her catheter bag and examined the urine critically.

"We're over-hydrating her," she said. "We might be drowning her right now. You need to go. I'll be sure to call you if she wakes up, even for a second, I promise I'll get a name." Gayle adjusted the woman's IV, lowering her fluid. "We want to find out who our friend is as much as you do."

CHAPTER 3

I WORKED THREE DAYS OF DOUBLES AT THE SITE OF THE FIRE, coming home to sleep and be told by my seven-year-old daughter that I smelled funny. The ash from the fire soaked into my clothes and my hair, which I was convinced was turning from blond to gray. Despite taking long showers, scraping the black out from under my nails, and washing my clothes twice, the scent clung to me, ground in. I figured I had another week of this before life reverted to normal, but on day four I arrived at the building site to find work stopped.

"Chemicals," Dave said. "Vats and vats of chemicals tucked behind an illegal wall in the basement."

My skin began to burn as I imagined all the toxins in the air. "Illegal?"

"The fire marshal said it doesn't show up in any of the plans filed at city hall." I watched as the fire department's hazardous materials response team carried tenting through the piles of bricks surrounding the building.

"Fire department says it's Tris—"

"Tris?"

"Yeah, some chemical they used to treat pajamas with until they figured out it caused kids to get liver cancer. Banned in the late seventies. Instead of spending money to dispose of it properly, goddamned Bernie Lawler stacked vats of this stuff behind a flimsy wall in the basement."

"In case his killing his wife left you with any doubt that he was a complete and total scumbag," I said. Bernie Lawler was another in a long line of owners who dumped chemicals into our land and water before decamping. Usually the companies moved to the South or overseas, not prison, although plenty deserved it.

"To be fair," Dave said, "it would've been there until the roaches ruled the earth if the place hadn't burned. We can't move until the fire department catalogs and removes the dozen or so barrels. You'll be sitting on your thumbs for a while."

The work being done down in the basement was hidden, detox tents covering the activities of the specially trained firefighters who were opening the barrels, examining and photographing the contents, and then wrapping the barrels in protective layers for transport. They had set up a well-lit staging area over the pit of chemicals. Reinforced scaffolding provided a scenic view of the dump site below, and a platform that rose and fell—a sort of elevator—carried barrels from the pit below up to the surface, where they were transported to the waiting trucks.

A worker wearing coveralls that I suspected were made of lead tried to calm our fears. "There's no evidence of airborne contamination."

"Fan-fuckin'-tastic," Dave said. "I feel my sperm count dropping already."

With the fire marshal handling most of the investigation into the fire's origin, we had little more to do than maintain the wide perimeter requested by the fire department. We talked about the burned woman, still unconscious at St. Peter's. All the local newscasts had carried her picture, but no real leads had come in.

"With the van destroyed we ran the partial plate. It didn't pop in the system," I said. "It was a rental with Nevada plates, and the big guns—Hertz, National, Avis—none of them report missing fleet." We stopped talking as a car approached, and I walked forward to intercept the vehicle. The driver's side window rolled down, and a young woman leaned out, hair pulled into a tight bun and her lips lined a deep brown.

"She's the owner," she said and pointed a blue-tipped nail at the elderly woman in the passenger seat. Small, the woman wore an Irish wool cardigan, cream colored with dark brown buttons, and a blue beret with a Claddagh circlet pinned to it. Elda Harris.

Everyone called this Bernie Lawler's factory, but in total he had owned it for only six years. On June 16, 1978 he married nineteen-year-old Luisa Harris and signed the final purchase agreements for the Sleep-Tite Factory, buying it from Luisa's parents. In August 1984, after Bernie had been convicted of murdering Luisa and Ted, Luisa's mother won a wrongful death suit and was awarded all of Bernie's assets, including his home, his boat, and the business. In July 1986, the Sleep-Tite factory went bankrupt and ceased operations, but the land and building remained in Elda's name, the fire finishing off what rust and decay hadn't taken care of.

Elda rolled down the window, and now sat watching the dump truck cart away bricks and beams. She had a halo of fuzzed hair and rheumy eyes, focused but teary. She appeared unaware of me, Dave, or the young woman who'd driven her here, despite the woman's repeated "Mrs. Harris! Mrs. Harris!"

Finally, in a voice stronger than I expected from such a frail person, she spoke.

"Good. *Good.* Now it's done. Take me home, Caitlin." She pushed a button, the window slid closed, and the two drove off.

"We'll have to interview her soon," I said.

"You think she torched the place?" Dave said. "I mean, everyone says she ran it into the ground intentionally. Maybe she burned it down."

"That can't be true," I said. "Unless she single-handedly orchestrated the fall of the manufacturing sector in the United States, in which case she *is* a criminal mastermind."

"You know, I start to believe you're a normal person, and then you start talking like you have a master's degree. Oh wait, you do!"

"Oh, give me a break. You majored in sociology, for God's sake."

"But Special Agent Lyons, I didn't log all those years in the FBI." He waggled his eyebrows at me. "Maybe Elda was a terrorist, destroying the US from the inside. Speaking of which . . ."

Another car approached, a black SUV the size of an ocean liner. It made a fast U-turn, splashing through a puddle that had formed in a pothole, and parked on the opposite side of the street. Hale Bascom emerged, trim and sharp in a Burberry overcoat, opposite in every way of his bloated car. I'd known him since our days at Quantico, fifteen years back, where he was the guy none of the women could resist, including me. We had our one night before he moved on to his next conquest and I moved on to my husband. I definitely got the better end. Except for laugh lines around his eyes and a touch more compassion, he hadn't changed a lot since then.

"Special Agent Bascom," Dave said. "To what do we owe the pleasure?"

"I was finishing up an investigation in Kinderhook and decided to stop by." Kinderhook's population was less than that of Hopewell Falls, and I wondered what someone could do there to get the attention of the FBI.

"Some hedge fund manager from Connecticut hid info on money laundering for a drug cartel in his summer house." Hale shook his head in disgust. "Forensic accounting was never my strong suit."

"Lots and lots of spreadsheets?" I asked. "That does sound like fun."

"Oh, it is. And we get to make spreadsheets to track the spreadsheets. Faced with such excitement, I decided to stop on by because you chose not to pull in our office officially, despite reports that the victim of this"—he waved his hand at the burned building casually, but his jaw clenched—"had a car with out-of-state plates."

"A van, actually," I said. "A rental. Hard to nail down since they cross state lines and aren't always rented where their plates are sourced. For all we know, she lived in Schenectady."

"Did you get the tags before they were scorched?"

I checked my notes. "Nevada 14 . . . and the rest was obscured."

"Obscured, or you forgot?"

Hale succeeded in life by not letting go of anything, but right now, I wanted to punch him. "Obscured. Mud all over the plate."

"Intentionally?"

"Maybe. Schenectady's got a lot of mud."

The site foreman called to Dave. Pissed that the fire department's hazardous materials response team had stopped work and, more importantly, cut into his crew's overtime, he had spent much of the day complaining to Dave, who was promising that demolition would restart soon. The second Dave was out of earshot, Hale switched topics.

"So I'm truly hoping"—the hard edge of his voice was gone, replaced with gentle coaxing—"that you've considered my offer to rejoin the Bureau . . ."

"I haven't decided yet. And if your management style is rolling over people, perhaps this should be a no."

Despite there being no one within thirty feet of us, Hale stepped close, and I could see the cowlicks starting the escape from whatever expensive gel he used to keep them in place. "Don't be hasty, June. Let's not cut off our options."

"So you're demanding an answer right now?"

"Only if the answer's yes. If it's a no, then mull it over a touch more."

"For now it's a maybe," I said.

Hale looked down at the ground. "Is this because of our past?"

I was caught off guard by his question. "Personally or professionally?"

"Either? Both?" His hand went to the back of his neck and I tensed. Hale didn't know it but he had a "tell," a giveaway when he was set to lie: he rested his hand on the back of his neck. But his fingers drifted up, massaging his head, and I realized how hard this conversation was for him. "I know that I wasn't much of a friend to you when Kevin was dying, and on a case I can be a little . . ."

"Dickish?"

"Aggressive." He glared but then smiled. "And perhaps I should let this go for now."

"Perhaps you should, Hale. But look, the answer isn't no. Some of the things you mentioned are issues, but they wouldn't keep me away."

"Well, that sounds like a win to me." Hale pointed at Dave, who was having an animated conversation with the foreman. "I'll refrain from inserting the FBI into whatever's going on over there and leave while I'm ahead." Hale gave me a backward salute as he walked toward the SUV.

"Lyons!" Dave shouted, waving me over to the ruins. I watched as the foreman clicked off his walkie-talkie and disappeared behind a pile of bricks. Dave followed.

I sprinted over, slowing down once I approached the demolished building. The engineers said the route was safe, but random bricks dotted the path, and I hesitated to touch the sides and cause a landslide.

Down below, EPA employees flooded the tent. A guy wearing a bright yellow hazmat suit held us back from the edge.

"You're about to do some real work," he said. "We found a body."

WITH THE CHEMICALS, WE KNEW WE HAD A CRIME SCENE—ONE
for the fire department and the EPA. With the body, we were now
in charge. The other agencies were unconvinced, allowing Dave and
me to go down into the pit only when we were kitted up like the Stay
Puft Marshmallow man and swore that we wouldn't touch anything.
We'd barely landed in the basement before they rushed us back to the
surface, accompanied by the barrel containing our victim. There, we
found the coroner, Norm Finch, and a crime scene tech, Annie Lin.

"Took you long enough," Annie said.

We'd taken photos of the body from the limited angles available,
but Annie repeated our work twice over. The victim was a woman.
In the sealed bin in the cool underground, undisturbed for years,
she'd mummified rather than decayed. Her skin was the color of
old oak, and for now, we couldn't determine her race. Patches of
orange mottled the red dress she wore where her bodily fluids seeped
out, and her brown high-heeled boots bagged loosely around her
shrunken calves, the skin coating the bones. Not even the fire had
harmed her, the concrete bunker sealing off her and the Tris from
the destruction above. The victim reminded me of the old ultrasound
picture of Lucy, curled in on herself, one hand against her chest, the
other half hiding her face and head.

Norm peered inside the barrel. "She'll break apart if we try to
lift her out."

"Let's get her back to the lab. I can have her cut out of there in
fifteen minutes," Annie said.

"Can we examine the barrel before you cut into it?" Dave said.

"Outside of the body itself, there's not a lot to see, and oxidized
metal does a very poor job of maintaining forensic evidence," Annie
said. "It's possible the barrel developed the power of speech. After it
tells you who put the woman here, the two of you can chat about
current events. It's doubtless wondering about the status of peace
talks in the Middle East."

"There's nothing else there?"

"Nope. I mean, I'll analyze it for trace evidence, but you should probably make a nuisance of yourselves with Norm." Annie began slotting her instruments carefully back into her case, looking up when no one replied. "He'll be the one to figure out what happened to Luisa Lawler."

Dave sighed. "Way to keep an open mind there, Annie."

"What? Like you all weren't thinking the same thing. There is a body of a woman in this factory. A factory that was owned, may I remind you, by a man whose murdered wife was never found." Annie picked up her case. "And not to be unkind, but I hope they find the boy in another barrel so both of them can get the burial they deserve."

As usual, Annie was saying what the rest of us filtered. I couldn't believe that after thirty years we'd finally found Luisa, and in a way, I was glad.

We stepped out from under the shelter, walking carefully along a path helpfully marked with flares. The sky had a glow, low clouds reflecting light, and it had begun to drizzle. Once clear of the rubble, I began to jog, anxious to get home.

Dave was in no rush. "It's nice to have a murder where our perp has been locked up for thirty years."

Dave's statement made me pause. "Is there a chance we're wrong?"

"Who am I to question Annie?" He clicked his key chain and his headlights went on, briefly blinding us. "Want to go grab a drink, Lyons?"

"Gotta get home and type up my report. And see my daughter." More importantly, I had to talk to my dad, tell him he could rest. We had found Luisa Lawler.

CHAPTER 4

I PUT MY GLOCK IN THE LOCKBOX, HIGH ON A SHELF IN MY front hallway closet.

"Hello!" I called. No one responded.

I peeked into the kitchen. Lucy sat poking an iPad, a gift from my sister to my dad, who viewed it with suspicion. Lucy had no such misgivings and commandeered the device as often as I'd let her to play Angry Birds.

I walked over and kissed her. "Where's Grandpa?"

She waved vaguely to her left. The house wasn't that big, and I figured I'd run into him soon.

Dad sat in his favorite chair, squarely in front of the TV. He slumped sideways, but he had no choice—the blue corduroy recliner was missing a few springs along the left side.

"Go get cleaned up and we'll order pizza," he said, never taking his eyes off the TV, where reporters stood in front of the factory. Luisa Lawler's picture flashed on the screen. So much for breaking it to him gently.

"We got the bastard." He beamed, and I could see the young cop in him, excited to bring a killer to justice. Without the fresh grief that usually accompanied a murder investigation, his expression was pure unadulterated glee.

He turned back to the TV. A photo of Luisa popped up. She was petite, and her red hair was cut in a simple pageboy, a conservative choice during the early eighties when big hair ruled. The screen showed old footage of Bernie Lawler in court, sitting up straight in a three-piece suit. Underneath the bad eighties feathered hair and the too large collars, he'd been a good-looking guy: tall, with a strong jaw and light-brown hair, bright blue eyes that came across even on TV.

If my family was going to eat, it was up to me to order. Lucy never paused from tapping the screen to get the birds to fly into a rickety structure as I placed the call, but shouted out her preference for plain cheese, which I passed on.

Upstairs, I peeled off my clothes, dropping them in a pile on the floor since putting them in the hamper would result in everything smelling like ash, possibly forever. Every day since the fire I had come home covered in grime and damp cinders that smelled like death. I touched the picture of Kevin, a three-year-old Lucy squirming in her father's lap, the two of them with the same laughing blue eyes. He wore a T-shirt, his FBI badge swinging loosely around his neck. With her chubby cheeks and short legs, Lucy was barely recognizable as the kid she was now.

"You'd find my dad freakin' funny right now," I said to his picture. "He's like a kid in a candy store."

I climbed into the shower, the hot spray a relief. I dropped a huge pool of shampoo into my hands, and washed my hair, and then washed it again when the water didn't run clear. I scrubbed extra hard under my nails and the back of my neck, where the dust built up. The water wasn't black the way it'd been the first day, but gray. I rinsed my hair again and shut off the faucet.

After changing into yoga pants and one of Kevin's old flannel shirts, I wrapped my dirty clothes in my towel and trudged downstairs. Lucy didn't acknowledge me as I passed through the kitchen to the laundry room. I returned to the kitchen and asked Lucy to set the table—her job for earning her allowance. She continued poking at the iPad.

"Away," I said. Lucy didn't hear me. I walked over and pulled the iPad out of her hand, and she briefly trailed after it, as if tethered.

"Set the table," I said.

While I made salad, we talked about her day, which, thanks to Angry Birds and winning a race at recess had been awesome as far as she was concerned. I had the salad made by the time the doorbell rang.

I paid the pizza delivery driver, who didn't meet my eye even as I gave him the tip. I'd stopped him on the road a few times when he'd been over-eager about getting the pizza into people's hands while it was hot, and I noted he'd made pretty good time tonight.

"Drive safely," I called.

Lucy leapt on the box with the plain pizza, and I reminded her of her manners. She kneeled on her chair, sitting back on her ankles and stretching out and touching the pizza.

"Dad?" I said. I heard no movement and walked into the living room, where my father flipped between channels. Several stations featured a college basketball player who had scored over fifty points in his third straight game—a local boy made good—but my father didn't care, racing past, stopping only when Luisa Lawler's face popped up. This was worse than Lucy and her Angry Birds.

"Dad, dinner," I repeated. After a moment he got up, leaving the TV on. He followed me into the kitchen, blinking as if he were emerging from a cave. We kept the conversation light at dinner. Even then my Dad didn't participate much, his head tilted, trying to catch snatches of the news. Lucy and I filled the gap, chatting about the two birthday parties she was attending this upcoming weekend, how Kailin was her second best friend and Sara was her most best friend. It involved an elaborate ranking system involving who sat where at lunch and teams at school.

After I'd wrapped up leftovers and won a heated discussion with Lucy about how she couldn't bring the iPad to bed—I could kill my sister—I got her tucked in. My father skipped his normal "pretending not to listen to the bedtime story" act, which resulted in Lucy watching the door rather than paying attention to the book. She settled down once she'd started her nightly ritual, begun three years ago during Kevin's illness when nightmares tortured her every night: She stood on her bed and touched the dream catcher my mother had sent her. My mother claimed her shaman made it especially for Lucy. Lucy didn't even ask what a shaman was and had been nightmare free since then, so who was I to question what worked, dubious as it was?

Tonight, she began by tracing the purple weavings that were designed to catch her bad dreams. Her finger followed down the ribbon hanging below. She reached the feather, there to help the good dreams slide down to her, when it snapped off. The feather spiraled down to the bed, landing on her pillow. She stared at it and then looked up at me. A child of habit and tired already, she burst into tears.

I grabbed her up and comforted her.

"But how will the nice dreams reach me?" she hiccupped. "Will Grandma send me another one?"

No way was I contacting my mother for a replacement. I wondered if they sold them on the Internet?

"Tomorrow, I'll sew that back on," I said. "I'll make it as good as new." I picked up the feather and ran it over her forehead. She giggled.

"Do it again," she said, and shut her eyes in anticipation.

I ran the feather back and forth across her brow. Steadily, her giggles settled into deep breathing, and eventually she dropped into sleep. I put the feather on her side table, safe until tomorrow.

I wandered downstairs and went to the living room. To my surprise, my father acknowledged me, holding out a glass of Irish whiskey in the Waterford crystal. He rarely drank since having the heart attack, and the Waterford crystal came out of the china cabinet once a year at Christmas. I took the glass.

"A toast," my dad said. "A toast to Luisa Lawler coming home to her family."

I swallowed. The Bushmills tasted wonderful, oaky and warm. I raised my hand for a second toast.

"And to closing your last case!"

Dad clinked his glass against mine. I curled into the corner of the couch closest to Dad's recliner, tucking my feet under me. My toes were chilled, but asking to start a fire would be admitting winter hadn't left. People were wearing shorts—wishful thinking in fifty-degree weather—but after the winter we'd had, I could see where they might want to *will* summer into being.

We settled into a comfortable silence, and I let Dad enjoy the moment. The TV was muted, but out of the corner of my eye I could see a commercial for the ten o'clock news, and a picture of Luisa and Bernie Lawler flashed on the screen, along with their son, Teddy. They'd probably had the portrait taken at Olan Mills: Bernie and Luisa in the forefront, Luisa perched on a stool wearing a corduroy jumper, Bernie standing behind her, arms wrapped around her waist, and in the corner, the silhouette of a young boy, his smile revealing a perfect line of baby teeth. My family had a similar photo, my shadow self beatific in a soft, hazy glow, an image with no resemblance to my personality. My parents had even gotten me into a dress.

Fair-haired like his father, Teddy had his mother's eyes, pale green, almost gray. I couldn't hear their announcements, but a scroll line read across the bottom said "Mystery solved!"

My dad broke the silence. "Did they find the boy?"

I shook my head no. "They're still opening bins," I said. "They're keeping an eye out."

"Teddy was such a little guy," he said. "There's probably not much left of him now. Luisa was a slip of a thing who tried hard to fade into the background, keeping the focus on her husband. That worked out fine for both of them: Bernie was an attention hog."

Dad settled into his story, describing how Luisa had come from some money. Her father, Stephen Harris, ran the family clothing-manufacturing business. The company was founded as a collar manufacturer in the 1800s, back when washing a whole shirt was a time-consuming chore. Each generation renamed it depending on what was in fashion—girdles were big in the fifties—before Bernie took it over and started manufacturing kids' pajamas, crib sets, and bath towels.

"He had his little empire and wanted the high-status lifestyle. A nice girl like Luisa didn't fit in with his plan."

"When did you figure out he did it?"

"I had some doubts about his guilt at first. They disappeared quick. A bunch of girls went missing at the time, young and pretty, and I was worried that we had some sort of serial killer on our hands. But most of those young women showed up alive. They just took off for a better life somewhere far from here."

"Like Dave's mom."

"Exactly. We got a conviction for Luisa because of the stories everyone repeated. Natalya Batko, their housekeeper, told me how Bernie shut Luisa in the house, cut her off from her friends and family. Even Sheila"—he took a deep breath after saying my mother's name—"said Bernie forbade Luisa from doing her hospital volunteer work. Of course your mother kept using the word 'patriarchy,' so I didn't listen much."

He reached for the bottle of Bushmills and poured himself a fin-gerful. "Anyway, the chatter about what a sleazeball he was, the blood all over the basement, and those bloody handprints in the trunk of his car like Luisa had tried, tried . . ." He paused, gulping down the whiskey. When he placed the glass down his eyes were bright with unshed tears. He cleared his throat twice and continued.

"So there was the stories about Bernie, the blood evidence in the basement, and bloody handprints in the trunk that looked like Luisa had tried to claw her way out, well, that finally convinced me beyond a reasonable doubt. Luisa's mother, Elda, was a woman on a mission from the get-go." He frowned. "I think she felt guilty."

"Why?"

"Well, I got the impression that she and her husband pushed Luisa into the marriage. Luisa's dad was struggling to keep the factory afloat." My dad sat back on his chair, relaxing into the story. "No one could figure out why Bernie bought it. He was such a smooth operator, working some excellent real estate deals, and here he picks up the Sleep-Tite factory, which even I knew was a few years away from death. Rumor had it he took on the business because Elda promised him Luisa if he took Sleep-Tite off their hands."

"Elda sold her daughter?"

My father nodded. "More or less. Most of Elda's fury was at herself. Families of murder victims have a certain amount of anger mixed in with their grief, but she was off the charts."

I'd lost my husband to cancer, and the sadness almost got washed away by the rage that came over me every day for the first year. I can't imagine what I would have done had he been murdered.

"I mean, there's nothing worse than losing a child. Elda, though, she took it to another level. She sued for the business and ran it into the ground . . ."

"That's true?" I said.

My father nodded.

"She salt the earth, too?"

"She would if she could. She put countless people out of work, ruined people's livelihoods, put another nail in Hopewell Falls's coffin all because she couldn't live with herself. She could've sold the business—Bernie got the place making money, and buyers were interested. Hell, just the land. Dan Jaleda? Big developer guy? He's been trying to get the land for condos for at least ten years. And before that some investors made an offer to Elda, a group put together by Bernie's brother, the judge."

"Judge . . ."

"Medved."

I knew Judge Medved, although he had retired before I started testifying in local cases. Leaving aside the different last names, he and Bernie had to be almost twenty years apart in age, but Dad was eager to explain. He was the world's leading expert on Bernie Lawler.

"Judge Medved's father died back in Ukraine during the war. A decade later, the Medveds are settled out on the Island, a couple of blocks from where Dave lives now, and his mother married a man named Lawler. It came up at trial that Bernie's dad liked to get loaded and belt his kids, beat Bernie and his sister Deirdre every day. At the trial, Judge Medved talked about how Bernie was like a son to him, but behind the scenes he was encouraging the DA to indict. Hardly brotherly love."

"That seems . . . odd."

"Well, the crime horrified even him. The Ukrainians, they didn't really trust cops since they equated them with the SS or Stalin's secret police or whatever showed up in the night to kill them, but they came forward in droves on this one. It was the little kid . . ." The TV caught Dad's attention, promos for the newscast set to start in a few minutes. "Dave's Aunt Natalya was more than just a housekeeper to Bernie and Luisa, she loved Luisa like a daughter, but even then it took me weeks of coaxing her before she finally agreed to testify. It was like the Wild West over there."

I thought of Dave, who talked about the Island as if it were an isolated outpost. Perhaps for him it was.

"Anyway, if the judge wouldn't even fight for him, Bernie must've been dirty."

Dad unmuted the TV, signaling that our conversation was over. A trumpet flourish blared, making the newscast sound grand.

"Lower the sound a touch?" I said. I pointed upstairs. "Lucy."

He dropped the volume. I watched along with him for the first fifteen minutes, deciding to go to bed before the sports and weather.

"You coming?" I asked. My dad usually woke at five, and he was up way past his bedtime.

"I'm going to watch the eleven o'clock report, but you go get some sleep. You've got to finish this once and for all for me, and Luisa, and Ted."

I touched his arm as I went to the kitchen to wash out the Waterford crystal. I hoped we'd find Ted's body soon and would have another reason to break out the good glasses and close the case file.

I WOKE UP TO THE SOUND OF MY FATHER'S VOICE, SPEAKING softly in the kitchen. I crept downstairs. He was showered and wearing different clothes, but I couldn't tell if he'd slept or not.

"Gotta go," he said. He stopped speaking when he saw me. "Uh-huh . . . uh-huh . . . take care . . . bye."

I poured myself some coffee. "Who was that?"

"Your mom."

"Interesting. How often do these little chats happen?"

"I don't note it on my calendar," he said. "When there's news. When something big happens."

I hadn't seen my mother for three years, at Kevin's funeral. I spent most of my teen years resenting her for leaving my dad after she claimed he was too caught up in his job. I stopped visitation. My father tried to force me, and my sister tried to guilt me into it, but my mother took the faux Zen approach: "She'll come back when she's ready." I added her attitude to the list of things to be mad about.

But in my late teens I softened. I didn't jump to reunite, mostly because I didn't want to admit my mother was right, but slowly we reconnected. I responded to her e-mails, and called to thank her for the grocery money she sent me in college. I visited for a couple of weeks on a college break and, to my amazement, almost had a good time. I had to make sure I didn't trip over Mom's crystal collection and I escaped outside for a break from the incense, but I began enjoying her for who she was. I even liked her "soul mate" Larry, who teased my mother while at the same time hanging up her wind chimes to "restore the chi in the guest bathroom." I invited them to my wedding, and encouraged her to visit for a long weekend a few months after Lucy was born.

When Kevin got sick, I thanked my Mom for the CDs on positive visualizations and the selenium she sent to help fight the free radicals in Kevin's body. She came from Florida to cheer us up. She did, unintentionally, as Kevin laughed himself to coughing after she gave "healing blue light" to his midsection, where his cancer was slowly crowding out his vital organs.

She swept into Kevin's funeral wearing muted linen earth tones, her hair twisted into a bun.

"You lost him long ago," she said to me in the mourning line. "I hope you can see how the universe needed to carry him home."

Stunned, I didn't say anything, focusing on the next mourner, Mrs. MacNeil. I took her condolences—"So terrible. Much too young."—and averted my eyes as my mother floated her hands above Kevin's dead body, "aiding him on his path into the next realm." Later, at the house, my mother explained how I shouldn't get caught up in the "negative energy" of Kevin's death, and how bad feelings would attract more bad feelings. I exploded.

"Please stop," I shouted, and the house, crowded with mourners, went still. "Can you for once think of how what you do, what you say, affects anyone but yourself?! You're always so selfish, caught up in your own crackpot ideas, you never once stop to consider what anyone other than yourself might need."

"You're speaking from a dark place. Your energy—"

"Shut. Up," I said. "I need you gone. Now."

My sister dragged her out of there, shooting judgmental glances at me over her shoulder. Over the last few years I've responded to Mom's e-mails briefly or not at all, and ignored all her invitations for me and Lucy to visit in Florida.

I didn't expect her and my dad to be buddy-buddy. "How was your chat?"

"Good," Dad said. I could see him struggle with whether to continue this conversation or not. I tried not to frown, and he continued. "She and Luisa were good friends, and she was happy Luisa's at peace. She said she'd make an offering at the temple later."

"She's Jewish these days?"

"Hindu."

I changed the subject. "You OK . . . with finding Luisa after all these years?"

He changed it back. "Your mom's planning a visit soon."

My father and I could both ignore the conversation. I waved at the door. "Gotta go."

I picked up Dave, and we drove over to visit our burn victim. We didn't stay long, as she was still unconscious and the smell in her room was almost intolerable.

"It's the dead skin," her nurse, Gayle, said. "And the open wounds. We're excising the burned tissue, but it's slow going, and it will be another three weeks, at the earliest, before we can do a skin graft. We've applied Silvadene and a xenograft—"

"Xenograft?" I asked.

"Pig skin," she said. I couldn't hide my revulsion. "Some burn centers utilize human cadaver skin. But pigs are readily available, have organs of similar size to humans, and don't transmit infections to humans very easily. They're perfect."

Dave and I were afraid of what else we might find out if we stayed, so we returned to the station, both of us agreeing we could skip lunch today. On our way, we passed the factory ruins. Six media trucks were parked out front, their transmitters sticking up like insect antennae.

"Traffic control and toxins down here today," Dave said. "Wonder what's waiting for us at the station?"

As I entered, I could hear Lorraine's voice bouncing off the walls of the empty room. The station's interior had been painted beige in 1990, the layer of spiderwebs in the corners deepening the shadows of an already gloomy room. I turned the corner to find Lorraine talking to Hale.

Hale wore one of his black suits. No longer required for agents, but as Hale admitted, "I look so nice." His good looks defied fluorescents, his skin golden, his green eyes sharp and bright.

Hale twisted around in the wooden chair he was sitting in, a huge grin on his face "Y'all are going to love me."

"Aw, G-man, we already do," Dave said. "Found us something good?"

"We got a line on your burn victim. Those plates on the van . . ."

The front door crashed open, and Annie Lin walked in.

"I called," Annie yelled over her shoulder. "The chief's expecting me."

Lorraine reached for her phone. "Let me . . ."

Annie didn't wait, racing across the squad room. She skidded to a halt when she saw us but then continued barreling toward the chief's office.

"Going to ignore us, Annie?" Dave called. "What about our deep and abiding friendship?"

Annie threw her shoulders back, steeling herself for war, and I braced myself for the comeback. Annie was more than capable of dishing it out, and fortunately she could take it, but nothing came, not even "shut up," which Annie used in place of hello and good-bye. Chief Donnelly opened his door.

"Ms. Lin," he said. "I appreciate you coming down here personally."

"Of course." She sounded sweet and respectful as she stepped inside his office. "This is important."

The door shut. We talked about the van found with the burned woman—Hale's big news was that he'd tracked down the partial plate to a Carfast rental agency, a regional outfit covering the southwestern United States—but none of us were completely engaged. We were all wondering what, exactly, Chief Donnelly and Annie were talking about.

Donnelly's door swung open. Annie bolted out of the office as fast as she had entered, leaving the chief hanging in the doorway.

"Detective," Donnelly said. He waved to Dave. "Can you join me?"

Dave raised an eyebrow to us before jogging over. He blew a kiss to Annie. "Hope you brought me a good one."

The door closed again. Hale spoke rapidly. "June, I think I came up with a compromise we can both live with. What if you consult for a very short time? We could make arrangements for you to continue on the Hopewell Falls police force."

I ignored Hale and instead watched Annie, who had her eyes glued to the door.

Hale continued. "Let me talk to Donnelly . . ."

Annie was listening for something. Hardheaded and harsh, she had great instincts.

"Be quiet," I told Hale, and he was.

A crash came from the chief's office, and I stood, unsure whether I should go in. I walked over to Annie, placing myself directly in front of her. She wouldn't meet my eyes.

"Annie?" I asked. Hale paced, his head cocked to one side, listening for another crash, a shout, a murmur. Lorraine stood at her desk, her ringing phone forgotten.

"Annie," I said, "I'm going to find out in a second what you told the chief. Give me a clue. What am I walking into?"

She looked left and then right, mapping a route of escape. Finally, she spoke.

"His mom." She didn't meet my eyes. "Dave's mom was in the barrel."

The chief opened his door. Behind him Dave slumped over a desk, its contents a jumble on the floor.

"Lyons, can you come in here?"

CHAPTER 5

T HE RING," THE CHIEF SAID, HANDING AROUND A PHOTO. THE gold ring was tarnished almost black, but the words "Ваш завжди" etched inside were still visible.

"Yours, forever," Dave said. I felt his shoulders tense and then relax under my hand. "That's what it means."

Donnelly continued. "So when Annie searched the missing persons files, Vera Batko's contained the note . . ."

"You found the report I filed," Dave said, "when I was twelve?" He reached into his pocket and pulled out a notebook and pencil, taking notes, more comfortable in cop mode.

"Annie did." Donnelly tried to pull Annie into the center of the conversation, but she kept her position against the wall. "The clothing didn't match—the original report listed her clothes as blue canvas work coveralls, and you saw her dress: shiny, red, polyester—"

"The manufacturer who made the dress went out of business in 1983." Annie marched into the center of the group. "The ring, though. Taras Batko—"

"My father."

"Yes, in your father's statement he says he purchased the ring for

Vera. Your mom." Annie moved around the room during the discussion, going from the window to the corner to the doorway, before she bumped into Hale and pinballed back. "It's not certain. Give me some DNA and I can—"

"It's her," Dave said. He finished writing a sentence. "I mean sure, go ahead, let's get the final evidence. But here, I know"—he touched his chest. "It's her. I just wish my father were still alive. He never had any peace." He tucked his notebook back into his pocket. "If it's not going to create a hassle, I'd like to tell my brother. Lucas is not going to take it . . . you know, I have no idea how he'll take it. He may dance with joy." Dave tapped the back of my hand. "You'll come, right?"

I agreed, and Dave stood. Rather than rushing out, he went to Annie, placing both hands on her shoulders.

"Thank you, Annie," he said.

In true Annie fashion, she argued. "Why are you thanking me for bringing you this news?"

"You were being a pal," he said. "I couldn't ask for a better friend."

Annie threw her arms around him, hugging him tightly, and after a second Dave hugged her back. They broke and she hustled out, Dave following close behind.

"Need backup, June?" Hale whispered.

"I'll keep you posted." I watched Dave grab keys off his desk and then pat all his pockets, checking for missing items. "He's going to need friends more than anything."

Dave didn't wait for me, walking toward the exit, and I jogged to catch up. He passed Lorraine, clear eyed, but with tear tracks running through her coral blush.

Dave was quiet on the drive. He flinched visibly as the car rumbled over the bridge, the river water high with spring runoff and recent rains. We pulled up in front of his aunt's house, and I got out of the car. Dave hesitated, but a curtain in the house moved aside—we'd been spotted.

The slam of his car door sounded loud on the quiet street. He paused on the sidewalk, looking up at the house. "What do I say, June?"

"You want me to do it? I can."

"I gotta, but what do I say? 'Lucas, Mom didn't run out.' Or"—and he laughed bitterly—"'Lucas, remember how you always wished Mom was dead? Well, now she is.'"

"Is that how you feel?"

He sighed. "No. My brother, though, he went through more of Mom's bullshit. By the time she left . . . was killed . . . he hated her."

"Stick to the facts," I said. "Facts are straightforward."

"Nothing with my mother was straightforward."

The front door opened. "You staking out my house?" Lucas called. His smile faltered as Dave got close. "What's wrong? Tara OK?"

"Tara's fine. Aunt Natalya here?" Dave asked. "We need to talk to you alone."

"Grocery shopping," Lucas said, his eyes darting from Dave to me. "June staying?"

"Yeah. She's here in an official capacity."

Lucas opened the door wide and we shuffled past. A plastic mat wound a path through the living room, keeping the cream-colored carpet clean. The brothers moved to a gold couch, the fabric squeaking as they sat down. A Stephen King novel rested open on the arm, and on the table sat a glass of cola, the color washed out with melted ice and, I was pretty sure, rum.

"It's Mom," Dave said, never breaking eye contact with Lucas. "She's dead."

Dave's brother frowned. "What? Where was she? How'd you find her?"

Dave explained that the woman found in the barrel in the factory that had been all over the news hadn't been Luisa Lawler, but instead their mother.

"Wait. She's been there since . . ."

"Yeah," Dave said. "That last run wasn't a run."

Lucas stood up, grabbing his hair and pulling. Dave rushed to intercept, clutching at his brother's elbow.

Lucas didn't pull away. "No!"

Dave grappled him into a hug. The two brothers rocked, Lucas sobbing harshly. They stood like that for a few minutes, and I tried to figure out how I could slip out. I shouldn't have come. They needed time to mourn.

Lucas struggled out of Dave's arms, pushing him away and running to the kitchen, a vomiting sound coming a moment later. I went to follow, but Dave held my arm.

"Give him a minute," he said. "Let him get himself together."

"Sure. You OK?"

Dave looked over my shoulder to where we could hear Lucas half choking and half sobbing. "That went . . . well, more or less as I expected."

"Really?"

"Well, it could have been nastier. A tirade on how she deserved it." Dave sounded bewildered. "Am I crazy, or did he seem sad?"

"He's a grieving son."

"I expected . . . not that."

The retching had stopped, and the two of us went into the kitchen. Lucas spat twice into the sink, before washing the vomit down the drain. He left the water running, sticking his mouth under the tap and drinking directly from the faucet.

"That stupid bitch went and got herself killed." Lucas wiped away tears with the end of his T-shirt. His breath hitched. "And I helped bury her."

Dave narrowed his eyes. "What do you mean?"

"It means exactly what I said." Lucas faced the sink. Rather than vomiting he stared out the window, to the backyard and the field beyond. "You found Mom behind a fake wall, right? Over on the right side of the Sleep-Tite basement?"

"Yes," Dave said.

Lucas took a hitching breath. "I helped build that wall."

Dave pulled his arms tight across his middle, clenching his eyes closed. Already, I regretted combining police work with helping Dave. He shook his head twice, opening his eyes and letting his arms drop to his sides before walking over, leaning back against the counter next to his brother. Unlike Lucas he faced me, gently bumping his brother's shoulder with his own.

I pulled out my notebook. "Lucas, when did you build this wall?"

"A few days after Mom went missing." I was surprised at how easily the date came to him, but realized that as much as he professed not to care, his mother's disappearance had never been forgotten. "Sleep-Tite always closed down the last week of summer to do cleaning and repairs. Me and a couple of other guys, Bernie hired us to pull apart machines, replace furnace filters, shit like that. And build the wall."

"Did you have any idea what was in those barrels, Lucas?"

"No." Lucas continued to stare out the window, entranced. The back field was filled with wildflowers, soft whites and greens, with purple dotted here and there.

"Not even the chemicals?" I asked. Dave opened his mouth to protest, and I held up my hand, silencing him.

"Those I suspected." Lucas turned, facing me. "I feel bad, especially when I picture Tara playing in places where the chemicals could be seeping into the ground. But back then, I wasn't sorry about it. Bernie said he would put in a good word with the Judge, who had his finger in all the contracts for the 787 extension back then. Deal got us our union cards."

"Who's 'us'?" I asked.

"Dan Jaleda was a sort of foreman, but the rest of the guys . . . I can't remember. Jake Medved dropped off the supplies—the plaster-board and sawed bricks."

Lucas explained that they hadn't built a real brick wall—"not enough time"—but rather a fake, sawed-in-half bricks covering a sheetrock base.

"Is Jake Medved related to Judge Medved?" I asked, realizing I might have stumbled on another half-brother in the twisted Medved/Lawler family tree.

"Ugh. Yes," Lucas said, pulling out his phone. "Which you just reminded me . . . I'm supposed to start my shift at the bar in thirty minutes. How the fuck am I—" He paused. "I can't lose this job . . . I'll lose custody."

"Tell them there's been a death in the family," Dave said.

"But don't mention anything about your mother," I said. "Not yet."

Dave and I returned to the living room. From the kitchen I could hear Lucas's voice: "Stop busting my balls, here. I'll cover your shifts next week."

"How come mentioning Jake reminded him to call in to work?" I asked.

Dave kept his voice low. "Lucas works at Jake's Social Club over on Ontario. Jake . . . Medved, owns the place."

"A social club?" I asked. "That serves alcohol?"

"That's all they do, really. Only reason they're a social club in-stead of a bar is because Jake Medved's racked up some felony as-sault charges back in the '60s. From what my dad said, if you found someone with their head bashed in on the Island, Jake did it." I heard Lucas say good-bye, and Dave added quickly, "Aunt Natalya always had a soft spot for Jake because they escaped the Nazis together. Or was it the Russians? Probably both."

Lucas returned, throwing himself onto the couch.

"That shithead Brian pulled one of his power trips. The guy's itching to fire me. If I lose this job, well . . . I can think of no more fitting tribute to our deadbeat mother." He grabbed his rum and Coke and took a long drink. "Bernie Lawler killed her, didn't he?"

"No question," Dave said. "He did his wife and kid, and then Mom. He placed the order to brick in the barrels, right?" Lucas nodded. "With this monster, we might reopen a couple of other cold cases."

Dave wouldn't be allowed anywhere near this case, but for now I kept my mouth shut. I planned to question Lucas further about the wall once we were alone.

"When did you last see your mother, Lucas?" I asked.

Lucas's fury had begun to seep out, a calmness returning, however briefly. "Me and Mom, we both had shifts at Sleep-Tite. Bernie Lawler came from the Island and gave jobs to his old neighbors, including me, a high-school dropout, and Mom, a slut famous for running off at the drop of a hat." Lucas rolled his eyes at Bernie's stupidity. "You could still do that then, get a job without a college degree. Nowadays, you even need it for construction, not that there are any *jobs*."

Lucas sat back in his chair, lost in the past. "Mom and me did different work, me in the loading area, and Mom at the cutting machines, slicing up pieces of fabric, cute shit with lambs or dancing sheep. Other ladies, they'd do the actual sewing. I tried to pretend we weren't related and stayed as far away as I could." He reached over and drained his glass. "We worked different shifts, so it wasn't hard. She took nights because she and mornings didn't get along. She could barely deal with eleven p.m." Lucas stood up, grabbing his glass. "I'm gonna make another. Want one?"

Both Dave and I said no, me because I was working, and Dave because he thought he was. We remained silent until Lucas returned.

I let Lucas resettle on the couch. "Did anyone report seeing her at work that last day?"

Dave jumped in. "There's mixed reports. Your dad did a check, Lyons, after I filed the missing person report. That was six months later, though."

"And I hadn't seen her since two days before she went away," Lucas said. "I was out partying with friends, came home and found Mom in the kitchen. Was one a.m., and she's sitting there smoking cigarette after cigarette, getting good and primed to wake up Dad and fight."

"She was drinking?"

"She usually was. But remember, Vera . . . our dear *mother,* was a nightmare stone cold sober, telling my Dad how he wasn't a man, that she hated being tied to such a useless loser for the rest of her life. That's what I meant about the mouth. She'd get into screaming matches with anyone, and she didn't need a drink to do it."

"Like with Mrs. Welgas," Dave laughed. "Mom found out her son pelted me with chestnuts. Mom went and punched her, said her son was next if he didn't stay away from me."

A key sounded in the lock. The door swung open, and a frail hand dropped plastic grocery bags inside the door. Dave stood up, moving to help his Aunt Natalya, who was struggling to collapse the granny cart she'd been pushing. He grabbed it, pulling three times before it shut, the cheap wheels spinning as he lifted it off the ground and slammed it together. She heaved herself over the door-jamb, twisting herself over the step.

She unbuttoned her black cloth coat, stopping when she saw Lucas.

"Your job! *Shcho z vami?*" She moved toward Lucas, but Dave blocked her way.

"There's nothing wrong with him, Aunt Natalya." Dave combed his hair with his fingers, trying to flatten his springing curls. "There's been some news."

Natalya reached up, stilling his hand. "Squashing your hair when you are afraid. Like your father." She looked back and forth between the brothers. "What has happened?"

"They found Vera," Lucas said, his comment lost as he gulped another drink.

"What?"

Dave gripped her hand in his. "Aunt Natalya, Mom's dead."

"Oh, my poor boys." She pulled her hand from Dave, covering her mouth. "After all these years." She composed herself quickly, pushing Dave toward the couch. "Sit down. I will make you tea." Refusing to listen to protests, she pulled herself through the living room, heavy step followed by a light one, stopping briefly in front of me.

"June, so kind you are to be with David."

"Lyons isn't here for me, *teta*," Dave said. "She's here to investigate Mom's murder."

Natalya frowned. "Now is time for the family to comfort each other. Not for police."

"*Teta*, you never think it is time for the police, but getting this solved fast? I would get comfort from that," Dave said.

"And opening old wounds? Do it fast and quick," Lucas said.

Natalya continued through to the kitchen, and I heard the sound of water running followed by a kettle slamming down on a stove. I decided to pick up where I'd left off, worried Aunt Natalya might shut down this questioning as being disrespectful of the dead.

I spoke low and quick. "So she was off booze?"

"Yeah," Dave said. "For about a year."

"Don't kid yourself," Lucas said. "Dad got pissed at me when he found a bunch of bottles in the basement, accused me of bringing booze into the house. That was all her, and I told Dad. He watched her like a hawk after that, dropping her off at work and picking her up, but she had her ways, slipping away while he worked."

"So she *was* drinking," I confirmed.

"And doing drugs. Enough dealers worked at the plant. I got my pot there, and cocaine was king back then. She *loved* cocaine."

"Where'd she get the money, though?" Dave said. "Dad took her paycheck."

"She could always scrape together cash for what she cared about," Lucas said. "I bet some new boyfriend bought it for her."

I could see Dave getting angry, slowly but surely. Natalya saved the day, carrying in a tray loaded with a whole almond cake that looked like it weighed more than Natalya, plates, and small cups of tea, the scent spicy and sweet. The china cups were ivory, birds painted in gold and blood-red enamel darting along the edge.

"Beautiful," I said, admiring the cup while Natalya handed out pieces of cake.

"One unbroken thing I smuggled out of Ukraine, my mother's teacups. Even my hip"—she tapped her flank twice—"the Soviets smashed that to pieces."

Lucas raised a cup to her. "You outsmarted the Red Army and the Nazis."

I offered her my seat. She declined, taking a straight-back chair. I asked her about Vera.

"She was troubled, our Vera. She was born in safety here, but she was raised by people like me, fighting for every meal, every breath. Ukraine was hard place. Stalin starved us, shipping grain from our beautiful breadbasket over Black Sea, to pretend he was a big man, a world leader. I lived because Stalin's force, his secret police, missed one sunflower, growing not in field but next to my home, hidden behind a post."

I thought of the sunflowers that lined Natalya's garden and realized they were for more than show.

"Every day, Mother gave me seeds from sunflower, a handful at sunrise and sunset. Between Stalin and Hitler, I spent my childhood dreaming of wheat, of food." Natalya got a faraway look in her eye before refocusing hard on me. "It is no way to live, and makes people desperate, like feral cats. That was Vera's family. That's where she came from."

"How long were she and Dave and Lucas's father—"

"Taras," Dave said. He was perched on the edge of the couch, and I didn't know if he wanted to be asking the questions or answering them.

"Yes, Taras. How long were they married?"

"Nineteen sixty . . ." Natalya shook her head. "Vera was no more than fifteen, pregnant with Lucas."

"Sixty-seven," Lucas said. "Knocked up and unmarried."

"Taras made it right. In that time, we Ukrainians got married earlier. Exquisite girl like that, it was almost worse than being crippled." She touched her hip. "This world gave her little, but she had beauty, and men, they wanted to use it up. Except for my brother. Marrying Taras was best thing she ever did."

"Were you and Taras close?"

"Taras was born when I was fourteen years of age. My three sisters starved, and my two brothers were stolen by Black Raven, Stalin's police force, Stalin's *thugs*, who came at night, grabbing people from their beds, never to be seen alive again. Taras was child of sorrow, born months after father was conscripted into Red Army to be slaughtered on fields of Poland. Mother died before Taras's first birthday, and he became my baby. I promised her I would do anything to save Taras. I did." She straightened her neck, imperial. "He and I escaped, following behind the Red Army and slipping into the American side before the Russians locked everything down."

"You got the Medveds out too, don't forget," Dave said. "I don't know how you did it."

"There is a saying, 'A hungry wolf is stronger than a satisfied dog.' I was wolf, but Taras, even starving and cold, he never lost sweetness or gentleness."

Dave smiled. "Dad liked to be nice to weaker things. Small animals, hurt birds."

"But Vera couldn't take kindness," Natalya said. "It is common. When everyone's fighting over scraps of bread, you believe others' kindness come with strings, that you will be tricked in trusting. Taras confounded her."

"Dad never gave up on her," Dave said.

"Except the last time," Lucas said. "He always told us she'd come back, that only death would keep mom away. That time, he didn't say it." Lucas put the tea down and picked up his rum and coke again. "Me, I knew she'd stay lost if she found a boyfriend with a never-ending supply of cocaine and vodka."

"Stop—" Dave said.

"She was a whore."

"You never . . ." Natalya's voice shook and she stood up, "use that word to talk about your mother in my presence again."

Lucas mumbled a barely audible apology. It was enough for Natalya. She returned to her seat.

"I'm sorry for outburst," she said. "Continue now, June."

Dave nodded, and I asked my next question. "Did you notice anything different about that last time she disappeared?"

Natalya hesitated. "After Vera stole my car . . . it went quiet. Usually we heard something, calls from her in middle of night, demanding money. Or police, holding her in cell, forcing us to take her back, not that Taras would have ever turned her away from his door."

I asked if they had any pictures of Vera.

"No. None," Lucas said. "I made sure of it. I never wanted to see her again."

"I do," Natalya said. She walked over to the bookcase that was topped with several framed pictures. Lucas with Tara grinned out from the first. In the second, Dave wore a cap and gown at his high school graduation, proudly flanked by his brother and father. The third was a woman pushing a young boy on a swing. Looking closely, I realized it was Luisa and Teddy Lawler. Dad had said Natalya took Luisa's death hard, but I was surprised to see their photo lined up next to family.

Natalya pulled out an album from a lower shelf. She flipped past black-and-white pictures from the forties and fifties, a young Natalya holding a toddler in her lap and an early picture of the house, the backyard overflowing with squash and apple trees. Suddenly, there was a burst of color. The sixties. She pointed to a photo.

"Wedding day," she said.

Color photography was wasted on Vera. She wore a white mini-dress, made even shorter by her protruding belly. Teased black hair spilled down her shoulders and framed her pale face, her eyes were lined black, and her lips, painted a nude tone, were set in a harsh line. Next to her was Dave's father, Taras, a man who could be Dave's twin if Dave grew a truly monumental mustache. Behind him stood Natalya, wearing a green plaid suit and a boxy hat. She looked grim, but then she didn't appear to smile in any photos I had ever seen of her.

"Who's that?" I asked, indicating the other person in the picture. A huge man, tall and well fed, his girth hidden under an expensively tailored suit. His hair was Brylcreemed away from his face, and his fleshy grin hid his eyes.

"Maxim," Natalya said. I brought the album close, staring. It was Judge Medved. Growing up I'd met him a few times, usually when my Dad dragged me to some political picnic. He'd always play umpire in the pick-up softball games, his voice booming, filling a baseball diamond.

Natalya continued through the album, and I saw pictures of Dave and Lucas, sometimes with their mother and father, more often with their father alone. There was one of Vera wearing coveralls, scowling, leaving the Sleep-Tite factory with a grinning Lucas, followed by a photo of a large group at a picnic table, toasting the camera with mugs of beer. Natalya gave me the names of these potential witnesses and told me whether they were living or dead. Most were dead.

"Natalya," I asked, "Do you remember the night Vera disappeared?"

"What Taras and others told me only." She leaned close. "You want me to tell you who killed her, yes?"

Between the picture on the bookcase and her testimony at Bernie Lawler's trial, I was pretty sure how she was going to answer, and I was right.

"Bernie Lawler," she said. "He abused and controlled women,

destroying Luisa, a lovely angel. There is no doubt for me that Bernie killed Vera as well."

"June," Dave said. He was slumped on the couch, drained. "June, I don't want to hijack the interview, but would you mind if we talked about the funeral?"

"What funeral?" Lucas said. "There's not going to be any memorial. No one liked her enough."

"There's people," Dave said.

"What people? Because I didn't see anyone real worked up when she left. No one cared."

"I cared," Dave said.

"You were a stupid kid."

"I'm not a stupid kid now, and I want a memorial."

"Well, we're not doing it. There's no place to bury her. Dad's plot is with Aunt Natalya, and there's not an empty spot."

"So we disinter him—"

"No."

"Your mother will have memorial," Natalya said. Lucas protested, but she shushed him. "And husbands and wives, they must be buried together. I will buy plot just for me."

I flipped my notebook closed. It was great to be on the inside of this family, watching them negotiate over burial space, giving me a sense of what price they'd put on Vera Batko's life. However, they needed time alone to figure this out.

I stood. "Dave, will you be OK if I take the car?"

"No, no," Dave said. "I'm going with you." Natalya protested but Dave went to her, leaning over to kiss her cheek. "I'll be here early tomorrow. We have a memorial to plan. Right, *teta*?"

"Don't be alone," she said.

"There's June," Dave said. Natalya gripped his sleeve, and he calmed her, even as he disentangled his hand. "My family's you, Lucas, and Tara. And June. I'll be fine."

"SEE THAT BILLBOARD?"

We'd just crossed the bridge back into town, when Dave pointed up the hill to a billboard advertising the services of a personal injury lawyer. "When Luisa and Teddy Lawler disappeared, Bernie Lawler bought that billboard, offering a $100,000 reward. And the posters! Taped up on every surface, from store windows to streetlights, and when they got dirty, someone came and replaced them."

I didn't tell Dave my mother had organized that poster campaign, enlisting people on the town's Christmas committee to hang posters instead of garlands.

"Now I can appreciate what they were trying to do, but the twelve-year-old me, he was pissed off! Because here was this woman, and she got all this attention, everyone searching for her. And my mom had been gone almost six months at that point, and no one gave a shit. So I went down to the police station, and your dad helped me file a missing person report. He gave me and Mom attention. He wrote down all of the information on his pad, and then recorded all the information on a missing person report, typing out what she was wearing, the color of her purse, how tall." He ran his hand up and down the leg of his wool pants, tracing the weave. "The ring she wore."

"It's a wonder you aren't still sitting there," I said. "My father wasn't the fastest typist."

"Wite-out was smeared across your dad's hand because he kept correcting mistakes while the page was still in the typewriter, but he was patient and treated me seriously, and for the first time I thought, 'What about being a cop?'"

My dad inspired two law enforcement careers, mine and Dave's. I wondered if he had any idea.

"The disappointing part," Dave continued, "was that after I filed the report, I expected the posters, the news coverage, everything, and instead . . . silence." He paused. "But your dad went around and

interviewed everyone. Once he heard more about my mom, he laid
off, figured the hoopla would hurt me more." Dave sat forward in his
seat. "Hey, hey . . . stop here."

I pulled to the curb in front of Gergan's liquor store. "It's after
nine."

"What's a couple of minutes between friends?"

He got out of the car and rapped on the window. Sparky Gergan
came to the door, opening up when he saw Dave. Dave talked rapidly. Sparky disappeared and reappeared with a brown paper bag.

Dave climbed back into the car, breathing heavily.

I pulled away. "Did you just suborn breaking the liquor laws of
the State of New York?"

"Nope. I explained the situation to Sparky, and he kindly offered
to donate a couple bottles of Stoli for my mother's memorial. I figured scamming liquor's the tribute my mother most deserved." He
paused. "I also told him I'd be by in a few days to buy a bunch."

On Dave's street, buds sprouted on the trees and maple helicop-
ters rained down—everything would be green in a few days. I pulled
up in front of his house and killed the engine.

"Don't," Dave said, grabbing my hand as I started to pocket the
keys. "Tonight I need to be alone."

"Is that a good idea?"

"It's a *very* good idea," he said. "I need to get my head straight,
think a little."

"Drink, you mean."

"That's when I do my best thinking. Look, Lyons, tonight it's
gotta be me and some Stoli and the memories of my mom. Tomorrow I'll be good old Dave again. OK?"

"OK. One condition, however." I reached over and removed one
of the bottles. "One's plenty for tonight. I don't want you doing too
much damage, OK?"

He hugged me too tightly, burying his face in my shoulder, and
then broke away suddenly. "You're a pal, Lyons."

He got out of the car and walked slowly up the walk. Once he was safely inside, I made a U-turn toward the station. The room was empty except for Leslie, Lorraine's sister, who worked dispatch at night. Vera Batko's missing person file sat squarely in the middle of my desk. The chief anticipated everything.

I typed up my notes for the day, digging up the phone number and address of Dan Jaleda with plans to interview him tomorrow about who ordered the construction of that fake wall. I tucked the folder into my bag for a little bedtime reading and left. I needed to get home before my father saw the news. He had been delighted when he thought the case was closed. Now it was wide open, and the knowledge that Vera had been murdered, the crime unsolved and undiscovered, might destroy him.

"June bug!" Dad called when I walked through the door. He was playing Blue Öyster Cult, quietly so it wouldn't wake Lucy, and reading a Lawrence Block novel. The TV was on, and a picture of the factory flashed past. Was word out? Dad smiled when he saw me.

"We need to talk," I said and flipped off the TV.

CHAPTER 6

Promptly at 7:27 a.m., the coroner's assistant wheeled out Vera Batko's body, draped in a sheet. The coroner, Norm Finch, wasn't due until 7:30—he liked to go to early mass—but his assistant arranged things so as not to waste even a minute of Norm's time.

"You got a file yet?" Chief Donnelly asked the young man, who shifted from one foot to the other, half in and half out of the door.

"Dr. Finch hasn't released his finding. He'll brief you at the appropriate time." He exited before Donnelly could ask another question.

"Well, OK then," Donnelly said to the swinging door. "I tell you, Lyons, this whole coroner thing doesn't work out, Norm's got a future as a cult leader. They would rather die than defy his authority."

Donnelly resembled my father, a big guy fighting gravity, his shoulders sloped as muscle tone disappeared. I'd never worked a case with him—he was too busy managing up and out, conferring with the DA and negotiating budgets with the city council. Donnelly would have preferred to be on the streets—again like my father— doing real police work.

Donnelly walked over and touched the computer standing next

to the autopsy table. He ran his finger up the stem of the microphone, tapping the mouthpiece.

"I spoke to Special Agent Bascom today," he said, still studying the device. I braced for a discussion about when I was leaving the police department.

"Can I ask you a question?" he said. I nodded.

"Why do we have a karaoke machine in the autopsy room?"

I let out the breath I'd been holding. "Autopsies are dirty work. This allows Norm to take notes without having to get gore on pen and paper. Congresswoman Brouillette arranged for a grant."

"Huh." Donnelly leaned back against the counter, body relaxed, scanning the room. "So Agent Bascom said he had a colleague in Phoenix visit the Carfast corporate offices who confirmed that the van found with your burn victim was rented at one of their shops."

"He briefed me on it," I said.

Donnelly chose his words carefully. "June, I know you can solve this case on your own. But the Hopewell Falls Police Department has successfully collaborated with the FBI, unfortunate as those circumstances were. And it's looking more and more like our burn victim crossed state lines, willingly or no. Given your proven track record with Special Agent Bascom, and Bascom's volunteering his services and the services of the Albany FBI district office, I'd like to have us collaborate again." He gave me a half smile. "I'd partner up with you myself, but I'm a few years out of date, plus I might have to stop everything to fight with the mayor over how many pencils we're allowed to have."

The chief went quiet, waiting for my response. I appreciated his presenting me with a choice, limited as it was. Between the budgetary pressure and the manpower shortage, how could I say no?

"That would be fine," I said, and Donnelly let out a breath. "Although it would have been fun to work with you, plus you know the history."

"You do have someone who's an expert on that time period sitting bored in your living room."

"Oh, he's not bored."

This morning had already been a long one. After arriving home last night, I'd stayed up talking with my father for an hour. It had been a one-sided conversation, my father mumbling "OK" or "Hmm"—he was trying to process the fact that the body found in the barrel wasn't Luisa. When our non-conversation finished, I went upstairs and read through Vera's file. My dad's case notes were small and neat, so unlike the messages he scrawled and left on the counter, like "Gone to park" or "Need milk." I took out my own pad and documented the names of witnesses and a timeline of Vera's disappearance. Taras had dropped her off at the Sleep-Tite factory for her shift at 9:45, wearing work coveralls. She had been spotted by several people punching in and putting her purse in a locker. After that it got sketchy: some people swore they saw her at her machine, others said she never manned her place on the assembly line, and one woman claimed she saw Vera slip out the back door halfway through her shift. I made a note of her name: Yolanda Zulitki.

I had intended to wake up early, setting my alarm for 5:30 so I could have another talk with my father before leaving. A good night's sleep would have let the bad news sink in, and he might have more questions than he had the night before. The smell of coffee woke me at 5:00.

I shuffled downstairs, still in my pajamas, and found Dad in the dining room, which was unexpected. Some people break out the fine china for holidays; we broke out this room, never using it otherwise. Dad sat at the table surrounded by papers, coffee forgotten as he rapidly jotted notes on a notepad.

He flipped a page. "I thought it would help you if I wrote up everything I remembered about the investigation into her disappearance."

I skipped asking whether he had slept, requesting that he read me his notes.

"Vera was a little wild. I picked her up a few times for public drunkenness, delivering her back to her husband, Taras. Back then, 'alcohol rehabilitation' was getting people home safe and pouring coffee into them. And most of those people I picked up . . . they weren't ladies."

I raised my eyebrow at him. He protested. "No, no. I meant not women. Here you go." Dad handed me the sheets. He had put together a list of witnesses.

I read through the names. "You have a good memory. These were all the people listed in the original file."

"You read my old notes?" He sat up straight. "If you show them to me, it would jog my memory."

I put my hand on his arm and glanced over his notes. "Why don't we start fresh. Tell me what comes to mind."

"Not a whole lot. Dave was the only one who thought she was in some kind of danger . . . something not self-inflicted." My dad sat forward, resting his arms on the oak table, which brought back a memory of sitting at the dinner table, my sister and I arguing with my mother about eating the manicotti she had "made gourmet" by adding raisins. Mom had banned Dad's notebook from the table, and he respected the letter of this law, but he got up every two minutes to go to the other room and make a note to himself.

"So I talked to the family and interviewed her co-workers until her family told us to stop. People were angry at her for running out, especially Lucas. Dave's dad, he'd given up. So we dismissed Dave's complaint, and . . . he was right the whole time." My father stared out the window into the blackness of the backyard, and I reached over and patted his hand. He had a faraway look in his eye, and I think he was back in 1983. "I was so caught up in the Luisa Lawler case that I fell down on the job. The Luisa Lawler case made my career, got me named police chief, and I completely missed another murder."

NORM BLEW IN AT 7:30 ON THE DOT.

"Hello, old man," he said, greeting the chief. "And Officer Lyons, Junior."

As he peeled off his rain slicker and put on his lab coat, I was struck at how big he was. Even in his mid-sixties, he had power. He was the kind of guy who would go out in a bar fight or from a heart attack. My father told me stories of how Norm's family had run all the cockfights in the north end of the county from the fifties until the seventies. Even though Norm was an MD, I could believe there were cockfights in his past. The fact that he knew where the bodies were buried—or at least the chicken carcasses—made him bulletproof politically. No one was going to run against him.

"So the cause of death was a skull fracture and strangulation." Norm washed his hands. "I can't tell if she was raped; however, she did have sexual intercourse in the hours before she died."

I found that unbelievable. "She's been dead thirty years."

"Vera Batko was remarkably intact, except for a crushed thorax and a smashed skull." Labeled bone fragments lay next to her body, clumps of black hair still attached. "The body's decay ended up not polluting the hair, and we got some of our best evidence."

"Like?"

"Carpet fibers. And paint flecks caught in the blood in her hair. Plus what wasn't there. No Tris. That drum was sealed as tight as . . . well, a drum. The tech didn't want to send them over to the labs in Albany for analysis. Said they could do it faster and better."

"Can they?" Chief Donnelly asked.

"I assume so. It's not my responsibility to make sure they do their job, and I've found they're resistant to correction."

"Ms. Lin, I take it?" Chief Donnelly said.

"Oh, yes. She doesn't take criticism, but of course, there's rarely a need for it."

Dismissed by Norm, the chief reluctantly returned to the station for a press conference, and I went to Dave's, buying him a coffee and a raspberry-filled donut to soak up the alcohol. I rang his bell twice, the chimes echoing through his old Victorian, but he didn't answer. I wrote him a note: "Thinking of you, call when you recover from the bottle of Stoli," and put the coffee and donut next to his door.

I arrived at the station to find the press clustered in the lobby, amiably chatting with Lorraine. The reporter from the *Troy Record* waved, and several of the reporters called to me—my last case had put us on a first-name basis, unfortunately. The chief's door opened, and he peeked around the corner and then ducked back, out of the sight line of the press, and frantically waved me over.

"Wrangle Batko for me, will you?" Dave sat in one of the chief's visitor's chairs, his feet on the desk. "I'll illuminate the fourth estate on recent developments."

Dave appeared incredibly fit for someone who had spent the night drinking himself unconscious. He strained for a smile, too wide and almost painful.

"Hello, Lyons."

"Dave, you shouldn't be here."

"When we have two cases to solve? How could I leave now?"

"You should try the window if you want to avoid the press."

"Before I give you a present, Lyons?" He held a slip of paper in front of him, waving it back and forth. "I put together a list of Mom's known associates."

I reached for the paper, and he pulled it behind his back. I was trying to be kind, but he needed to leave—right now. In the same firm tone I used on Lucy that time she tried to coax a wild rabbit into the house using a trail of carrots, I said, "Dave, it's been one day. Go spend time with your brother, your aunt." I rested my hand on his shoulder. "Let me take care of everything for you."

"I can—"

Outside, the press got loud, calling out "Chief! Chief!" I used the distraction to grab the paper. He jumped up, ready to make a grab for it, when the door opened. It was my father.

Dave stopped his assault, walking toward my father. "Chief Lyons. You're here."

My dad threw an arm over Dave's shoulder, quite a display for a man who was more of a handshake kind of guy.

My dad held out a Price Chopper bag, an apple crushing a sandwich through the plastic. "June forgot her lunch."

In no universe would I expect my father to bring me lunch. I raised an eyebrow at him, and he raised one right back.

"Dave needs lunch. Or maybe breakfast," I said. "Why don't you two get something to eat?"

Chief Donnelly returned. He didn't come in, holding the door open. "You need to leave, Batko. You too, Gordon. We'll take your statements later."

"Like we're nothing more than witnesses," Dave said.

"You're so much more than that, which is why you can't be here." Donnelly waved them out. "Go home."

Dave was holding fast, but Dad relented.

"C'mon, Dave. Lemme buy you a pancake." Dad guided Dave to the door. "Between the two of us, I bet we can come up with some new leads."

Donnelly shut the door behind them, walked behind the desk and made a call.

"All clear," he said and hung up.

I dropped into his guest chair. "That was cryptic. Who'd you call?"

"Special Agent Bascom. I told him to wait outside until Batko hit the road. Didn't want Dave to feel shoved out the door." Personally I would have called it dragging rather than shoving, but I did want to be sensitive to Dave's feelings. "I give Dave and your dad twenty-four hours before they're trying to solve this case, so you two should move forward with, what's the phrase? All deliberate speed."

"I'm ready when you are," Hale said, coming in and shaking Donnelly's hand.

I explained to the two men that I planned to revisit any of the witnesses from Vera's original missing person investigation who were still alive, plus two additional people Dave had identified on the list I stole from him. Dan Jaleda, who helped brick in Vera back in 1983, was my priority, but calls to his office implied he would be out until late this afternoon. We had more than enough to do until then.

I wanted to add one more interview to this group, the most important person: my chief suspect. "Can we arrange a visit with Bernie Lawler in prison?"

"I'll call Defoe," the chief said. "With such a press heavy case, our illustrious DA will be put out if we don't include him."

Oh, joy. Jerry Defoe. While Jerry had stopped actively trying to undermine me after our success on our last case together, we were far from friendly. The chief read my mind.

"You don't want to be here when Jerry arrives. Get out there and do some police work."

CHAPTER 7

I SPENT THE NEXT FOUR HOURS LEARNING UKRAINIAN PRO-
fanities.

"*Suka,*" Famka, Vera's friend from grade school called her. Neither Hale nor I spoke Ukrainian, but we guessed by the way she spat
out the word that it wasn't a compliment. Everyone on the list had
spent most, if not all, of their lives in the United States. They spoke
flawless English, talking about the neighborhood, their home, their
family, and even the TV shows they liked in uninflected English.
However, the mention of Vera got them back in touch with their
roots, and out came the Ukrainian word for "slut."

"Beautiful woman, so beautiful she had no kindness in her. She
slept with my husband." Famka met our eyes frankly. "He was no great
loss. He could not keep jobs, and ran around with loose women. Like
Vera. Vera's husband, Taras, it killed him, her and her . . . drunken
behavior."

"You knew Taras?" I asked.

"A bit. His sister, much more. Natalya was almost like mother to
him. Not like huggy, kissy mother," the way she twisted her mouth

made clear Famka's distaste for hugging and kissing, "but like mother bear. Strong, and fierce, and protective."

I'd seen Natalya's mama-bear routine with Dave, petting him and then smacking him around when he got "brainless." I wouldn't have described Natalya as fierce, however.

"No, it's true. She's a fifteen-year-old girl, an orphan with a two-year-old brother, and she gets them plus Maxim and Jake Medved and their mother over the border. My sixteen-year-old granddaughter plays shooting video games all day, thinks she's tough, but she doesn't know anything. Judge Medved, he always says he'd be dead without Natalya since his mother was a saint but a mouse and would have waited patiently at home for the Red Army to return so they could shoot her in the head and conscript the boys. Natalya got them all into Germany."

"The Red Army were shooting their own citizens?"

"They didn't consider the Ukrainians citizens. Half of us were ready to join the side of the Nazis."

A shocked look must've passed my face. "It wasn't ideological," she said offhandedly. "The Soviets starved the Ukrainians, and then sent the Black Raven to grab us in our beds in the night. We thought the Nazis would be an improvement." She rolled her eyes. "Boy, were we wrong. Anyway, it's good she got her brother and the Medveds onto the American side at the end of the war because she found her way here and saved even more lives. Between her and Maxim, er, Judge Medved, no one ever went hungry. Natalya's garden overflowed, she said, but I suspect she would go without food rather than let others starve, and she could arrange a doctor to visit, help you with paperwork you needed for immigration."

"Paperwork?" Hale asked.

"Yes, fixing IDs or writing letters for people who didn't have strong English. She'd arrange for what you needed, and then Judge Medved, he'd give you all the things you wanted—a job or maybe a loan for a car." She paused. "They couldn't aid Vera, though. She was beyond help from the day she was born."

"Were you aware that we found her in a barrel in the basement of the Sleep-Tite factory?" Hale asked Vera's old friend? Enemy? It was hard to tell.

"I know." She stuck her chin out. "You know I didn't work there, right?"

ONCE SHE GOT THE OBLIGATORY PROFANITIES OUT OF THE WAY, Olga, a woman Vera worked with at the factory, gave us more information. She claimed Vera was absent from work the night she disappeared.

"Vera was the laziest woman alive, always ducking out for a smoke," Olga said. Now fifty-nine, Olga had been a few years younger than Vera, and had worked in the factories until she was disabled. She claimed that the heat from the factory had left her lungs sounding like she smoked three packs a day, two more packs than the one she smoked during our visit.

Olga took a drag on her cigarette. "But the rules that applied to the rest of us didn't apply to her. She disappeared for a few hours one night, and our team got written up for missing production targets. I complained to my supervisor, and he told me to take it up with the owner himself, Bernie Lawler, if I had a problem. He said he wasn't going to put his neck on the line." She sat back in her chair. "I never brought it up again."

"Who was her supervisor?" I asked.

Olga didn't say anything for almost a minute, before slapping her head, ash from her cigarette sprinkling across her and the chair. "Now I remember. Ilan Petrovich. He died back in the eighties. Killed himself."

"Killed himself?"

"Yeah, he couldn't get work after Sleep-Tite closed. Couldn't support his family." She shrugged. "You do what you have to do."

"THOSE WERE HER FRIENDS?" HALE ASKED AS HE DROVE US through the winding streets of the Island.

"And to think their opinions have mellowed. Imagine how they felt thirty years ago."

Hale laughed. "The only folks we can exclude as suspects are dead."

"Well, the dead and Dave." I flipped through my notes, trying to decide who to visit next.

"We did pretty well back there," Hale said.

"Hmm?"

"As a team. We worked well together. You got some great questions in there—"

"And you had my back." Before Hale could take a victory lap, I pointed to a street coming up. "Wait. Wait. Make a right up here."

Hale turned without question. As we drove to the north edge of the Island, the houses grew bigger. On the left, the lots backed onto the Hudson River; they must have beautiful sunrises. On the right, the houses were set far back from the street, shaded by tall oak and maple trees. We parked in front of a line of privet hedges that grew high and almost wild, obscuring the house from the street.

Hale leaned over me to get a better view. I could smell his cologne faintly, tobacco and sandalwood, so subtle it had to be expensive. "What've we got here?"

"The house where Bernie Lawler murdered Luisa."

We got out and walked to the driveway, cut off from the road by a rusty chain with a faded No Trespassing sign attached.

The house had cedar shingles, most faded or fallen off, giving it a mangy dog quality. It was big, but not as gargantuan as the McMansions popular in the nineties, and without their Mediterranean accents.

"Can I help you?" A slight man limped toward us, carrying a pair of hedge clippers. "That's private property you're on."

"We're the police," I said and pulled out my badge. "Do you take care of the property?"

"A bit. Judge Medved, he asks me to keep it from being an eyesore. Elda Harris owns it, but she don't care about maintaining it."

"So Elda owns this," I said. "She doesn't mind the work you're doing?"

"We can't go inside or nothing, just keep the hedges clipped and the lawns mowed, what she said was OK after the city fined her a couple thousand bucks for not maintaining her property. That's too rich for even her." The man shifted from foot to foot, nervous in a way that made me suspect he had some jail stretches in his past. "If you want to get in, I don't got the keys."

"No need for a visit right now," I said, "We may have to come back."

As we waved good-bye, Hale said, "So the Lawlers—or should I say Medveds?—that family is an interesting bunch. If I understand correctly, half the clan plays cops and the other half are robbers. On the one side you have Bernie and Jake. The one that did a stint in prison?"

"That's him."

"And on the side of good you have Deirdre, Bernie's sister, a lawyer who represented him on his appeals, and Judge Maxim Medved." Hale rolled through a stop sign but I didn't protest—out at the edge of the Island there was very little traffic. "Both of whom seem to have escaped the taint of having convicts at Christmas dinner. The judge still on the bench?"

"No, he stepped down five years ago."

"Those crony guys usually are more about scratching the right people's backs than making good law."

"He wasn't a lawyer," I said.

"What?!"

"You don't have to be in New York. My dad gave Judge Medved high praise, calling the judge 'reasonable' on the bench. But the politics part . . . the machine isn't as lockstep as it once was—Republicans occasionally win, and no one drives people to the polls anymore— but back then Dad thought the judge crossed a lot of lines."

Hale came to a complete stop at Ontario Street. Traffic crossing the river from Hopewell Falls to Troy was heavy here, and we almost missed the bar, the car behind us beeping when Hale made a sharp turn into the lot.

Hale looked at the two-story house, white aluminum siding stained with rust, a glassed-in porch on the second floor. He frowned. "This is Jake's bar?"

I walked to the wooden door and, like Vanna White, underlined "Jake's," pasted on in square sticky letters. The door was unlocked, and we pushed inside.

I blinked twice to let my eyes adjust to the dark room.

A voice came out of the gloom. "Got a membership?"

A young man stood behind the bar, his long blond hair falling past his chin, obscuring his face. With a layer of fat over an already big frame he must have been handy in a bar fight. He washed glasses, his thick fingers pushing a rag into a glass before dunking it into clean water and picking up a second.

"A membership?" Hale said. "Is this a country club?"

"A social club."

"Are you Jake?" Hale asked.

"Brian. Jake's son. But don't tell me how you're long-lost friends of his to try to get around rules." He tucked his bangs around his ears with a wet hand, and I could see his face: handsome, with pale blue eyes and a straight nose.

"You need a membership here. Five dollars, and we give you a card, and you show it when you come in."

"We're not going to drink," I said.

"No exceptions. You still need a card." Brian gently placed the clean glass on a rack.

"No, we're the police. We're here investigating the murder of Vera Batko."

He stopped, picked up a towel, and dried his hand. "Lucas's mom, who got killed. The one I hear stories about."

"From whom?" Hale asked.

"The old guys, mostly. Call her a good-time girl, making a fool of herself with booze and men. They even say stuff in front of Lucas. He doesn't give a shit." He heaved the rack of glasses to his left. "Me, I'd kill a man before letting him talk about my mother that way, dead or alive."

I walked up to the bar, a dark oak marked with cigarette burns and water rings, but unsticky, a nice surprise. "Can you give us the names of the people you heard talking?"

"Sure thing," he said. "Or hang around for an hour or two. They'll be in sooner or later."

"How 'bout your dad?" Hale said. "He around?"

"Pop's in the office." The young man gestured toward some swinging doors. "Gimme a sec."

The windows were blacked out with heavy shades, blocking most of the light, but efforts had been made to decorate, with scenes of mountains and beaches mounted on poster board, the corners curved up and splitting. Several Ukrainian beer signs hung behind the bar, and the hallway was lined with pictures of softball teams spanning back thirty years, the beer guts under the "Jake's Social Club" black jerseys giving the impression they were not the most competitive team.

"June." Hale crooked his finger at me. I walked over to where Hale was looking at a picture of a young army recruit, blond and blue eyed. He was wearing his combat camouflage uniform, with the tans, browns, and grays of the desert, "B. Medved" on a name tape attached to the slanted pocket.

"The guy in the kitchen?" I asked. He bore little resemblance to the man in the picture, who had hair shaved close under a cap and a hopeful look on his young face.

Hale pointed at the insignia Brian was wearing in the picture. "A Crab. Part of the Fourth Brigade, First Armored Division." He paused. "The boy was responsible for clearing explosives."

"Explosives that could have caused a fire like the one in the factory?"

"No," Hale said. "With his expertise he would've done a better job."

The front door swung open, and the daylight was almost blinding. An older gentleman wearing a three-piece suit stood in the doorway, a cloth bag swinging from his hand. He had a lined face and huge eyebrows that seemed to be making up for his retreating hairline.

"May I help you?" he said.

"Jake Medved?" Hale asked.

"I am Judge Maxim Medved. Jake would be my brother." From behind us hinges creaked, and Jake emerged through the swinging doors, as tall as his son but wiry, muscle mass gone with age.

The judge walked forward slowly, embracing his brother and kissing his cheek.

"Am I interrupting business, brother?" He asked, squinting at Hale and me.

"Police officers, right?" Jake frowned "Been a long time since I had a visit from you. Here about Vera, right?"

The four of us took seats around a table in the far corner.

"I'm June Lyons, from the Hopewell Falls PD, and Hale Bascom—"

"Before we start," the judge said, despite the fact that we already had. He handed the bag to his brother. "Natalya made your favorite soup. Beef borscht."

Jake opened the bag and smiled. "She even included sour cream."

"She has always taken care of us," the judge said to me, winking conspiratorially. "A container waits for me in the car." Without look-ing, the judge called over his shoulder. "Brian!"

The young man moved from around the bar faster than I would have expected of someone with his build. Only when he approached our table did I realize he was limping. One foot was in a scuffed suede military boot, and the other was prosthetic.

"Brian, put this away for your father, so he has something to eat later." He shoved the bag into Brian's hands and patted his nephew's belly. "And do not eat it! You have had plenty!"

Brian ducked down behind the bar with the food, I assumed to put it in the refrigerator, watching us the whole time.

"So we're here today, gentlemen, to ask you about Vera Batko," Hale said.

The judge didn't hesitate. "That was a long while ago, but no one could forget Vera," he said, easing into his telling. "When she was a girl, she was the prettiest thing you ever saw, if a little cheeky. I introduced her to her husband. I thought I made a love match: she was a little wild, and I thought Taras would calm her down, settle her. Taras, he needed a little joy in his life." He nudged Jake in the ribs. "Broke my brother's heart."

"So you knew Vera?" I asked Jake.

"Everyone knew everybody, out here on the Island. I tried to protect her when she was young . . ."

"Because you were sweet on her," the judge teased.

"I was no such thing," Jake said grabbing his brother's elbow and pushing it away. "She was a child. Of course later, much later, she'd disappear from town and then show up again, all hollowed out. See that table, next to the jukebox?" I twisted, looking at a scarred wooden table shoved in a corner. "She'd get drunk and dance up there."

"The lady had problems," Hale emphasized "problems," "and you served her?"

The judge threw his thick arm over his brother's thin shoulders, forcing Jake to slump down. "Do not blame Jake. Better she get it here, where there were people who could watch out for her."

"We usually cut her off before things got rough and made sure she got home safe," Jake added. "None of the guys she ran off with were from the neighborhood."

"Yes," the Judge said. "A social club like this, we can keep the riff raff out."

Considering the owner was a felon, I doubt they were worried about how classy their clientele was.

"So you worked here?" I asked Jake. "After you got out of prison."

"A long time after, in fact."

"I thought ex-cons couldn't bartend?"

Jake's nostrils flared at Hale's question. "That's at a regular bar. We don't follow the same rules at a social club like this. Maxim here helped me apply for a certificate of relief of disabilities"—*the disability being two felony convictions for assault,* I thought—"and I bought the place, got it running."

A group of five men came in, calling out to Brian, dropping their voices when they saw us. The men all wore train uniforms, the bar a quick hop over the bridge from the Rensselaer train station.

"Freddie," Jake yelled, pointing to a man who hung in the doorway, hesitant to join the rest of the group. "I don't need to tell you what will happen if we have a repeat of last time?"

The man shook his head frantically, joining his friends in the corner.

"Sorry, officers," Jake said, still staring at the man who was trying to duck behind his friends. "A troublemaker. Please continue."

"How about your other brother, Judge Medved?" Hale asked. "Bernie?"

"Bernie and Deirdre," the judge said. "My stepfather treated them so cruelly. When our mother died, I took custody of the two little ones. I moved heaven and earth to make sure their father could never hurt them again."

"May that black dog rot in hell," muttered Jake.

The judge leaned in close. "My stepfather beat my mother. He taught Bernie you could treat women like nothing."

"He stopped beating them once I paid him a visit," Jake said. "Didn't like it so much when he had someone who could hit back."

"I tried to teach Bernie to respect women when I took the children in, but . . . it was too late for Bernie."

A dozen people crowded in, the men in pressed khakis and the women in sweater sets. State workers if I had to guess. Brian, delivering fries and wings to the train employees, called out to the second group, "You all getting your regular?" When he was concentrating on work, his limp almost disappeared.

I dropped my voice. "Did Bernie abuse Luisa?"

"No," Jake said. "Absolutely not."

"Nothing physical." The judge added, "But my brother, he kept her a prisoner in that house. Bernie liked to control women."

"Including Vera?" Hale asked.

"Including Vera," the judge said. "Him hiring her? It was not charity. Back in high school she would not give him the time of day. He liked making her beg for her job every time she came crawling back."

For a politician, the judge didn't talk about himself much, but he had no problem trashing his brother.

"When was the last time you saw Vera?" I asked.

Jake flicked his eyes to his brother, snakelike. The judge ignored him.

"We think," the judge said carefully, "it was the night she disappeared."

"There was a poker game at the bar, but they were all amateurs"—Jake shook his head in disgust—"and I cleaned them out quickly. They all wanted beers on credit, so I decided to take them to where there was plenty of free booze: Bernie's. Vera was there." Jake shook his head. "Following Dan Jaleda around. He brought her along to Bernie's even though everyone knew it was a bad idea."

"She liked male attention," Judge Medved said. "A room full of men, having a few drinks? She was in heaven."

That matched up with what we knew. "Who did she leave with that night?"

"She didn't," Jake said. "She was still at Bernie's. She'd taken some Quaaludes. Vera was out cold."

"You talking about my mother?" Lucas stood behind me. We had been speaking softly, so I hoped he hadn't heard any details. He rested his hand on the back of my chair. "Hi, June. Dave here?" He noticed Hale. "Hi. You're Hale, right?"

Jake and Judge Medved both stood and moved to embrace Lucas.

"Young man, good to see you," Jake said, clapping him on the shoulder. "What can we get you?"

"A beer would be good," Lucas said to Brian as Brian passed on his way to deliver five vodka tonics.

Brian never paused, the drinks on his tray perfectly balanced despite his hitching gait. "You know where it is," he called over his shoulder. "Serve yourself."

The place was packed. Despite the crowd, no one got within three tables of us on any side, keeping their distance from Jake and the judge. Between Lucas and the crowds, this interview was over, and we stood to go. The men ignored us, focused on Lucas.

"We want to be here for you in your time of need," Jake said.

"You know you can count on us," the judge said. "We owe Natalya our lives."

Lucas reached out, embracing both men.

"You," he slurred. "You're family to me."

CHAPTER 8

WHEN WE ARRIVED AT HIS OFFICE, DAN JALEDA'S ADMINISTRA-
tive assistant was on the phone, giving detailed instructions on how
to defrost stuffed peppers.

"Not the microwave," she said. "The bread crumbs get all sticky."
She noticed us standing in the door, mouthed "one second," and dismissed her caller.

"Gotta go," she said. "The cops are here."

She didn't wait for introductions, rapidly typing into the computer. "Which of the guys are you looking for this time? Bail skipper
or outstanding warrant?"

"Neither," I said. "We're here to see Dan Jaleda."

The woman took her hands off her keyboard. "Dan?"

"I think you and I spoke this morning." I held out my hand. "I'm
Officer June Lyons with the Hopewell Falls police department, and
this is Hale Bascom, with the FBI. You mentioned he'd be in this
afternoon."

"I'm Ashley," she said. "And this morning? Not me. I was running some paperwork to the notary." She paused. "We're not supposed to give out Dan's schedule."

I had the sense I was getting someone fired. "We explained we were the police and it was important."

Her eyes traveled up Hale's body, eventually reaching his face. "FBI-level important?"

"Agent Bascom is on loan to us for this investigation."

"Let me try to track Dan down." She motioned to fabric-covered folding chairs in the corner. "Make yourselves comfortable."

I heard her leave a message for her boss, and then she dialed a work site, using her pencil so as not to damage her long burgundy-tipped nails. She called two more numbers and put down the phone.

"All three sites say he's 'just left.'" She sighed, her inability to find him a personal failing. "He's been the boss for twenty years now, but he spends half his time at sites."

"Keeps things running smoothly," Hale said. "Good thing in a boss. We'll sit here entertaining ourselves. Don't let us disturb you."

She went back to typing, but slowly, keeping half an eye on us. I didn't mind waiting. Catching him off guard might be our only chance of interviewing him without his wife, Deirdre Lawler. Deirdre was both Bernie's sister and his lawyer, and she could make my life difficult in any number of ways, cutting off this interview, or worse, keeping me from seeing Bernie. I didn't want her here, but I also didn't want to conduct this interview with her in the room.

I slipped out to the hallway and called the hospital about our burn victim: no change. When I returned, I found Hale tapping away on his BlackBerry, so I spent my time reading through my notes. A few guys came in and out requesting paychecks and paperwork, and with them Ashley was easygoing, calling them "hon" and quizzing them on their plans for the weekend. Having finished reading my notes, I cast around for something to do. A table in front of us displayed a magazine from four and five years back, when Gwyneth Paltrow was still with her husband and Lindsay Lohan was in trouble with the law, which could be any time in the last decade. The rest of the office was designed to look low rent, but I sensed it was intentional. The industry awards lining the walls—almost twenty by my count—undid the "aw shucks" atmosphere.

Dan Jaleda entered talking. "Yeah. I get it. But the bond issue won't carry us over, and they have severely underestimated the cost per square foot on that HVAC system." He stood in front of the desk. He wore the men's business-casual uniform—khakis and a blue button-down shirt, and his gray hair had a crease where he had been wearing a hard hat. He picked up the mail and began to flip through as he spoke, giving us a brief nod even as he reamed out the person on the other end of the phone.

"I've laid this out for you. Multiple times. This was not included in your bid instructions, and we can't be held to those cost estimates." He never raised his voice, but his sharp clipped tones made clear that the other person's opinion was invalid. "You send out an RFP asking for a hot dog, and then get mad when a steak isn't delivered. Join us in reality anytime you'd like." He listened. "Get back to me by six or this deal is off."

He hung up without saying good-bye and pulled the earpiece out of his ear, put out his hand, and to my amazement, smiled. "C'mon in, officers. I was expecting you."

Like his nephew Brian Medved, Dan limped, his foot dragging behind him, although if I had to guess I'd bet his injury came from a construction accident instead of battle. Dan wore heavy work boots, steel toed and ungraceful. He went around the side of the desk, gathered up a stack of rolled-up architectural plans, sliding them into a wire rack. His office was utilitarian, one wall covered in whiteboard and the other three posted with architectural plans.

"My wife is going to kill me when she hears I was talking to the police without her present." He sat down. "She's a lawyer and doesn't think you should pay a parking ticket without counsel present, but I don't always like her knowing the details of my deals. It makes her nervous when she sees how much money's involved, like if it doesn't work out she'll have to go back to waitressing at Jake's bar."

I wasn't sure what kind of deal he was referring to, but I played along.

"Informational interview only," I said. "I promise."

"That's what cops always say." He pulled out a folder full of papers. "Here's the info on the proposed sale, including the plans and all correspondence between me and Elda Harris. It includes the deed search, showing how she took ownership of the property once Bernie went to jail." He flipped forward a few pages. "And here's the contract for sale, signed by one party, me, and a letter in which Elda explains that as a memorial to her dead daughter and grandson, and to punish Luisa's killer, she wanted the land to remain forever empty."

I pulled the documents to my side of the desk, and Hale leaned in close—we read together. It seemed that Dan Jaleda had spent several years trying to coax Elda Harris into selling him Sleep-Tite and the land it sat on. His proposal consisted of an offer for the property, with plans to knock it down and build a combination retail/housing space.

"So despite the rumors you may have heard"—I had heard none, but I nodded, acting as if I had—"Elda turned down my very lucrative offer. Like a dog with a bone, Elda is." He shook his head. "So any ideas you might have had that I hired that woman that got burned up to torch that factory need to be put to rest."

I closed the folder and slid it under my notebook. "That's very helpful, thank you. I have a few more items on my list—"

"About the wall." It wasn't a question.

"About the wall," I said.

"Well, let me start by saying I had no idea chemicals were in those barrels."

I could understand his desire to establish deniability, particularly with the EPA cranking up their investigation. "Our investigation is focused on Vera."

"Right. So Bernie hired me to do some cleaning and 'light construction' at the Sleep-Tite factory. Annual maintenance, he said. We get there, and Jake gives us a bunch of sheetrock and some bricks and tells us we're going to build a wall. Didn't talk about the barrels behind the wall, and we didn't ask."

"You were able to build a brick wall in a week?"

"We got it up in two days. No permit means no inspection means who cares how crappy the work is." He pulled a piece of paper out of a drawer and began sketching. He drew the dimensions of the basement, and squares at the end to represent the barrels, his lines straight and angles perfect. He then drew a dotted line in front of the barrels. "It was like a veneer, looked substantial, but flimsy underneath. We put up a sheetrock wall, floor to ceiling, and then plastered sawed-off bricks to the sheetrock." He dropped his pencil and sat back. "They wanted it to match, not hold up a building."

I slid the paper close, studying it before handing it to Hale.

"May we keep this?" I asked, and he waved it away. I picked up my notebook. "Do you have the names of the people you worked with?"

He listed several names, including Lucas Batko. "Bunch of dopes we were. High school dropouts hustling to get into the trades, and Jake promised we'd all get a shot at construction work if we did right on this job."

"So Jake hired you?"

"Officially, yes, it was him, but Bernie was paying us, and Maxim dangled the better jobs in front of us. Jake was there to do the dirty work, playing to his strengths, you know?"

We needed some sort of direct proof. "Did Bernie write you a check for this project?"

"Jake slid an envelope of cash across the bar. That was payment."

Hale leaned forward. "And did Bernie ever comment on the work you did?"

"Not before it was built or after." He reached for his mechanical pencil, punching forward two leads before speaking. "The only time I saw Bernie during that week . . . I think it was the night Vera was killed."

"Which night was that?" I asked.

"The Friday before we sealed the barrels in the basement," he said. "At Bernie's."

So far this matched up with the statement of the Medved brothers. "Tell me about it."

"Vera . . . she was always up for a party, you know?" I did know, it being the sole thing people remembered. "Jake's had been pretty dead, with most people getting away, celebrating the last week of summer. Jake announced we were taking the party to Bernie's. He invited me along. I didn't like him much, but I was trying to get in with the brothers, so of course I said yes."

I thought of Lucas building the wall to get a better job. "Were you trying to get work?"

He paused, a half smile on his lips. "No. I was trying to get in with Deirdre. Back then she was whip smart and had the nicest green eyes I'd ever seen, and I was trying real hard to impress her, so I was playing nice with the Medveds." He smiled to himself. "Found out later that spending time with her brothers *hurt* my chances, but back then, I had no idea."

"So we show up at his house, and our friend Bernie didn't look happy to see us *at all*. He had luggage and a blow-up raft in the living room, all set to join his wife and child out on the Cape. He kept repeating 'Luisa is going to kill me,' over and over."

"Afraid you'd bust up the place?" asked Hale.

Dan laughed. "Pretty much. We were a rowdy bunch back then, Jake leading the charge. Bernie had eased off a bit since becoming a father, and Maxim made sure nothing got out of hand, knocked everyone upside the head when they got too out of bounds, or made calls, getting people out of trouble later."

"But both Bernie and Jake went to prison," I said. "If he couldn't get charges dropped against his brothers, he didn't do a very good job."

"But remember," Dan said, "Bernie could have gone away for

life, and Jake's assault charges—bullshit as they were—were origi-
nally attempted murder."

Felony assault was rarely bullshit. I asked him to explain.

"Well, it was before my time, but the story is that some contractor
did a shitty job of paving the streets on the Island. Worse, he didn't
hire anyone from the Island on the job. Maxim was a councilman
back then, but he wanted what was best for his constituents, if only
to get re-elected. Jake didn't want his brother to be disappointed, so
he went to persuade the guy to re-do the work for free. With a lead
pipe." He shrugged. "The contractor is still around—I worked with
him on a job back in October—so it couldn't have been that bad."

Dan handled lead pipes to the skull with considerable equanim-
ity.

"Anyway, back to Vera. Things got going in Bernie's party room,
his pride and joy. Had a big black glossy bar, white shag carpeting,
and a white leather couch. That couch was where things started to
go downhill."

"Why?"

"Vera was all over that night, three sheets to the wind by the time
things got rolling."

"Who'd she arrive with?" I asked.

"Honestly, I don't remember." Sentences started with "honestly"
rarely had much truth to them, but I let him continue. "She stumbled
downstairs mid-party like she had been there the whole time and
settled right in. She was doing cocaine, talking ten thousand miles a
minute, sharing with everyone what a genius she was and how she
was about to be a rich woman. She was off on a rant and she let a
cigarette burn down on the arm of his couch. Bernie went through
the roof."

"What did he do?"

"He was ready to kick her and the whole crowd out of there,
but the judge talked him down; the night went downhill, with arguments over a poker game, and Vera picking a fight with Oksana,

Jake's girlfriend. Oksana was a meek little thing, but Jake took offense and was on the warpath with Vera, too. Someone must have decided to defuse the situation and slip Vera a Quaalude, because she went from motormouth to out of it in a few minutes. I decided to get out of there before things got ugly. When Bernie walked me to the door, he thanked me for treating his sister right. Said he was jealous, that he was supposed to do a night drive out to Cape Cod to avoid the traffic and now he had a house full of drunks.

"So when you left, Bernie, Jake, the judge, and Oksana were the last ones there?"

"The judge may have been gone, and Oksana and Jake walked out a few steps ahead of me and were sitting in the car when I drove away. That left Bernie and Vera, alone in that house." He paused and seemed to be struggling for the right words. "Bernie's my brother-in-law, and Deirdre would kill me if she heard this, but with him, alone in the house with her? I think he did it."

I asked him for the names of other witnesses who were at Bernie's that night, looking for people who could validate either Dan's or Jake's story. As I put away my notebook, he offered to answer any additional questions we had.

"One more, if you don't mind," I said. "You don't seem very protective of your in-laws."

"Do you think those brothers need protection?" He didn't look at us, pulling blueprints out of the rack. "Bernie, I always liked the guy, but he's been in prison for thirty years for a murder I think he's good for. Maxim, he's okay in small bursts, but he goes into judge mode and is a huge pain in the ass. Jake, though. Jake's a thug. I don't like him now, and I never did." He paused. "And he dragged his son down with him. Me and my wife, we were ready to do anything for Brian when he got back from Iraq, his leg blown off, get him back his life." He shook his head. "But Brian has no life. Jake locked him away in that new house of his, gave him the keys to the bar, and tied him to the Island for the rest of his life."

CHAPTER 9

THE SUN WAS SETTING AS WE DROVE UP THE HILL TO COLONIE, the glare through the passenger side window blinding. We were driving west, past the border of Hopewell Falls, to talk to Tanya Zulitki. Tanya had left the Island, but she'd known Dave's mom, and more importantly, she was the daughter of Yolanda Zulitki, the woman who saw Vera leave the building the night she disappeared. We hoped that if she saw Vera leave, she might also have seen who she went with.

We had agreed to meet her after work, but when we pulled up in front of her house, it was dark. We rang the bell to be sure. No answer.

The sun dropped over the horizon, and Hale took off his sunglasses. With the hard angles of his face, the shades made him harsh and unreachable—it was nice to be able to talk eye-to-eye. As we waited, my phone rang. The chief.

"Officer Lyons"—Donnelly's voice sounded tinny and faraway—"I've got you on speaker here with the DA."

"Hello, Officer Lyons," Jerry said. We had made a certain peace after the Brouillette case, but we were hardly friends. "You're going to be *very happy* for this phone call." Somehow Jerry managed to make good news an insinuation. "We've arranged for you to get in to see Bernie Lawler tomorrow."

That *was* good news. "How'd you swing that?"

"We made a little deal with his lawyer. She's been pushing to have the blood evidence retested, everything we collected from the basement and the back of Bernie's car. There's no chance she'll find anything, so there's no harm in indulging her. I mean, your father did thorough police work, and he wouldn't have made a mistake *that* big, would he?"

Ah, there's the Jerry I knew and hated. He would have fought that retest tooth and nail, but on the off chance that my dad had made a mistake and Jerry could humiliate him? No way would Jerry let that opportunity pass.

"The blood types in both the basement and Bernie's trunk matched," the chief said. "Gordon did everything right. Bernie's lawyer did put some stipulations on the meeting, however. She will be present. And also, Hale Bascom can't be in the room. It's you and them, June."

I looked over at Hale, who mouthed "what?" Had he heard?

"She can't prevent you from visiting," the chief said.

"But she could delay it," Jerry said. "I greased the wheels for you."

A sedan came up the street, pulling into the driveway, and I quickly agreed to the terms.

"Thanks—to you both," I said, hanging up. That was as close to appreciation as Jerry was going to get from me.

Spotlights went on in the driveway, revealing a pearl-gray Audi. A tall African-American woman got out of the car.

"What'd they say?" Hale asked, but my answer was cut off by Tanya Zulitki.

"Sorry for the delay," she called, pulling her purse out of the backseat. "Things got crazy at work and I underestimated the commute."

She jogged up the walk. The pink reflective panels on her zip-up jacket, exercise capris, and sneakers glowed bright, even in the weak light. She scaled the steps and opened the door, punching in a security code and hitting the lights.

Her hallway was clean, but not scarily so—mail was dropped on an entry table, and shoes had been kicked off next to the door, including her current pair.

"Gimme a sec," she said. "If I don't get some protein, this interview ends fast. Settle yourself in the living room and I'll be right back."

We sat on a suede couch, its muted browns letting the bright textiles, pictures, and masks that hung on the wall really pop. Magazines were piled under a side table almost to tipping, but the desk tucked in a corner was completely clear, without even a pencil.

She walked in carrying a tray of sparkling water, cheese, and crackers. "Thought you might be hungry. I'd offer wine, but I'm working tonight and need to stay sharp." She cracked open the sparkling water and poured some for the three of us without asking. I placed mine on a coaster next to me, keeping my hands free to take notes. She dove into the cheese, cutting off several slabs.

"Manchego, my favorite." She swallowed her cracker and cheese and took a long drink of water. "So, Vera, right? Dave and Lucas's mom?"

Hale sat up straight. "Yes. Your memories, but also if you recall anything your mother said about the night Vera disappeared or who might have put her in that barrel."

Tanya pulled her legs onto the chair, settling into her story. "I was about five when my dad took off, and Vera left the same week. She and my Mom had been thick as thieves. Oh, before I forget . . ." She walked over to her desk. Unlocking it, she retrieved a folder from the top drawer and handed us a photo.

It was a picnic, the picture's focus close enough that it could have been anywhere, the leaves of a maple tree hanging low, putting the group in shade. An African-American woman—Tanya's mother,

Yolanda—talked to Vera, who sat across the table, an open bottle of rosé between them, next to the hamburgers, hot dogs, chips, and potato salad spilling across the rest of the table. Vera wore a red shirt-dress, the same dress she was wearing when her body was found in the barrel. Big loose curls framed her face, and her burgundy lips twisted in a half smile, sharing a joke with Tanya's mother. Across the table, Yolanda laughed.

"Vera was always nice to my mother, a rare thing on the Island. When my father brought his lovely, young, *pregnant* black bride home, she wasn't welcomed with open arms. They'd insult her in Ukrainian, thinking she didn't understand what they were saying. She could guess." Tanya crossed her legs. "So could I."

I studied the picture. Next to Vera was Dave, drinking from a can of generic soda, "Orange" stamped black on a white can. Taras hunched over Dave, putting mustard on his hot dog, revealing Taras's balding head, black hair thinning to reveal the pale skin below. He was wearing a white button-down shirt, cuffed at the elbows, and black pants. Across from him, almost out of the frame, was Lucas, reaching for potato chips. Only Tanya, with her huge brown eyes and her yellow sundress, smiled for the camera.

"My memories of Vera are mostly superficial," Tanya said. "I liked her because my mom liked her, but Vera was one of those people who didn't get kids, talking to me in a loud voice, and petting me, but at arm's length. I loved her clothes: high-heeled clogs and these beautiful peacock feather earrings." She laughed and waved to the room. "I like things a little different, design wise."

"That painting over there," Hale said. "Cambodian, right?"

I was a little confused as to why Hale decided now was a good time for a discussion on home decorating.

"That it is. I've very impressed, Agent Bascom." He gave her a shy smile and my alarm bells went off: Hale smiled, but shy was not in his emotional repertoire.

Tanya pointed to the screen in the corner, three monstrous pup-

pets in front of a delicate brown paper screen. "That's my last purchase. Picked it up two years ago in Indonesia. I try to go on one big
trip every year, but it's getting harder and harder as my firm grows—
the cases are higher profile and don't always have a defined deadline."
She took a sip of her sparkling water. "It was easier to do when I was
setting up divorced guys in bars."

"You're a PI?" I asked. Dave had failed to mention that. Even so,
I'd never met Tanya, and usually we tripped over the PIs when criminal charges turned into civil.

"I am. Followed around old Harvey Sanger for a few years, part
of a crew of honey traps, batting my eyes at men stepping out on their
wives. That was small-time, though, so about ten years ago I set up
my own firm, focused on insurance, and in the last few years, corporate spying and espionage."

I was surprised that she was admitting she did corporate spying
straight out, but she laughed, merry and bright.

"Oh, to see your face," she said to Hale. She hadn't noticed my
reaction. "No, not doing it. Hunting it down. Biggest part of my
work now—big pay and big clients. I wouldn't cross paths with
you, Officer Lyons. With my clients, I'd tangle with Special Agent
Bascom." She winked at him. "Although generally my clients prefer
to settle these things out of court. Less bad publicity."

I decided to steer the conversation back to the original topic. "I
was reading through the original case file, and your late mother said
she saw Vera leaving through a back door. Did she ever tell you anything about that night?"

"She did," Tanya said. "Mom was a safety rep for the union, and
there had been an injury. She had gone to the office to pick up a form
and saw the tail end of Vera sliding out the side door in high-heeled
boots and that red dress right there." Tanya tapped the photo. "Not
that anyone believed her at first."

"Why wouldn't they believe your mom?"

She sighed. "No reason, or should I say no *real* reason. Back then, people thought Mom was lying because that's what black people did. They kept her around because they drank beer with her husband. They weren't so prejudiced that they thought black people should be sent back to Africa." She crossed her arms and her legs. "But Albany would be far enough. Outside of Albany and Troy this area's really white. Really, really, really white."

She was right. After spending time in New York and California, it was a shock for me to come back to my hometown. Diversity for us was when the Irish mixed with the Italian Catholics.

"Anyway," Tanya said, "after a week of Vera being gone folks allowed that maybe, possibly my mother was telling the truth. Then they started hitting her with all these questions—When did you see her leave? Who was she with?" She shook her head. "What they were really trying to find out is the name of her new boyfriend so they could call him and tell him to bring her home."

"Dave mentioned your dad might have been close with Vera," Hale said.

"Everyone thought they were *screwing.* But he was a deadbeat, not a cheater. Because of the timing, people assumed they took off together. I gave him a call last week—"

"He's alive?" I asked.

"Alive and kicking in South Carolina with his third wife. I usually call him at Christmas and his birthday, so he was thrilled with a third call. He was cagey about Vera, not wanting to sully my virgin ears"—at this she laughed—"but he did say Vera was 'in a bad place' when he last saw her. In Dad-code that means drugs or possibly sex and drugs. I confronted him straight out, asked if they'd been dating, and he denied it. Then I hung up, because that was plenty of time talking to the old goat."

I asked for her father's number, and she pulled out her phone, reading it to me.

"A second?" Tanya said, typing something into her phone. She finished and placed it on the arm of her chair. "Any more questions?"

Hale and I looked at each other.

"No?" she said, looking from me to Hale. "So now you can help me solve my very first case."

She reached out and handed me the file. I opened it up and was greeted with a picture of five women—one blonde, one redhead, and three brunettes, one of whom was Vera. The pictures of two of the brunettes were X-ed out.

"When my dad left, I became a little fixated on missing persons, to say the least. By the time I was eight, I investigated disappearances in my neighborhood: my dad, Vera, and several other women." She shifted closer so her knees brushed Hale's. "The two brunettes crossed out there? They came home to their families. The blonde and the redhead, both from the neighborhood, they didn't come back. Neither did Vera."

I examined the pictures more closely. Both women were pretty—clean, shiny hair, smiling. Families had given photos like this before. Later, when I went to the station and ran the person through the database I found mug shots, people too thin, cheeks pockmarked or scarred the mark of drugs and hard living.

"Those last two never popped anywhere. It's completely possibly that Oksana, the redhead, ran away. Her father was a famous bastard."

Was this the same Oksana who was there the night Vera disappeared? I pulled the file closer, Hale leaning in to get a closer look. "Did she date Jake Medved?"

"She did—risky behavior back then. Hold up a second." Tanya picked up her phone, texting something. "I'll have to run in five, so I'll talk fast. Anyway, Oksana might have taken off, a lot of reasons to, but Jeannie?" She pointed to the blonde. "She had the bohunk boyfriend, was in secretarial school, and had a part-time job at Brouillette Paper. No way would she have taken off. The cops treated her like a runaway. I checked with my cousin, who still lives down the street from her brother, and he says she never came back."

Tanya stood up. "Unfortunately, I've gotta go. One of our targets has left his office, a flash drive full of intellectual property in his pocket, and I have to pretend to be a jogger out for a run, make sure those company secrets don't end up with the competition. Do I look nondescript enough?" She twisted her hair into a baseball cap, showing off her beautiful cheekbones, and I thought Hale was going to fall over. His usual types were blondes with big breasts, but he seemed willing to make an exception for someone as gorgeous and smart as Tanya.

On her way out of the driveway, Tanya beeped. We made a U-turn and followed, but she quickly outpaced us.

"You're not going to the prison alone," Hale said when I told him about the visit to Bernie tomorrow. "We know Bernie killed his wife and son, and the evidence we have so far points to him as Vera's killer, too. The man's a psychopath, and sometimes—"

"I don't feel like waiting, Hale. His sister—"

"I think in this particular case she's acting as his lawyer—"

"Well, whether she's acting as his sister or his lawyer, Deirdre could block this for weeks if we don't go tomorrow."

Hale shook his head. "We need a second set of eyes, a second set of ears."

"Got a handheld recorder? Hopewell Falls doesn't have money for fancy electronics in their budget."

"I do, and I can bring it along when I go with you."

"Hale, if you come, we'll be shut out."

I wanted this interview. While I wasn't sure how wise it was to give Hale six hours to try to talk me into rejoining the FBI, I was willing to make a deal.

"You can't come to the interview, but we can drive out together. So you know, it's a three-hour drive each way—"

"Deal," Hale said. "And while you're visiting Bernie, I'll drop in unexpectedly on the Syracuse field office. They'll *love* that."

On the way home, we called Chief Donnelly.

"I recall Tanya," he said when I told him about her file. "She's hard to forget. Firecracker. Ten years old, and she announced she was starting a detective agency. I expected lost dogs or stolen lunch money, but she clued me in to a money-laundering racket run out of a video store."

I told Donnelly about the missing women.

"I know those cases," Donnelly said, "We re-examine the evidence from time to time, but your dad, he could tell you more."

Great. Convincing my dad to stay out of the investigation would be hard if I kept pulling him back in, but the chief was right.

Hale dropped me off, and I promised to pick him up promptly at 6:30.

"Can't we take my car?" he said. "It's roomier and has a CD player."

I was still unhappy that he was going at all. "Bring your cassettes," I said, and slammed the door.

It was past Lucy's bedtime, and I was half wishing it was past Dad's, too. But the downstairs was lit up, and more ominously, Dave's car was parked out front.

Inside, I didn't bother stopping in the kitchen, but crossed through the living room to the dining room, which had been converted into a sort of incident room. Dave sat on one side of the table, Dad to his right. In front of them files spilled across the table, brown with age and labeled in Dad's neat script: basement pictures. Witness testimony.

I grabbed one labeled "Blood spatter." "Which of you stole these from the station?"

"Not me," Dave said.

"They're copies," my father said. "I've had them forever. Since the case."

Between Tanya and these two, I felt surrounded by vigilantes. I was lucky they didn't have gun permits. Oh wait! They did!

"Look, Lyons," Dave said. "We're digging through old details, trying to come up with a connection between Vera and Bernie Lawler. If Bernie's willing to murder his angelic wife Luisa and his son, he wouldn't blink at killing Mom."

I thought of the judge, his earlier comment on how Bernie was raised to control and abuse women. They might have something.

"So you two promise"—I looked back and forth from my dad to Dave—"not to go out there and get in the way of the investigation."

My dad held up his hand in pledge, and Dave followed. They were both good cops. It would be a huge help and might keep them off the street.

"Here," I said, holding out the file Tanya had given me. "Add this to your pile."

Both men hesitated—I think they thought it was a trick. I put it on the table between them and they pounced.

"Jeannie Saranov," Dave said, admiring the blonde. "I had such a big crush on her. Never saw her in the open files."

Dad's voice gentled. "Jeannie was a sad case."

"Murdered?" I asked. "The way Tanya describes it, she had the world to live for, and Jeannie's family hasn't been in contact."

"There's more to that story," Dad said. "Jeannie had a nice little life. But she started to hear voices, voices telling her there was evil in the world."

"Schizophrenia," I said.

"That it was. She did go missing for a while, but we found her nine months later when she got arrested for stabbing another woman, thankfully with a plastic knife, but it was enough to get Jeannie committed."

"And she's still in a facility somewhere?" Dave asked.

"Most other patients like her have been mainstreamed, but she's noncompliant with her meds, so her family pays through the nose to keep her someplace where she's monitored." He frowned. "And where she's away from them. When neighbors and friends ask, the family claims they have no idea where she is. They know. They want to avoid the taint of the illness."

I pointed to the redhead. "What about Oksana?"

"That one's tougher. Another island girl. Rough family, but Oksana made good, with a job and friends, and a boyfriend, if you want to call him that, in Jake Medved." He studied her picture. "Disappeared in 1985? Eighty-six? Her family didn't put in a missing person report, but a friend filed one in 1989. Couple months after that she started sending letters home, so we let it go." He shrugged. "Provided there's no fraud, adults are allowed to disappear."

Dave pulled the file close. "Her family was kind of a mess. I'm not judging." He hunched over the pictures. "Mine was, too."

I told them about my trip to Auburn the following day.

Dad sat forward. "You're seeing Bernie?"

"And his lawyer," I said.

"Deirdre," Dave said. "I don't envy you. I went up against her once, and I felt like my head"—he clapped his hands together hard—"was in a vise."

"You know she's Bernie's sister, right?" Dad said. I didn't want to mention my talk with Dan, so I just nodded. "She's a sharp cookie. Did criminal defense work way back when, and teaches over at SUNY. I hope for your sake she's lost her edge."

"She'll never lose her edge," Dave said. "She's all edge."

CHAPTER 10

HALE GAVE A LOW WHISTLE. "DICKENS CALLED. HE WANTS HIS prison back."

The gates of Auburn Correctional Facility loomed in front of our car, iron bars towering up twenty feet—old-fashioned but effective.

"What, no moat?" Hale asked. A guard in front gave us the stink eye as we switched places, with Hale sliding behind the wheel of the Saturn.

"Two hours. Over there." I pointed across the street to the prison's visitor's center, a low-slung building that, in contrast to the prison, had the architecture of a seventies bus station.

"I know, I know," he said. "Several of my biggest fans are in that prison right now."

My gun was in a locked chest in the trunk, and I left my phone, keys, and purse in the car—everything except my ID, notebook, pencil, recorder, and five dollars in quarters. I didn't want to risk getting stopped at the gate.

I introduced myself to the guard and showed my ID, and the officer radioed for confirmation before unlocking the gate. It swung open electronically—I would have expected the jailer to have a big skeleton key.

Once through, I was greeted by a second guard, a large man wearing a shirt that cut into his formidable biceps. He couldn't carry a weapon within prison walls, so his too-tight shirt was a way to signal to the prisoners that he could take them down.

"The lawyer lady's here." His voice was without affect, although his lip quirked at the corner. "Think she wanted to have a few minutes alone with her client, but I didn't want to give them an unfair advantage. He's looking good on another murder?"

"It's likely," I said as we entered the waiting area.

"Likely?" a woman's voice said from across the room, her voice clear and sharp, bouncing off the linoleum. "If you've made up your mind to convict him without conducting an interview, I'm glad I'm here."

I would have put Deirdre Lawler in her early fifties, but it was hard to tell from her CV. She finished college in the late seventies but didn't go to law school until much later, graduating in 1988. She had a stellar reputation, both as a defense lawyer and as a professor at SUNY, where she ran their Innocence Clinic, a group of law students representing prisoners who claimed to be wrongly accused. Knowing prisoners, I was amazed they weren't representing the entire prison system.

I walked forward and put my hand out. "Ms. Lawler?"

She didn't take it.

The guard wagged a finger. "Now you two get along."

"Are you going to tell us how much prettier we are when we smile, too?" Deirdre said.

"I meant . . ."

"You wouldn't have made a comment like that to two men." She walked toward the door to the holding area. "Shall we get this show on the road?"

Without another word, the guard walked us down the long hall-way, the stone walls painted bluish white and cold when I brushed against them. This prison was the oldest in operation in the country. The walls were thicker, stonework that no one would escape, but it had the same smell as all prisons: industrial cleaners, male sweat, and urine. The smell got stronger and stronger as we walked down the hall. By the time we reached the interview room, I was breathing through my mouth, trying to avoid the worst of it.

Bernie Lawler—shaved head bowed, eyes closed—sat at a metal table, which had all four of its legs bolted to the ground. His hands weren't cuffed, but he held them clasped in front of him as if they were. It wasn't a large room, but the ceilings were high, and the room dwarfed the lone man sitting at a single table.

He opened his eyes as we walked in, and surprisingly, smiled, crow's-feet creasing the corners of his eyes. For the first few years, prisoners were a ball of fury, ready to smash it up at "hello." Those in for a long stretch looked beaten down. Bernie looked peaceful.

"Bernie," Deirdre Lawler said. She sat next to him, and he leaned close, obeying the rules forbidding touching, but barely. He was shorter than his half-brothers, and his denim shirt had been neatly pressed.

Deirdre Lawler was explaining the parameters of the interview, when I pulled out the recorder.

"No recordings," she said, pushing it back at me.

Cameras tracked our every move from every angle, and she knew it. She was trying to score an early win. "This little machine isn't going to make any difference."

"Let her keep the recorder, Dee," Bernie said. "This lady's right." He smiled, encouraging. "Sure you got enough tape?"

"Digital," I said.

He laughed at himself. "Not up on the latest technology in here."

I went to hit *record,* but he stopped me.

"Hold up. You related to Gordon Lyons?"

There went cooperation. "Yes. He's my father."

"Your dad put me away here. Didja know that?" I nodded, waiting for the speech. Prisoners had a lot of time to think, and in interviewing them, I found they often had the responses prepared in advance, having spent a lot of time thinking of everything a police officer might ask and how they might answer. Those folks in for long stretches were also big letter writers, penning thoughtful replies with better spelling than I had.

"For the first several years in here, I hated your dad's guts. Cursed his name every night, and wished pain and suffering on him and those he loved. It was wrong." He clasped his hands together tightly. "Your dad probably doesn't care about my good opinion, but if it's appropriate, tell him I appreciate what a fair guy he was. After time spent with the rest of the law enforcement profession"—he glanced up at the cameras—"I have come to appreciate him." He half reached across the table and pulled back. "And you turned out OK, so my curses weren't good for much."

The eye roll Deirdre gave was more sisterly than lawyerly. "My client, the Zen master. Still have your sensei?"

"It's a spiritual teacher, not a sensei. And yes. In here, acceptance keeps you alive. You fight it, you end up hurting yourself."

"Yes, yes. That's why you have me to fight for you." Deirdre tapped the table, and for a moment I thought of Jake Medved. Looking at Deirdre and Bernie and comparing them to Jake and Maxim, it was hard to see much physical resemblance between the siblings apart from their pale blue eyes, but Deirdre shared Jake's need to make his point physically, and I wondered if she, like her brother, wouldn't mind breaking a few skulls with a pipe. If so, I was probably at the top of her list right now.

"Shall we?" Deirdre asked.

I hit *record*. A soft low whir sounded, so much less jarring than the crackle of tape. I gave everyone's names, including Bernie's. He shifted in his seat as I recited his prisoner number.

"Tell me about your relationship with Vera Batko," I said.

"Sure." He paused. "That's terrible, what happened to her."

"How'd you know her?"

"We grew up together, and later, I gave her a job. I always tried to hire from the neighborhood as much as possible, give people a leg up. Vera worked for me for about a year—I want to say in seventy-eight or seventy-nine?—and then took off, and then came back and worked for me again for about six months in eighty-three. Up 'til she died." He paused. "The business closed, and the old employment records . . . maybe Elda might know where they are. Although"—he smiled—"she probably burned them. Maybe the whole factory. Did you check her alibi?"

"Let's stick to the topic of Vera Batko, shall we?" Deirdre said.

A look of hatred passed over the face of the guard working the far door. Seeing him, I worked harder to keep my expression impassive. "Did you date?"

Bernie looked at his sister, who shook her head no. He answered anyway. "She dropped out of school pretty early. Had a son."

"No, I meant did you date in the early eighties, right before she died?"

"We—"

"Caution," Deirdre said.

"Yeah, yeah. It all came out in the trial, anyway. I cheated on my wife, my Luisa. But I didn't cheat on her with Vera. Vera was fast, even for me, and I couldn't keep up with the way she partied."

"And how was that?"

"She went to my brother's bar all the time. You hang out at Jake's, you start to notice who's going to the bathroom, coming back a little hyped up, maybe a dusting of powder on the nose. Plus, toward the end there, she went pro."

"Pro?" I asked.

"Yeah, pro. Professional." He lowered his voice. "Prostitute. She wasn't out there walking the streets, but she was willing to give a guy a blowie on his break in the back of his car."

"Bernie . . ." Deirdre said.

"Did you ever pay her for sex?" I asked.

"Don't answer, Bernie." Deirdre stared at me. "That question is off limits."

Bernie talked over his sister. "I'm not implicating myself if I say no, I didn't pay her for sex, right, Deirdre?" She quieted, and he patted her hand.

"No touching," the guard said.

Bernie quickly pulled his hand away. "How Vera lived? No way was I risking picking up a disease. That was pre-AIDS, but God, if I'd brought something home to my wife? I couldn't have lived with myself."

"Luisa didn't approve of your . . ." I tried to think of a polite way of saying "affairs," " . . . outside relationships. That must have caused friction in the marriage."

"Don't answer, Bernie," Deirdre said.

"Deirdre," Bernie said, "I know you're doing everything to clear me, but they've convicted me of Luisa and Teddy's murders and can't do it again. Double jeopardy, right, Officer Lyons?"

"That's true."

"And the fact that I was a terrible husband all came out at the trial. So yes, Luisa didn't approve of my affairs, but when she disappeared . . . when she died, I'd been on the straight and narrow. I hadn't fooled around with anyone since Teddy was born because my boy-o . . ." He closed his eyes tightly and took a few quick breaths. His breathing slowed, and he opened his eyes. "I wanted to make sure he had the best life. And I loved Luisa. The day I first saw her, I was willing to do anything to get her . . ."

"Bernie, there's no time for dredging up memories of Luisa.

Later," Deirdre said, not unkindly, "when it comes out you were innocent and this woman's father wasted years focusing on the wrong suspect"—she pointed at me, and I wanted to grab her finger and break it for implying my father was a bad cop—"that will be the time to share with people like Officer Lyons how much you've lost."

The air in the closed space was stifling. The vents in these places usually sounded like aircraft taking off, but they were kept off when an interview was taking place. The heat made me crankier than Deirdre.

"Bernie, tell me more about Luisa."

Deirdre swung her arm protectively in front of Bernie, as if it could keep away my questions. "No! We're done with that discussion."

"It would be nice to talk about her," Bernie said. "And maybe if Officer Lyons understood how much I loved her . . . I would never kill my sweet Lou, she would . . ."

"No," Deirdre said. "Bernie, we agreed you would always take my advice when I was acting as your legal counsel, and in this situation, I'm telling you we're not talking about Luisa anymore." She slid her arm in front of her brother. "Officer Lyons, stick to Vera, her character and behavior, or this conversation ends now."

She was right. I had no reason to talk about Luisa. Bernie's crime and punishment were never going to change, no matter how many DNA tests of the basement or the blood in the trunk she ordered.

Direct questions weren't getting me anywhere. I decided to see if he would lie. "Bernie, were you there the last night Vera worked?"

"I—"

"Don't answer," Deirdre Lawler said.

I shut my notebook and threw down my pencil. "Ms. Lawler, why did you agree to this interview if you were going to block every single question? Let me do my job, or I promise you, we will block that DNA test."

"The DNA test is happening because we're following the terms of my agreement with the DA. He denied our request for immunity. Without that, we agreed my client will answer questions about Vera Batko including her character and reputation, but Bernie will not answer questions about himself, up to and including where he was the night she disappeared."

I reopened my notebook but left my pencil on the table. I didn't expect him to answer, and the recorder would catch everything anyway. "What can you tell me about the barrels in the sub-basement?" This time his sister didn't have to caution him—he remained silent. I pushed. "The chemicals and the barrel with Vera were put there around the same time. You ordered the burial, had your brother Jake and brother-in-law Dan Jaleda"—I saw Deirdre flinch—"brick in those barrels."

Deirdre was furious, and I watched a flush rise up her neck and over her cheeks, but when she spoke, she was calm. "If I'm not mistaken, the chemical dumping falls under a federal jurisdiction, the very reason I didn't want that FBI agent tagging along. We're not answering."

"So we're done," I said. Count on Jerry to work a deal preventing me from doing my job. Whether through incompetence, spite, or a combination of the two, Jerry had fixed it so we weren't going to get any good information, not with a lawyer like Deirdre Lawler in the room. I hit the button on the recorder and waved at the cameras. The guard reappeared.

"Oh, we're not done," Deirdre said. "This interview was supposed to be sixty to ninety minutes."

The guard's arm muscle twitched in restrained anger, although he remained expressionless. "You done, Officer Lyons?"

"I am."

Deirdre protested, but Bernie stood. "Good-bye, Dee," he said. "Thanks for fighting the good fight. And Officer Lyons, it was nice to meet you. You're a chip off the old block, a good thing in my book. If I hadn't been set up . . . well, we'll never know what would have happened, will we? That path is closed." He walked toward the door, standing at a safe distance as the guard unlocked it. It opened, and I heard shouts, not angry but demanding respect, or at least acknowledgment. Bernie walked through the door, staring at the ground.

Deirdre Lawler's eyes never left her brother. When he was out of sight, she picked up the briefcase at her side. I tried the door, but it was locked. After a short buzz we were able to open it up, a guard waiting for us on the other side.

"That was quite helpful," Deirdre Lawler said as the heavy steel locked behind us.

"Helpful?" I said. "It was the farthest thing from it."

"Now Bernie and I know what avenues law enforcement are pursuing. So yes, helpful." She slowed her pace, walking leisurely so that both the guard and I were forced to wait for her when we reached the far door. "Were you expecting him to walk in and confess he killed her, and oh, yes, the chemicals were his, too? You have no concrete—"

"The chemicals can be dated."

"Bernie owned the factory for a short window. Perhaps Luisa's father put them there?"

"And Vera's body?"

"Another employee?"

The guard opened the door, going into the waiting area first to make sure no one was ready to jump us on the other side. The room was empty, a bolted door with bulletproof glass at the far end.·

As we walked, Deirdre said, "We petitioned for immunity on the Vera Batko info, and your DA denied us. I told him it was a waste of time, but he insisted. Who am I to turn down a deal like that?"

I wouldn't have expected Jerry to waste my time during a case when he had the chance to grab press, but if for some reason he thought the DNA evidence would screw over my dad? Totally.

"Officer Lyons," Deirdre said, "I appreciate that you're approaching this as a law-enforcement professional. And I appreciate that

you're approaching this as your father's daughter. But Bernie's conviction . . . It was a travesty. Completely based on circumstantial
evidence."

The two of us arrived at the outside door. We waved through
the window to the officer in a cage at the end of the hallway, who
hit a buzzer, letting us in. The guard who had been escorting us
held the door as we passed through to the hallway and then locked
it behind us.

"They never found the bodies of Luisa and Teddy, Officer Lyons,"
Deirdre said. "Never."

"They found plenty of blood, including the handprints in the
trunk of the car. Did you see pictures of those, Ms. Lawler? Someone
who was bleeding copiously was trying very hard to escape from
where they'd been locked in. Your sister-in-law and your nephew
had the same blood type, and the blood in the trunk matched it."

"But the blood DNA will not. I know it."

We passed a sign announcing that this was a No Hostage Zone,
which meant that if this place was taken over by the prisoners, Deirdre and I were on our own. There was a second buzz and we were
let out the door.

We stopped in the lobby. "Officer Lyons, trust me, I've seen
guilty. When I was a public defender, I went on the assumption that
most of my clients were guilty. I tried to make sure we got justice
rather than vengeance. The system works if everyone has a compe-
tent defense attorney."

"As I recall, your brother had very experienced counsel."

"He was paid extravagantly, but as to experienced? He was one
of my brother Maxim's cronies who mostly did wills and divorces.
Bernie and everyone on the Island may think our dear brother the
judge can do no wrong, but in that case he did—his decision guar-
anteed that Bernie went to prison. That injustice needs to be miti-
gated."

"Is that what you're trying to do with your brother? Mitigate?"

"No." She walked across the street to the visitor center trailer. Families huddled outside, in line for the van that would drive them fifty feet into the prison to visit their loved ones. They could have more easily walked across the street, but rules were rules. A young woman balanced a child on her hip and kept stepping sideways to prevent a blond toddler from making his escape, the sweatpants she was wearing sliding down two inches before she reached across and yanked them up: no strollers were allowed. The rest of the group were dressed in jeans and sweatshirts, except for four older African-American women, wearing dresses that skimmed below the knee and orthopedic shoes, naked without their banned purses.

Deirdre Lawler looked ready to hand her cards out to the crowd. A van pulled up and the people piled in. We cut behind it, thick exhaust hitting us in the face, temporarily silencing both of us. She didn't say good-bye, just hurried toward the Jaguar parked at the far end of the lot. Academics were broke, but her private practice was obviously lucrative. Not surprising. She made sure I made no progress at all today, a good quality in a defense attorney.

CHAPTER 11

I WAS SCANNING THE STREET FOR A COFFEE SHOP TO KILL THE hour. Maybe it would even have a pay phone so I could call Hale. Not having a cell phone was viewed as antisocial behavior these days, although I might get lucky—the prison was right there. I made it five steps toward a chicken-wing place before I heard my Saturn sputtering up the street.

"You still OK to drive?" Hale asked as he climbed out of the car. I waved him around to the passenger side. I could feel eyes on me as I walked around the car and realized that stopping in a no parking zone opposite a prison was not our brightest move, even if we were law enforcement. I scanned the towers of the prison and saw guards with machine guns aimed toward the yard, inside the prison. Facing out was a metal figure, a replica of a Revolutionary War soldier. He had watched people come and go at the prison for almost two hundred years—mostly come. When the prison was built in 1818 the soldier was wood. The elements took care of him, so prisoners who worked in the foundry molded a stronger, more resilient jailer out of copper. He now stood guard.

Hale climbed into the car next to me. "I got here early, figured it would be an unproductive interview, what with Jerry setting it up and all."

"What makes you say that?"

"Well, he's not very bright, is he?" Hale pulled out his smartphone. "Should we bring Chief Donnelly up to speed at the same time you brief me?"

Donnelly didn't wait for us to get out a hello. "Just got a call from the hospital."

"Our burn victim? Did she wake up?" I asked, afraid to ask if she'd died.

"We aren't that lucky, but something went our way: The hospital thinks that the second-degree wounds on her hands have healed enough that you can pull a print."

"Piece of cake," Hale said. "I can have my people over there in thirty minutes and we can get her prints in the system in an hour. Unless," Hale hit the *mute* button and talked rapidly. "Do you want to be there? This is your deal."

"No, no. Sooner rather than later is better. We can stop by at the end of the day."

"Hello? Hello?" the chief called. We unmuted him and told him our plans for Hale's agents to take care of it. The chief seemed happy with the result. He was much less happy with the results from our visit to Bernie.

"As lovely as the Finger Lakes are, did you get anything valuable out of him?" he asked.

"Other than the fact that his lawyer—his sister—is convinced the DNA will exonerate him? Nothing. And she was gleeful to get information on Vera's case so she can prep before we come at Bernie."

"But does she realize the DNA can help prove he committed a second murder?" Hale asked.

"She must," Donnelly said. "She has that much faith in her

client." He paused. "Any problem coming in tomorrow morning to write it up? I want to have a sharing and caring discussion with Jerry about what constitutes helpful in this case."

I promised to type up a report first thing in the morning, and had my own request. "Any chance we could get into Bernie Lawler's house with a crime scene team? It's been empty for thirty years, and there might still be evidence of Vera's murder."

"Let me line up a warrant and a crime scene unit," he said. "I'll call you back in a bit."

On our way out of town, we drove past a bunch of small machine shops and foundries. All the guys who served time developed skills, and there were opportunities right outside the prison wall. In the nineteenth century, it was small trades: shoes, leatherwork, saddles. When the big industry moved to town, the ex-cons found jobs there or in the small businesses serving those factories. In the nineteen seventies Columbian Rope, ALCOA, P&R Spaghetti, and a bunch of other factories moved South, wooed by lower wages in those states that were less favorable to unions, and then overseas by even lower wages. The city stayed afloat thanks to the prison jobs, but prospects were about even with those in Hopewell Falls.

Hale listened to the recording of the interview as we drove, periodically pausing the machine and making notes. He stopped it when his phone rang.

"Hale Bascom," he said, and then sat up straight. "Yes, of course. Hello there."

Hale had a sweet smile on his face, trying to charm the person at the other end of the phone.

"Yes, we'd like that very much. Should we pick them up tomorrow?" He shifted in his seat, and I could hear a feminine voice on the phone. "Well, if it's not putting you to any trouble . . . No, no, it's very secure. Yes, ma'am. We can tie up this investigation and move on to other things. Absolutely. Thank you kindly."

He hung up. "Tanya."

"Didn't realize you two were friends."

"We're not. She dug out some more pictures for us, a few of Vera and one of Oksana. Tomorrow could go sideways, so I asked her to drop them at the station." He turned to me, his broad shoulders straining at the seat belt. "I'm sure she would have called you next."

"Oh, I'm sure."

As we crossed the Albany city limits, Hale's phone rang again. It was his people calling with bad news: prints from our burn victim were impossible.

"They got some detail, but not enough to get a match with anyone in CODIS. It would seem that our victim has been 'sloughed' of a couple of layers of skin, with another scheduled for later today." Hale shuddered. "A hospital visit today looks like a bust."

I made a U-turn and drove Hale home, toward old townhouses that were part of the first settlements in Albany, clustered around the Ten Broeck mansion downtown. Built in the last century, the townhouses were beautiful, but most had fallen into disrepair. The neighborhood scared off all but the most intrepid of yuppies.

"I'm carrying," Hale said. "And one of the old ladies in the neighborhood made sure to announce to all and sundry that the neighborhood's new homeowner was an FBI agent. The drug dealers moved away right quick."

"You bought?"

"I'm not going anyplace anytime soon, and even if I have to pick up at the last minute, I can maintain two residences for a bit." I didn't know if that was a comment on Hale's family money or the neighborhood's low cost of real estate. "Plus, I like being so close to the bus station. It's a great way to keep track of the criminals who are in town."

I craned left and right, trying to find a parking space. I was getting ready to double-park when Hale nudged my arm. "Hey, why don't you come in for dinner?" I was about to decline when he added,

"C'mon. I haven't had a chance to show my place off to anyone. You can be my housewarming party."

I hadn't thought of Hale as someone who might lack for company, but most of the people he'd met in this area worked for him, so socializing could be awkward. I agreed to his invitation.

"Really?"

"Yes . . . however"—I scanned the block—"there's no parking nearby."

"Oh, wait 'til you see this," he said and directed me to an alley that led back behind a series of row houses. At the end was a garage.

"This right here," I said as I pulled into one of the two berths, "doubled the value of your place in downtown Albany."

Hale unlocked his back gate. It was an iron affair dating from the Civil War era, which in this historic neighborhood could be considered a modern addition. The yard was empty but mowed, and we walked up the back steps to the townhouse door.

Hale unbolted three locks and held the door for me. I walked through to a beautiful kitchen. Original wide oak floors were polished to gleaming. The cabinets were made of the same wood as the floors, and the countertops and backsplash were green marble that gleamed in the late-afternoon light. Flowers sat on the counter.

"Cleaning lady came today," Hale said. "She had to go through security clearance to get this job and thinks she's a spy. She always brings groceries and flowers from her garden." He pulled off his jacket, hanging it over the back of his chair, and removed his tie. "You want the tour first or food first?"

I hadn't eaten since breakfast. "Food. Now."

"Yes, ma'am," Hale said, opening the refrigerator and pulling out ingredients.

Hale poured me a glass of pinot grigio while I called my Dad. He encouraged me to take my time, suspiciously pleased that I was eating dinner at Hale's.

I hung up. "They're up to something."

Hale raised an eyebrow. "Your dad and Lucy?"

"No, Lucy's fine. It's Dad and Dave I'm worried about. The Hardy boys swear they're going to hand over any information they find to me, but . . ."

"It matters too much to them." Hale looked up from where he was whisking together a marinade of soy sauce, orange juice, and honey. "They're good men and good cops, but you can't trust 'em to do the right thing at the moment, June."

Hale put rice on to boil and dropped salmon steaks into the marinade. He picked up a mango, squeezing it briefly before splitting it along its length, the green skin giving way to golden flesh. We chatted about Lucy, Albany, and old friends from Quantico while he diced mango and a red pepper into small uniform pieces, scattering cilantro on top.

He slid the salmon into the oven.

"That'll take five minutes," he said. "Want the quick tour while that broils?"

He led me through a dining room with a farmhouse table made of recovered railroad ties, its roughness offset by the detailed ironwork holding it together. One chocolate-brown wall was almost entirely taken up with three posters, each showing the lines of battle on a day in Gettysburg. The living room was lined with bookcases made of the same recovered railroad ties as the dining table, filled with history books and Thomas Pynchon novels, three shelves taken up with vinyl records. He had a modern leather couch, brown with clean lines and sharp edges, and an oriental rug, worn in places, with rich blues and golds running through it. I'd vouch for it being a certifiable antique.

"Nice," I said. "Was it hard to move from your old place?"

"Didn't have a place, honestly. Everything's new except for the rug, a legacy from my great-great-grandmother on my mother's side." He reached over and straightened a book. "When we were working the Brouillette case, well, I figured out I wanted to put down roots here."

"If you can say that after suffering through two blizzards, you're committed."

"Don't forget the ice storm. Ruined my favorite pair of Donald Pliner loafers," he said, looking pleased when I laughed. He touched my shoulder and said more seriously: "No, June. Right here is where I want to be."

The oven buzzed, and we returned to the kitchen, where Hale prepared plates. I was just about to pour more wine when Hale stopped me.

"Why don't we go up to the deck? It's the nicest part of the house." He pointed up. "Well, except for the garage."

I followed Hale up the narrow staircase. He took the short stairs two at a time—it seemed that the American colonists were much shorter people. I found him waiting for me on the landing, eager to show off the second floor.

"The guest bedroom is down there," he said, gesturing with his elbow to the far end of the hallway. My feet sank into the thick carpet as we passed the bathroom and a locked office. We arrived at the base of a second staircase, directly in front of his bedroom.

"It took me months to get permits to knock down the wall," he said, pointing to a spot midway down the room where the planks of the wood floor didn't line up exactly. "Before it was two cramped little rooms."

That was hard to imagine. Hale had painted the walls a navy blue, but the room was so big that the dark color didn't make the room feel closed in, but instead secure, an unassailable fortress. His sheets were a light blue, and taking up much of the wall over the bed was an abstract painting, splashes of rust-red paint bursting at the boundaries of the canvas.

"Food's getting cold." He slipped around me, his broad chest brushing my shoulder as he negotiated the tight landing, before striding up the stairs.

I followed him up to the roof, which was as spectacular as he promised. The sun was starting to set, and the gold sky was streaked red and purple. We would have rain tomorrow, but tonight was perfect. Hale waved me over to a teak table tucked under a pergola. I poured wine while he lit a citronella candle.

"Too early for mosquitos," I said. "Not hot enough."

"My southern training—I assume there's always a gruesome bug lurking in the shadows. Plus, you know, atmosphere." He picked up his wineglass. "To Albany."

"To Albany."

The salmon was perfect, the smooth fish offset by the sweet, sharp relish.

I shoveled in another mouthful. "Where did you learn to make this?"

"Miami," Hale said.

Hale explained he had been assigned there five years back after doing a long stint in Detroit. He did antiterrorism in both places, but in Miami the antiterrorism overlapped with gang activity, since some of the terrorist groups were raising money through the drug trade.

"I loved the people of Detroit, but after those winters, Miami was a kindness."

I told him the story of working with an informant in Missouri who had infiltrated the Banditos. Fang proved to be one of our best sources; he slipped out right before we were able to indict him on weapons, human trafficking, and racketeering charges, going to California where he returned to his life of crime. I was transferred to California and was still doing anti-gang work when I knocked on the door of a person we were watching, acting like a drug-hungry tweaker, and met Fang again. I described how he kept calling me June, even though my contacts knew me as Maggie. Eventually, I had to pull a screwdriver on him as Maggie didn't appreciate being mistaken for some skank called June.

"He dropped his beer and ran out the back door." Hale threw his head back, laughing, the hard lines of his face softening, reminding me of when I knew him over a decade ago, long before Kevin and I became a couple, the three of us trainees at Quantico. One night Hale and I were studying for our computer crime class—Kevin skipped out since he could basically teach the class—and we ended the night not just sharing notes, but with a kiss.

I wasn't stupid. I knew he was a player. I knew it would be good because his ego wouldn't be satisfied unless I admitted the sex was fantastic, but the great sex was paired with a surprising intensity. When I thought about it—and I *had*—I imagined that he would be a couple of orgasms and a laugh. Instead, he wouldn't stop kissing and touching me: my neck, my breasts, and less obvious places, like my fingers and the soft gap behind my knee. He slept wound around me and kissed me awake in the morning.

I pushed my plate away, satisfied. A breeze came up, bringing with it the smell of lilacs and wood smoke. Spring had sprung but people still used their fireplaces.

"So, when we tie this up," Hale asked as he leaned back against the bench, "what did you decide?"

I was honestly surprised he had held out as long as he had, never once mentioning his offer during the trip.

"I didn't want to trap you," he said, as if sensing my question. "We were working your cases. I thought . . . to me, it seemed like things were going well. Teamwork and . . . trust."

"I'm still on the fence," I said. He waited, his face expressionless, knowing the best way to get a perp to talk was to remain silent, but he shifted in his seat and leaned forward on the table.

I leaned away. "You're offering me a fantastic opportunity and I really appreciate that you've gone to such lengths to make me think you're a better man—"

He flinched. "I am a better man, June."

"You are. There's no question you've changed. But, and I don't mean to offend you when I say this, but there's no way it can live up to what you've promised. It can't. Opportunities to challenge myself, but keeping travel to a minimum? Exciting cases, but no danger?"

"Since I've been working with you in your small town, you've almost died of hypothermia and were trapped in a burning building."

"But those were anomalies. Once-in-a-lifetime events."

"Which you have had two of in the last five months."

"So I'm done for this lifetime."

Hale raised an eyebrow at me. "June, you're making all these excuses, but we could make this happen. You have your father. You would have me. And I bet if we talked about it with your chief, we could ensure some job security. Of course, I'd be happiest if you signed back on full-time, but my wishes aren't the most significant thing here. However, they are"—he smiled—"important."

My phone rang. It was Chief Donnelly. I tried to draw out the conversation, but Donnelly kept it short and sweet: he had secured access to the Lawler home and assistance from crime scene units at 8:00 a.m. tomorrow. I hung up, ready to use the excuse of an early morning to escape, but I knew it was a bad idea: I would spend the next few weeks expecting Hale to bring it up again. I took a deep breath and dove in.

"What I can't understand," I said, "is why you want me back so badly." He started to protest, but I cut him off. "I was a good shot—"

"A great shot," he said.

"And I was good on the anti-gang work. But out here, we've got a couple of Hell's Angels, some Five Percenters, but nothing like LA or Oakland. Soon you'd have me doing other assignments, ones I'm not qualified for, and I'd end up botching them. I'd lose the faith of the other agents. You would, too, for being nice to an old . . . friend."

Hale dropped his voice low. "June. Here's the deal. You got top scores on the shooting range. You have deep experience in organized crime, and a grasp of cybercrime having been married to Kevin." At the mention of Kevin I pulled back, but Hale reached forward and wrapped his fingers around my arm, gently holding me in place. "Your mind, your dedication, your skills—with the new stuff, there would be no learning curve."

"I haven't retained much knowledge about explosives," I said.

"We'll keep you away from the C-4." He patted my hand before pulling back, fixing me with his gaze. "Listen to me, June. I say this absolutely: there is no one I trust more. No one."

The two of us sat quietly. I watched as offices in the State Tower went dark, leaving a patchwork of light. I could hear cars down on the street and traffic on 787, a few blocks away, and beyond that the river, lapping at the shore, as quiet as a breath. The temperature was dropping, and a chill was traveling up from the base of my spine. Hale broke the silence.

"I understand, June, that you might want to stay a small-town cop. Knowing your neighbors, your friends, your local criminals? It has appeal. And we can still be friends. But here's the thing"— the sun had set and there was only his voice—"if you think you don't have the resources to do this, that's bullshit. And if you think I would jeopardize my first regional direction position so you felt comfortable, you're flat-out wrong. So think about this. Seriously." Hale picked up his plate. "C'mon, let's go inside where it's warm."

I offered to help with the dishes, but Hale refused and walked me to the garage. The car was running when he knocked on the glass, and I rolled down the window.

"I'll see you bright and early tomorrow," he said. "I know your thoughts are on these two cases, but I will need your answer soon. OK, June?"

"Yes, Agent Bascom."

I backed out of the driveway. My headlights caught Hale, standing in the center of the alley, shielding his eyes against the glare. He never once moved, staying in place until I turned onto the street and was gone.

CHAPTER 12

LUISA LAWLER'S HEAD HAD HIT THE WALL HARD.

In the pitch-black room the luminol glowed bright. The flashes from the crime scene techs' cameras blinded me as they crammed as many photos as they could into the thirty-second window we had before the chemicals stopped working and the spots faded.

"Again!" Annie called out of the darkness. There was a low hiss as the chemical was applied, and the blue reappeared, a solid stain of color at the center, with spots arcing out smaller and smaller, blood evidence for Luisa Lawler's murder, the evidence as revealing as it had been thirty years ago. I saw Annie's shadow scraping blood flecks off the wall to get DNA evidence that Deirdre Lawler hoped would absolve her brother Bernie of Luisa's murder, and that I hoped would convict him of killing both his wife and Vera Batko.

I'd seen a Polaroid of this image before in Luisa's murder file. My father had discovered the blood evidence first, and it had been the clue that tipped him off that something very bad had gone down at the Lawlers' house. There were other pictures of this room taken by a police photographer, glossy black and whites that captured the room's early eighties tackiness in all its glory. A white shag carpet covered the floor, and one whole wall was taken up by wallpaper that was a photo of a true-to-size forest. Bernie Lawler had put in a glossy black bar that dominated the far corner, and a white leather couch sat opposite a forty-inch TV that looked heavy enough to crack the building's foundation, the rabbit ears reaching almost to the ceiling.

Nobody would have looked at the room twice, but then the Lawlers' housekeeper, Natalya Batko, told my father that it had recently been repainted and the furniture rearranged. My dad and the officers moved the couch, taking away a layer of paint and revealing flecks of blood on the wall and a section of the shag rug that had been cut away. Dad sprayed luminol, revealing the same pattern we saw here today. Back then no DNA testing was available, but when he scratched off some blood, the type matched that of Luisa Lawler. From that moment, they stopped searching for an anonymous assailant and concentrated on Bernie Lawler.

"Lights!" Annie called.

Spotlights went on, and the room was bright white, unchanged in many ways from when my father first gathered evidence on Luisa's murder. The couch had been removed by the police, and the TV had been taken years ago by muscular thieves. A pipe had burst above the bar, cracking the shiny black glass, spiderwebs spanning its surface. Brown rings on the formerly white rug marking a flood that had receded, and the forest on the wall was obscured behind a layer of dirt that upon closer inspection proved to be black mold. I was beginning to regret not taking Annie up on her offer of a protective suit.

"We done?" Annie was more of a demand than a request kind of person, and if she was going to request my permission, I would agree.

"Annie likes you," Hale said as we trooped upstairs, the techs following behind with the lamps and a generator. The living room had the same trapped-in-amber quality as the basement. Sure, the stereo was long gone, but the house was still decorated in the latest fashions from 1983. This room showed Luisa's feminine hand, with pastel couches and a brass planter, that, if I had to guess, had once held a spider fern. The room dropped into darkness as techs put blackout curtains over the windows and sprayed the luminol. Nothing.

There continued to be nothing through the rest of the first floor. We walked up a half flight to the second floor and walked down the hall, lined with pictures of the family.

Hale looked at the photos of Teddy, tracking the Lawlers' son from birth until age three, a few months before he died. "Why didn't Luisa's mother take any of this?"

We walked into the little boy's room, blue with a bed shaped like a race car, the sheets disintegrating with age. Another small bedroom across the hall contained Teddy's crib and changing table, and at the end of the hall was the master bedroom. Luisa and Bernie's room had gold carpeting, and the bed was still made, a green satin comforter faded in places where the morning sun hit it. They put up the blackout curtains and again sprayed the luminol.

"Where are the pentacles?" I asked Hale in the darkness.

He gave a sharp laugh. "You think Bernie was flirting with the lord of the underworld? Sacrificing goats, maybe?"

"No, no," I said. "An abandoned place like this, where a murder took place, would be catnip to teenagers, either carrying a Ouija board or a case of beer. But other than a few missing electronics, there's nothing."

"Was the murder brutal enough that they stayed away? Afraid of the ghost of Luisa Lawler?"

"Or more likely, afraid of Jake Medved, ready to kick the ass of anyone who trespassed on his brother's property."

Annie grabbed a single blackout curtain, a bottle of luminol, and a camera and locked herself in the bathroom, muttering something about getting out of this hellhole. The door swung open not twenty seconds later.

"Get in here!" Annie ordered. Three of the techs sprinted toward the door. "No, not you," she said. "The cops."

Hale and I slid past the group and into the cramped bathroom. Annie closed the door and the room went black.

"Pay attention," Annie said. The hiss from the spray canister filled the space. The bathtub started to glow, and then *flash*. I saw stars.

"Can you hold off on the photos for a second, Annie?" I asked.

Annie stopped. Out of the blackness an image appeared, brighter and brighter, blood smeared across the tile, marking the path of a slumping body. Several small handprints appeared at the edge of the basin along with one large one and there were rings in the tub where blood had sat and then drained.

Annie vibrated with restrained energy. "So can I do my job?"

I agreed and she sprayed again, taking pictures of the wall, careful to get close-ups of the corners and drains. She brought in the lights. No blood was visible under the glare.

"Bleach," Annie said. She grabbed a lamp and aimed it toward the drain, standing on her toes to change the angle.

"I want the pipe under this tub," she said. "Where's my wrench?"

As Annie and one of the techs worked on the plumbing, Hale and I followed the others out into the hall, which proved clean of blood.

"So I hate to ask this," Hale said when we were down the hall out of earshot, "but is there any chance at all that your Dad might have missed this," he waved in the direction of the bathroom, "during the initial investigation?"

"All the spatter analysis and the luminol tests were in the file—I re-read them this morning. With the exception of some trace elements, the rooms on the second floor were tested for blood and were clear." I paused now, worried that I was making assumptions about my Dad's initial investigation and jotted a note to myself to double check the results. "There is the possibility that the blood we found in the basement and Bernie's trunk belonged to Vera—and we can know definitively with the DNA tests—but Annie's discovery in the bathroom? It wasn't here during the initial investigation."

Leaving Annie to finish up, Hale hit the flashlight app on his phone and we made our way down the stairs and out the door. We stumbled out into a world filled with light, and I took a deep breath of the fresh air. I needed to get out of 1983.

ELDA HARRIS'S HOUSE WAS CLOSE TO THE RIVER, ONE OF A SERIES of Victorian mansions built by the first mill owners. It was no longer prime real estate, and most of the houses had been cut up into apartments, with Elda's being one of the few exceptions. Luisa Lawler's childhood home was perched on top of a steep slope, giving it excellent views. Both Hale and I were panting by the time we rang the doorbell.

The door was opened by the same young woman who had driven Elda down to the factory. In addition to her nursing duties, Caitlin acted as maid, leading us to the living room, which was papered in green and gold brocade and filled with expensive furniture built in the nineteenth century to last into the twenty-first. The spindle-legged tables were topped by a sea of pictures of Teddy and Luisa. Now I understood why Elda hadn't taken any photos from Bernie's house.

Elda Harris limped in. She didn't need a cane but moved between pieces of furniture, catching herself like a toddler learning to walk. She wore matching green knit pants and a turtleneck under a gray cashmere sweater. We introduced ourselves.

"The FBI's involvement is what my daughter's case needs," she said. Before I could explain, she rushed ahead. "Please know, Officer Lyons, I'm grateful for your father's work." She squared her shoulders. "Bernie was slimy enough to slither away from the charges, but my son-in-law didn't realize he had two bigger foes: me and your father."

During the investigation into Luisa's murder, the phone had rung constantly at all hours of the day and night. Then I'd hear my father's tired voice from the downstairs hallway: "Yes, Elda. First thing in the morning."

Elda hopscotched past a few more chairs before landing on a settee, the brocade fabric matching the wallpaper. I sat down on a chair opposite her, my legs folding up like an accordion. Everything in this room had been built for a petite person. Hale continued standing.

I explained as kindly as I could that we were there to investigate the death of Vera Batko and the fire at the factory, not Luisa and Teddy's murder.

"And why not?" Elda said. "You never found their bodies. Maybe the professionals at the FBI could change that."

I didn't want him to promise Elda things we couldn't deliver, particularly when we had two major crimes we were trying to solve, but Hale plowed on. "The deaths are very likely related—"

"Did you know," Elda said, "when they found that body in the burned factory I was hopeful. Can you believe that? I was hopeful that a dead woman in a barrel was my daughter."

She picked up a picture of her daughter. I gave her a moment to collect herself and started my real line of questioning. "We need employment records from when Sleep-Tite was a going concern. Anything to prove Vera Batko—"

"Who?"

"The dead woman in the barrel. We want to interview every employee who worked with her on her last shift, try to lock down a timeline on her movements both at the factory and when she left, find out if she talked to anyone about her plans. I realize it's been more than twenty years since your company went out of business—"

"Since I let Sleep-Tite die. I wanted to burn it to the ground . . ." She paused, as if suddenly realizing what she had said. "Not that I did. I let it die a slow death."

"Why not sell?"

"That business never brought anyone anything but pain—it broke my husband's heart and was the reason my daughter died. I drove a stake into its heart, finished it off forever."

I bit my tongue, wanting to point out that when she did that, she also killed off hundreds of jobs and the hopes of many people employed by Sleep-Tite.

"Do you know if the employment records were kept?" Hale asked.

"Did you put them in storage?" I added, "Or can you tell us where they are?"

"Oh, yes," she said. "I have them."

"All of them?"

"Well, from the last ten years it was a going concern. The accounting department was rigorous and there was always a chance for an audit—Bernie was dirty and the books probably were, too. By the time the statute of limitations passed, it was too much trouble to throw them away."

"Where are the files, ma'am?" Hale asked.

Elda crooked her finger and Hale approached. She patted the seat next to her and Hale sat, balanced on the edge of the delicate furniture.

"Are you the person who decides whether the FBI will make an effort to find my daughter?" Elda asked.

"I am," Hale said.

"Can you dedicate resources to find them?"

"We'd have to look at the current caseload—"

"Yes or no, young man," she said. "It seems only fair that if I do something for you, you do something for me."

Elda was threatening to withhold evidence. I was ready to protest when Hale spoke.

"I think we can find some manpower to investigate your daughter's case."

Elda took a pillow and propped it behind her back, shifting until she found the perfect spot, relaxing into the couch.

"The Sleep-Tite records are in my attic," she said.

CAITLIN LED US UPSTAIRS. LUISA'S HIGH SCHOOL GRADUATION picture hung on the landing; she looked not so much ready to conquer the world as to approach it slowly and hope it didn't hurt her. It was hard to believe that she would be married to Bernie within a year of the photo's being taken.

Caitlin opened a door at the end of the hallway, flipped a switch, and waved us upstairs. The attic consisted of a series of small rooms off a hallway—old servants' quarters. Caitlin called up to us, telling us that Elda suggested we check in the third, fourth, fifth, and sixth rooms on the right.

We opened the first door, finding a room filled floor to ceiling with bankers' boxes. Faced with the wall of cartons, Hale took out his phone. "Now's the time to avail ourselves of the Bureau's manpower. As one half of the joint task force, I vote we delegate."

"Won't Elda be concerned that you're taking people away from the search for her daughter?"

Hale put his phone away. "Can't believe I got strong-armed by a little old lady."

The containers were carefully labeled by department, the nature of the records, and the year. The boxes appeared to be in pretty good shape, so I made a deal with Hale: try to locate Vera's employment records, and if we don't find them in fifteen minutes, we could call in the cavalry. He agreed.

None of the boxes in the first room dated from the important years, and we ducked into the second. I pulled a box marked "HR March 1983–June 1983." Threads of spiderwebs pulled away, and a fine layer of dust coated the pile of yellowed papers. I pulled a file at random and paged through it—carefully typewritten sheet, thin and mimeographed, including the employee's name, Social Security number, birthdate, start date, end date. This place would be a gold mine for an identity thief.

Hale's phone rang.

"Hale Bascom," he said and walked out to the hallway to talk. He had a lot of business outside this case, and I wondered how he was getting it all done. He came back, hand over the mouthpiece.

"June, can I borrow some paper?"

I considered handing him a piece from one of the thousands in these boxes, but pulled out my pad and pencil. Using the wall as a writing surface, he wrote down a time, thanked the person on the other end, and hung up.

"We got a line on the burned woman," he said. "Possibly. Louann Bazelon of Taos, New Mexico."

The name Bazelon was familiar to me. They weren't local, so maybe they were from one of my FBI assignments? I'd never been to New Mexico, and I doubted they were from Missouri, but maybe Los Angeles?

"From the TV show," Hale said. "*Global Adventure*. The two brothers, both park rangers, who made a name for themselves saving that idiot CEO who went on a vision quest with only his personal chef as a guide and got himself stuck on top of a mountain. It was high drama, and that CEO made sure they got plenty of attention."

I'd seen the TV show several times, and I'd caught the newscasts that covered their daring rescue.

"They definitely had the whole hero thing down," I said. "Plus they were pretty hot."

"And they had loyal steeds, cute puppies, and they loved their mother." Hale took a breath. "That last part's true. They're pretty wrecked about their momma's disappearance."

"Did they have any idea how she might have ended up here?"

"No idea. Last time she was seen or heard from she was at home, gardening with her rocks."

"Gardening with rocks?"

"Yeah, it's high desert up there. No hydrangeas, so if you want something decorative and environmentally sound, you go for rocks and pine trees and cactus." Hale tore the page out of my pad and returned it to me. "As it happened, the CEO they saved still has a fond spot for them, and he lent them his plane. They should be here in a few hours."

I returned to my document search, and found Vera's HR records without too much effort. She had two stints at the factory—one for fourteen months a few years before she died, and the second for six months right before she went missing. I didn't find the timesheets, but I did find the payroll records. Double-checking the dates, I was able to pull payroll for every employee who worked at the factory at the same time as Vera. The fifth room held nothing of interest, and the sixth was a jumble. There were pens and pencils, old safety signs and a lost and found box, which contained a jumble of old shirts, three brown shoes, all matching, and a red purse.

"I'm taking this," I said, holding up the purse. "It doesn't match the one described in the missing persons report Dave filed exactly, but I could see where a twelve-year-old might confuse vinyl for leather."

"These you definitely want." Hale held up two of the shoes, boring beige lace-ups that were a practical choice for the factory floor. His finger traced the edge, where a name was written.

Vera.

If what Tanya's mother said was true, Vera walked out of Sleep-Tite the night she died in a red dress and high-heeled boots. No need for practical rubber-soled brown shoes where she was going. But who picked her up for the party at the Medveds'? And did they kill her?

THE BUZZ HUMMING THROUGH THE HOSPITAL ALMOST drowned out the beeps and hisses of the machines. A low murmur, an awareness of celebrity muted by the attention to the patients.

"Did you see them?" I heard someone ask as our group passed the nurses' station. They weren't talking about Hale and me. Theo Bazelon had light brown hair and green eyes, and he was tall—almost 6'3". Nate, the younger of the two, had red hair, but the same green eyes and was short and muscular. Their eyes could be the same color as the burned woman lying in the hospital bed, but it was hard to tell.

It was odd to feel like you knew someone you'd never met. In preparation for meeting the men I'd read a *People* magazine article in which Theo talked about his love of popcorn and Nate cuddled with his pixie-cute girlfriend. I'd watched the show: Theo was the wiser of the two, advising caution. Nate would push, faster and faster, forcing Theo to keep up. The combination allowed them to save that CEO and worked to an even greater advantage when they were on *Great Adventure*. Nate provided the speed, and Theo made sure they didn't make a mistake.

With them was a tall African-American man, gray dreadlocks spilling over a fine blue linen shirt. Theo introduced him as the woman's husband.

"Can we go in now?" Nate said.

After donning the paper scrubs and face masks, we went in. Our burn victim had stabilized in the two weeks since her injury, and the smell of rotting flesh was almost gone, a blessing for these young men who might be identifying their mother. Even so, the nurse remained, monitoring the victim's fluids and checking her vitals. The patient looked even smaller than before, the nutrients in her saline drip no replacement for real food. Pink hard skin obscured her facial features, but her hair had started to sprout, a light red fuzz.

"She might be Mom," Theo said softly. "Same . . . size. I think."

Nate disagreed. "Red hair. Mom's hair is kind of dishwater blond. Like Theo's."

Darius went around the other side of the bed. "She dyed her hair."

"Her hair went gray ten, fifteen years ago?" Nate said.

"No, I mean she dyed her hair from the day I met her." Darius stepped close, examining her. "She was a pretty down-to-earth woman, never vain, but she spent money on hair dye. She didn't need it. She was a knockout." He reached for her, taking her unburned hand in his. "Still is."

"Do you believe this is your wife, sir?" Hale asked.

Darius paused, running his finger gently over her fingertips.

"These hands. I watched those hands do everything, from potting plants to changing your diaper, Nate." He caressed her wrist. "It's her."

"But she's hurt so badly," Nate said, near tears. I got the sense it wasn't that he didn't think the burn victim was his mother, but that he didn't want it to be.

Theo walked around the bed, resting his arm on his brother's shoulder. "Look closer, Nate." He traced her arm, inches from Darius's hand. "Freckles. She could never tan." Nate sobbed, and Theo hugged him. "It's her, Nate."

The nurse stood up and checked the monitor. "I'm supposed to change the dressing, but—"

"Now?!" Nate stalked toward the nurse. "We just find out our mother is almost dead . . ." He stopped, taking a step back. "I'm sorry. You don't deserve my rudeness, miss."

Theo spoke, his voice kind. "We're sorry for inconveniencing you, nurse . . ."

"That's fine," the nurse said. "It's a difficult day." While younger, she was no more taken with these minor celebrities than nurse Gayle was. Spending enough time with doctors who had huge egos made anyone unflappable.

Darius had started to hum a song, sweet and low. "Coma patients have their hearing, mostly. I figure if she hears some Marvin Gaye, she'll know I'm here."

After agreeing to take the brother's statements the next day, Hale and I decided to leave, giving the men time alone with the woman they'd been searching desperately for, no matter how damaged. We exited to the sounds of Darius singing "How Sweet It Is to Be Loved by You."

CHAPTER 13

THE NEXT MORNING, CHIEF DONNELLY WATCHED WARILY AS A dozen seventy-year-old women arranged a roast, cold cuts, dumplings, and coleslaw on the pink plastic fake lace tablecloth, food for fifty rather than the twenty people roaming Natalya's house.

"I served in Vietnam," Donnelly said. "And I can safely say less planning went into the TET offensive."

Two women walked by, each holding one handle of a soup tureen, their hands shaking. I almost stepped in before they safely hefted it onto the table.

During Vera Batko's requiem mass at the Ukrainian church, these same practical women had been the source of a sublime sound, their voices layering in song, filling the empty corners of the church and bounced off the icon panels, the gold leaf, and the deep reds of the pictures, giving the saints more gravity than the stained-glass variety.

Dave's family had huddled close to the casket. It was small, Vera having shrunk to the size of a child while in the barrel. The bushy-bearded priest spoke over her casket in Ukrainian, his robes spilling over his 6'5" frame, skimming the floor and wearing a hat that put his final height over 7 feet, easily. The Ukrainian rolled out of him, a steady thunder of words, and the women joined in, their voices light, skidding around his voice. I wondered if their masses always had this much singing or if it was saved for funerals. Bells tolled through the song, and the voices rang out, followed by one last chime.

A contingent from Jake's Social Club had showed up, a group of men who refrained from drinking long enough to get through the service. The rest of Dave's friends and I sat in the back, including people from the station, several deputies from the sheriff's department, state troopers, and cops from neighboring towns. It was only respect for Dave that kept law enforcement from arresting the guys from Jake's bar, but I did receive several passed notes with their suggestions of who had stuffed Vera in a barrel, most of which said "Jake Medved." Even my dad came, making a quick exit after the service with a lie about having to meet someone—my dad had no social life. Annie emerged as the go-to person on what to do. She wore a lace scarf, and it being church, the whisper she used was lower as she explained the different parts of the funeral mass. I was wondering where she'd learned all this. One of the state troopers asked.

"Dave's aunt."

Annie now hustled through Natalya's house carrying a basket of rolls, politely obeying an older woman who told her to move the bread to the other side of the table.

"Help yourself!" Dave said. "Aunt Natalya's been cooking for days. She's got a bit of a reputation to uphold, having been the unofficial caterer for the Island over the last forty years." He waved his hand in front of the table. "I give the bar crowd twenty minutes to get here. Eat up now, before the locusts hit."

I laughed.

"I'm exaggerating. Slightly," Dave said.

We loaded up plates and grabbed a corner, the chief sitting at a small table and the group from the station crowded around. Next to us were two pictures of Vera, the frames surrounded by six religious icons. Both Vera and the icons were beautiful.

I picked up a picture of Vera that I guessed was from the late 1970s. Dave, probably five, beamed from the seat of an amusement park train, his mother sitting next to him, gripping him tightly. In the seat behind Vera and Dave slumped young Lucas, an island of misery in a sea of candy-colored gaiety, his straight hair feathered back in a way that made me suspect he had a comb stuck in the back of the cut-off jean shorts he was wearing.

"Lucas wasn't enjoying the train ride?" I asked.

"He wasn't enjoying much of anything, I don't think." Dave lowered his voice. "Mom was three days back from a few months . . . out of town. Me and Dad were ecstatic to have her back. Lucas was not."

I picked up the second picture. Vera was much thinner than in the first, all high cheekbones and dead eyes. She was wearing a lime-green sleeveless shirtdress, the polyester clinging to her slim frame, and was perched in front of a handpainted sign that read HAPPY JULY 4TH 1983 in childlike script, backward flags lining the edge. I looked closer, trying to get a hint of what would leave Vera dead before the end of the summer, but there was nothing. I placed the photo back in the nest of icons.

"Aunt Natalya took an icon-making class at the church," Dave said when he saw me studying them. "She wasn't religious, but every time she made one it was a big 'fuck you' to Khrushchev."

"Stalin." I hadn't heard Natalya coming. "And do not use profanity."

The chief stood. "Thank you for your hospitality, Ms. Batko, but I need to return to the station."

Dave shook his hand. "Thanks for coming. The ladies auxiliary here"—he pointed to the women in the kitchen—"will be sorry to see you go. Fresh meat."

Dave's joke couldn't have been farther from the truth. While the younger crowd welcomed us warmly, the older women who buzzed around Natalya gave us a wide berth, distrusting law enforcement on principle. I doubted if this group had so much as jaywalked in their lifetime, but they looked at us as if they expected the chief and me to round them up and take them away. I think in their minds I was close kin with Stalin, which was not a comparison I appreciated.

Chief Donnelly had to fight his way past the crush at the door. Jake and Maxim Medved had arrived, accompanied by the barflies. Lucas greeted several of them warmly, introducing them to Tara, who spun tightly around her father's legs. Judge Medved carried a ring of lilies over his arm like a racehorse, the smell of the flowers filling the room.

"Our crowd was getting hungry," Jake called. "Good thing we followed our noses."

"It is a wonder you could smell over those flowers," Natalya said. "Ostentatious arrangement, the scent overwhelms." She waved to the backyard. "Put it out there, Maxim."

The guys from Jake's bar that trooped in after the Medved brothers, sticking to the plastic path running through the living room, afraid to step off. One of Natalya's handmaidens brought the judge a plate, piled high. Clearly Natalya wasn't holding the fact that the prime suspect in Vera's death was Maxim's brother against him. No other plates were forthcoming, and Jake led a contingent into the dining room. The men weren't grief stricken, and there were happy sighs when they spotted the food.

Dave nudged Hale. "See that guy?" A man in his sixties, small and gray, made a sandwich and dropped it into his pocket. "That's Tomas Wolschowicz. Oksana's brother. The last woman who, maybe, possibly disappeared."

"We should go get his contact info," I said.

"He'll dodge you. Cops make him nervous. Grab him now and take him to the backyard. It's pretty quiet."

We approached and introduced ourselves, asking to talk about his sister.

"Can I bring my food?" When we agreed, he followed us happily. We slipped out the kitchen door to the porch, but even out-side the judge's wreath was sickeningly sweet. We walked farther out onto the lawn.

"Natalya's house is such a sweet place," Tomas said, taking in the land. "My parents would have killed for property like this. They were about Natalya's age, always afraid of starving. Our whole back-yard was a garden." He nodded approvingly at some asparagus that were pushing through the earth. "My mom was a housekeeper; no way could she afford a place like this."

I looked at the back door where I saw Dave hovering. I dove into my questions about Oksana's disappearance, confident that Dave couldn't hear.

"I'm not sure why you want to talk about my sister," Tomas said. "She moved."

I relaxed, relieved there wasn't another missing person. "When did you last talk to her?"

"Talk?" Tomas shook his head. "It's been a while."

"Since she left?"

"No. But she sends letters, all classy and typed. She's a legal sec-retary now."

I pulled out my notebook. "What's the return address?"

"There is none." He shoved a large piece of pork roast in his mouth, chewing and swallowing so quickly I worried about him choking. "She sends me a hundred dollars for my birthday every year, not on my actual birthday or nothing, but it's the thought that counts. I think she likes to show off a little, how good she's doing, but doesn't want my dad to track her down. Wish I could give her the all clear. The rat bastard died ten years ago."

"She and your dad fought?"

"For a while, yeah. But she dated Jake Medved for a few years, and Jake threatened to kill my dad if he touched Oksana again."

"He was scared of Jake getting violent?"

"Jake used to get his kicks beating the shit out of people, but that wouldn't have stopped my dad. No way Dad was going to cross the judge, though."

"So just to clarify, Tomas, other than the letters"—*which could be faked by anyone,* I thought—"you haven't had any contact with your sister Oksana in over twenty years?"

"When you put it that way . . . no, I guess not." He paused, food forgotten. "Do you think something happened to her?"

"It would be good if we could rule that out," Hale said. "Any chance you'd be willing to take a DNA test?"

Tara bounced out of the house, her dark blue dress now replaced by a too-large cotton shift that was a swirl of hot pink and orange, a princess dress if the princess was from 1973. Lucas chased her outside with the judge and Jake on his heels.

"Oh, sorry," Lucas said. "Didn't realize . . ."

"Tomas!" the judge called. "A smart man you were, coming out here on this beautiful day instead of being trapped inside." He smiles at me. "I hope we are not interrupting, Officer Lyons and Agent Bascom."

Jake stared at us. "A bunch of us are leaving, Tomas. Come now if you want a ride."

"Be there in a sec," Tomas yelled. "They're asking me a bunch of questions about Oksana!"

Lucas and the judge were trying to corral Tara, but Jake stopped, staring at us. "Oksana? Something happen to Oksana?"

"We should let you get back to your friends," Hale said to Tomas, patting him on the back. "But let's keep this conversation just among us. And let me know when you're ready for the test and we can fix you right up."

Tomas didn't answer, shuffling his feet.

"What's wrong, Tomas?" I asked. "It doesn't hurt if that's worrying you."

"No, it's just . . . this woman I slept with says I'm her kid's father."

I was at a loss. I wasn't too impressed that he was trying to dodge his parental responsibilities. "They didn't request a test before?"

"She didn't want much to do with me. But she could change her mind and come after me for child support."

"How old's your daughter?"

"Twenty-four."

While I still wasn't impressed, at least I had a solution. "Too old. No child support for a child over eighteen."

"Then that's OK. I might even try to talk my daughter into getting one herself. Get proof she's my kid."

INSIDE, THE CROWD HAD THINNED. THE LADIES HELPING WITH food were still there, but the guys from the bar had left along with Dave's friends.

"You should take off," Dave said. "Things around here are about to get real boring. They're talking about who has cancer, and in a few more minutes, we'll be discussing who died. I'd leave if I could."

"Dave, we have the investigation, but we're also your friends," Hale said and Dave grinned, too brightly. "I don't know if I said this before, but I'm so very sorry about your mother. To lose the person who was there from the first, who named you." Dave's face softened, his smile blurring as he looked at the ground. "Well, it's a big loss."

"We'd stay for you," I said. Dave flinched. Everyone who remained was Island, and he knew they wouldn't relax until we were gone. I gave him an out. "But we do have a lot of work to do." Dave met my eye again, and I knew I was on the right course. "Want to meet up later?"

Dave agreed, propelling us toward the door. I had to force him to stop so we could say good-bye to his aunt.

On the way home, I stopped at the station to type up my notes on the interview with Tomas. It sounded like Oksana had a lot of good reasons to disappear—violent father, ex-con boyfriend, and a brother who at the very least was a deadbeat. My curiosity was piqued not because Oksana had left, but because she'd made the cursory attempt to stay in contact with her brother. Perhaps I was giving the letters she sent too much weight, but with Dave's mom showing up dead after being a missing person for so many years, I was beginning to assume the worst about Oksana.

I mapped out my plan for the next few days. I'd hit the dead end on Dave's mother, having gone through all the forensics and interviews, and planned to switch to Louann Bazelon's case. Now that we had a "who" with the burned woman, we could start to investigate the "how" and "why."

I waved my good-night to Lorraine, who, based on radio codes, was arranging a welfare check on Ernie Hollaran, a mean drunk whose family didn't like him enough to visit but still cared enough to make sure he wasn't dead. The streets were dim and quiet—except for a few old-man bars, we didn't have much of a night life. I arrived home to find my spot in the driveway taken up by a new white Honda. As I opened the front door, I heard laughter from the kitchen, the conversation cutting off as I shut the door. I took off my shoes and padded in. My father was at the kitchen table, and Lucy was playing with a dream catcher, sitting on the lap of our guest. My mother.

CHAPTER 14

ISCRUBBED HARD AT MY FACE, RUBBING MY CHEEKS VIGOROUSLY with the cold water. I had escaped upstairs, ostensibly to "clean up after the funeral," but really to get my head together. I felt ambushed.

I had to prepare for my mother at the best of times. She was always so impractical, "off with the leprechauns," my dad used to say when she would talk about "setting intentions" or walk through the house with burning sage to clarify the energies.

My dad would sniff the air. "Smells like church," he'd say, which infuriated her.

I heard the stairs creak, and figured my dad must be coming up to apologize, or at least to explain. My mother and I hadn't spoken since Kevin's funeral, and I had no interest in restarting the relationship. I'd given her too many extra chances for this lifetime. It was hard to see why Dad would have let my mother come, especially when things were crazy. There was a knock at the bathroom door.

"Come in," I said.

It was my mother. She was wearing a loose shift in a golden sage color I guessed was Eileen Fisher, the embroidered cuff slipping to expose age-spotted hands.

"I have to change," I said, trying to slide past. I always reverted to fourteen and pissed around her. She wouldn't give way.

"I wanted to tell you," she said evenly, "that I came up because I thought Gordon might need support at this time."

"Dad has support."

"You don't think about supporting your father's emotional needs because you're his daughter. And your father, with his cop lifestyle, and his cop friends, and his cop daughter, he doesn't have anyone to talk to about what's really going on. In here." She tapped her chest. "You can tell by how stiff his back is that he's not at peace." She rolled her shoulders, as if to give my father relief from a distance. "And I figured he would need a friend."

"You're his friend?" I said.

"I am. One of the few close ones he has."

From below I could hear my father and Lucy banging around in the kitchen, Lucy offering to set the table.

"June, I don't know if you remember what it was like last time—"

"How could I forget?"

"He never slept, taking Elda's calls. You remember her? Luisa's mother?"

"Yes, I remember her. I visited her yesterday."

"Or he'd be up through the night, pacing from room to room, practicing the arguments he was going to make to the judge to secure a warrant."

"If only he'd had someone to support him back then," I said meanly. "But you ran off with Larry."

"Now, June, that's not true," she said.

"Don't try to rewrite history."

"June, your father and I, we stayed together all during the trial. Both of us knew the marriage was over. We'd been young kids when we met, and our love, it felt like a lightning strike. But those lightning strikes are usually bad news—the sickest part of you speaking to the sickest part of another person. And once you get past the heat and power, you're left with two people who don't bring out the best in each other."

As always, my mother couldn't stick to the facts—names and dates—and instead went for the grand metaphor.

"Let's make a deal, June," she said. "I'll stay at the hotel, although I hope . . . it would be so nice . . . if you would let me back into your life."

I was unmoved. She had spent so much time yelling at my dad back then. "Trying to get a reaction, any reaction," she would shout. My dad would stop, tell her to pull herself together and leave, going for very long walks. One night I thought he wasn't coming back, and when I opened the door, I found him sitting on the chair on the front porch.

"Sorry, June," he said. "Didn't mean to scare you."

That was a bad time, and talking to my mother brought it all back. I wanted her gone, but my father hadn't thrown her out. Driving her back to the airport probably wasn't an option.

"Leave now," I said. "I need a break, and I'm not up to negotiating with you right now."

She nodded and, surprisingly, didn't say anything.

We went downstairs where Lucy was spinning around the living room, the feather from the dream catcher streaming behind her.

"I've had a very long day, Lucy," my mother said as she put on her coat. "Plane trips take a lot out of me—so much unhealthy air! I need a shower and some meditation. Why don't we plan on meeting tomorrow after I get a good night's sleep?"

"You could stay," my dad said from the doorway.

"No, no," she said, meeting my eyes briefly before looking away. "I do need some sleep. Since we're both early risers, let's have breakfast. Is Marie's still there, and does she still make those sublime banana pancakes?"

"It's her daughter's place now, but she kept the recipes," my dad said. "How about six?"

I wanted to protest, but it seemed unfair to remind him I needed him to get Lucy on the school bus at 7:30.

My mother walked over and kissed him on the cheek—he looked shocked, but recovered fast, returning the kiss, and walking her to her car.

The three of us ate dinner, ignoring the empty place next to Lucy. After dinner, Lucy and my father hung up her new dream catcher while I did the dishes, and he hauled the garbage to the curb while I read her a story.

I considered going to bed, but I could hear him in the dining room, flipping through papers, no doubt rereading the file, and knew we had to talk about my mother tonight—I wouldn't sleep otherwise. I made a cup of tea to fortify myself for the confrontation. As the water boiled, my phone rang. Hale.

"My techs scraped the VIN off the van and were able to track down the specific Carfast office where it was rented. Las Vegas."

"Why would she rent it there? Vegas isn't New Mexico."

"Well, it's closer to New Mexico than Schenectady is."

I stayed silent. The longest longshot in the world slotted into place. "Can the place send us video?" I said.

"Sure can," Hale said. "I have a local agent there picking it up for us. The only problem—and thankfully it's temporary—is that the owner recorded with videotape, not digital."

"Videotape?" I said. Not only was it years out of date, it was expensive. Digital imaging was more or less free once you set up the system. "Is it recorded on Betamax?"

Hale laughed. "No, but close. As you might imagine, a franchise owner too cheap to install a new digital security system is also not going to be shelling out for new videotapes very often. We have the tapes, but they've been taped over and over and over so many times that the video of the person renting the van, such as it is, is difficult to make out."

I groaned.

"Don't despair now, June," Hale said. "You have an in at the FBI. Our agency has technology available to transfer the video to a digital format, and then pull clear images out of that digital file."

"That's nice of you to expedite the transfer."

"The faster we close these cases, the sooner you're on my team."

"Hale. Seriously."

"Give it a rest," Hale said. "I got it, June."

I hung up the phone and ran smack into my father.

"You're rejoining the Bureau?"

"Absolutely not," I said, and then reconsidered. "The chances aren't zero, but they're close."

"Why?" he said. "You're through . . . the crisis." Dad still avoided mentioning Kevin's death. "And you liked the work. More than what you're doing now."

"I might end up on the road."

"But around here?"

The kettle whistled, and I walked over and poured my tea. "Between Vermont and Buffalo."

"Overnights?"

I couldn't believe this. "It doesn't matter. Yes, there are overnights, and they're not an option. And neither are undercover operations. And the first time I did mob or gang work and they came hunting for me? Who do you think they would find? Lucy," I said, furious at even the thought of it. "And you."

My father didn't protest, and I thought the conversation was closed. I was wrong.

"Does no one in the Bureau have families?" he asked.

I took a deep breath. "Some. Not all of them thrive."

"You and Kevin did. Successfully, as I recall."

"Kevin did cybercrime, following trails through the Internet, not across a desert or up a mountain. He covered home base."

"You have me now."

"I know, I know." I pulled the teabag out of my cup and threw it away. "But Hale offered me a position as a consultant, anyway. It wouldn't be permanent."

"Wouldn't that be a positive? Try it out, see how it goes?"

"And what if it fell through? Would you enjoy your *unemployed* daughter living with you?"

My father squinted at me. "You're afraid."

He was talking about feelings. My mother *was* a bad influence on him. I decided to change the subject to something I wanted to argue about.

"So, Mom? Your new best friend?"

"The lady you were rude to? Yeah, we're friends."

"I would have appreciated a little warning. I could have gone and done some overtime. Run some errands. Anything other than coming over to talk to that woman."

He crossed his arms. "Twenty years, June. Let it go."

"I did. I let the divorce go a long time ago. But at Kevin's funeral . . ."

"It wasn't so awful," he said. "It wasn't silent-treatment awful. Forgive her."

"For what she said at Kevin's funeral?"

"For that. And for the time in your twenties she invited you to a healing circle. And for when she let you ignore her. And when she left . . . left me, not you." He paused. "Which was the right thing to do at the time."

He stood up and walked past me, picking up my cup and loading it into the dishwasher. I listened to him shuffle toward the dining room and expected him to dig in for another night of research, but he flipped the light and returned, stopping to place a kiss on the top of my head, the way he did when I was younger and shorter.

The carpet muffled his steps as he went upstairs, but his tread was heavy, crossing between the bathroom and his bedroom. I waited until he was completely settled before walking upstairs myself, flipping off lights as I went. Sleep came fast.

NATE AND THEO OFFERED TO COME DOWN TO THE STATION TO make a statement about their mother's probable abduction, but Nate had a request: he wanted to see where the fire happened. Doing the interview at the station made my life easier so I was happy to oblige;

Hale and I picked them up at the hospital. Darius stayed at Louann's bedside, and we planned to get his information when we returned the brothers to the hospital.

As Hale drove, Nate gave us the information they had.

"She and Darius own a nursery and landscaping business, and a neighbor planned to bring over a half-dead plant for mom to fix," he said. "Mom can grow *anything.*"

We were close to Hopewell Falls, but I decided to let Nate keep talking. Theo added nothing, staring out the window at the river.

"So the neighbor called Mom, let Mom know she was running late. Mom didn't pick up, and the neighbor arrived to find the garage wide open, and the door to the house unlocked. The house was normal except for a bowl of persimmons smashed all over the hallway."

"So she answered the door for a neighbor and . . ."

"And someone grabbed her." Nate was getting agitated and spoke faster and faster. "We're celebrities, sort of, and someone probably took her, thinking they would get rich. She always told me and Theo that being in the public eye was a bad idea. She was right." Nate closed his eyes, and his voice wavered. "I wanted the money."

I expected some sort of reaction from Theo, at least some comforting words for his brother. Nothing. I stepped in.

"Nate, you can't possibly know the motive for this crime. It may very well have had nothing to do with you or the TV show."

"She was a *landscaper,*" Nate said. "What, she put in an ugly rock garden and someone decides to knock her off?"

I put a "no" next to that question. We were a few blocks from the station, and I'd be through my list by the time we arrived. "Did you get any threats—"

"Hold up a second," Theo said. "Stop here!"

Hale pulled to the curb and put the car in park. Theo shook his head, as if trying to dislodge a memory, and I was hoping we'd finally get some useful information out of him. He pointed out the window.

"Did there used to be a store there?" We had stopped in front of a closed department store, a nondescript black marble box with bolts marking where it had been stripped bare of the space-age silver letters. "A Jupiter's?"

I faced Theo directly, my shoulder jammed into the headrest. "Yes . . . but it's been closed for more than a decade. Do you want to get out and take a look?"

Theo shook his head "no," and Hale began driving. We made it half a block before Theo again called for us to stop, this time asking for us to turn left.

"I'm having a weird case of déjà vu," Theo said. Hale raised one eyebrow at me, but we continued.

"Cannon," Theo said as we passed the old armory, the weapon out front an iron replica. "Hey, is there a bridge nearby?"

"The one to the Island," I said. I tapped Hale's arm and he turned.

No one spoke as the car rumbled over the bridge. Nate shot worried glances at his brother, who twisted in his seat, first left, than right, tugging at his seat belt so he didn't miss a thing.

"Was there a bakery around here?" Theo asked.

"It's been gone for a while, but it stood right"—we passed an empty lot—"there."

"Left here!" Theo said at the next STOP sign. Following his orders we turned, passing tightly spaced apartment buildings before we got to the more spacious houses.

"One . . . two . . . three . . . four . . ." Theo was counting houses. "Here! Stop here!"

Hale braked suddenly, throwing his arm across my waist as I jolted forward. We were in front of the home where Bernie had murdered Luisa so many years ago.

"I lived here as a kid," Theo said. "Before Mom and I moved, this was my house."

I turned around, ready to correct Theo and then stopped. Theo. Theodore. Teddy.

Theo was Teddy Lawler.

CHAPTER 15

SWEAT POOLED AT THE BASE OF MY SPINE. THE RADIATORS IN the 116-year-old courthouse had stood the test of time, but the air conditioning, touch and go at best, was no match for a day that had reached eighty degrees before 10 a.m. The windows were cracked to let in a breeze, but if we opened them a few more inches, the reporters pressed against the glass were likely to crawl in. That said, all two hundred spectators remained silent, refusing to risk being ejected for what promised to be a great show. After thirty years, Bernie Lawler was getting out of prison because his wife and child were alive.

Theo Bazelon's ID of his childhood home had seemed unbelievable at first, not only to us but to him. He kept trying to rationalize his memories into a truth he could live with—he had come to Hopewell Falls on vacation, he was remembering another Jupiter's store in the chain, he was a child and making things up, *anything* to prove that he wasn't Teddy Lawler because that would mean his mother had at the least lied, and at worst faked her death. Nate ended up being the practical one.

"Test my DNA. Test his, too," Nate said, pointing at his brother. "Send it to an outside lab and charge it to us if they can get the job done faster. Better to know for sure than spend months agonizing."

Within five days we had the results, which proved beyond doubt that Bernie was Teddy and Nate's father and that the woman lying in the hospital bed was Luisa Lawler. From there the wheels of justice cranked into gear, as we informed the DA, the DA informed Deirdre Lawler, and she demanded release of her brother with all deliberate speed, meaning yesterday. Now here we sat, eight days after Theo first identified his childhood home, waiting for Bernie Lawler.

Next to me, Hale looked cool and dry, the crease still sharp in his black wool pants. I was glad to be plainclothes today, not only because it was cooler than the uniform but because I had some hope of fading into the background.

I scanned the crowd, ducking so as not to draw attention to myself. I was on the watch for Lucas and Dave. At the prospect of his mother's killer getting out of prison, Lucas had spent the last few days swinging between rages and long walks to the river's edge, returning home tight jawed, only softening when his daughter climbed into his lap. Dave went into cop mode, amassing a file of evidence against Bernie.

"Maybe he didn't kill his wife and child," Dave said when I visited him at home, "but that motherfucker *slaughtered* my mother."

I thought he was right, but I needed to back him away from any truly stupid decision. "You don't know that."

"I do. Luisa Lawler is out cold in a hospital bed, not in a shallow grave somewhere. She didn't die in that house, but we're both smart cops, and there's no denying someone did, and that someone was my mother. You saw the pictures from the basement—"

"You saw your mother's file. Dave—"

"No!" He stood suddenly, walking across the living room, kicking over a pile of old newspapers. Dave was a neat person, but trash was accumulating, and even from the next room I could smell that he needed to do dishes.

"It was twenty years ago," he said. "When I was starting out, studying what your dad did to try to learn how to be a good cop, I read the file. I saw the blood . . . splashed on the walls and seeping between the floorboards. It . . . took a long time for my mother to die. The head wounds that were identified in my mom's autopsy? Someone smashed her skull against the basement wall."

"Dave," I said and waited until he met my eyes. "You're a smart cop. Your involvement could wreck this case in court. Please stay away from Bernie."

Today, Dave seemed to be doing just that. Eight sheriff's deputies walked the courtroom's four aisles, doing quick patrols. They were less concerned about violence and instead searched for electronic devices, people trying to capture video they could sell to the highest bidder among the fake news websites.

A low buzz started in the back of the courtroom, and Jake rushed up the aisle, head down. He wore a suit and had his salt-and-pepper hair slicked back. For the first time I could see the resemblance between Jake and Maxim, the brothers sharing the same large nose and jutting jaws. Jake was followed by Brian, who had his hair pulled back in a neat ponytail, the tailored jacket straining across his shoulders and arms. The two men slid into the seat opposite us next to three law students and Dan Jaleda, who had ignored my earlier greeting and stared forward toward the empty jury box. Maxim Medved was slower, stopping at almost every row to say hello or shake hands. He reached the front, and the deputy ushered him into his row with a flourish, clapping the judge on the shoulder.

"Bet you wish it was you sitting on that bench, about to set your brother free, Judge."

Maxim Medved didn't correct the deputy's use of "Judge," and I realized that more people used his title than his name, including me. He gave a half wave to the bailiff who stood at the front of the courtroom. "I would unlock his shackles myself."

The prison transport entrance opened, and Bernie shuffled to the table flanked by two guards, followed by Deirdre and a young law student carrying two document boxes. Bernie strained his neck, surveying the crowd, greeting several people who waved. I knew the instant he saw his brothers: he tried to break away. The guards gently guided him back to the table.

"Check out his suit," Hale whispered.

Of course Hale noticed the clothes. "Not bespoke?"

"Not even close."

Someone had arranged for Bernie to get a pale gray linen suit, but they missed on the size, folds of cloth hung at his back, and the tie hung around a collar with a several-inch gap. His sister, in low heels, appeared taller than he was, but of course she wasn't. She just had more substance.

Judge Keveney entered the courtroom. We barely had a chance to stand before Keveney waved us down. Court proceedings could be ponderous, but Keveney worked at a quick clip, completing the formalities in less than a minute: he asked Jerry, the DA on this case, if he would like to withdraw charges, since the two decedents—Luisa Lawler and Theodore Lawler—were in fact alive. Skipping even the perfunctory protests that prosecutors usually threw out when prisoners were going to be released, Jerry agreed. Keveney announced that charges against Bernie Lawler had been dropped and he was free to go.

The crowd erupted. Deirdre shoved the law student aside, grabbing her brother into a hug that bunched his baggy suit. When she pulled away, I could see she was crying. Bernie reached out and wiped her tears away, kissing her once and then twice, less a "thank you for getting me out of jail" kiss one might give a lawyer and more an "I missed you" from a big brother.

The crowds surged forward to meet Bernie, forcing Hale and me to step sideways, out of the crush. As Bernie crossed the bar from the courtroom to where the spectators sat, Jake grabbed Bernie's arm. He seemed unsure, but Bernie pulled him close. Bernie ruffled Brian's hair, despite Brian's being several inches taller, before reaching for the judge. The judge rested his hand on his brother's shoulder and left it there even as he and Bernie pushed forward through the crowd. Despite getting pulled forward by his brother and pushed by his sister, Bernie stopped, again and again, to listen to well-wishers and greet old friends. After thirty years in prison, Bernie had lost his sense of urgency.

"Got a cattle prod?" Hale asked as the crowd made its slow way through the dimly lit marble corridors of the courthouse.

"He's been in institutions long enough that if law enforcement ordered him to, he would pick up the pace, but that seems . . . unkind."

After the slow trip through the dimly lit marble corridors of the old courthouse, stepping outside was a shock, the sun's glare beating down and destroying shadows. A microphone had been set up, and a large crowd fanned out down the steps to the sidewalk, spilling into the street. Hand lettered signs reading JUSTICE FOR ALL or FREE BERNIE bobbed above the crowd.

"How vicious is this going to get?" Hale asked.

"Most of the people who might be enraged by this verdict are dead."

With the exception of an occasional flossy champagne blond or home-dyed matte black hair—usually sported by men—it was a sea of white hair. I spotted several of the former employees of Sleep-Tite and a couple of guys from Jake's bar. The only people genuinely agitated were the law students, and that was mostly for the cameras. I was scanning the crowd for Lucas and Dave when I saw my father, tucked in along a row of hedges on the left. I was shocked. Last night, he had said he wouldn't be here, and I had believed him.

"I sent a man to prison for thirty years, Juniper." Dad had pulled the paper label off his teabag and was folding it, ripping it in half, and then folding the torn pieces in half again. My mother and I waited for him to speak, which involved a lot of long silences as Dad struggled to find the words to express his grief. Mom was still, feet on the floor and palms up, meditative. I had to sit on my hands to keep from grabbing the shredded paper out of his hands.

"I took a man's life," he said.

From my perch atop the courthouse steps I tried to catch my
dad's attention, but his eyes were glued to Bernie. Dad wore a blue
raincoat despite the clear day, and his old pair of eyeglasses, the bent
wire frames sitting askew on his nose.

I tapped Hale's wrist and nodded in the direction of my father,
afraid that saying his name, even in a whisper, would draw attention
to him. I didn't need to worry—everyone was focused on Bernie or
his sister, who stepped up to the podium.

"Today, an innocent man," Deirdre's voice boomed, and the
audience flinched before one of her law students reached over and
lowered the volume. "Today, an innocent man has been set free.
My brother, Bernie, should never have been arrested, and his time
in prison robbed him of life. For those of you, who, unlike my law
students, were alive thirty years ago"—the crowd chuckled—"think
about what has happened in your life over those last thirty years.
Births. Marriages. Maybe a job you love. Holidays spent around a
table with family, sharing stories." The people in the audience smiled
up at her as I worked myself toward my father. "Now imagine if all
those experiences—your life—were taken for you." The judge put
his arm over Bernie's shoulder, gripping him fiercely. "The Innocence Clinic has walls lined with the pictures of people like Bernie,
imprisoned or even put to death. While we have so much more work
to do, today we can celebrate my brother's freedom. It is a joyous day
for my family, for Hopewell Falls, for the people of New York State,
and this country."

The crowd clapped, and the law students cheered as if it were
a sporting event. Hale and I were stuck in the crowd, clustered so
tightly we couldn't pass. I watched as Deirdre pulled Bernie forward.
He stood mute in front of the mic as the clapping went on and on,
the crowd matching the enthusiasm of the judge and Jake. The crowd
quieted, and he leaned forward, speaking, but the mic didn't pick up
his voice. His sister nudged him forward, and his nose bumped the
metal. He jumped back as feedback screeched out, shrugging help-

lessly as one of the law students reached over and upped the volume.

"It's a beautiful day, isn't it?" Bernie said. "The sky, it's gorgeous! And there's so much of it!" The crowd laughed as he gazed up, smiling, and he looked like a boy instead of a man of sixty. The smile on his face stayed as he looked at his sister. "I want to thank Deirdre, although now I think about it, maybe she should thank me." Bernie held out his hand to Deirdre, who grasped it tightly.

"Deirdre here would never have gone out there and gotten her law degree if she hadn't seen where bad lawyering will get you. And to all her little worker elves"—the law students cheered again—"who worked tirelessly for years to make this day happen, I hope I get the opportunity to shake each and every one of your hands."

"What's next for you, Bernie?" a reporter yelled out.

Deirdre dropped Bernie's hand.

"No questions!" she said, but Bernie had already started talking.

"Well, first I'm going for a walk. A long walk, down by the river. Then I'm going to eat a lot of vegetables. You try to get a fresh cucumber in prison." The press scribbled in their pads, and I bet Bernie's vegetable comment would lead off several newscasts and newspaper articles.

His smile faded. "And then, I'm going to get reacquainted with my family." Jake was crying openly at this, comforted by Brian. "My brothers, and my nephews and nieces. And maybe, eventually, my sons. I have two boys." His voice cracked, and he paused, the microphone catching his hitching breath until it eased. "I'm ready to meet them whenever they're ready, but I . . . I hope it's soon." He laughed. "Oh, but first, a shower, which can be as long and hot as I want, with no guards watching."

State troopers cleared a path as Bernie and his sister stepped into the crowd. The judge followed, with Jake and Brian close behind. Reporters continued to throw questions at Bernie, but he concentrated on shaking the hands of the old Sleep-Tite employees and childhood friends he met. He even kissed a baby.

"This way," Hale said, skimming the crowd's edge, the quickest path to my father. Bernie and his sister were moving rapidly in the direction of my father thanks to the intervention of the state troopers, and I wanted to prevent what might be a terrible confrontation. I was still ten feet away when Bernie stopped, turned, and broke away from his entourage. Within seconds, he was nose to nose with my father.

"My worthy foe," Bernie said. "Officer Lyons." Flashes went off, reporters getting pictures of the two men shaking hands. Bernie rested his hands on my father's shoulders, saying something only my father could hear, my father nodding once, twice, before whispering something back. Hale held me back, while to my left the judge and Brian corralled Jake, who muttered in a voice roughened by cigarettes and tears, "He's the one who should be locked away for life."

"Bernie. The civil suit," Deirdre said. Bernie pulled away, and Hale and I rushed forward, but my father didn't notice, frozen in place. I expected him to joke, say, "Think the photographers got my good side?" or flip into action: "No question, he killed Dave's mom. Let's nail him!" But this helpless version of my dad wasn't right.

Hale grabbed my father's arm and pulled him across the grass. "Come along, sir." Some reporters debated following us, but in the end they didn't want to lose a minute of Bernie. Hale ducked through a break in the bushes, and we crossed the lawn, bright green thanks to the recent rains. I looked up. Bernie was right. It was a beautiful sky.

We spilled out onto the sidewalk twenty feet down from the crowds, and Hale led us at a rapid clip across the street. From a distance, I saw Bernie talking with Susie, who served me coffee every morning. She had come from work and was still wearing her Dunkin' Donuts uniform.

My father stopped in the middle of the street, shaking off Hale's grip. "Oh, God. Susie was a juror at his trial."

"I'm sorry. I'm so, so sorry," Susie wailed, and Bernie hugged her close.

A car approached, and we hustled to the far side and scaled the steps of the parking garage. Hale packed my father and me into my car.

"You gonna be OK?" Hale asked, watching my dad the whole time.

"Yes." I gripped the steering wheel harder to calm the shaking in my hands. "I think so. Let's meet up in a few hours, once everyone is settled."

Hale tapped the top of my Saturn. "Well, call me if you need to change plans. Everyone would understand."

I rolled up my window, gliding down the ramp to the exit, out onto the street and past the line of news vans, toward home.

"What did Bernie say?" I asked. Dad didn't answer, rubbing his glasses on the hem of his sweater. I repeated the question, talking louder. No response.

"Dad!"

He jolted. "What?"

I felt guilty for shocking him. "Bernie. What did he say to you?"

My dad put his glasses back on. "I apologized. He wouldn't accept my apology. He said that faced with the same situation—a missing mother and child . . . the blood evidence . . . that he would have sent the guy away for life." His voice dropped, his words scratched and faint. "How does someone do that?"

"Do what?" I asked gently.

"Forgive. Something like that." He struggled to find the words. "Forgive the person who sent you to prison for thirty years and destroyed your life."

We turned the corner onto our block and I stopped. The reporters hadn't chased down my dad at the courthouse because they had the second brigade in place to jump us at our house. I made a U-turn. I didn't know where we would go, but it wouldn't be home. Out of Hopewell Falls would be best. Maybe Hale's house?

My phone rang. It was an unfamiliar number, and I was going to let it go to voicemail when my Dad grabbed it out of my hand.

"Your mother," he said, hitting *send* and saying hello. I had no idea my mother had my number and was stunned Dad knew how to use a cell phone.

"You were right," I heard him say, "it was a huge mistake." He dropped his head back on the rest. "It's on the news already?"

I listened as my father avoided answering questions about what happened, his replies getting shorter and shorter until he was down to "Yeah" or "No." I was about to suggest he hang up when he said a complete sentence: "That's a great idea. I'll let June know."

He mashed the face of the phone, ending the phone call by hitting all the buttons. "I'm going to your mother's hotel. The Kelly Suites. She's got a room in her name. We'll be untraceable."

I had to admit it wasn't a bad idea. We drove to the hotel, parking in the back and taking the stairway up to the second floor. I scrutinized the hotel. I liked it. Her room and the parking lot weren't visible from the street and my dad—and my mom, I suppose—could come and go as they pleased.

"Come in, come in," Mom said. The room smelled sweet and spicy—not the quasi-floral scent of commercial disinfectants, but the sandalwood incense that had always been her favorite. The TV was off, but the cup of tea in front of the sofa gave away the fact that she had been watching. She was willing to brave the cancer-causing rays TVs supposedly gave off for something this important.

"I chose this place because it has a full kitchen," she said. "Restaurants are so unhealthy." She pointed to a pair of doors at the far end of the living room. "There are two bedrooms with two beds each. You could all stay if you wanted."

"Maybe for a few hours," I said. "I have to go to the station for a bit." I didn't want to tell my dad, but Hale and I were planning to re-interview Theo and Nate Bazelon, trying to get more information about why their mom might have dyed her hair, changed her name, and fled across the country. "I'll pick Lucy up after school and then swing by and get Dad."

"Gordon and I can get her, bring her over here," she said. "I have a pool. It'll be an adventure."

"Real nice adventure," Dad said, dropping into a blue and pink pastel chair that sat in the corner. He took off his glasses and began cleaning them.

"Did you eat lunch, Gordon? How about you, June?" Mom went to the fridge and pulled out food: hummus. Bread. A daikon radish.

"I have to go," I said to my mom, and then dropped my voice, mouthing to my father: "You OK with her?"

"I'll be fine." He blew nonexistent dust off the lenses and put the glasses back on, frowning.

"You know that's your old pair, right?" I said. He took them off and examined them before propping them on the table in front of him and closing his eyes.

"Gordon, where can I pick up a bathing suit for Lucy?" my mother called from the kitchen. "Is there still a Caldor around?"

"The Gap," he said, keeping his eyes closed.

"I don't approve of their child-labor practices. Do you have a Costco?"

I left the two of them to fight out the labor practices of the different retail outlets and went to meet Hale.

CHAPTER 16

Darius watched the ventilator instead of Luisa, still unconscious in her hospital bed. The oxygen reservoir rose and fell, shallow but steady, and Darius took a few breaths, matching his wife's slow pace. We sat in silence for a moment, the machines pinging and chirping like a flock of birds. He took another slow breath and finally answered our question: "What is your wife like?"

"Louann wants to leave a light footprint on this earth. She makes others feel loved and special."

Elda sat near Luisa's head, her gnarled hand gripping Nate's. "Luisa was never one to grab attention."

"Louann." Nate pulled his hand away. "Mom's been Louann longer than she was Luisa."

"Well, actually," Elda said, and then a sad smile crossed her face. "I'm sorry. If you prefer Louann, I'll do my best. Anyway, from the day she was born, Lou . . ." She looked to the two men, checking to see if the nickname was acceptable. It was. She continued. "Well, Lou kept her light tucked under a bushel basket. I'd have to push her to wear lipstick, and at school assemblies she would go mute."

This was the third question Elda had answered instead of Darius.

If I was going to get answers out of him rather than her, I'd need to talk to him alone.

"Darius, I'm worried we're disturbing Lou's sleep. Would you mind talking to us in one of the waiting rooms? Just for a minute." I had learned from Elda's error, but it was an easy one to make—"Luisa" almost came out of my mouth. I was less focused on the woman she'd been in New Mexico and more concerned with the person she'd been thirty years ago when she made the decision to fake her death. She'd obviously planned it carefully, lining up new identities and going someplace where no one would ever find her. And despite the sweetness Darius and Elda described, it took a certain ruthlessness to stay lost even as your husband was sentenced to forty years in prison.

Darius didn't protest our request, but Nate objected. "I can come, too."

"Your mother needs a friendly face by her side," Hale said.

Nate wasn't willing to give up so easily. "Theo said he was going to grab lunch and that was over an hour ago. He'll be back soon." His lip quirked, a half frown. "He didn't take off, did he, Darius?"

"Your brother's fine, and you will be too." Darius stood in front of Nate, placing his hand first on Nate's neck and then resting his hands on his shoulders, the outline of a hug, before speaking to Elda.

"Will you be OK, ma'am?"

She gripped Nate's hand again. He grimaced.

"I'll be fine," she said.

A lounge at the far end of the hallway was usually empty, and we went there. Today there was a guest, Theo curled up in the far corner of a green vinyl couch. The TV was off, and he stared straight ahead at an egg-yolk-yellow wall.

Darius sat right next to Theo. "How you doing, young man?"

"Not so bad," Theo said. The dark shadows under his eyes gave away his lie. "They here to arrest Mom?"

"Absolutely not," Hale said.

"Oh. You gotta wait until she wakes up?"

"No, Theo." I took one of the chairs at the far side of the room and dragged it close, sitting a few feet to Theo's left. "We're still putting together the story of what happened to your mother. And I'm pretty sure the reason she was kidnapped a few weeks ago and burned is closely related to why she left Hopewell Falls way back then. I'm here today to ask Darius some questions about her early days in New Mexico. You too, if you'd agree." Theo nodded absently at this, which I took as a yes.

I decided to start with Darius, asking him a bit about his history.

"I went on a vision quest," Darius said, "back in the sixties. Why a black kid from Chicago was going on a vision quest is a story for another day, but I came out of that with a mission to get in touch with nature. I discovered I had a way with desert plants, and I figured starting a nursery was a way to honor the forces of the universe and make a little cash. Did OK for myself." Theo was watching Darius intently, and I hoped he was catching the storytelling bug.

"Then Lou showed up," Darius said. "Here's this little bitty thing, pregnant and chasing a three-year-old, who comes to me begging for a day's work so she could feed herself and her boy." He smiled at Theo. "The two of you were living in a Ford Pinto, you remember?"

"She called it camping, so I thought it was fun," Theo said. He pulled his hands inside the sleeves of his fleece jacket, despite the room's being almost stifling. "She loved that car. Held onto it for years. Strangers would come up to us, telling us it was a deathtrap, and she'd thank them for their concern and roll her eyes."

"I gave Lou a job repotting plants for the day, this one underfoot the whole time." Darius patted Theo's knee. "She did excellent work, and I invited her back the next day. And the day after that."

Theo picked up the story. "And then you gave her a full-time job, with benefits."

"And two days later Mr. Impatient was born," Darius said.

Theo smiled. "You wooed her with health insurance, smooth operator."

Darius nodded. "Your mother's and mine has been a slow romance. We're not officially married," he explained to Hale and me. "Common law, though. She didn't want to be formal about it, despite my numerous requests."

"You were winning her over," Theo said. "Any day . . ." But he suddenly frowned, reaching out and touching Darius's arm, a comforting gesture. "But of course, that would have been bigamy."

I didn't want Theo to dwell on the legal ramifications of marriage between Luisa and Darius. "Theo, are there any other details about your life in Hopewell Falls you remember, other than the house?"

Theo described images, memories from a kid's eye view. "A woman who smelled like lilacs made red Knox blocks with me, letting me sweeten the gelatin. She wasn't very tall, and she kissed me too hard." *Natalya,* I thought. "Men who smelled like cigars, talking loudly. In a foreign language." He paused. "My father is Ukrainian, right?"

"Born here," I said. "He has brothers, though. Maybe you are remembering them."

"And I lived in a house with a yard I thought went on forever and ever. I remember walking outside and being surrounded by green. For years, Mom, Nate, and I lived in these shitty apartments in New Mexico, places filled with people who weren't staying long—students, military, sometimes illegal immigrants. I kept the memory of the yard. I just didn't know where it was."

I thought of his career choice—park ranger—and wondered if he liked having miles of green space.

"I tried to get her to move in with me," Darius said, as much to Theo as to us. "I tried to pay her more, but she never took it. She always wanted to live simply."

"Did that ever change?" I asked.

"A bit. She liked having a garden, liked planting, for fun, creatively." Darius threw his arm over the back of the couch, settling into the story. "I had her design my yard. She did a beautiful job, and it got her and the boys over to my house, which I loved."

"Over the years, did Lou ever go out of town?" I asked. "Any unexplained trips?"

"She didn't travel much," Darius said. "We went to Peru last year. And either she or I would go to a trade show every year. Those could be anywhere." He frowned. "She wouldn't go to the one in New York City and got sick the year it was in Boston."

Those cities might have been a little too close to Hopewell Falls for Luisa's comfort. "How about people contacting her? Phone calls she avoided, or any odd people showing up?"

Both men shook their heads, but I pushed.

"Even after you got famous, Theo?" Hale asked, and Theo rolled his eyes.

"Not me." Theo nudged Darius with his shoulder. "You hear of anyone?"

"Only the lovelorn, begging me to put in a good word with Nathaniel. And even they were rare. Me and Louann preferred to leave the spotlight to the boys."

Theo frowned. "But now that you say that . . ." He stood, Darius's hand thumping to the couch as Theo got to his feet. "She got angry when we saved that CEO's life. She didn't want him to die, but she hated how quickly it went from a story about a rescue to a story about me and Nate."

"I remember when you got that idiot off the top of the mountain," Hale said. "The news channels went from 24-7 coverage of the CEO to 24-7 coverage of you and your brother. You two came across like guys I'd invite to a barbeque."

"That's almost word-for-word what the producers of *Global Adventures* said, kept going on about our likability factor in the eighteen-to-thirty-four age group. They really pushed for us to be on the show."

"Why did you agree?" I asked.

Theo blushed. "A million dollar prize."

As we talked about the case, Hale typed a message into his phone, paused, and sent another. I continued to question them about the media or odd contacts but kept getting the same answer. They didn't know anything.

Nate skidded into the doorway. Theo and Darius were up, Darius rushing toward the door.

"Nate? Your mother?" Darius asked.

"No, there's no change. But I couldn't take another minute with the old woman. She told me to call her 'Nana.'" He had a frantic look in his eye. "Elda Harris is not my grandma."

"I'll go back," Darius said, stopping short of the door. "I want to hear about Louann's childhood from Mrs. Harris, find out where Louann got that wicked sense of humor."

Theo sat down, and Nate slumped next to him. "Where the fuck have you been?"

"Don't start," Theo said, crossing his arms and glaring at his brother. I was worried that Theo would stop answering questions, so I threw one at Nate, asking him if he had any idea that his mother had another identity. Considering he was in utero when everything happened, I didn't expect much of a response, but he had one.

"My mother always said she was from Philadelphia. No family alive. She moved away after our father died."

Theo scoffed.

"Anyway," Nate said, "I did the great American road trip after college and asked about places to go, not just tourist attractions but places she loved, her childhood home, or my father's grave. She spaced, couldn't think of a thing, until a couple days later she comes back to me and lists things like a tour guide—Liberty Bell, the Rocky

Steps, the Mummer Museum, cheesesteak. I figured the family stuff
was too painful."

I was stumped. Nothing the three had said gave any indication
that they knew Luisa . . . er, Louann . . . was on the run. We weren't
going to get anything.

As we were leaving, Theo stopped us. "Are we obligated to talk
to Bernie Lawler?"

"Has he contacted you?" I asked.

"Not him, but his lawyer," Nate said. "Who's our aunt, right?"

"She invited us to come to the courthouse today, but the whole
thing . . ."

"Too many cameras," Nate said.

It was interesting to hear the two brothers discuss their feelings
about their father. The more the brothers talked, the more their opinion melded into one. It was the same connection that came through
in their TV appearances, where the two were so tightly bonded they
communicated with a look, responding as one.

"And I'm not sure whether I even want a reunion with our . . .
father. With the aunt and uncles," Theo said. "They're not family.
Not really."

"But aren't you curious?" Nate said. "Don't you want to meet
our father, find out who we are?"

"Bernie Lawler didn't have anything to do with making us who
we are," Theo said. "And my mother? Until I hear the real story from
her own mouth, I'm not passing judgment."

The two men agreed to contact us if they thought of other details.
We followed the brothers down the hall to Luisa's—no, Louann's—
room. Despite being several inches shorter, Nate threw his arm over
Theo's shoulder, causing Theo's knees to buckle.

"Come visit Mom," Nate said.

"Gimme a minute," Theo said.

"That's what you said four hours ago."

"Has it been that long?"

"Yup. And I'm likely to tell off the old lady if you're not there to sigh and tell me to be tactful. C'mon."

"OH, THERE YOU ARE!" WE HEARD ELDA CALL TO THEM. WE made a fast exit.

CHAPTER 17

Hale made his pitch before I started the car. "Want to go to the Albany field office?"

I buckled my seat belt and put the key in the ignition. "Still didn't make my decision about consulting, Hale."

"I have inducements," he said, pushing the seat back several inches so that he was almost lounging. "You know how I've been promising the clear video from the car rental place?"

"Yeah?"

"I don't have that."

"I don't think 'inducements' means what you think it means."

"However," he said, giving me a cocky grin, "I do have grainy images of the guy who leased the van."

That was enough for me. We wound our way out of the hospital parking lot, braking as a pair of exhausted interns skittered across the street to a Starbucks. We drove through to Arbor Hill, the African-American section of the city. This area of town had the same colonial townhouses as the section where Hale lived, but without the self-conscious gas lamps and ironwork the developer had used in Hale's neighborhood to make it old-timey. We passed the Palace Theatre.

I'd taken Lucy there to see a Christmas spectacular a few months back, carols sung by people dressed as elves and a visit from Santa. Lucy lost interest in the dancing snowmen, endlessly amused by the fact the place had a couch in the ladies' room. I had made a note to myself not to shell out for tickets next year, but instead to find a bathroom with interesting architectural detail.

At Hale's direction, I made two quick lefts, putting us in front of the Federal Building, and continued down a one-way street. Midway down the block was an unmarked parking garage, one I'd never noticed before. We pulled up to the gate and were met by a guard with a gun who studied Hale's badge closely, writing down the number on a log sheet. A camera flashed, taking a picture of me, Hale, and my license plate, and we were through.

The lot was full, and Hale told me to take his space, a reserved spot near the elevator.

"Fancy," I said.

"Wait 'til you see the digs."

He punched a code into the elevator and then hit the button for the twelfth floor. The door opened on an airy lobby. A wide blond wood desk was manned by a smiling receptionist who was no doubt armed to the teeth. The young man had me sign in and buzzed us past the security door.

We entered what could have been a cubicle farm at an insurance company, the same burnt-coffee smell, but with wanted posters instead of actuary tables tacked to the cubicle walls. The only other difference was that all the employees wore black suits. Part of this might have been because Hale was now the special agent in charge of this field office, and people were trying to emulate the boss, but the sharp suits also came in handy during investigations: when the agents walked on scene, they demanded attention. It made me wish I'd polished my shoes.

Hale walked through the office at a rapid clip with me scuttling behind, the hum of voices rising as we approached, everyone trying to look busy. I remembered when Hale was the guy being sent out for sandwiches. Agents snapping to attention seemed odd. It was funny: more than my obligations to Hopewell Falls, Lucy, and my father, the biggest stumbling block to my rejoining the FBI would be the respect for the chain of command, with Hale sitting on top. I didn't know if I could muster that kind of reverence.

A distant boom sounded, and I felt a low vibration.

"Firing range," Hale said before I had the chance to ask. "We share it with the DEA and the ATF."

"Are they testing rocket launchers?"

"Not today. This whole place is concrete reinforced—"

"A really tall bunker?"

Hale's pace quickened. "You gotta do what you gotta do in these urban areas. Concrete will help us in a bomb attack, but it doesn't provide the best soundproofing. The floor below is empty, partially because of downsizing, and partially because the IRS wants to stay far away from the rest of us."

Hale stopped suddenly in front of a cubicle where a woman sat in front of her computer, earphones on, intently watching a reality TV show. Unfazed by a slacking employee, he introduced me as a liaison from the Hopewell Falls Police Department.

He peered over her shoulder at her computer. "Got that research for me yet, Agent Harrison?"

"Yes, sir." Harrison flipped between screens, notes with dates and times popping up even as the TV show continued playing. She rewound the video past a promo that had Theo and Nate hanging from a cliff in Ireland and froze the image. Theo sat on a couch in front of a bookcase, mouth ajar, caught mid-word.

"Ready?" Harrison asked.

The screen came to life, with Theo telling a sweet story about how the love of nature was instilled in him at an early age, a puff piece meant to humanize the reality show contestants.

"Mom and Darius, my stepdad, they used to take me and Nate

on long hikes into the foothills of the Sangre de Cristo Mountains. They wanted us to slow down, take in the natural world around us." He laughed. "Instead, Nate and I raced to the top as fast as we could."

A photo filled the screen as Theo's voiceover continued. In the picture he looked about four, his hair the same blond shade as in the pictures we had seen on the walls of his abandoned house—there was no doubt that Theo Bazelon and Teddy Lawler were the same boy. Next to him in the photo, his brother squirmed in his mother's lap. With blond hair that was harsh against her freckled skin and a relaxed and happy expression, she was harder to identify. The agent froze the picture on the screen and panned in.

"That's definitely Luisa," I said. "And if I could ID her, anyone could."

The agent unpaused the show, and Theo talked more about how his mother was too shy to be on camera, but sent her thanks to all the fans who were rooting for her sons.

The agent paused the video again and handed Hale some printouts. "Here's a few newspaper articles on the brothers. There's nothing revealing in the text, but there's another photo"—this picture showed Darius, Luisa, Theo, and Nate digging in the dirt. "This one talks about how Louann grew up in Philadelphia and was a young widow when she moved." Harrison folded her hands in front of her, putting on a faux earnest expression. "It was a very inspirational story."

"Quite the fairy tale," Hale said. "Great work, Agent Harrison. Report in with any additional sightings of our missing woman."

Hale continued down the hall, talking the whole way. "When Theo started in about how publicity averse his mama was, I asked Agent Harrison to go through old video from the TV show, see if pictures of Luisa showed up anywhere."

Agent Harrison had produced evidence that it would have taken me weeks to track down. "She did all that in forty-five minutes?"

"We have all the finest resources around here . . . a firing range, working computers . . ."

"Yeah, yeah. Do you give your employees ponies, too?"

"No, but I'm sponsoring a little trip up to Saratoga in August to watch the races. You join in time, you will get an all-expense-paid trip to the Whitney. Sitting on lawn chairs, of course." He opened the door to the corner office. "Shall we?"

Hale's office was big, with a large desk and a meeting table. Unlike his home, this was strictly by the book, with midnight blue carpets and recently painted walls. Service commendations and a picture of President Obama hung behind his desk. His back would be to the awards most of the time, but it was no loss: a wall of windows looked out over the Hudson.

"Do you *require* spectacular views?"

"I earned this," Hale said. "In an ironic twist, my office in Miami got no natural light. I'm making up for years of being vitamin D deficient."

He pulled a chair behind the desk so we were sitting shoulder to shoulder. I averted my eyes when he punched in his password, but I needn't have bothered as the computer had facial recognition software. The screen came on, and grainy video popped up on the screen.

Images flashed in and out, ghosts from Vegas's past. The static got lighter and out of the fuzziness came an image of a man.

"No audio?" I asked.

"Don't be greedy."

The employee bustled back and forth behind the counter, printing out paperwork, pointing at a signature line, and standing close as the customer counted out bills on the counter.

I couldn't believe my eyes. "Cash?"

Hale nodded. "Yup. Cash."

"Who takes cash anymore?"

"The owner. He's the guy behind the counter, and he has a policy in place where you can pay in cash if you leave a $5,000 deposit. Gamblers *have* been known to ruin their credit."

I squinted at the screen, but the suspect's image faded and warped. "I can't make out the suspect's face *at all*. The owner get an ID?"

"ID was fake. The rental agency kept a copy, and when we tracked it down, it was some army ranger who'd never set foot in Vegas, let alone Hopewell Falls. The owner did get the guy to remove his sunglasses and said his eyes were blue, the same color listed on the license."

"How is this even possible? You can't pick up your dry cleaning without three forms of ID and a background check." I wanted to walk out right now. "We've got nothing."

"That's not entirely true," Hale said. He switched views to a camera positioned across the street from the rental place. A cab pulled up and despite the distance, I was able to make out every number on the license plate.

"The casinos," Hale said. "Thanks to them, there's not a single place in the whole of Las Vegas without surveillance."

"Facial recognition software?"

"Impossible to avoid, but our guy did a nice job of hiding under sunglasses and a hoodie. Witness identification didn't go much better. Cabdriver could only give us tall, sunglasses, and 'wearing a lot of clothes'—unhelpful to say the least." Hale opened a separate file. A police sketch. Our guy who rented the van looked vaguely like the Unabomber.

I watched as the path of the car was tracked backward to its origin, the camera from Caesars Palace following the car to the place where the camera from the Parisienne picked it up. Someone in the FBI had done some good footwork, going from casino to casino, collecting footage. Unfortunately, their work hadn't given us the result we needed: I couldn't make out the guy's face.

The cameras shifted, and we were now in the airport, everyone walking backward. I spotted our guy, still in sunglasses, despite being indoors. He backward-marched through the airport, but slowly: he had a pronounced limp. I pushed my chair close to the computer trying to get a better view. Was it Dan Jaleda? Or Brian? He arrived at the Southwest terminal, going right past the Minneapolis gate to the one arriving from Detroit. "How can you be sure he didn't connect through Detroit from Minnesota?"

The screen flashed again and we were in a different airport. "Detroit," Hale said. Our suspect rode an electronic sidewalk through the flash of fluorescents in a mile-long passageway.

"That's gorgeous," I said. "It's like you're underwater." It made me want to visit Detroit.

"One time my flight to Atlanta was delayed and I took the walkway back and forth three times," Hale said. An instant message screen popped up in the corner of Hale's screen, and I watched him type "5 mins," before minimizing the dialogue box.

"Watch this," he said.

The suspect took off his sunglasses, dazzled by the lightshow. The shot was grainy, and the lights played havoc with the images, but it looked like Brian Medved.

I almost smacked Hale. "Why didn't you start there?!"

"I wasn't convinced."

I was. Brian had the straight stance of a soldier, as did this man. He put his sunglasses on, retreating up an escalator, down a hallway to a gate marked ARRIVAL: ALBANY.

"The plane from Albany didn't convince you?"

"It did, it did," he said, spinning around in his chair to face me. "But then I remembered. The leg." Hale tapped his knee. "The metal joint-work would set off TSA alarms, and he would have to take the leg off for inspection. We interviewed a bunch of TSA agents who were working the gates the morning he was traveling, and there are no records of someone with a prosthesis."

I stepped closer, and without asking, Hale rewound, stopping at the second where the guy took off his glasses.

"With the limp, there's a chance it might be Dan Jaleda . . . but it looks like Brian . . ." My face was inches from the screen. Brian made a lot more sense than Dan Jaleda—despite his injury, his military training would give him the skills to overpower most people, but especially a small woman like Luisa. And anyone who did patrols in the desert wouldn't blink about driving a hostage across country.

"Are you sure his leg would set off the alarms?" I asked.

"Definitely," Hale said. A message popped up in the corner of his screen and he typed "on my way." He picked up a file from the desk. "I have a four p.m. meeting, but I could go to the bar with you later."

"We'll be crashing a party," I said. "Bernie's homecoming, and I'm guessing that Maxim and Jake have pulled out all the stops for their brother's shindig. Pulling Bernie's nephew outside might start a riot." I followed Hale out of his office and down the hallway. "Plus I really want to get home and check on my dad."

"I may do the same with Dave. Our friend is looking a little hollowed out, and it might do him some good to get out. How's your dad taking it?"

"It's weird. Normally I'd expect him to be stoic, or to leap into action. Instead he's sharing his feelings." I thought of him in the car, unable to navigate Bernie's forgiveness. "I blame my mother."

Hale stopped short. "Your mother? You have a mom?"

I was offended. "A lot of people do, you know."

Hale laughed. "I had thought you sprang full-grown from your father's knee. You never talked about her, that I remember."

Explaining my mother was hard, starting from when my parents met, my dad arresting her at a peace rally. There were the homemade granola bars in my lunch bags long before they were fashionable, and the time she attended the policemen's ball wearing an Indian print dress. But those were easy compared to the big things: leaving us and moving to Florida, and her selfish behavior at Kevin's funeral. The funeral still made me wince, but no way was I talking about it with Hale. Hale and Kevin had been close, but during the time Kevin was ill we hadn't been friends—we'd almost been enemies—and Hale missed the funeral.

"I should go," I said, pointing at the exit. "Family awaits. Thanks again for putting the FBI at our disposal."

"Consider it a recruitment trip. All this could be yours if you decide to return."

"Even the parking space?"

"Well, maybe not everything."

CHAPTER 18

I STAKED OUT MY HOUSE. TWO NEWS VANS WERE PARKED END to end out front, and a reporter fiddling with his phone was talking to a bored cameraman who sat on the back bumper, smoking. It would be easy to get in the side door before they could get any footage. I could rescue my dad and Lucy from my mother, and everyone could sleep in their own bed tonight.

At the hotel, I discovered they didn't needed rescuing. My father was nowhere to be seen, and Lucy was sitting at the dinner table, quiet and still. Usually her silences worried me as they preceded all hell breaking loose, but this was different. She was listening to my mother.

"June had been begging for a treehouse for months," my mother said. "For her seventh birthday, your granddad and I built one. Up she went, scaling the ladder, poking her head out of the window and waving down at us. But that wasn't high enough for our June."

"It would be fun to climb to the top of a tree," Lucy said, and I choked back a protest. As a child, playing in my treehouse was my favorite thing to do. As a parent, it would be a cold day in hell before I let my daughter hang ten feet above the ground on a couple of hammered-together two-by-fours.

"No, not to the top of the tree," my mom said. "Onto the roof of the playhouse. She was having a grand old time right up 'til she realized she was stuck up there." Mom made a cartoonish shocked face and Lucy laughed. "Your granddad and I were too big to fit through the hole, and we were almost ready to call a fire truck when your mom's cat decided to join her on the roof."

"Were they both stuck?" Lucy asked.

"No, and we can thank the cat for that. It guided June down, showing her the safe places to step until she'd shimmied back to the ground. I'm convinced that cat is her spirit animal."

"Grandma, can we build a treehouse this summer?" Lucy asked before noticing me. "Oh, hey, Mom." She wore clothes I'd never seen, a striped shirt over a T-shirt, with a polka-dotted skirt and leggings that had the same pinks and oranges as the stripes in the shirt. It almost matched, a first for Lucy.

I reached out my hand to Lucy, who ignored it. "Ready to go home?"

"I like it here," Lucy said. "I want to live here forever."

"Because they have a pool?" I asked.

"A pool and Grandma."

My mother beamed. "We've had a wonderful day, June. Lucy told me all about her best friend Kaylie and starting judo next year, and I told her stories of when you were a little girl." She waved me over to a chair. "Let me make you a plate. It's mushroom risotto, and there's plenty."

"That's OK, I'm not hungry." A statement that was about the farthest you could get from the truth.

"Are you sure? Lucy isn't finished." My daughter was pushing stuff around the plate rather than eating. My mother hadn't gotten smart to that trick yet.

The food smelled delicious, and I didn't want to leave without my father, so I dropped my bag onto a chair, draped my coat across the back, and took the plate my mother offered.

"Where's Dad?" I said between mouthfuls. It was very good.

"He went to visit Dave," she said. "Your friend needs a father figure right now, and your Dad is as close as he might get."

I didn't think any such thing was true, and I wondered if she had just made assumptions about Dave or my dad's emotional state. She liked to do that.

"And Dad's doing OK?"

My mother put down her fork. "No, he's not. We both know that, June."

It wasn't hard to avoid conversation with Lucy next to me babbling about her day. She showed off her bathing suit and the artwork she and Grandma had done, where half the page was Lucy's abstract versions of houses and a sun, next to my mother's mellow beach scene, all soft blues and greens with a dolphin visible on the ocean. I was happy to let Lucy chatter away if it meant I didn't have to discuss the elephant in the room—or rather, the one that was out trying to keep Dave from hunting down Bernie Lawler and thrashing him.

"I want to go to Florida and visit the dolphins," Lucy said. I shot a look at my mother, but Lucy had captured her complete attention, babbling on about flamingos, Grandma, swimming pools, and summer before suddenly changing subjects.

"I made dessert," Lucy announced. She ran for the kitchen and returned with three bowls of strawberry rhubarb crumble topped with vanilla ice cream. It was perfect, if a little early in the season.

"It's always in season at Whole Foods," my mother said. Normally I would have tried to knock my mother off her high horse, pointing out the gas she burned driving to Colonie to buy organic produce, but Lucy knelt next to me, bobbing up and down on her chair, and asked, "Do you like it, Mom? Grandma said it was your favorite."

I'm not a dessert person, but the tartness of the rhubarb made it perfect. "I love it! You did a great job."

"Grandma gave me the recipe so me and you can make it any time we want."

"That reminds me of the first time I served this to June. June and her little pals took their bikes out . . ." My mother continued telling a story of how my friends and I rode our bikes down a hill as fast as we could, splashing through a mud puddle in the final stretch. My bike got stuck and I tipped over, getting completely coated in a layer of mud.

"Which delighted her," my mother said. "I had to hose her off outside. I have a picture of her, wet and happy, hanging above my desk at home."

"And then we ate dinner," I said, "and you served this to comfort me."

"It was mostly consolation for your sister, who was devastated that she hadn't fallen in the mud puddle, too. Oh, I forgot, your sister and I talked." Mom hesitated, and I waited for the message, no doubt a mix of New Age and sentimental. "She offered to come out, support your father."

I was surprised. Catherine's relationship with my father was about as good as mine with my mother. "Maybe she should hold off."

It was getting late. I called my father. I'd thought he might pick up—he kept his cell phone for an emergency, and this situation certainly qualified. No answer. I called Dave, but he didn't pick up either. That worried me. He always kept his phone close by, even at night. Finally, I tried Hale.

"You with Dave?" I asked.

"Couldn't raise him. Worried?"

"He's with my father, which could be . . . trouble."

"Aw, they'll be fine," he said. "Your dad had a hard day. It's good for him to help out Dave a bit, let your dad get his mind off his own troubles."

I hung up. Lucy was about twenty minutes away from collapse. I could take her home, but Dad had borrowed Mom's car, and I didn't want to leave her stranded. We were staying, if not for the night, than certainly until my dad returned.

"I'll get changed," Lucy announced, returning moments later with pajamas with purple sheep frolicking across them.

"How many outfits did you buy her?" I asked my mother.

"A week's worth." She raised an eyebrow at me. "Consider the clothes overdue Christmas gifts."

Lucy climbed into bed, and my mother pulled out an iPad. Lucy tapped the screen, picking a bedtime story. I nestled next to her, reading, Lucy flipping the pages when I proved inept until finally dropping off to sleep, despite being in a strange place. I crept out to the living room, desperately hoping that Dad had returned. He hadn't.

Feigning sleep seemed like a good option, and my mother was willing to give me an out: "You are welcome to take the bed in Lucy's room tonight if you want."

Never one to back down from a challenge, I forced myself to sit on the couch next to her. The fluffy cushions looked plush, but that was a lie; the stuffing was packed so tightly it was almost painful to sit on.

"Do you want some tea?" Mom offered. I agreed. She walked the ten feet to the kitchen, but we both remained silent, and she might as well have been in the far wing of a mansion.

I spoke first. "Did you have to buy all the kitchenware?"

"Oh, no. They gave me all the china and most of the cooking equipment. I went out and picked up an aluminum skillet—the non-stick kind they had will chip off and give you cancer." She paused. "I'm going to gift it to your father when I leave since it sounds like he has embraced cooking."

I snorted. "If you use that term loosely." I felt bad for putting my father down, as if I'd betrayed him. "Not that I'm any great shakes. But I suspect he's gotten most of his recipes from the 1972 edition of a Betty Crocker cookbook."

"He very well might have," Mom said. "I believe my aunt gave it to us as a wedding gift, noting all her favorite recipes, most of which involved suspending things in Jell-O. It's probably still tucked somewhere in the kitchen."

The kettle whistled, and she poured two cups of a spicy sweet tea, a scent I connected with my childhood.

"Sweet, the way you like it," she said, handing me my mug. I hadn't added sugar to my drinks since I got out of high school. Not that Mom knew.

We sipped our drinks quietly, but by the way she frowned, I could tell she was thinking. I was seconds away from having a heart-to-heart about my Dad, or worse, discussing our mother/daughter relationship. I needed to take the offensive.

"What can you tell me about Luisa Lawler?" I asked.

My plan worked. "Well," she said, "if she did what they say she did, she must have hated her husband."

"But . . . but why wouldn't she get a divorce?" I pulled a leg onto the couch, a barrier between me and my mother. "It *was* done. She could have moved to Florida, like you. The two of you could have formed a commune."

"That would have been a very seventies thing to do, and we were modern women of the eighties." My mother quirked a smile. I'd never seen her make a joke at her own expense.

"But June," she said, "for a lot of women, the awful ones are the hardest to leave. The men hunt you down and they hurt you, and if they have a powerful family—like Bernie did—it was practically impossible."

"Did he hit her?"

"I wouldn't have stood for physical abuse." She reached forward and grabbed her mug. "Luisa was always watched, though, first by her mother and then by her husband and his family, handed from babysitter to babysitter. I knew her from the Hopewell Falls Hope Committee. You would think a group dedicated to running bake sales and hanging bunting on streetlights at Christmas would be above reproach, but sometimes Jake Medved would stop by claiming to be interested in our work." She raised an eyebrow. "Do you really think an ex-con bartender had any interest in how many Arbor Day sponsors his sister-in-law secured?"

"So she missed a lot of meetings?" I asked.

My mother tilted her head. "Not too many, now that I think about it, but she had to push hard to attend. Luisa wanted nothing more than to dye hundreds of Easter eggs or stick American flags on cupcakes, and I would have been happy to leave her to it."

I had a memory of my mother sitting up late at the dining room table gluing yarn hair onto clothespins for a fall carnival game, muttering, "I don't need this bullshit." She still made the most clothespin people. I could get why some people might not enjoy it—I certainly wouldn't—but it wasn't like Mom was chained to the chair and forced to continue.

"Mom, I was alive and reasonably aware during this time. Luisa had options."

"Not many. When your father and I divorced, he could have chosen to make my life miserable—cutting me off from you and your sister, ruining me financially. But when you were under someone's thumb, like Luisa—back then it was almost impossible to pull off. In those days no fault divorces didn't exist."

"But if he was as bad as you say he was, surely someone—Dad, the courts, someone—would have helped her get free."

"Bernie didn't beat her. He controlled her and treated her like a child, but law enforcement and the courts would never intervene in that. To get away from that type of situation, Luisa would have had to be aggressive, and Luisa? She'd do anything to avoid people getting mad at her." My mother pulled her legs up so she was sitting Indian style. "Sounds like hell to me, June."

I had to agree. In my work I'd learned the importance of silence, both to keep secrets and to let criminals have time to run their mouths, but having to keep my mouth shut in every area of my life would drive me crazy.

"So you found out how emotionally abusive Bernie was at the trial? The way Dave's Aunt Natalya described it in court, Luisa barely left the house."

My mother leaned forward. "Luisa confided in me. We were paired up stuffing scarecrows for the hayride, and she mentioned how she wished she could come to more meetings, but Bernie wouldn't let her. After she disappeared, it came out that she'd gone to a lot of people, telling them how much of a tyrant her husband was." She paused. "Although now that I think about it . . . if she set him up, she might have been planting the information." Her eyes got wide. "Everybody seemed to know . . . because she told them."

Mom was absolutely right. What I still didn't get was why Luisa had resorted to such extreme measures.

"There are two odd things about this situation, June, details that make me believe someone else came up with the plot." My mother took a sip of her tea. "First of all, as I said, Luisa avoided confrontation."

"Ah," I said, "but this was about as far as you could get from direct confrontation. I don't have all the details, but it was more a sideswipe, a sneak attack against her husband. The perfect option for someone who wanted to get out without having a confrontation."

"However, my dear Watson"—Mom held up her finger—"there was the blood."

"We now think the blood in the basement came from Vera," I said. I didn't mention the blood we'd found in the bathroom of the Lawler house. That was law enforcement's secret until Annie got DNA results.

"I'm talking about the blood in the trunk of Bernie's car. The bloody handprints. Luisa couldn't have pulled that off."

"Why?"

"The Hope Committee did a volunteer blood drive. Poor Luisa fainted at the sight of blood—any blood. And when I say faint, it was more like a seizure, eyes rolling back, shaking."

"A vasovagal response," I said. "We're told to keep an eye out for them at crash scenes."

"Right. We had a volunteer blood drive. We put her in the cookie room, thinking it would keep her from collapsing. It still wasn't enough. Down she went. We had loads of orange juice on hand to boost her blood sugar, but she was done for the day. Anyway, the point of all this is that bloody handprint in the trunk. No way could it be her blood."

This was interesting, and it added to my sense that someone was in on it with Luisa. The question was whether that person was invested in keeping Luisa disappeared, going so far as to kill her.

"I hope the information helps you solve the case fast, June." I was about to thank her when she added, "I don't want you falling into the same negative patterns as your father. Focusing on the job at the expense of everything else."

Rage rushed through me, filling my chest, choking me. I pulled my arm away. "So running away from the situation would be the better option?"

"Running away, no. But setting boundaries between yourself and your father, yourself and this work, would give you more balance in your life. You could have fun with Lucy, or develop a spiritual practice, or date a little. It's been three years—"

"Are you saying I don't spend enough time with Lucy?"

"Juniper, you are a very good mother doing a very good job. But the time with her will be gone before you know it, and you will regret it for the rest of your life." She reached out and grabbed my arm. "You can't make this right for him, as much as you'd like."

I stood up. This fight was bound to happen sooner or later, and it might as well happen now when Lucy was asleep and Dad was out. "Mom, you need to realize I will never, ever take any advice on how to treat family from you."

My mother let her voice go low and even. "You need to let your anger go. It's poisoning you."

"You know, I like you better when you are being a real person, not lapsing into this magical earth mother thing."

"I'm your mother."

"Barely. Dad was always there for me. Always." I lowered my voice so as to not wake Lucy. "He made sure I got to the dentist to get my braces off, took me to watch the *Star Wars* movies, explained the birds and the bees to me. That was fun: Dad explained the mechanics of making babies and then offered to pay for the pill." I felt myself start to hyperventilate and struggled to talk. "He helped me, day in and day out, when my husband was dying."

"I tried to help, but you wouldn't let me."

"You helped in the ways you wanted, not in the ways I needed."

My mother dropped the serene act. "You didn't know what you needed."

"I was pretty clear, Mom. Helping me change the sheets when Kevin threw up bile on the bed. Picking up late-night prescriptions. Making me sandwich after sandwich because Kevin couldn't stand any cooking smells in the house. Getting Lucy off to preschool. That's what real family does."

"When are you going to let this go, June? I've apologized. I've reached out. I've invited you into my life."

"But it was always your life. You would crash into my life periodically and make assumptions about me and what was important. And I had made peace with you for the stuff that happened when I was young—"

"No, you haven't. You have never forgiven me for leaving your father."

"Listen! For once. I was good with your New Age cures and your free spirit ways and the fact your marriage to Dad was a bad idea for everyone involved. But when you showed up at Kevin's funeral and did your mumbo jumbo over the body, making yourself the center of attention on the day that should have been all about him—"

"No one noticed," she said.

"*Everyone* noticed. And your lack of respect would have been funny, except you took it to the next step, making that comment on how I had lost Kevin months ago. I hadn't lost him months ago, Mom. He was with me right up until the end, and even when he couldn't speak, he could listen. He was with me." I felt tears pricking my eyes. "He still is."

I brushed the tears away, but I was helpless to stop. My mother went to the kitchen and brought me a paper towel. I rubbed hard, and the skin on my cheek was raw. Mom left again and returned with a washcloth soaked in cold water. I settled back on the couch, the washcloth resting over my eyes.

"I . . . I'm sorry," she said. With my sight cut off, I focused on her words. "I am sorry if I caused you pain at the funeral. I was trying to comfort you."

I didn't say anything, letting her words wash over me.

"You and your father, June, the two of you were always a team. I wanted the two of us to be that close." She paused. "When your father and I separated, I knew you'd pick him. I never doubted it for a minute."

She was quiet, and I thought she was done, but then she took my hand, gently folding it between both of hers.

"I will have to meditate and journal on what happened at the funeral." I tried to pull my hand away, and her grip went from tender to fierce. "No. Please don't. Please don't pull away, just as I understand . . . everything. I need to think hard on how I'm going to make this right. But between now and then . . ."

She went quiet again. I pulled the washcloth from my face with my free hand. Normally, I described my mother as willowy, with strength running through her airy grace. Right now, she looked fragile.

"Mom—"

"Sorry," she said, lifting my hand and kissing it. "I just love you so much."

I thought of Bernie, absolving my father of guilt, and Dave, whose mother had left a trail of wreckage through everyone's lives before disappearing forever, and I left my hand in hers, not pulling away.

"Let's try," I said. "Let's both try."

My phone rang, and I jolted, pulling my hand from hers. I stretched forward and grabbed it from the table.

"It's Dave," I said to her. "I have to take it."

It wasn't Dave.

"Hold on, June," my dad said. I heard a car door slam, and then my father was back on the line, breathing heavily. "There. Sorry."

"What are you doing with Dave's phone?"

"Went over to his place to talk, but he was gone. I drove around a bit and saw his car parked outside Jake's tavern. Dave was going to help with Bernie's welcome home."

"Oh, no," I said.

"The gods were smiling on us though," Dad continued, "because Bernie Lawler decided to skip his own welcome home shindig, and I only had to protect Dave from dirty looks by the bartender, Jake's son?"

"Brian."

"Yeah. He looked ready to kill Dave, but he didn't. We're leaving now, and I'm going to take Dave home and get him settled in."

My dad sounded like his own self, not chipper, exactly, but like a man ready for action. My mother and Hale were right. Maybe letting Dad help out Dave was for the best. "Sounds like a good plan."

"You at home?" he asked.

"No. Mom's."

"She alive?"

"Yes," I said. "I thought we could sleep here, at least for one night, make sure the press have cleared out."

My dad thought that was a wonderful idea. "I have a key, so no need to wait up."

I hung up, and my mother emerged from her bedroom carrying a pair of pajamas. "Thought you might need something to sleep in."

"Oh, I can't," I said.

"Go ahead. And there's an extra toothbrush in the bathroom." She pushed the blue-gray pajamas into my hands. "June, I'd like to continue the conversation, but after I've had time to think, and when you're not in the middle of two cases. So let's call a truce, at least until after the cases are done."

I didn't know if it was a reprieve or a threat. I thanked her for the pajamas, went in and brushed my teeth with one of the four toothbrushes she had lined up on the sink, and changed for bed. Her pajamas, cotton and impossibly soft, protecting me against bleached hotel sheets, and my daughter's sleeping breath rising and falling next to me lulled me into sleep.

CHAPTER 19

MY PARENTS WERE AWAKE AND DRINKING TEA AT THE DINING table when I got up. It was six a.m., but I hoped to be able to go home and change before the press showed up. My mother hadn't bought a week's worth of clothes for me.

"Want some?" Dad said, raising his cup at me halfway before letting it drop back down. With dull eyes and the beginnings of a gray beard covering his pale face, he looked sick. It had been almost three years since his heart attack, but a trip to the cardiologist might be a good idea. The stress couldn't be good for him.

I declined his offer of tea. If I didn't have coffee first thing, my brain never woke up. Tea would just confuse it.

We talked through the day, my dad grunting one-word answers, my mother embellishing his statements, finalizing Lucy's school plans, and offering salmon for dinner.

"We can work around your plans," Mom said a little too eagerly, but I was willing to give her points for trying.

I grabbed my purse and notebook from the chair and gave each a little wave. With Lucy still asleep, no one was in the mood for hugs.

The sun was up by the time I got home, and I moved quickly

through my routine: coffee, shower, dress, coffee, and more coffee. I wanted to get to work, but I also wanted to get away from my quiet house. Before Lucy was born, Kevin would periodically go on assignment. The time alone was like a holiday. I watched five seasons of *The Wire* in eight days and ate Mexican food for dinner—Kevin, that freak, refused to eat cilantro. But when Kevin died, I became afraid of the quiet. Silence became a punishment. I poured my third coffee into a to-go cup and raced out to meet Hale.

Hale and I decided to have a friendly early-morning conversation with Brian, bringing a file with a DVD labeled "Detroit airport" and a video labeled "Carfast Car rental" along with some prints. I'd used videos before—sometimes real and sometimes blank. Often you didn't even have to push for a confession; the guilty blurted out explanations.

We'd strategically timed our visit to Jake's bar for 9:30 a.m. so we'd arrive after the post–swing-shift happy hour, people having a couple of beers before heading home, pulling the blackout blinds, and sleeping the day away. We congratulated ourselves when we arrived to find no cars in the parking lot, but our victory was short lived. The bar was closed.

"The Medved family is celebrating Bernie Lawler's release from his unfair incarceration and thanks the community for their warm support." The last sentence had been wedged at the bottom of the page and was difficult to read. "Jake's Bar will reopen tomorrow."

"Well then," Hale said.

I had Lorraine pull Jake's address. Jake's Camaro was parked in front of the house, half on the grass and half on the street, and we pulled up in front of the neighbor's house. As we got out, we were greeted by a handyman, the same one who'd been hired by Maxim to do Bernie's yard work. I could tell the moment he recognized us—he looked ready to drop his hedge clippers and run. I went with the assumption that the judge wouldn't hire someone with outstanding warrants and decided to let him be.

"Judge Medved isn't here," the man blurted. "He's at the office."

We explained that we were there to see Jake rather than the judge and the man relaxed visibly, wishing us good-bye and running behind a bush. The driveway of Jake's house was dominated by Brian's four-by-four. Wheelchair accessible, it was another indication about how far Brian had come in his recovery since his injury.

"I was really hoping to avoid having this conversation with Jake hanging around," I said.

"C'mon. They'll be delighted we came to them. Saved them that trip down to the police station." Hale smirked. "For now."

We walked down the broad sloping path, widened to accommodate a wheelchair, an upward curve at the end gently depositing us at the front door. I rang the doorbell. No answer, although I heard a strange clanging echoing through the house.

Hale punched the bell again.

As the chime's echo disappeared, I heard a voice. "We're in the garage, Dan!"

The clanging continued as we walked to the garage. The door slid up, Jake Medved gripping the strap.

"Wouldn't have opened the door if I knew it was you," he said. He wore a sleeveless shirt. In his early seventies, Jake had reached an age when it was hard to develop muscle tone, and his arms were skinny, almost stringy. They were tanned a deep brown, a strange look in a bartender; they were usually as pale as deep sea creatures.

Brian sat on a leg press, the weights crashing as he finished a set. Behind him sat a weight bench, barbell propped at its head, 150 pounds of plates loaded on to each end. Brian was wearing a green army T-shirt stained with sweat and gym shorts that hung almost to his knee. The clothes did nothing to hide his prosthesis, and I had a chance to study it for the first time. Unlike the heavy plastic versions I had expected, this one was sleek black metal with a curve at the end, aerodynamic, but in no way resembling a foot.

Jake squinted at us. "Can I help you?"

"We need to ask Brian some questions," I said.

Jake yanked at the canvas strap, preparing to pull down the door. "He doesn't have to talk to you."

Hale raised his left arm and stopped the garage door's descent. "The other option is for us to take Brian to the station and conduct the interview there." He bumped the door back up. "Your choice."

"So this woman can try to stick my son with a crime the same way her father did Bernie?"

"We never mentioned a crime," I said.

"Go take a walk, Dad," Brian said, climbing down from the machine. He waved us inside. "Let's go talk in the kitchen."

Brian didn't wait for us, hurrying through a door leading to the house, his step even and free of the limp. Scuff marks dotted the concrete of the garage marking the path of his prosthesis, a circuit that traveled from the leg press to the barbells and back to the door, and the house's hallway had square imprints cutting through the vacuum lines in the tan carpet. I caught sight of an army poster in his room as we walked through to the kitchen, updated with the pristine marble countertops perfect for noncooks.

Hale, Brian, and I settled around the kitchen table, and I asked Brian about his whereabouts in mid-May.

"Went fishing at Lake George," he replied without hesitation, not asking for the specific dates.

"Did you catch anything?"

"Fish."

"See anyone while you were fishing?"

"No one. Only me and the fish."

Who needed Deirdre? A confession was going to be impossible with a guy who had been trained to resist interrogation.

Sliding doors separated the dining area from the backyard, and out of the corner of my eye I saw Jake, hose in hand, watering the three-foot patch of grass right outside the glass. Lawn care was not his strong suit.

"A lot of green up in the Adirondacks," Hale said. "Must have been a relief after the desert. Were you in Afghanistan or Iraq?"

Brian sat back in his chair. "Who told you?"

"Picture at the bar," Hale said. "Desert camos." He looked down before meeting Brian's eyes. "Your leg."

Brian spoke rapidly. "When I was over in Iraq, a sea of brown in every direction, I would dream of going to the lake. Quiet, with the hills providing plenty of defensible positions."

I laughed. "Defensible positions are key to a good time."

Brian glared. "They were where I was stationed."

I felt my misstep, but Hale picked up the slack. "And you worked with explosives?"

"Yeah." Brian smiled for the first time, unexpected and sweet. With his injury, I would have thought bad memories would outweigh the good. But his pleasure was genuine. "I signed up for another tour, made sure my brothers got home safe. Then this happened." He pointed to his destroyed leg. "IED, hidden in a soda can." He looked away. "Coke is life, right?"

We were silent as Brian pulled a paper towel from a roll propped in the middle of the table between the salt and pepper and mopped up sweat from his workout. "I got lucky, I guess. A leg is better than a head."

While we talked, his eyes darted to the file in front of me, squinting to read the labels on the videos. Hale had done a nice job of getting Brian talking. I wrote "GO ON" in capital letters in my notebook and slid it to where Hale could see.

"You didn't go out to eat? Buy bait? Go to a bar?" Hale asked.

"I spend enough time in a bar, thanks, so my vacations include time away from the crap. And the bait shop . . . you stick your cash in a box and take the bait out of a cooler out front. The guy who owns the place hates getting up at five a.m." He paused. "I did have dinner with my Uncle Maxim one night. Nothing fancy. Burgers up the road from the cabin."

I opened the file, putting the tape and the DVD in full view, and slid off the top sheet to reveal a picture of the Detroit airport concourse. The fluorescent tubes warping in the still photographs, bent waves capturing where the light had been, where it was, and where it was going. Our guy—Brian—was staring up, the hood of his sweatshirt hiding the top half of his face, long hair ghosting his chin.

Brian remained silent, twisting the photo left and squinting.

I could hear the front door open, Dan Jaleda calling out. There were footsteps down the hall, but instead of Dan, Deirdre marched in, her husband following close by.

"Very nice, Officer Lyons," Deirdre said. She wore a pressed white blouse over khakis, and her gray bob swung when she pointed a finger at me. "Less than twenty-four hours, and you've already picked up your father's vendetta."

"I didn't tell them anything, Aunt Dee," Brian said.

"And why were you being questioned in the first place? Brian, they could turn hello into a criminal case, if they wanted."

Brian half stood, wobbling briefly. Deirdre stopped her rant, gently guiding him back to his chair.

Jake opened the back door and still had one foot outside the house when Deirdre started quizzing him. "Dan called, told me a cruiser was parked out front. Why didn't you call me, Jake?"

"I tried to reach Maxim—"

"Of course. You called our brother, the ex-judge without a college degree, instead of me."

"This is none of your goddamned business, Dee," he said. "This is family—"

"And I'm not family?" She was furious. "I'm your sister. I worked in your bar—"

"And never let me forget that it was beneath you," Jake said.

"And spent twenty years trying to get our brother out of prison."

"Your brother. My half-brother." He marched around the table. "And you went on and on about how Maxim and I did such a shitty job keeping Bernie out of jail."

Brian tried to pull his father away, but it was Dan Jaleda who stopped the fight, resting his hand on his wife's shoulder.

"Deirdre," he said. "Police."

Deirdre and Jake turned on us, and whatever they might think of each other, the family resemblance was clear. Both looked as if they were ready to destroy us, Deirdre in court and Jake with his bare hands.

"You need to get out," Deirdre said to us. She began sweeping up the files, but Jake stopped her, pulling a fuzzy image from in front of the Parisienne in Vegas, our suspect dwarfed by the mock Eiffel Tower.

"Got some pictures of my trip to Vegas, I see." He slapped his son on the back, and Brian cringed, I suspected because his father was so obviously lying. "Sorry for not telling you before, big guy, but I snuck off when you went fishing."

"Really?" I said. "Tell me about it."

"Don't say anything, Jake," Deirdre said. Dan Jaleda peeked at the photos and shook his head, moving toward the far end of the kitchen and leaning against the counter.

"What's to say? Vegas is all the best things about America, rolled into one."

"Tell us about the van," I said.

"Jake," Deirdre said.

"Shut up, Dee. You're not my lawyer." He sat down next to us and pulled the folder close.

"The van . . . I rented the van because the flight out was so awful." Deirdre reached over and tried to grab the folder but Jake pulled it close. "I rented it because although I've been in the US over fifty years, when they hear *w* where a *v* should be, or vice versa, they assume I'm some Russian spy. It's a whole lot better than it was in the eighties, but the TSA still want to give me the complete pat-down. So I didn't want to fly again, decided to drive back."

"Wouldn't an economy car have been more practical?" Hale asked. "Better gas mileage?"

Jake hesitated, nodding his head before breaking into a wide grin. "With a van I could sleep in the back! No hotel rooms."

I took notes rapidly so I would have exact quotes when we were nailing him for his lies. "And what happened to the van once you got back here?"

"Stolen off the street. Probably someone from Troy."

"Did you report it?"

"I couldn't find the contact information." He didn't break eye contact as he said it, but I realized it was intimidation rather than honesty. "It was all in the van, and the van was gone."

"And what name—"

Brian stood. "Shut the fuck up, Dad!"

Jake opened his mouth and then snapped it closed. Deirdre grabbed the folder out of his hand and flipped through the pictures, facing the sliding door where the light was better. She held up the grainy photo from the Carfast agency, holding it an inch from her face and squinting. "There will be no more questions without me acting as counsel. For either of them."

"Does the same go for your husband?" I said. If I hadn't been watching Dan for a reaction, I would have missed it, his jaw clenching and relaxing. He had no prosthesis, and unlike Brian, he was alive when Vera was killed and Luisa ran off. "Dan, we'd like to talk to you about your whereabouts the week of May twenty-third."

"Now you're desperate," Deirdre said. "I can't remember where I was during a random period in May, but I can tell you where I will be next week. Filing a lawsuit against your father, and you, too." She paced back and forth across the room as if she were making a case to a jury. "Why don't you investigate the real crime here. Where was Luisa? And how did your father miss Vera's murder?" A triumphant smile crossed her lips. "Go do your job."

CHAPTER 20

"HIGH FIVE!" HALE SAID, HOLDING OUT HIS PALM WHEN THE CAR was half a block from the house.

I gripped the steering wheel. "I'm sorry. Were you in the same interview I was?"

"It's not what they said—"

"Which was close to nothing, although I think we have them getting desperate about the van, and finding out whether Judge Medved took Brian to dinner is at the top of my list—"

"Brian's leg," Hale said.

"The prosthesis?"

"It wasn't a normal prosthesis. One of those dynamic pieces, captures the energy of the user. Costs about ten times what the older models did, but truly state of the art."

I pulled to a stop at the light as cars sped past on the far side of the bridge. "It would still set off the metal detector."

"No, it wouldn't." He bit his lip, trying to stifle a smile, but gave in, grinning. "Carbon."

I sat stunned, a car's horn reminding me the light was now green. "Are you sure?"

"Pretty much," Hale said. "I've flown into and out of the Albany airport often enough. The agents there don't have full-body scans. If they sent him through a metal detector, he would sail through."

Crossing the bridge, I stopped, unsure whether to turn left or right. I wanted to track down the judge while at the same time trying to do an end run around Deirdre and confirm exactly where Dan was that week in May. Deirdre would take us apart in court if we didn't explore all suspects, even if those suspects included her husband. Hale and I decided to divide and conquer.

"Let me work my mojo," Hale said. "Get pictures of Dan, Jake, and Brian, put them in front of the Carfast guy. Get their phone numbers, see if I can get a judge to give me a warrant, find out where the towers they were pinging on were closest."

"See if any were pinging in Las Vegas or New Mexico."

"It's a long shot," he said. "I'll also visit Dan's helpful assistant Ashley, try to get her to let me take a gander at Dan Jaleda's calendar for that missing week. I'm betting Ashley has his days planned down to the minute."

"And I'll try to get to the judge, hopefully before his family does. Find out if dinner at Lake George happened the way Brian said it did."

"NO, I DID NOT GO FISHING WITH MY NEPHEW," THE JUDGE SAID. "Jake, he enjoyed it, said it was calming and good to have a steady source of food, but that is old world thinking, and his son, he apes whatever his father does." Judge Medved leaned back in his chair, rocking contentedly. "Me, I like waiters who call me 'sir.'"

I faked a laugh. I was easing the judge into the topic of Brian's fishing trip. The room had a giant window facing the courthouse, but it received afternoon sunlight, and the whole office was in shadow. As we talked, people stopped and gave Judge Medved a quick wave, and he responded with a mock salute or a mouthed hello.

"So you don't join your family for any non-fishing activities up in Lake George?"

"Sometimes, yes. My brother Jake is a simple man, and despite his previous problems, a good man." Maxim Medved spoke without Natalya's accent but had the formal sentence structure of an immigrant. It probably served him well on the bench, giving his judgments greater weight. "Many times my brother or my nephew have invited me, and I like to make the effort, go along."

"But during the May trip?"

"During the May trip, no, I did not. The nights there get cold, and I feel freezing weather in my bones." He tapped the leather desk pad that topped his gigantic curved oak desk. "Do not get old, Officer Lyons."

This time I laughed for real. He'd shot Brian's alibi through of holes, and I tried to hide my glee as I wrote down the details.

There was a knock on the window. The judge waved to Elda Harris, who was wearing a cream-colored beret and an Irish sweater, a wash of pale except for her coral lipstick.

"She is coming back to life," the judge said. "First time in years. May I inquire, what do you plan on doing to Luisa? She committed fraud—"

"That's an ongoing investigation," I said. "I hope you'll appreciate—"

He waved it off. "Of course. Procedure."

There was a knock, this time at the door and the receptionist called through the door.

"Enter," he said. She did, halfway, tilting sideways so her frizzy permed head was inside, the rest of her body hidden.

"Your nephew is on the phone," she said.

"Tell Brian I will return his call later." He raised one bushy eyebrow. "It is Brian, correct?"

She agreed to pass on the message, closing the door silently behind her.

"I am not used to having multiple nephews," he said. "Bernie and Deirdre say that we are to leave his boys alone, but if they reach out . . ."

I decided to keep him talking and away from Brian's phone calls for as long as I could. I pointed to a picture behind him, a blown-up photo of the ribbon cutting for the 787 extension. The judge was standing in front of a five-foot-tall yellow ribbon, a bold choice when a giant shovel might be more appropriate.

"Is that snow on the ground?" I asked.

"It is," he said. "There were so many false starts over the years that we did not want to risk waiting until the new legislature took office in January, when they might put the project on hold. Construction could be delayed for weather, but not stopped."

"Can I take a closer look?" I said. "I think I see my father."

"Of course, of course," the judge said, delighted. He stood close to the photo, identifying the mayor, a few council members, a congressman, and even a state senator. My father was on crowd control, despite the risk of unruly crowds being practically nil.

"It was the most important day of my life. The day I brought hundreds of jobs to the area. The day I arranged so Hopewell Falls would be connected by a four-lane highway, bringing trucks and trade."

"Is that Lucas?" I asked. He had feathered hair and mirrored sunglasses and like his fellow workers wore a puffy blue coat.

"It is. His first job off the assembly line. And that is my brother-in-law, Dan. Before marriage, of course."

I squinted. Dan had worn a bright red scarf, standing out from the rest of crowd

"My brother-in-law has changed, has he not?" The judge rocked back on his heels. "He was a rough young man, not caring for much beyond beer and women."

"Construction jobs are pretty sweet," I said. "How'd he line that up if he was such a punk?"

"Jake came to me, asked me to get them assigned to the projects. He told me Dan was likely going to be our brother-in-law, and Lucas was proving to be a go-getter. I made some calls." He folded his hands in front of him. "For family, you do that."

The secretary knocked again, coming in without waiting, and placed a pink message slip on the desk.

"Message from Brian," she said. "He'd like you to call."

The words "dinner" and "Lake George" were clearly visible on the note. I started peppering Maxim Medved with questions to keep him away from the desk.

"Were Jake and Bernie at the grand opening of the thruway?"

"Is your question a trick?" His voice was harsh, the politician's solicitous charm now gone.

I was worried I'd blown it. "Not in the least."

"No, of course. My brother had such pride in his business, he would never go a day without opening, even on a day of such importance to me." His hands shook as he unhooked the photo from the wall, not an old man's tremble, but anger. "But Bernie. This is the day everything changed. This is the day Luisa went missing."

He moved quickly toward his desk, carrying the photo, and I was relieved when he dropped it on top of the pink message slip. He tapped his temple. "Of course, I may be mistaking details about that day. I have had too much crammed into my head for too long and, of course, I am an old man."

I hoped he hadn't seen the message from Brian, but my hope was short lived.

"For example, now that I think further on the topic," he said, "I believe I misspoke before. You inquired into the trip Brian took in mid-May, correct?"

"I did," I said.

He slipped a pocket-size book out of his jacket and flipped it open. A calendar.

"I really should not have commented on Brian's trip without

checking. He goes up so often, I may have given you the wrong information." He licked his thumb and pushed the pages to May. "Yes. I was right. I gave you the wrong information. I did meet Brian in Lake George." He jabbed the page. "It says so right there."

This lie couldn't stand, but I needed more details to make sure his "doddering old man" act wasn't used in court. "Where did the two of you eat?"

Brian and I went to the Stanhope Lodge." Judge Medved leaned back in his chair. "I love to visit whenever I am in Lake George. Wonderful food, beautiful views. Classy in every way."

The Lodge was gorgeous, built in 1906 by New York City socialites trying to recover from tuberculosis. With the invention of penicillin, the sanitarium was repurposed as a hotel, an escape from New York's stifling heat. I had a hard time picturing the judge there, let alone Brian. Perhaps the judge had a secret life where he hobnobbed with the rich and famous. It was nothing like the hamburger stand Brian had described.

I was ready to call his bluff. "May I see your calendar?"

He held out the calendar and I flipped back to the week Luisa was kidnapped in New Mexico. Several appointments were jotted in, all in Cyrillic.

"That one," he said, pointing to Wednesday. It could have said he was playing first base for the Mets for all I knew. "I am sorry it is not in English. I'm Americanized in every way except in this one small area. A small way to stay in contact with my roots. Natalya would be so pleased."

A loud voice demanding to see the judge could be heard through the door. Was it Brian? Lucas rushed in, grabbing the judge's lapel.

"My mother's killer is strutting around free. I ran into him on Silliman Street—"

The judge rested his hand on Lucas's shoulder. "Do not trouble yourself."

"You said justice would be served! I want to destroy him—"

"Now, Lucas," the judge said, his eyes flicking to me. "You do not mean that."

"Yes! I want—"

"No, take it from an old judge. What you have described is vengeance." He walked Lucas to a chair. "Back in our childhoods, your aunt and I lived through an endless cycle of vengeance, each time hoping we would have peace if one more Soviet official died, one more Red Army soldier was buried in a shallow grave, the right Nazi burned alive. It never worked."

The judge's deep voice rolled over me. It had the steady cadence and deep tone of the one Medved used from the bench, as if you were hearing the voice of God. Lucas looked hypnotized.

"We escaped it, and I refused to live that way. Law and order are to be trusted, or we will have chaos." The gravity of his statement sunk in, and I hoped Lucas heard it so he would give up his vigilante role. The judge held Lucas's gaze as he made the next statement: "Do you agree, Officer Lyons?"

"I do," I said, although for a statement I believed in wholeheartedly, it was hard to get out. It was the truth, but it had been extracted from me. I wanted out.

"I have all the information I need," I said. "Would you mind if I made a scan of that picture? It would tickle my father."

"Of course." He waved toward the outer office. "Marlene is responsible for all the new technology. Have her do it for you."

"And your calendar?" I held out my hand. "It would be good to have documentation."

"That I cannot do," Judge Medved said. "I advise people, in confidence, sometimes on legal matters."

"But you aren't a lawyer—"

"True. And if you find you need more than my word, than you can get a warrant," he said.

The new technology the judge referred to didn't include scanning capability, but Marlene was able to remove the picture from the frame and without the glass make a pretty clear copy. Taking an inventory of the office, I could understand why the judge considered a Xerox machine pretty cutting edge, with a computer whose plastic was taking on a yellow cast, cases of heavy paper, a typewriter in the corner, and three walls taken up with law volumes from the seventies. He was no lawyer, and I wondered if he had ever read the books, or if they were just for show. While I waited, I checked my phone for texts from Hale: "Got the warrant." "Got Jaleda's calendar." And three minutes ago: "I'm outside judge's office."

The lobby of the building was dim, and I almost missed Hale.

"That was quite a visit you had with the judge," he said, his hand resting on a wooden globe that topped the banister leading to the second floor.

"It would have been longer, but Lucas paid a visit, demanding that Bernie go back to jail in the next ten minutes. The judge seemed to be trying to calm him, but I got the sense it was just for my benefit. He didn't say no."

The bulb came off in Hale's hand, the joints of the handrail so loose that the bannister wobbled when he gently placed it back. I peeked around the corner and then glanced up the staircase. It was carpeted with a threadbare oriental rug, the floors above in shadow as the judge's office was the only one still in operation. This hallway would be the one private place we'd have for a while, so I told him about my interview, including the destruction of Brian's alibi as well as how the judge came to hire Lucas and Dan way back when.

"Jake."

"You don't say," Hale said. "My money was on Bernie."

"Me, too, but no. So the way things stand now, we can confirm that Jake purchased the materials for the wall that bricked in Vera, lined up the manpower, and then rewarded the people who did the construction."

"Interesting," Hale said. "Ashley gave up Dan's calendar without a warrant, and he most certainly was not in Las Vegas. I don't believe for a second that Jake went to New Mexico and kidnapped Luisa, but I now have little doubt that Brian did. And if I had to bet, I'd say he did it for dear old dad. So he's at the center of the Vera murder and close to the center of the Luisa kidnapping."

"And don't forget his old girlfriend Oksana," I said. "We don't know she's dead, but we can't confirm she's alive either."

"For the simple reason that we aren't working with decades-old evidence, Luisa's kidnapping seems the easiest to prove," he said. "We should try to get that one locked down."

"Did you get the phone records so we can confirm Brian and Jake's whereabouts that week?"

"Put in a request to the Department of Justice," he said. "All that's left to do is wait for them to say no."

He was right. The chances were very slim that they'd see justifiable cause. We had to come up with more proof, but I wasn't sure what. I suggested we take a break and get lunch and hope inspiration struck.

We were half a block away from Maria's diner when we saw Bernie weaving up the sidewalk from the other direction, bumping into a NO PARKING sign before righting himself. Arresting him for public intoxication would be a PR nightmare. But no, he wasn't walking off a drunk. He was staring straight up, surveying the buildings, smiling. I couldn't figure out what was making him so happy—half the stores were boarded over, and I'd hardly call the check-cashing place a tourist destination. We were right in front of him before he saw us.

"Officer Lyons," Bernie said, "and . . ."

"Special Agent Bascom." Hale put out his hand and the two men shook.

"Recovered from yesterday?" I asked.

"What's to recover from? It's the best day of my life." He reached out, running his fingers over the letters on a plaque identifying the building as the original site of the Simmons Axe Manufacturer. It had closed in the twenties; a dry grocer, an electronics store, and most recently an optometrist had all opened and gone bankrupt in the century since the axe company closed.

Bernie pulled his hand away from the wall. "Had a tough time talking my family into giving me a few minutes alone. Deirdre thinks if I'm unsupervised the press or the police will grab me off the streets." He raised his eyebrows at me. "You're not here for that, are you?"

"Just lunch, Bernie."

"Lunch for me, too. I've been fantasizing about Maria's banana pancakes for thirty years, and I'm going to get some now, breakfast hours be damned."

He hesitated, and I assured him we wouldn't question him during lunch. He relaxed but still hesitated before going inside, and I was thinking Hale and I would need to find another lunch spot. I was ready to talk Hale into pizza when the door opened and someone exited. Without touching the door, Bernie ducked in, and I remembered the prison: Bernie hadn't been allowed to open a door for himself in thirty years.

Like an Old West saloon, the diner got quiet as we entered. Bernie went to the lunch counter, and Hale and I grabbed a booth in the corner. People's eyes darted between us and Bernie, trying to figure out if this was some sort of last meal before we arrested him again. I ordered grilled cheese and tomato and Hale had a tuna melt, and like the rest of the people in the diner, listened as Bernie had a conversation with Janelle DuMurier, taking her lunch break before returning to driving her bus route.

"So what have you been up to?" Bernie asked Janelle.

Janelle struggled to answer. "Since . . . 1983?"

Bernie laughed. "Yeah, well. You know what I've been up to. You haven't changed a bit. You look great!"

Janelle considered her bus driver's uniform. The clothes were neat and pressed, but they wouldn't flatter anyone.

"You've been in prison for a long time, haven't you?" she said.

Bernie laughed again. "Sorry, my small talk's rusty. But you do look great." He carefully placed his knife and fork to his left, grabbing some napkins to rest the cutlery on. "If you tell me about yourself, I promise to shut up."

The rest of our meal was spent listening to a free man absolutely delighted to be eating his banana pancakes and talking to a bus driver about her biannual trips to Civil War battlefields. Not a bad way to spend a lunch hour.

CHAPTER 21

As EXPECTED, OUR REQUEST FOR A WARRANT FOR THE PHONE records was denied.

"It was a long shot," I said. "It was all circumstantial."

Hale continued frowning down at his phone, which had delivered the bad news about the warrant.

"Something up?" I asked.

"Nothing related to this case. I could tell you about it if—"

"Yeah, yeah," I said. "Why don't we assume every conversation will include some element of you begging me to rejoin the FBI, and me saying no, and we can save each other the trouble."

Hale went to take care of business and I decided to visit Dave, more as a welfare check than to move the case forward. His cell phone went right to voicemail, and he didn't answer the door. I banged on the door again, louder, but there was still no response. It was four p.m., and Dave's car was in the driveway. If he didn't answer the door in thirty seconds I was going to let myself in. Luckily for him, I knew the location of his spare key and wouldn't have to smash a window.

I followed the path around to the back, past a pile of two-by-fours under a blue tarp, treated and waiting for Dave to build a pergola. When Dave's leave was extended, he made plans to do some home improvement, but those plans were long forgotten. Last year Dave had grown enough squash to keep the department in zucchini bread until Armageddon, but right now his yard was a patchy mess, barren except for a pink rose bush that Dave swore he was going to pull up by its roots one of these days.

Dave kept his spare key hidden in his tool shed. I found it behind some rose fertilizer—Ha! I knew he was trying to keep it alive!—and let myself in. The kitchen was no longer a public-health disaster. While the recycling was spilling over with beer bottles, dishes had been washed and the floor was swept. I wound my way toward the dining room, dim in the afternoon light with all the shades drawn. I felt my way along the wall and flipped on the light.

And then wished I hadn't.

Dave always claimed he was a visual learner, and for any case that wasn't easily solved he would often take over one of the interview rooms in the station, creating a timeline with tape marking relationships, actions, and evidence. I had appreciated it when we worked a murder together earlier this year, the crisscrossing tape marking the intersection of victims and suspects and revealing snarled relationships and gaps in people's alibis.

Here, Vera topped the evidence tree, the picture of her in the green dress, smoking and hollowed out, the point from which everything else flowed. The lines of tape shot down in four threads, with pictures of the factory, Dave's childhood home, Jake's bar, and Bernie's house posted midway on the wall. From there the four lines snaked together and broke apart, crisscrossing awkwardly, with visible gaps where the tape had been ripped off the wall and repatched, the layers creating a thick broken line that converged on one suspect: Bernie.

Below Bernie were different pictures of Vera, dead and decaying: curled in the barrel; small and shriveled on an autopsy table; a close-up of her mouth, decomposed skin exposing a row of perfect teeth; and skull fragments lined up on white background, clumps of black hair clinging to the bone. Autopsy photos.

I furiously ripped the autopsy pictures off the wall, tearing them in the process, but I didn't care. Dave shouldn't have these, Dave should never have *seen* these, and when I found out who had given them to him, I would do anything within my power to have them fired.

I balled the pictures up and continued to the living room where I found Dave on the couch, passed out in sweats and an old Yankee shirt. The TV was on mute, light bouncing off his skin, the screen showing Paul Newman eating fifty eggs.

"Dave!" I yelled. He sat up suddenly, squinting despite the low light.

"Lyons. Hey." He rubbed his head, his curls flat and dirty, heavy with oil, and smiled up at me. "Whatcha got there?"

"What does it look like?" I wanted to throw them at him but was afraid he would unwrap the pictures, flatten them, and hang them back up. "Where did you get these?"

Dave pushed himself up into a standing position, faltering briefly before he was steady on his feet.

"I have my ways." He waggled his eyebrows. "You'd be surprised how few people can resist my charms."

"This isn't charming, Dave. Did my dad see these?"

"No. I took them down when I was expecting visitors. Today . . . I was expecting to be alone."

"And how long have you had them?"

"Almost two weeks. You'd know if you ever visited."

"How can you say that?!" I was about to list all the things I had been doing to find his mother's killer when I really looked at him: slumped sideways on the couch, empty cereal dishes and beer bottles clustered on the side table, blocked off on every side by newspaper articles about his mother's death and the release of the man Dave believed had killed her.

"I'm sorry," I said. "You are absolutely right." I had been trying to be the best friend I could to Dave by finding his mother's killer, but Dave needed more. I would start by getting him away from that ghoulish mural. "How about you get cleaned up and we go out and get some dinner. Will you slip and smash your head in the shower?"

"No more than it's already broken," he said. "And no need to eat out. Make whatever there's a pan of in the fridge. Annie's been dropping off a casserole every other day. She throws out the old food, so we can avoid food poisoning, no problem."

"Good to hear," I said. I wondered if Annie was the source of the gruesome photos. Had Dave put on a sob story, manipulated her into bringing over copies? Annie seemed like the opposite of a soft touch, but Dave had a refrigerator full of food proving otherwise.

I found a lasagna on the second shelf of his refrigerator, a post-it note taped on all four sides to the aluminum foil: "To heat up, bake in a 400 degree oven for 30 minutes, or, if you insist, in a microwave for 3. Take post-it off before you put it in the oven. Eat with a salad." I pulled out the tub of spring mix I found next to the lasagna. "Dressing is optional." And then underlined. "Do this instead of drink."

I cranked the oven up and put the lasagna in. Upstairs I could hear the shower running for a long time. I worried if he had slipped and fallen, then the pipes went quiet and I heard him pad to the bedroom.

I went around the house collecting empty beer bottles. Dave's trash and recycling pickup was the next morning, so I dumped all of them in a barrel and dragged them and the trash out to the curb. When I returned, he was at the kitchen table, freshly shaven and with a glass of water in hand. I applauded his beverage choice.

"I read Annie's note and figured I'd try to follow her instructions," he said. "I owe her big time."

I tried to keep things light, but I needed to know where he'd gotten those photos. "How much do you owe her for supplying you with the autopsy photos?"

"She didn't supply me with photos from the investigation. I helped myself." He took three huge gulps of water. "Plus, Lucas wanted to see the pictures."

"You showed Lucas?!" I was back to being furious. "Dave, that could destroy the investigation."

"I had to. Lucas was ready to jump Bernie outside the courthouse, demanding answers. I had to throw him a bone."

A bell pinged, announcing that the lasagna was ready. It was burnt around the edges, but was edible. I served two plates while Dave served himself a vodka tonic.

"Don't let Annie find out about that drink."

He pointed at his meal. "There's a dinner plate *right here*."

"I think she was encouraging you to eat instead of drink."

Dave shrugged. "Life's about compromise."

He dug in, but the cheese was too hot and he ended up burning his tongue. He blew on it twice and took a gulp of his drink.

"I'm sorry about the photos, June," he said.

I put down my own fork. "I know. And I know why you did it—any feeling person would. That said, I'm going to have someone cut off your access to the system."

"But—"

"This is not negotiable. I'm doing it to keep you safe."

The two of us ate in silence for a while. If he had his way, we'd talk exclusively about the case. Me, I wanted to know how he was. I asked.

He finished chewing his food, swallowing. "To be honest, I have no idea. I feel like Aunt Natalya and I are constantly on alert, waiting for Lucas to blow." A reasonable fear from what I'd seen this afternoon. He put down his knife and fork. "In a way, it's a lot like the way my dad was with my mom."

"What do you mean?"

"My father, in his whole life with my mother, he never had a moment's peace. She didn't like him, and he certainly wasn't loved.

Mom was always telling him about how his love was a burden, and if she hadn't been foolish enough to get knocked up with Lucas, they would have never been married."

"Your father told you that?"

"Oh, no. Never. But my mother had these conversations loud enough that the whole house could hear them—loud enough that everyone on the Island knew what she said." Dave took a drink. "So I heard how much of a loser my dad was, and Lucas got to hear, over and over again, how he ruined her life. It fucked him up."

I thought the situation had fucked Dave up pretty successfully as well, but I held my tongue.

"With his wife . . . his *wives,* Lucas anticipated them leaving, and when they didn't, he pushed them into it. His last wife, she was patient and she loved him, and his behavior . . . well, I'll skip the details. You saw the police reports."

I was happy when Dave reached for the food again instead of the booze. "You turned out OK."

"I got off easy. She tolerated me, and she took off . . . disappeared before I understood how much of a monster she was. And I had my dad. He worked, and he did all the housework, he made sure I was bathed and fed, and then he had to listen to her rage about how no one appreciated everything she did around the house and how we forced her to drink due to our ungratefulness. Today, she'd be diagnosed with something. Back then, we called it misery." Dave took a sip of water. "And my dad who had been through so much worse, had been through the Nazis, he thought you should be grateful for what life gave you and make the most of it. When Mom went on a tear, he would say, 'You're right. I don't appreciate you enough. Let me take you out to dinner somewhere. Go put on a dress. I want to show you off.'

"When she would run off, every time my dad told us not to talk bad about her, that she wouldn't abandon us, ever." Dave looked me directly in the eye. "That last time, he never once promised she'd return."

"Did he act different?"

"No . . . yes. He got quiet." Dave tilted his chair back until his shoulders brushed the wall behind him. "I thought he was like me but was afraid to say it."

"How's that?"

Dave rocked back and forth on his chair and I worried it might shatter under his weight. "I thought maybe he was afraid if he said her name she'd come back, like a witch. That he didn't work hard to find her because he didn't want her to come back. So we didn't search and this," he waved in the direction of the dining room, "happened."

"Dave, you did more than any twelve-year-old could be expected to do."

He shook his head. "That was after. Before, I prayed she'd stay away. With her gone, Lucas wasn't as angry, my dad was less worried, and we could go places without having to be braced for a scene, or braced for a story," he said. "But then I saw the billboard of Luisa. Once I saw what normal people did, people who loved their relatives, I felt bad. But it wasn't because I was desperate. It was because I felt guilty that I had wanted her to go away and never come back."

"Dave—"

Dave let his chair drop back onto all four legs. "I've had enough for today, Lyons. Why don't you talk for a while. Tell me about your day. Tell me about your *feelings*."

Dave resisted my efforts to restart the conversation, helped himself to more lasagna, and dug in with fierce gusto. I struggled with what to say. Both cases were untouchable, and the drama with my mother was completely superficial in the face of what he was going through. I decided to tell him about Hale's apartment.

"Been there often?" he asked.

"Just the once."

As I described the roof deck and the garage, he ate three-quarters of the pan of lasagna, and I wondered when he had last had a meal.

"Think Hale would give me the name of his cleaning lady?" He scraped the plate with a fork. "Since she's got security clearance and all."

His phone rang. Not his cell, but his landline, an old rotary phone bolted to the wall.

"Aunt Natalya's hotline," he said, moving around the table. "She prefers wires to wireless."

As he talked to her on the phone, he swayed, as if tilting with a breeze. "Haven't seen him today," he said.

"Lucas?" I mouthed, and he nodded.

"What did he do now, *teta*?" Dave said, rolling his eyes at me. Natalya must have sensed it.

"No," he protested into the phone. "Of course I'm concerned about my brother." Dave opened the door to the basement, stepped inside, and closed the door. The phone cord forced the door open a crack, allowing me to hear him as he tried to calm his aunt, swinging between explanations and excuses for Lucas's behavior.

The basement door opened, and Dave slammed down the receiver. "Judge Medved is over at Natalya's. Neither of them can find Lucas, so I gotta go be the cavalry." He pulled a pair of sneakers out of the pile next to the door and shoved his feet into them. He was stuffing his keys into the pocket of his windbreaker when I offered to drive.

"June, I'm fine."

"You've had a few. More than a few." I punched him the in the shoulder. "Make an old lady happy."

"Aunt Natalya?"

"No, me."

He snorted and put his keys away.

We passed Jake's bar. After today, I was 100 percent sure my membership at Jake's was canceled. I half wanted to go in there and take Brian into custody, but we didn't have enough evidence for a warrant to search his house, let alone arrest him.

The judge was stopped at the corner as we made the turn onto Natalya's street.

"Maybe Lucas is home safe," Dave said. "Maybe you can take me home." The sun was almost behind the hills, the last gasp before dusk, pink and orange rays streaking through the black sky.

"Pretty," Dave said. I put the car in park and looked over at him. He was watching me closely. "Thank you for being here for me, Lyons."

"I feel like I haven't been much of a friend to you."

"You are trying to find who killed Mom, and you are the best when it comes to police work." He smiled. "Whereas you're a terrible cook."

"Yeah, well, Annie's got that covered. I gotta say, I didn't realize you two were such good friends."

"No one did. Not even me." He unhooked his seat belt. "I'll take a certain amount of yelling if it means I have good evidence. And good lasagna. And a good friend."

He kissed me on the cheek but wouldn't make eye contact.

"You're planning something stupid, aren't you?" I said.

The creak from the car door almost drowned out his response. "Never."

"Stay here tonight," I said, trying to get in a last word before he slammed the door. "Keep an eye on Lucas. Play bridge with your aunt."

"She's more of a chess player."

"Even better. The games are much longer."

"Goodnight, Lyons." He shut the car door and jogged up the walk, went into the house, and waved through the window. I fully expected him to leave the moment he saw me drive away. Little did he realize I would be staking out his house.

I was disappointed to see a white car sitting in the spot on the next corner where I planned to park and do my surveillance. As I drove past the car, preparing to make a U-turn, I peered inside. The Toyota Corolla had someone sitting in the driver's seat. My father.

CHAPTER 22

I HEARD THE "CLICK" OF THE CAR LOCKS WHILE THREE FEET away. Dad kept his eyes trained on the house even as I climbed in and slammed the door. I expected him to acknowledge me, apologize, *something*. Instead, silence.

"So," I said, trying to lead him into conversation. "Keeping an eye on Dave?"

He didn't respond. I fished for a response. "Lucas done something?"

Still nothing. I responded the same way I usually responded to fear: humor.

"Is it Natalya? Running her drug empire with an iron fist between making dumplings?"

The front door of Natalya's house opened, and Dave exited, bouncing down the steps and cutting across the lawn of the house across the street. Off to get into trouble, no doubt. Dad grabbed the door handle, but I stopped him.

"Dad, answer the question. What are you doing?"

He kept his eyes on the house. "I need to talk to Natalya alone."

"Is Dave in trouble? Lucas?"

My father clenched his fists and relaxed, his hands trembling in his lap. "I read your notebook while you were asleep."

"You what! Jesus, Dad, how—"

"Natalya was a part of it."

"Part of what? Vera's disappearance?"

"I don't have a lot of time," he said, scanning the street. "The judge had just left when you and Dave arrived. I need to go now."

"You're going nowhere," I said. "Tell me."

Out here there were no streetlights, and I could just barely make out the outline of his profile. Dad opened and closed his mouth twice, until finally he spoke. "Luisa. Natalya helped her disappear."

I pulled out my notebook and flipped back to my conversation with Natalya, trying to find something giving away her involvement. Where had he pulled this idea?

"The Pinto," he said. "That piece of shit car gave away the whole deal."

I flipped forward, to my interview with Theo and Darius, where they described the Pinto, how Luisa had lived in it, how she could never let herself get another car.

Dad's bulk kept him from facing me. "That car would blow up on people, and she wouldn't let it go? Who does that? Especially with those two kids. I'm betting she knew if anyone ran the numbers, it would pop up as Natalya's car."

I stopped. I didn't have to read my notes. "Natalya's Pinto went missing."

"Almost four months before Luisa disappeared."

"Right around the time Vera was murdered." I paused. "So, was Natalya involved in Vera's disappearance? Was Luisa?"

"I have no idea," Dad said. "That's what I wanted to find out."

"So you were going to do what? Confront Natalya? Hog-tie her and take her down to the station?" I snapped my notebook shut. "Or were you even going to involve the police? Was this going to be a situation where you were going to work outside of the law?"

"June, you don't understand . . ."

"I understand fine. You crossed a huge ethical line—"

"I'm not bound by the code of ethics. In case you forgot, I'm retired—"

"You're my father!" I shouted. Right at this moment I was glad Natalya lived at the ass end of nowhere with no near neighbors, because this on top of Dave's stealing the photos of his mother left me apoplectic. "You were the person I wanted to be like more than anything else in the world. I modeled my life and my career after you, and now I have you sneaking around, reading my notebook—"

"I sent a man to prison for thirty years, June." He slumped back in his seat. "Can you fathom what that means? Independent of the fact that Deirdre Lawler is probably gearing up to sue me into kingdom come . . . June, all that time I was worried I wasn't doing right by Luisa, when what I should have been worrying about was destroying Bernie Lawler's life. I failed him, in every way a cop can fail. And I failed Vera. And you. And everyone."

He sat panting. Condensation pooled on the window, fogging out the moon. I tried to think of how I might comfort him, but my solutions were inadequate.

"Dad, you may have sent Bernie to prison for a murder he didn't commit, but he's looking like a suspect in Vera's murder."

"That's not . . . don't you make the same mistakes I'm making, June. Don't assume he's guilty."

"Wouldn't it be better if he was?"

"It doesn't make things right," he said. "Vera is dead, but we have no proof as to why or how. Natalya has the answers—"

"You've done enough, Dad."

"But—"

"*Enough*. You will not be there when I question Natalya." I laughed bitterly. "The way things are going, it's questionable whether I'm the cop for this job, but I don't want to restart the investigation. So I need you to leave."

"The papers," he said frantically. "She used to do the papers of people on the Island. I bet she got papers for Luisa and Theo."

I wrote it down in my notebook—it matched up with what Vera's "friends" had said. "If you think of anything else, call me, and I can move on it. Right now you need to go home. Got it?"

HALE LEANED AGAINST THE CAR, LOOSE AND CASUAL. HIS UN-characteristically relaxed attitude and the peepers croaking away around us were calming, much needed after the run-in with my father.

"I'm pretty sure you can take an old lady," he said.

"Not this one. Plus you'll need to run interference if Lucas or Dave show."

"I'm pretty sure you can take them, too."

"Not funny, Hale." My voice echoed in the empty street. "This could destroy Dave."

"Hey now. Let's listen to what she has to say first." Hale brushed nonexistent dust off the arm of his jacket. Keeping his eyes fixed on Natalya's house, he said, "Something else going on here?" He slid his leg forward, touching his foot to mine. "C'mon, June. You don't lose your cool. Not ever."

I tried to regain the supposed cool I possessed, taking deep breaths before launching into the background of the Pinto and how my dad was able to find the information by reading my notebook.

"Your dad got a little overeager—"

"Obsessed, you mean."

"OK, maybe. But obsession is a strength sometimes."

"Deliberate police work is a strength. Obsession leads to mistakes."

"And it would be terrible if your dad made a mistake, huh?"

His comment felt like a punch in the gut. I had few illusions about my father, but one thing I always believed was that he was a good cop. The best cop.

"This case. His behavior." I struggled to find the right words. "And all along, my mother squawking in my ear about how screwed up my father is."

"Were those her exact words?"

"No. But when she talks about how cut off he was from the world, how the job was such a big deal to him, how he didn't have a life—"

"You thought she was talking about you?"

"No!" I spun around, taking a deep breath before facing him again. "Maybe. But I'm having a hard time redoing his work."

"June, your father and I have only met briefly, but I can say without hesitation that he would never choose being right over the truth."

"And how do you know that?"

"Because he raised you. And that's what you would want."

I pointed at Natalya's house. "We should go talk to her before Dave and Lucas gets home."

"Your father also raised you to avoid emotionally charged conversations," Hale said, not unkindly, and walked toward the house. "C'mon killer, let's go talk to Natalya. I'll put on my kid gloves and try not to rough her up too much."

"No, we're about to get rough," I said. "Natalya has avoided capture her whole life, from the Nazis to the police. We're taking her head-on. She can't run."

CHAPTER 23

HALE AND I WERE HALFWAY UP THE STEPS WHEN NATALYA opened the door. She couldn't hide her disappointment.

"I thought you were one of the boys." She peered down the street. "Dave is out searching for Lucas."

"Can we come in?" I asked. "We have some questions."

She frowned briefly but opened the door wide, offering us tea before the door was even closed.

"No tea," I said.

"I insist. A host always—"

"This isn't social, Natalya."

Natalya hesitated, watching Hale. He had moved to the middle of the room and stood, dropping into the wide-legged "at rest" he learned in military school. She placed her hand on her chest and asked, "Is there news about Vera?"

"No. Luisa."

I could see her running rapidly through her options. She went for concerned friend. "She woke? A *good* sign." She paused. "She told you what happened?"

"No, Natalya. But I bet you can."

She staggered a step toward Hale, letting him catch her. "Luisa's burn injuries? I do not understand what you think I might know."

"Not the fire, Natalya. Her escape to New Mexico." Her eyes went wide, mock confusion.

"The Pinto, Natalya," I said. Her eyes darted between Hale and me. "You gave her your Pinto. You faked the theft right after Vera was killed and handed the vehicle over to Luisa." Natalya's expression became blank, a wall in the face of authority. "Vera didn't steal your car, Natalya. Your original story was a lie."

"It was not!" She edged along the wall, but Hale blocked her way.

"The VIN number," he said. "Luisa got rear-ended in 1985, and we have a copy of the ticket."

Hale was lying. Today there might be a chance the information was in a computer system somewhere, but back then a ticket like that would have been disposed of within a year.

"And the fake IDs," I said. "We're betting you're the source of Luisa Lawler's—or should I say Louann Bazelon's—Social Security cards."

"We have a group of agents going through her home, top to bottom," Hale said. Natalya's face went blank as he continued talking. "Her tax records could be a *wealth* of information."

The stillness in her face spread to the rest of her body. I remembered my dad telling me that many of the Ukrainians had a distrust of any official authority, and Natalya's wall was going up, brick by brick. I circled her, staying close until we were again face to face, Hale fading back toward the dining room. This time I wasn't going to try to batter her with reason or facts.

"Natalya, I think you had a very good reason for doing what you did. You were trying to protect Luisa in some way. Forget leaving town, it would have been tough for her to get a divorce. You need to tell me what happened."

She raised an eyebrow at me, as if to say "Make me."

"If you don't, there will be repercussions," I said. "I'm betting whoever went and kidnapped Luisa, it was payback for what happened to Bernie. And if this person was willing to drive across the country to grab her, they will have no problem driving across town to grab you once they figure out you are involved." I paused, wanting my last words to hit home. "You are playing God, but you are not infallible."

"I am not!" She pulled back, not flinching but furious. "*Vin tse zasluzhyv.*"

"What?"

"He deserved it," she said.

"Who?"

"Bernard."

"Why?"

"The remains."

Hale came and stood next to us, overshadowing both me and Natalya. "You saw the body?"

"Not Vera dead, but after. Her absence." She took a halting half step away from Hale. "At my home, my real home, *Ukrayina.* I learned to spot signs of"—she flicked her hand in the air— "vanishings. Stalin and Hitler, master teachers they were in making those you loved disappear. Bullet holes in wall. Drag marks leading to field. My brother's . . . favorite pen in hands of another." She balled her hands into fists. "When I saw blood everywhere, Vera's purse discarded, I knew. *I know.*"

"You found Vera's purse?" I couldn't hide my frustration. "Natalya, why didn't you go to the police. My father—"

"Your father was not in charge during that time. Even if he were . . . Bernard was rich. powerful. He hired his childhood friends at factory and made them crawl, begging for jobs. Luisa's family . . . they sold Luisa to him. His brothers counseled him, and he ignored them. Even Maxim! Maxim the judge!" She advanced on me. "No law would keep a man like Bernard locked up."

Her read on the situation was wrong in every way. My father

would have ensured that Vera got justice. I decided to stick to the facts. "How did you find the purse?"

"I did not find it, not really. Luisa did."

"Where did she find it?" Natalya didn't answer. "C'mon, Natalya. We have all the puzzle pieces. Show us how to put them together."

She didn't speak.

"I don't know about you, June," Hale said, "but I could go for some of that tea right around now." He waved to the kitchen. "How about you tell us the story in the kitchen, Natalya?"

Standing in front of the stove, Natalya relaxed. She pointed to chairs at the table, two large, for Lucas and his brother, and two small, Natalya and Tara size. We took the large ones.

"Luisa and Teddy had returned from a seashore trip. Bernard had joined them for one week and two days, leaving morning after Vera was last seen alive, and they gave me week off from housecleaning, which meant extra work when they returned. Dirty house, dirty clothes—Luisa and I had much to do after her time away." Natalya measured spoonfuls of tea into a pot. "That first morning back, I heard Luisa scream."

"Scream?"

"Shout. Profanity. 'That dirty whore!' Luisa yelled." Natalya looked down at the ground when she repeated Luisa's curses. "Luisa was proper and quiet lady, but on that day, Luisa shouted like she was stabbed with ten thousand knives." Natalya paused from pulling tea-cups out of the cupboard. "Most days, I walked slowly down stairs, but on that August day I raced, not caring if I fell." Natalya shook her head. "Never in my life have I wished to be whole as I did that day. Never."

"What happened when you got down there?"

"Luisa was holding purse in her hands, garish and red. 'Taras's wife!' she shouted, and demanded to know if I had suspected that Bernie and Vera had an affair. I could not understand what made Luisa ask such question, until I went to purse"—unconsciously,

Natalya took a step toward us—"and looked inside. It belonged to Vera, holding her driver's license, her wallet, her lipstick.

"Vera's disappearance was family matter still. Shame kept us silent, and knowledge that when the hungry wolf inside Vera killed satisfied dog, she would return to us again. We waited. But that day I saw Vera's purse and I knew. She would leave family, job, home, but she would not leave purse behind. Our Vera, *pishov*. Dead."

"What did Luisa say when you told her?" I asked.

"I told her nothing at first, and Luisa paid me no attention. Luisa acted wilder and wilder. Luisa threw cushions to ground, tearing at seams, the handbag forgotten. She shoved couch, hard and furious, her nails broken, her arms scratched. She was small, but the furniture moved releasing from wall, along with layer of paint stuck to the back of leather."

"Paint?" Hale asked.

"Bernard did arrogant man's job of covering up crime. A little paint, and done!" She waved her hand back and forth. "Did not wait for wall to dry, and his laziness, it undid him. When couch moved, paint came with it. Underneath, there was blood."

I thought of the stains that had appeared when Annie sprayed luminol in the basement, illuminating through the paint, revealing the crime. To the naked eye it looked like a few flecks of blood. With the luminol, it looked like carnage.

"And your father found what we found, June. The destroyed rug, hidden under couch. A large hole cut through, old black blood soaked to roots of rug." She shook her head. "And smell of death over everything. Old blood." She squinted at me. "You know."

I did. It was sometimes hard to distinguish at a murder scene. The smell of rotting flesh fills the room, but the scent of blood hangs on the edges, acrid.

"All of it. A struggle ended, a life taken. That is what rug and wall and purse told me. And that is what made Luisa realize who she married. And she wept, her heart broken. She didn't love him because of his selfishness, but she realized that the father of her child was a monster and she must escape before he realized that she was carrying another child."

"Is that when you two came up with your plan?" Hale asked.

"It was. Luisa had not wanted to marry Bernie, and to defy him was impossible. He was rich, and his family powerful. We two, we decided that we would punish Bernie for killing Vera, and we would do it in way that Luisa would be free."

"Natalya, we have reports of a party at Bernie's house the Friday she disappeared. Any one of them could have done it—"

"Why must you complicate this?" she said. "Vera was in Bernie's home. And then she wasn't. He killed her, and I had proof."

Natalya explained how she had brought the purse to Taras so he would stop waiting for Vera to return. "When Vera was teenager, he planned to court her when she reached marriageable age. She seduced him, an innocent man, and refused to marry him for six months into pregnancy, a lifetime for my brother, who would die before being dishonorable. Her marriage vows came only when she had huge belly, Lucas almost born without his father. And then torture for whole marriage. Going away. Returning. And he waited, always."

I wasn't sure I wanted the answer to the next question. "What did he do with the purse?"

"Nothing. I knew my brother, he would obsess, turning it into relic for woman who was no saint." She raised her chin. "I took it. I have it. Still."

"What?" Hale exclaimed, at the same time I said, "Where?"

Natalya pointed to a door at the far side of the kitchen. "Basement."

"And when we found Vera's body, you didn't think to hand it over?"

"Bernard was in prison, and coming forward might draw unwanted attention from authorities for me, and for Luisa."

We asked her to take us to where she had hidden the bag, but she declined.

"No handrail," she said. "Stairs are not possible without at least one banister." She walked to the door and held it wide. "I will tell you its location."

Hale looked at Natalya and then the steps. "Ma'am, would it be inappropriate if I offered to piggyback you downstairs?"

Surprisingly, she laughed. "Gymnastics are . . . unwise."

"But Officer Lyons and I might get lost down there," Hale said. "And we need to have some sort of chain, linking the purse in the basement to Vera. When we go to trial to try to send Bernie back to prison."

Natalya nodded and turned off the burner. We'd convinced her. I created a sling with my hands where Natalya could step, and on her third attempt she successfully climbed onto Hale's back. I toyed with the idea of going first, catching them if Hale flipped forward, but honestly, I was going to be useless if that happened. Instead I followed behind, ready to support Natalya if she slipped backward and boosting her gently if her arms gave way.

Once in the basement, Hale put her down. We passed a set of bookcases with Tara's old toys piled neatly on the shelves. A living room set and a TV were wrapped in plastic, Lucas's share of the furniture split in his divorce. A few racks of men's clothing that I'd bet had belonged to Dave and Lucas's dad hung nearby, and in the back corner there was a series of boxes, each labeled in Natalya's faint Cyrillic script.

Natalya patted a trunk shoved in the corner, mahogany with leather straps. "Retrieve for me."

Hale dragged out the heavy piece of furniture. He'd flipped the first clasp when she stopped him.

"No." She indicated a box tucked behind where the chest had been. "That one."

I crawled back. The basement was dry, and the box and the documents inside were covered with dust and spiderwebs. Natalya dug in without hesitation, pulling out tax documents from 1952 through 1995, copies of Taras's will, and insurance documents for expired policies. Underneath was a purse, cherry red, the bright vinyl cracking. No one would mistake it for Natalya's. Hale produced an evidence bag, and we slid it inside, planning to do a close inspection later.

Upstairs, we heard the door open, footsteps sounding above us.

"*Teta!*" Lucas called.

"Down here!" She grabbed the purse, dropping it into the box and covering it with files, and Hale scooped up the box, holding it close.

Lucas crashed halfway down the steps and then called again, following Natalya's voice to our corner of the basement. He stopped when he saw us. "I wondered how you got yourself down here. What are these two doing here?"

Natalya lied easily. "Employment records. From my time with Luisa and Bernie. The police plan to compare document signatures, so I give them documents."

Lucas smirked. "But *teta*, what if the IRS audits your 1972 taxes?"

"You are not helpful, Lucas," Natalya said. "Your brother? He found you?"

"No . . . why?"

"I sent him to bar."

"No, I was at Felicia's. She wanted to hear what's going on."

"Your ex-wife doesn't watch news?"

"She does." Lucas looked offended. "But Tara did some interesting reporting of her own, and Felicia wanted the real story."

"Well, how wonderful she has true story. It is important she remain informed." Natalya wasn't warm and fuzzy, but I'd never seen her be unkind until I realized that she was intentionally trying to drive Lucas out. "Make yourself of use. Retrieve David."

Lucas stood his ground. "How are you going to get upstairs?"

"Officer Bascom carried me down. He will return me as well."

Lucas bounced from one foot to the other, unsure whether to stay or leave.

"Go!" Natalya said, and he stopped hesitating, bounding up the steps. Once we heard the front door slam, we moved upstairs. I asked her about the blood the police had found in Bernie's trunk.

"Luisa cut her hand in morning before Bernie awoke," Natalya said from her perch on Hale's back, the blocks from her orthopedic shoes dangling in front of my face. "She made marks inside."

"Even with her blood phobia?" I called to her.

"Luisa had courage. More courage than you could know." We had reached the top, and Natalya brushing her skirt after Hale put her down. "Luisa practiced a method recommended by a doctor she saw about her fainting spells—she clenched every muscle of her body. Only then did she cut hard across palm of her hand, and marked Bernard's trunk with blood. Only her blood would fool police. That stupid man never noticed. He never paid attention to anyone but himself."

I didn't know how many people even opened their trunks on a given day, but I gave the women credit for anticipating the blood-type analysis, the latest in police forensics in 1983.

"What arrangements did Luisa make?" Hale asked. "And where did you keep your car, ma'am? Dave said it went missing four months before Luisa did."

She walked over to the sink and rinsed off her hands. "From the moment we discovered Bernard's butchery, Luisa planned. We wanted to be sure she escaped and that Bernard was punished for his crime."

"But he wasn't punished for his crime," I said.

"He was punished for murder, was he not? I counseled Luisa on how to present false front, to influence those around her so that the worst was expected of Bernard. We planned escape route, and I took her to the hidden car, smuggling the two to freedom." She gave a resigned shrug, and her bun brushed the edge of the collar of her white blouse. "Driving Luisa's car back to her house, it was last time I drove car. I miss having freedom to travel but with this," she indicated her hip, "my driving days ended."

Natalya explained how they had intentionally picked that day to transport Luisa and Teddy to the garage in Troy since everyone would be on the Albany side of the Island, celebrating the ground-breaking of the new leg of 787.

"Everyone cheered at new road, Maxim preening at new jobs and money. We were cut off from Hopewell Falls but not from Troy."

We heard Dave and his brother coming up the street. Not their steps, but their voices, loudly singing a Def Leppard song. Natalya picked up her purse. "Please let me explain it to Lucas and David. On the worst day of my life, the Black Raven took my brother and I never said good-bye. At least let me explain my imprisonment."

Natalya was prepared for an arrest. I had other ideas.

"We need to get several things lined up before we consider ar-resting you. The purse alone, especially when it's been sitting in your basement for thirty years, is likely useless as evidence. And we don't want to tip off anyone yet, especially Dave and Lucas." There were too many vigilantes around here already, and I didn't need more. "We know you can keep a secret, Natalya. Keep it for one more day."

The front door clattered open, and Dave and Lucas fell rather than walked through the door.

"He wasn't there," Dave said, hanging off his brother. He stood straight when he saw me. "Lyons." He tapped Lucas on the chest. "Uh, oh. Now I'm in trouble."

"We're not here for you, Batko," I said. "Although don't think I didn't notice that you took off for the bar the second I left."

"Sorry, June."

"Hey, man," Hale said. "Feeling no pain, I see."

"G-man," Dave said, propelling himself off his brother in the direction of Hale. "June told me you have quite a nice bedroom."

It was time for Hale and me to leave. Outside, Hale walked me to my car, both of us facing the house to make sure we weren't overheard.

"You need help processing the handbag?" he said.

"No, I got it. I also want to have a conversation with Annie. I hope she's working."

I booked the purse into evidence, calling Annie to let her know we needed a check for trace evidence, blood spatter or, if we were lucky, fingerprints. The fact that Natalya had removed it from the house thirty years ago wasn't good for the chain of evidence, but from here forward we would follow proper procedure.

Annie buzzed into the station fifteen minutes later. "What do you have for me?"

I held out the purse.

"Yes, very tacky. Are you offering me fashion advice?"

"This is Vera Batko's." I explained where we had found it.

"Oh, joy," Annie said, reaching for it. "I'm sure the courts will be happy to admit evidence that's been kept in a housekeeper's basement for thirty years."

"It may not be admitted, but I need you to check." I paused, trying to figure out a way to make my next request tactful. Then I remembered that Annie despised tact. "Tell Dave nothing about the purse."

Annie was half paying attention, writing notes to herself on a pad. "He's not assigned to the case. I should be able to control myself."

"That's right. So no access, no photos, nothing."

She rested the purse on the table and carefully placed the pad next to it. "What are you implying?"

I told her about the photos Dave had on his wall.

Her elbows jutted out when she crossed her arms tightly. "I didn't give them to him."

I held up my hands in surrender. "I figured. But you've been dropping off food, and I'd prefer to be safe rather than sorry."

"No. No. Where's a computer," she said. She pulled up Vera Bat-ko's files electronically, tabbing through to the access page.

"So these photos have been accessed by you twelve times, and you printed them . . . three times? Are you trying to kill *all* the trees?" She advanced to another set of initials farther down the screen. "That's Dave helping himself to the same images, printing once."

"Can you cut off his access?"

"I can't, but I know who can." She opened her phone.

"Hi Brendan, it's Annie. No, surprisingly enough the network isn't down. But we need to cut off remote access for an employee. Last name Batko . . . yes, Dave. He's meddling . . . yes, his mom. Are you going to keep talking over me?" Annie blew out a sigh, the air ruffling her bangs, and I could hear a male voice speaking rapidly. "That is a challenge, Brendan. Do you think you could *find* a computer? Rumor has it you are the system administrator for the city." She made the hurry-up gesture with her hands, not that he could see it. "No, I won't owe you a beer. I have presented you with the opportunity to help solve a murder and protect one of your fellow civil servants. Yes. Yes, much more gratifying work than resetting passwords all day. What, it's done?"

I could hear Brendan saying good-bye as Annie hung up.

"Done," she said, and stood. "And now, the purse. That moron Dave is going to drink himself to death if we don't get this solved soon."

She wasn't wrong.

CHAPTER 24

THERE WAS NOTHING MORE TO DO TONIGHT, AT LEAST UNTIL ie analyzed Vera's purse, and I half suspected she wouldn't sleep until it was done. I went to my desk and typed up my report, getting every last detail in. It was the longest report I'd ever written, not because of the level of detail, but because I didn't want to go home.

The house was quiet when I walked in, no chatty Lucy, the TV off for the first time since we found Vera in the barrel. I secured my gun and hung up my coat, listening for my father. I found both my parents sitting in the dining room. A lit candle sat in the center of the dining table. Squat and pale yellow, the candle wasn't romantic. I would have normally pinned something like this on my mom, but my father had a secret fondness for Yankee Candle, and I bet this was his doing.

"Mom, I'd like to talk to Dad alone," I said, standing in the doorway.

Dad put his hand over my mother's. "I'd like your mother to stay for this, June. Your mom helped me practice my apology, and I want to be sure I get it right."

"You came up with the words, Gordon," Mom said. "I helped

you set the intention, so you and June can both feel the healing light of the universe."

My father stifled laughter, and my mother swatted him on the arm.

"Laugh all you want," she said. "But this is important, Juniper."

Dad patted the seat next to him. "C'mon, Juney. Sit down so I can apologize to you."

I stayed standing. "I'm furious with you."

"I know. And I deserve it. I'm going to make an apology that, yes, I practiced with your mom, and then you can say your piece."

"Anything at all, June," Mom said. "You don't have to worry about hurting our feelings."

"She's never been one to hold back," Dad said.

I sat. He closed his eyes, took a breath in and out, and said "Amen." He was a very lapsed Catholic. If he was scared enough to pray, that alone made my wall of anger crack.

"Go ahead," I said.

He talked quickly. "What I did was wrong, and I am heartily sorry for having injured you." He didn't continue.

"Tell me exactly," I said. My father was a wrecking ball these days, and I wanted to make sure he hadn't done damage I knew nothing about.

"Well, I shouldn't have read your notes. I felt shut out of my case—"

Even now, he wouldn't give it up. "It was my case, Dad."

"It still felt like mine. Especially when I found out justice hadn't been served."

My dad sounded like he was apologizing to the universe.

"There's something else. Something bigger," he said. My mother knitted her brow—Dad was going off script—and I braced myself, ready for him to tell me he'd run over Bernie Lawler with a car earlier this evening.

"I'm sorry I forced you to be a police officer," he said.

I sat back in my chair, crossing my arms. "Mom made you say that."

"I didn't!" she said.

"I've heard you say those exact words, Mom."

"She didn't make me, June," he said. "I've thought it for a long time. I feel like I made you feel like this work was the only choice, and it's not. See what it did to me, Juniper?"

"What did it do, Dad?"

"It made it so I was never anything but the job."

My mom jumped in. "You were also a wonderful father."

"When I wasn't caught up in the job."

"That was between you and me. Not the girls," Mom protested. I could tell she needed the healing light of the candle right now. "Where is all this coming from, Gordon?"

I wondered that, too. As angry as I was about the notebook, he was still a good man. "Dad, you were a wonderful father. I know I'm back here now, but you didn't bully me, not into living here *or* law enforcement." I pointed to the picture of my sister with her boys. "Catherine's a marketing manager at a biotech company. You gave us choices."

My mother chimed in. "And you are a lifesaver with June, now. Without you here, day in and day out, someone she could count on—" at this she hesitated. "Well, she would have very few options." She raised an eyebrow at my father. "Let's return to the original script, shall we?"

"OK," he said and took a deep breath before meeting my eyes. "June, what I did was unethical. Even worse, I inserted myself into the investigation and made a mess of things. I'm sorry."

No one said anything, and I realized it was the end of the apology. I wanted to say "thank you" and escape, but the problem would be here tomorrow, ready to ambush me at breakfast.

"There was no mess." I thought of what Hale had said earlier. "You made a mistake. The one mistake of your career, as near as

I can tell." Mom nodded along. "Whether you were a good father is not up for debate, because you were. And as a cop I will tell you that Hopewell Falls would be in a lot worse straits than it is if you weren't around. Despite the problems the city has"—and they were many—"you never gave up hope. You made it a community. You made people feel safe."

"But not a place where you yourself would want to stay," he said. "You never wanted to be tied here. You always wanted to go out and live your life."

"Which I did. Before." I threw out my hands. "This is my life now."

"So why don't you go and do it again?" he said. "Does the Agent Bascom guy still want you to rejoin the FBI?"

Mom looked from me to my father, and back to me again. "Rejoin the FBI?"

"Consult," I said. "It wouldn't be permanent. It would be on a shortened basis, and possibly project by project."

I was half hoping Mom would start in on how I shouldn't be so law enforcement focused so we could have an old argument instead of a new one. I was disappointed.

"So you could possibly," Mom offered tentatively, "work on a project-by-project basis?"

Dad looked triumphant. "She could. She could try it out, and if it doesn't work, return to the Hopewell Falls Police Department."

I think I liked it better when my parents weren't speaking. "It's not that simple, Dad. And Mom. I like the small town policing. I do the job, and it's quiet except when there's an insane case."

"Haven't there been two like that this year?" Mom asked.

"There have," Dad said. "And you never know when you'll pull another."

"Did Hale coach you two? It's different. As bad as the last few months have been, work wise, it's nothing like what it could be. Undercover work that goes on for months. Monstrous people telling me they were going to find where I lived and teach me a lesson."

Mom looked shocked. "They said that?"

"No, Mom. They said worse. I was trying to spare your sensitive ears."

"But if you consult," Mom said, "don't you get some say in the cases you'll work? Can't you specify 'no undercover work' or 'no murderous thugs'?"

"Hale could *probably* swing the first, but not the second."

"Do you not trust Agent Bascom?" Mom asked.

I thought of Hale, who had pulled me back from the edge of a snowy death a few months before, and who made me be honest today when I wanted to disappear into the work. "I trust him."

"Is it me?" Dad looked upset. "Is it because you can't trust me . . . with Lucy?"

"No, Dad. As a father, as a grandfather, there's no one better." My mother started to rub my father's shoulder, and I don't know if it was her touch or my words that helped him relax. "As a cop . . . well, if we were partners we'd be doing some rebuilding. But since one of us"—I pointed a finger at my father—"is no longer on active duty, that's not a problem."

"So you trust your father, and you trust Agent Bascom," my mother said. "Do you not trust yourself?"

I was ready to protest—"No! Of course not!"—but realized what she said had an element of truth.

"I'm rusty."

My dad laughed. "Yeah, not so much."

"No, it's true. Hale throws himself into cases. I used to be like that. Now I hesitate. I second-guess."

"Deliberate and steady investigative approaches are better, not worse," Dad said. "And honestly, after seeing how destructive rushing into action might be, it's not a bad way to go."

"What if I moved back," my mother said. "What if you had someone else, backup for your backup."

"That is kind of you," I said. "But that doesn't change the nature of the job. Plus, what would Larry say about moving back up North?"

"We could be snowbirds," she said. "We're almost old enough. Summers up here and winters down there." She laughed. "Actually, I kind of like the idea of getting out of Florida during hurricane season. C'mon, June. You always wanted to work for the FBI. Say yes to this opportunity."

"Maybe," I said.

"Say probably," Dad said.

"OK. Probably," I said. I looked between the two of them. "Is this what it's going to be like if Mom moves back?"

"I promise to let you be an adult, make your own decisions," Mom said.

"I don't," Dad added. "You'll always be my girl."

I stood up. "I should go to bed. I'm expecting results on a piece of evidence early tomorrow."

Dad pursed his lips, withholding questions through force of will. I felt like I needed to throw him a bone, show my trust, at least a little bit.

"Between you and me, it is something that will ensure that we put Bernie Lawler away for the crime he DID commit."

My dad held up his hand. "I can't believe I'm saying this, but don't get so focused on Bernie. The other bloody scene in his house, it couldn't have been him. He's not some ex-con. There's no pattern of murder." He folded his hands in front of him, and I saw how a generation of police officers saw their chief. "You can do right by him, Vera, and Dave."

"And you."

"Whatever action you take will be right by me. I believe in you." He patted my hand. "We good?"

"We're good."

"Then I'm going to bed," Mom said. Dad had set her up in the family room with an air mattress. It seemed she was here for the long haul.

Dad blew out the candle. "Spending those nights at you mother's hotel, it was nice of her, but in the end, it wasn't home."

No, it wasn't. I checked the locks on the front door while my father checked the back. From the second-floor landing I heard my father jiggle the front door handle, unable to keep himself from making sure we were safe. While my father went in to brush his teeth, I went to say my good night to Lucy. Her purple bedroom had a low glow from the nightlight in the corner. She was tucked into her canopy bed—thanks to her grandfather—underneath her dream catcher—thanks to her grandmother. I went over, smoothing back her hair. She was still in her purple nightgown phase, refusing to give it up despite its cutting into her shoulders. She was getting too big for it. She would be grown up before I knew it.

I kissed her forehead and went and changed for bed, combing my hair out of its bun and brushing my teeth slowly, not out of any sense of fantastic personal hygiene, but because it was peaceful; normal, even. I flipped on the bathroom's nightlight and felt my way along the hallway to my room. Bumping my hip on the dresser, I slid along the side to my mattress, settling in and sinking into the softness. I took one breath and the second, and then was out.

CHAPTER 25

I RECEIVED A TEXT FROM ANNIE AT 5:30 A.M. "ARE YOU UP yet????" and then at 5:35: "Are you always this lazy?"

I texted her back, and received a *request* to join her at her lab. I offered to pick Hale up and meet her at 7:00 so she could show us the evidence and then go home and get some sleep. On my way out the door I grabbed a cup of coffee from the kitchen. Everyone was in the backyard, my Dad sitting in a lawn chair drinking coffee, my mother doing a series of yoga poses, Lucy next to her, still in her nightgown. It usually took dynamite to get Lucy out of bed in the morning.

"Sun Salutations, Mom!" Lucy said, delighted as she tipped forward onto her hands. I watched the two of them bend and stretch before saying my good-byes.

Hale and I called Chief Donnelly on our way to give him an update. It was early, but he had said I could call at any hour so I took a chance and dialed. He answered, not only up, but in the office. And he wasn't alone.

"Batko's here, re-upping his paperwork to extend his leave, and surprise, surprise, he's doing it voluntarily. He smells like a brewery and his eyes are bright red. But he's on leave, so I won't ding him for being drunk on the job."

Annie was waiting for us, hands on hips. "Is it the special agent who needed the primping time?" She buzzed around the room, alighting at one table before moving to another, stopping briefly to grab one of the coffees Hale had picked up on his way. She handed the camera to a young man, instructing him to load it onto the server without screwing it up. Unlike the other young techs, this one seemed delighted to have his intelligence questioned.

"Sure thing, Annie," he said.

"Well, come on," Annie said, waving us over to a table. Spread across it were a series of evidence bags, each containing a separate item: the purse and a wallet, with one dollar and change bagged next to it. A one-inch mirror, broken along one corner, and a bright orangey-red lipstick. I picked up the tube, reading the label: Flame.

"This," Annie said and thrust a bag containing a piece of paper under my nose. "The rest is unimportant."

I held the evidence bag up to the light. I would have expected a piece of paper this old to be yellowed and faded, but having been tucked away in Natalya's basement, the writing was visible and clear.

"J," it said, the top of the letter looping up tall and fat. "You have done very well for yourself. Too well. Give me"—and here "$5,000" was crossed out and replaced with "$25,000"—"or I will tell everyone who Lucas's real father is. You've gotten away with pawning me off on that half-wit Taras, but those days are over. You are going to pay up, and I am going to get the life I deserve."

"Jesus," Hale said. "Does Lucas know about this?"

"I don't think so," I said. "Dave certainly didn't."

"It was in the lining," Annie said. "That mirror had cut through the fabric, and this slipped inside."

I read the note again. J. Jake. The judge. Dan Jaleda? I could exclude Bernie. Or could I? Was J the start of some sort of pet name?

"So, blackmail," Hale said. "Money, sex, and security. All very good reasons to kill someone."

"Yes," Annie said. She faded the second she was no longer in motion, jolting herself awake. "So you have that note, and I've given you a lot to do. Why don't you go do it?"

"We'll go," I said. "But do me a favor? Pull any pictures related to the note off the server, and don't tell anyone. It could be a disaster if Dave found out."

"Did you hear?" Annie shouted to the tech.

"I did," the young man said. "And is that what you want me to do?"

For the first time since I knew her, Annie smiled. "Please pull the pictures." I was marveling over her use of "please" when she added, "And if you tell anyone about the contents of that note I will find you and I will kill you."

FEARING THAT A VISIT TO DAN JALEDA COULD TIP OFF DEIRDRE Lawler, we decided to drive to the Medved brothers. The cars were gone at Jake's, so we started with Maxim. The judge's front door was wide and red, and the bell echoed through the house. A minute passed, and we were beginning to give up when he called to us from the side of the house.

"Hello!" he said. He was wearing a blue track suit, matching top and bottom, the three-piece suit of athletic wear. "What brings you to my humble home?"

"We hope we're not too early . . ."

"Oh, no. I garden before the sun gets too high in the sky."

Hale put his hand out, checking for rain. "Even in weather like this?"

"You ignore a garden, even for a day, and you end up losing the battle with weeds and bugs. I get out here, walk around a bit, try to keep my joints loose and get some roses to bloom."

We followed him around to the back. He, like Natalya, had quite a bit of land, but it was taken up by a large in-ground pool. The garden lay off to the side, curving around Jake's property next door, a fence of flowers.

"I spoke to Bernie. Elda signed over his house to him, the factory, too. Said he was going to rent space for a new clothing factory. I asked him when he was flying to China to find workers." He laughed, and Hale gave him a polite smile.

I didn't. "We have a few more questions about Vera Batko."

"About the night she disappeared? I told you about the party at Bernie's house, and I'm not going to say another word. Bernie's been through enough grief."

"It's Vera's wedding we were interested in," Hale said. "We saw the pictures. Vera, Taras, Natalya, and you were the only people there."

"Oh, that was a happy day. Vera and Taras were a love match despite the . . ." the judge skimmed his own broad belly, mimicking a baby bump. "Jake was unable to attend the wedding that day and I offered to attend in his place. Someone needed to stand up for Vera. My brother took a special interest in her."

I looked closely at the judge, ruddy cheeked and smiling. His comment could be innocent, but he'd been on the bench for twenty-five years and knew plenty of cops and how they thought.

Hale took the bait. "When you say special interest . . . ?"

"Oh, nothing like that." He chuckled as if Hale had made a very funny joke. "He was thirty and she was a girl of fourteen. Her family let her run wild, and she needed a steadying influence in her life. That was Jake." I doubted that anyone, up to and including Jake, would describe him as a steadying influence.

The judge continued. "My brother would have been very displeased if I'd allowed Vera to remain an unwed mother." He paused, his face pink from exertion. "Do either of you young people mind getting a little dirty? I want to tie up my wife's rose bushes. They can get heavy with the weight of the buds. Sonya and I didn't have children, so caring for her plants is a way to remember her."

Hale's suit had probably cost in the four figures, so I volunteered. The judge handed me some string and gardening shears. He knelt in the mud and encircled the bush in his broad arms. Bald patches showed through his slicked-back hair, and age spots dotted his hairline.

"You have so many people you cared for like a father," I said. "Jake, Bernie, Deirdre, Brian, and Lucas . . . the list could go on. You never thought of having children of your own?"

"Sonya and I were desperate for them, even researching a Ukrainian adoption. But adopted children are never the same as flesh and blood. I had mumps as a child, and, well, children were not possible for us. Perhaps it was for the best. Sonya had her gardening and her volunteer work, and I had my civic responsibilities." He tightened his grip on the bush, and I wondered how he could stand the thorns. "Could you pull tighter? I want to keep the flowers exposed to the sun."

I took the string and wrapped it around the bushes, and Hale made a tight knot, cutting off the end. Hale offered his hand, and the judge pulled himself up.

"Thank you, young man. Gravity is having its way with me these days." He removed his gardening gloves. "Would you like to come in for coffee? I usually get to the office around ten these days. Now that I'm no longer on the bench hearing cases, well, time has no meaning. I can come and go as I please."

With the judge unable to have children, no way was he Lucas's father. Our time could be better spent with someone who might be, and we declined.

Hale and I walked around the house to the car. The grass in Jake's yard was longer than that in the judge's, and it was easy to make out the property line. Jake's property was boxed in on three sides by flowers.

Hale climbed in the car. "Jaleda or Jake next?"

"Let's visit the bar and talk to Jake," I said. "Since he had a 'special interest in Vera.'"

"Plus, the man liked a lead pipe to the skull," Hale said.

We were almost at the bar when my phone rang.

"Dave," Hale said. I didn't want to give Dave a report when we were so close to solving his mother's case, and I let it go to voicemail.

Hale's phone rang.

"He's going to swap back and forth until he gets one of us," Hale said and, putting his phone on speaker, he answered.

"Hale, you with Lyons?" Dave sounded shaky. This was one of the few times when I was hoping for a hangover.

"He is," I called out. "How are you doing this morning?"

"June, we have a problem. A big, big problem. Lucas found out about the purse."

At Dave's announcement I swerved to the right, almost hitting a parked car, before pulling to the curb.

"How is that possible?" I said. I thought of the young tech. He seemed like a nice enough young man. Too bad Annie was going to kill him.

"I saw the pictures in the electronic case file," he said. "On the server."

"You're lying. You're cut off from the remote server, and even if you weren't, those pictures aren't loaded. I made sure of it."

"At the station, this morning. The photos popped up, then disappeared."

"God dammit, Dave," I said. "You say you want this case solved, but everything you do undermines our efforts. And to tell Lucas!"

Hale leaned in close to the mouthpiece. "I get that you were emotional, Dave"—he mouthed "you, too" to me before continuing—"but did it occur to you that telling Lucas would be a misstep?"

"I didn't mean to tell him," Dave said. "He overheard."

"Then who were you telling?" I pictured Dave at Jake's bar, drunk and reciting the note's message.

"Natalya. I came home and . . . June, how could she hide the purse for so long? If she'd come forward immediately when Mom got murdered . . . Bernie got away with it . . . But to lie to the police, and me, and Lucas? How could she?"

Dave jumped from topic to topic, making little sense. I had to stop him.

"So you confronted her at the house, Dave?"

"Yeah . . . out in her garden. Lucas was asleep, and I was trying to keep him from finding out, but I got loud. Yelled." His voice was starting to rise. "I mean, June, she owed me! And Lucas, this must be ripping him up—"

"Are you positive he overheard, Dave? Maybe he just went out."

"He was gone, June . . . just gone. And he's not answering his phone—" I started up the car again and began to drive quickly toward the bar to try to intercept Lucas. But was there a chance Lucas was after Bernie? Or Dan?

"Dave, you need to tell me exactly. What did Lucas overhear?"

"I can't say for sure. But I had told my aunt how if she had given it to the police the day they found it, it would have made the case and now the purse was as good as inadmissible. Then she started to cry, so I stopped yelling, but June . . . that note. It could have given us our killer *decades* ago."

I drove toward Ontario Street, a byway to both Jake's Social Club and the bridge off the Island.

"Where do you think Lucas went, Dave?"

I could hear Dave breathing, short and rapid. "He's had it in for Bernie from day one. Bernie hired Lucas to do that basement job. And Dan. Lucas seemed even more mad at Dan, blaming him for making Lucas brick in Mom. My money's on one of them."

Hale and I whipped a U-turn, racing toward Colonie, where Bernie was living with Dan.

"Go home, Dave," I said. "Go to your Aunt Natalya's and stay there until I call you."

"I can't even look at her."

"Do as I say, Dave. You've screwed this up enough. From here forward, you need to stay out of this. I mean it."

I waited for his acknowledgment. Instead, he hung up.

"Shit," I said. "Call him back while I radio the Colonie police."

I listened to Dave's phone go to voicemail even as I explained to the Colonie police the nature of the threat and requested their assistance.

The dispatcher patched me through to a patrol car, who was hesitant to go to Deirdre and Dan Jaleda's house. "That lawyer told us if we harassed her brother, she would take us all to court for human rights violations. She told us not to set foot on the property."

"Then sit out front. And if you see a guy forty to fifty with light brown/grayish hair try to get in, detain him. Trust me, the lawyer will thank you."

I called the chief and filled him in, in case we needed to worry about jurisdictional issues. I briefly told him where we were going and why.

"Christ on a bike," he said. "I should have known when Dave showed up this morning. I may go and arrest him myself."

"Save it for later," I said. The chief, Hale, and I coordinated protection at the locations, Hale offering extra manpower for the judge's house and Jake's. The chief was extremely grateful.

"We don't need another death," he said.

When we pulled up in front of Dan and Deirdre's house, the two officers were guarding the ends of the front gate, covering the perimeter without setting foot on the property.

"Quiet," the first said.

"Anyone here?" I asked.

"Backyard," said the second.

We wound our way around the back, past a fountain made of stacked rocks and a multilevel deck. Whereas Dan's office looked like a glorified cargo container, the fantastic yard clearly belonged at a house owned by a contractor.

Bernie Lawler didn't see us at first. He wouldn't have noticed anyone, including Lucas armed to the teeth. Sitting at a picnic table on the far edge of the lawn, a cup of coffee sitting next to him, he was hunched over, petting a frog.

"Bernie?" I said when we were still ten feet away.

Bernie gently captured the frog. Holding it close, he turned. "Hello, Officer Lyons. What brings you here?"

CHAPTER 26

WE HAD SPENT THE LAST TEN MINUTES TRYING TO CONVINCE
Bernie the threat to his life was real. Bernie didn't doubt us, which
made his refusal to let us move him anywhere because we were police
officers especially galling. I was relieved when I heard Deirdre was on
her way. Deirdre would probably make Bernie run away from both
Lucas and us. I could live with that. He would be safe, even if it was
for Deirdre's paranoid reasons.

I decided I would try to get as much information as I could out of
Bernie while we waited. "Bernie, have you ever met Lucas Batko?"

"I knew him from when he was a little guy, and I remember all
the employees from Sleep-Tite. I didn't make many new memories
in prison so everything from that time is crystal clear." He took a sip
of his coffee but dropped his cup when the frog made a break for it.
"Is this about Vera?"

"It is," I said.

"Lucas thinks I did it."

"He's come to that conclusion, yes," Hale said.

"Because they found her in my basement."

"Yes, that . . . and some other things that have come to light."

Bernie pulled the frog close. "Don't suppose you put those ideas in his mind?"

"No, we didn't," I said, firmly, leaving out the detail that another cop had. I pointed to the bench opposite him. "May we sit down?"

Bernie waved us toward the seat, and I sat down. Hale straddled the bench, facing the rest of the yard, and I relaxed, knowing he had my back. Bernie caught me watching him pet the frog and then laughed. "Found this guy back here in a puddle in the garden. I had a pet frog in prison."

"They let you keep a pet?"

"Let me? No, of course not. But Lassie—"

"You named your frog Lassie?" The frog hopping around had a lot of energy, but I wouldn't have credited it with a personality.

"I did. He was very loyal. Lassie climbed up through the prison plumbing one day, and I figured any frog that went to such lengths to be with me deserved the best of everything. I spoiled him. Caught flies for him to eat. The waste, the sweat . . . prison had no shortage of flies." Over my shoulder, Hale laughed.

"No, it's true," Bernie said. "I made him a little pool out of a plastic bowl, so that he'd have swim time, and I hid him when guards came hunting for the croaking. But one day we went into lockdown, and they flipped over my locker. I never saw him again, but I heard him, his croak echoing through the pod. Now I have Lassie Jr. here."

Petting the frog calmed him, so I let him keep it. "Bernie, what do you remember about 1967?"

"What do I remember about being fourteen? Girls . . . and more girls. They were all I paid attention to. And it was the year my mother died. There was grief, but Dee and I went to live with Maxim and Sonya, which made my life loads better. I had my own room, and after the craziness of living with my father, living there was kind of heaven." He smiled. "Maxim encouraged us in school, and Sonya was so nice to us. She would have been a great mom."

"Sounds like Maxim was a great brother. How about Jake?"

"Jake meant well, but he didn't have the best impulse control. He had always been the cool brother, great car, beautiful women, but with the prison time," he shook his head, "we never got close. Until I went to prison. Then he visited me regularly, and he wrote. He surprised me, telling me stories about the people at the bar, how proud he was of Brian." He peered over my shoulder. I expected to see Deirdre, or worse, Lucas, but it was the Colonie cop, who disappeared back around the side of the house as soon as he was spotted. "When Brian was injured, it almost killed Jake. But a couple of years ago the letters got hopeful after he worked a deal with Maxim where Maxim got title to the bar and Jake got money to buy a house that was handicap friendly. He was so proud of his son."

"But in 1967 he was a little rough."

"Jake was the family embarrassment until I took over that title."

I tried to think of a way to phrase my next question so he wouldn't get defensive and shut down. "Did Jake spend time with Vera?"

Hale's phone buzzed, and he looked down. "Dan Jaleda is safe and secured. Agents are escorting him here."

That was good news. "See, Bernie? Dan doesn't mind the protection."

Bernie looked past me to the pond dotted with leaves where koi kissed the surface, looking for food. "Good for him. Dan hasn't been in prison for thirty years. He couldn't possibly know what it means to lose your freedom. What you need to understand is that I would rather be dead"—he choked out the word, swallowing before he continued—"than be back in the custody of the police."

This was the first hint of unhappiness I'd seen in Bernie, and it was more realistic than his serene act.

"I can't even imagine, Bernie," I said. "It's a wonder you didn't break out."

He laughed bitterly. "Despite my reputation, I'm not a criminal mastermind."

Hale spoke, still facing the yard. "I bet you'd do anything to stay out of jail."

"Not anything," he said. "I've never lied, and I'm not going to start now."

I decided to take Bernie at his word.

"Did you sleep with Vera, Bernie?" I asked, thinking of his long speech in prison on how he didn't want to bring a disease home to Luisa.

"Yes," he said.

I was shocked. "Bernie, you said you didn't lie, but at prison you told me—"

"In prison you asked if we dated in high school. I said no, which was true. Then you asked me if we slept together during those last few years. I said no. Also the truth."

"Cash register honesty, instead of real honesty," Hale said. "Very nice."

"I didn't volunteer information because cops can use information against you and ruin your life." He didn't break eye contact with me. "Even when they aren't out to get you, Officer Lyons."

We weren't here to talk about my father. "When did you sleep with Vera, Bernie?"

"When we were teenagers. Before she had the baby."

A look of disgust crossed Hale's face. "When she was thirteen?"

"She was fourteen. I was too. It wasn't a crime then"—Bernie shook his head—"although it probably should've been."

"Tell me how it happened, Bernie," I said.

"I was home after school one day. I had the place to myself and was rebelling by playing Monkees records too loud on the hi-fi in the living room. I was *not* a cool kid." Bernie petted his frog for almost thirty seconds. Hale cleared his throat and Bernie continued. "Vera showed up at the front door. She asked if Sonya was home, then Maxim and when I said no, invited herself in. She seduced me," he shook his head, "No, there was no seduction. She led me to Maxim and Sonya's bedroom and we had sex . . . I didn't even realize what was happening until it was over."

As he recounted the story, Bernie looked profoundly sad. "How long did your relationship last, Bernie?"

"It wasn't a relationship, at least in the boyfriend-girlfriend way." He placed the frog on the table, touching its ridged back, and I got a glimpse of the boy he'd been. "I wanted it to be, and she laughed in my face. Said I was a foolish boy, that it was just sex, and I shouldn't have gotten attached. At the time . . . it hurt." He gripped his coffee cup and took a swig. "Now that I'm older, I'd bet she'd heard that speech from some man and was parroting it. She wasn't a virgin."

"And there was no chance you got her pregnant?" I asked.

"I remember doing the math when I heard she was having a baby, and I figured she was already pregnant when we . . ." Realization crossed his face. "Hold up. She married Taras who I thought . . . Are you asking if I'm Lucas's father?"

I felt bad, as if I were divulging Lucas's secrets, but I had to know who Vera was trying to blackmail that night. "There's a question about Lucas's paternity that's directly related to Vera's death."

Bernie looked horrified. "Is that why Lucas is hunting for me? He thinks I'm his father? Jesus! Why would he think . . ."

I leaned across the table. "The identity of Lucas's father is the key to Vera's murder."

"How?"

"For now, I can't tell you. But Lucas is out to get the truth, which means he might come looking for anyone who might possibly be his father."

"Wait. Dan slept with Vera?" Bernie asked. "I know he and my sister weren't married, but if he's the guy—"

Next to me, Hale stood up. "Hello, ma'am."

"Wonderful," Deirdre Lawler called from across the lawn. "I told you I would bring a suit if you harassed us. Between this and Brian? Consider yourself served."

Hale moved across the lawn to intercept her. "We're doing the best we can to keep your loved ones safe."

I whispered, "We have no proof that Dan slept with Vera when she got pregnant, but we think Lucas's father was one of the men at the party that last night she was alive. At your house."

"So me. Dan. My brothers." Bernie stared into space. His frog used the distraction to hop across the table and back into the grass. Next to a willow tree, Deirdre and Hale were laying into each other.

"You two are the biggest threat to Bernie," she shouted.

"We're completely within our rights, ma'am," Hale said. "You can't stop us."

I used their argument on constitutional law to try to get an answer out of Bernie.

"Lucas's father, Bernie. Of the men who were there that last night, who could it be?" He didn't answer, and I gripped his arm. "Don't lie, Bernie."

"I don't know," he said rapidly. "I'd tell you if I did."

"Guess, Bernie. Go with your gut."

"Well, Jake was protective of her, almost territorial. He chased other guys away."

"So you think it's Jake?"

"Maybe. Possibly. But the other possibility would be the guy she chased. He ignored her, but she liked a challenge."

"Who was it, Bernie?"

"Dan. Deirdre's husband, Dan Jaleda."

I could hear Deirdre get in the last word, and she came tearing across the lawn, followed by Hale. Bernie rose to meet her.

"Bernie, don't answer any more questions," Deirdre said breathlessly, pushing her brother behind her.

"He's in danger, Deirdre, and so is Dan," I said. "Lucas Batko has come to believe they were involved in his mother's death."

"Dan!" Deirdre called. Dan Jaleda crossed the lawn, followed by two agents. Deirdre rushed toward them. Instead of reaming out the agents, she threw herself into her husband's arms.

"I'm OK," he said. "Deirdre, I'm safe, but we need to get out of here."

Hale walked over to confer with the two FBI agents who stood back, scanning the yard from behind mirrored sunglasses. I hung close to Bernie, keeping an eye out for Lucas, hoping he wouldn't show up. The FBI agents were trained in deadly force, and I was afraid they'd have to use it.

Hale's phone rang, and he walked a few feet away, holding his ear, at the same time my phone vibrated. It was Lorraine at the station. I answered.

"We're using phones. Dave is monitoring the radio," Lorraine said. "We have a report of a shooting at Jake's bar."

God. Lucas got to someone. Jake, if I had to guess. I had wanted more than anything to prevent this, make sure everyone made it through alive, including Lucas.

Hale shoved a finger in his ear, talking rapidly to the person on the other end of the phone. "You're on scene?"

"We haven't confirmed the victim—" Lorraine said. "EMTs have arrived."

Deirdre's phone rang. She pulled it out of her purse and answered, her voice low and even, back in lawyer mode, although it didn't last. "Hello? Who is this? Oh my God! Jake?"

So Lucas had shot Jake. I prepared to go down to the scene, start the investigation. I felt sick. Deirdre hung up the phone.

"Brian's been shot."

CHAPTER 27

A CROWD WAS FORMING. CRIME SCENE TAPE CORDONED BACK thirty or so people who were no doubt coming up with elaborate stories about why the FBI might be investigating a bar shooting on the Island. Everyone craned their necks to get a better view except Dave, who was skimming the edge of the crowd and scanning the streets and passing cars, searching for his brother.

"On the radio. I heard," Dave said, jogging up to us. "The sheriff's department said Lucas did this?!" He grabbed the police tape and shook it so hard I thought it would snap. "Is there a warrant for his arrest?"

"No, but I might arrest you," I said. "You seriously impeded this investigation."

Hale unwrapped Dave's hand from the tape, lifting it up. We both ducked under and dropped it in front of Dave, who reared back from the piece of flimsy plastic.

"One of Hale's men is going to take your statement and then you have two choices: you can go home, or you can wait out here on *that side* of the crime scene tape. Pick."

He ran his shaking hands through his hair. "I'll wait here."

Chief Donnelly called. "I'm at the hospital. Brian is being prepped for surgery. We've got Bernie, Deirdre, and Dan here under guard, and I'm about to join them." He dropped his voice. "There's no Maxim. And worse, no Jake. I've gotta go, but I've alerted the state troopers to keep an eye out for Jake's car. Jake was following his son's ambulance. He should be here." He hung up.

"We have a witness," the agent guarding the door said. "Guy who found him is back in the kitchen, sobering up. Tomas Wolschowicz."

"Oksana's brother?" I asked.

"Didn't mention a sister," the young agent said.

The bar was a blood bath. Blood had sprayed against the bottles along the back, the backlight giving the rows of bottles a pink cast through the blood spatter. The front row of bottles had fallen, Brian having taken down a whole row when he fell.

As we walked around the bar, the scene was worse. Plastic mats behind the bar meant to prevent slipping were coated with blood, and there was a heavy pool at the center of the bar. Based on where he fell, Brian didn't get a chance to run, or even duck. He was too good a soldier to let that happen.

I took in the destroyed bar. "Any signs of robbery?"

"Not a one, and it's unlikely a robber would leave a big pile of twenties behind."

In the kitchen, Annie stalked back and forth between the bar entrance and the back door, mapping the path of not one but two sets of bloody footprints, a heavily treaded bootprint sliding into the path of flat-soled shoes, the two crisscrossing and overlapping in their path to the door.

"I hate this," Annie said. I was beginning to suspect that she didn't need sleep. "This makes no sense. Both sets of footprints stop right here," she pointed to the base of the steps leading up to the old apartment. "But neither go up."

"Are you sure?" I peered up the narrow staircase. The walls had swaths of gray, streaks where decades of people had braced themselves going downstairs, sandpaper nailed to the steps to prevent slipping. Blood would have been impossible to miss.

Bringing the errors made by others to Annie's attention was like throwing red meat to a lion, but I had to ask. "Is it possible the blood wore away when our guys went upstairs to do the sweep for suspects?"

"Agents tromping over everything, the blood would have smudged, not been wiped clean. Plus, an exit is right there. Criminals are notoriously stupid, but in this case they did the smart thing and headed right out the door."

"Maybe we can follow bloody footprints to the shooter?" Hale said.

"We tracked both sets to the parking lot. Your people," she said, "are capturing tire imprints."

"Can we go upstairs?" I asked.

"With no immediate threat, no, you cannot." She knelt down, waving over her shoulder to our witness. "Go talk to that guy."

Tomas sat half on and half off the stool, penned in the corner of the kitchen. His shirt was clean, but blood soaked one leg of his jeans where he had knelt, and his hands were shaking. Even allowing for the shock of the day, it was easy to tell he was three sheets to the wind.

Tomas took a deep slug of his coffee and described what he found. "I came in for my lunch and a drink."

We were several hours past lunch. "Little late, isn't it?"

"They always have the stew going, and I have a hard time eating in the morning, nothing sits right. Would have been earlier, but I didn't want to get in the middle of the fight."

"What fight?"

"Lucas and Brian," he said. "The main door was open, and you could hear them all the way out to the street. They were really going at it."

"What did they say?"

"I heard Lucas yelling 'Where is he?!' and then Brian, he shouted, 'Like I would want you for a brother!'" Tomas cocked an eyebrow. "What was that about?"

"Did you hear anything else?"

"Nope. The back door slammed, and Lucas took off, bat out of hell. I waited outside, letting Brian calm down—he has his father's temper, I tell you. I came in, but no Brian. I settled myself in at the bar, all patient, but Brian didn't show."

I waited for him to go on—clearly he was leaving something out of the story—but he remained silent.

"And then?" I asked.

"Oh," Tomas said. "After that I waited for . . . at least five minutes, and then I decided to serve myself. That's when I found him."

I doubted that Tomas had hesitated five seconds before helping himself to beer. He would have heard Brian, gasping or crying out. Dying of a gunshot wound was rarely a quiet activity, despite what showed up on the news, but Tomas's eagerness for beer saved Brian's life.

Tomas took a long slurp of his coffee. "I was trying to stop the bleeding, grabbing some bar towels, when Jake came in. Then it's a blur for me. He gave me the phone and told me to call an ambulance, stanching the blood himself. He was weeping, holding his son close. Then the ambulance came."

"Then what did Jake do?" Hale asked.

"Then he got very quiet."

"So did he—"

"I forgot!" Tomas raised a finger and almost poked me in the eye. His gestures were getting broader. "He told me to call his sister."

I stepped around the still-raised finger. "And he went to the hospital with his son?"

Tomas frowned. "Well, of course."

"Out the front, or out the back?"

"Back."

"You two." Annie snapped her fingers at us, and I glared. Sometimes she tipped past assertive into obnoxious. She and I both knew she had crossed a line.

"I wouldn't do it if it wasn't important," she said. "Come here."

Annie was right—she rarely slipped into pure rudeness unless there was a very good reason. I wanted to see what she'd found, and I also wanted Tomas to sit for a while longer—the lack of detail in his story made me wonder if I was getting the whole truth, or any truth at all.

"There," Annie said triumphantly once we were next to her. She had a point—this was a big deal. The step with the bloody handprint was open on hidden hinges, which in itself was interesting. I peered inside and saw a makeshift box with two spent 12-gauge shells, a half-empty box of unused shotgun shells, along with a cleaning kit.

Annie ran a swab along the edge. "Shotgun residue everywhere. Give me an hour and I'll compare it to what's at the bar."

"This isn't big enough to contain a shotgun," Hale said.

"But a sawed-off shotgun?" I said. "That could fit."

Hale shook his head, a sharp no. "But why would Jake and Brian not keep it behind the bar? Back here it doesn't do much good, self-defense wise."

"Because Jake, as a convicted felon, wasn't supposed to have a firearm," Annie said. "This was a nice hidey-hole."

"A hidey-hole that's now empty. If you're saying their shotgun residue is there, then the weapon should be there, too. Where is it?"

Annie fished the spent shell casings out, dropping them in an evidence bag. "Upstairs?"

I hopped over the open step. The steep stairs were difficult to scale for someone healthy—I can't imagine how someone with a prosthesis might manage them. I emerged into a light-filled apartment. The space wasn't fancy, but its views were spectacular. With the Hudson River rolling by on the left, the Mohawk rushing toward its end on the right, I could see to the southern end of the Island, the small houses giving way to marshes.

"This is one stylin' bachelor pad," Hale said.

A single bed was tucked in the corner, a New England Patriots stadium blanket covering an unmade mattress, stains peeking out from the base of the quilt. Handy for late-night trysts or early-morning naps. We continued through to the dining room, furnished with a card table, metal folding chairs, and an elaborately carved credenza with curlicues along the top and fifteen drawers of different sizes and shapes opening out.

"That monstrosity will be here forever," I said. "I can't imagine how the furniture got up here in the first place."

We opened up the drawers and found short pencils and score sheets in one and a pile of receipts in another.

"Bet the IRS would be excited to see those," Hale said, pushing several decks of cards aside and reaching back, fishing for anything at the back of the drawer.

Trays of poker chips filled another drawer. I lifted the first one out and discovered two pieces of paper. The first was cream colored and heavy, almost bond weight, folded over multiple times. Pulling it open I noticed a cursive watermark reading "BP" that had been traced over by a blue pen and a map of New Mexico, an address written along the top. The second had a diagram of a house, arrows marking the front door, garage, and two windows. A list ran down the side: "Rope. Gloves. Heavy pipe."

"Pipe?" Hale asked.

"To beat her to death. I don't think the kidnapping was plan A. Probably wasn't plan B, either."

Hale nodded. "Someone panicked."

If the evidence under the first tray helped us understand what was planned, what we found underneath the second was damning: an unused plane ticket for the return trip from Vegas and a driver's license. Covering the name, I held up the ID to Hale.

"Who's that?" I asked.

"Brian."

"No. It's the Wisconsin man whose name is on this ticket."

Hale took a close look. "It's real. Brian doesn't exactly match the picture, but close enough."

I dropped the note into an evidence bag, and we continued through to the kitchen. The old refrigerator hummed, still working, but when I opened it, I found only mold, the moisture a breeding ground for the spores coating the inside. The smell was disgusting, and after slamming the door I was able to pick up another scent. Gasoline.

The bathroom was dark, and the light switch didn't work. Without the flashlights carried by Hale's agents, I lit the room the old fashioned way. Opening a window, I knocked a roll of toilet paper resting on the frame down into the parking lot below, beaning one of the crime scene techs. I gave him a wave and he waved back. No harm done.

In the sink, rust stains showed a path where the hot water had dripped, possibly for decades. Hale looked disgusted. "They used this?"

"There's no other bathroom. Unless they decide to trek down to the bar, this is it." I pushed aside the shower curtain and was met with six gas cans, piled halfway up the edge of the tub.

"I'll get Annie," Hale said.

WE STOOD BY THE WINDOWS IN THE LIVING ROOM. AFTER THE dark bathroom and the cavelike bar, it was nice to be able to look out on blue skies and the river where a fleet of rowers sculled past.

"I'm beginning to think Brian didn't set fire to Luisa and the factory," Hale said.

"I'm pretty sure that the evidence we found in the dining room sealed it for me—Brian's our man." I was tired and wanted to sit, but the folding chairs in the dining room were being used and the bed in the corner looked disgusting. "Plus there's all the other evidence. Brian disappeared for a week. His carbon prosthetic meant he could have slipped past the TSA without notice. The videos from the airport look like him. And finally, the way he was slinging around cases of beer means he had the strength to overpower Luisa, and his army training ensured that he had the skill."

"Oh, I'll give you that he committed the kidnapping," Hale said. "But as for the fire, I don't believe it. The man was trained in explosives. He wouldn't have set such an amateurish fire. Honestly, if he wanted to blow something up, he'd have better ways than a low-rent gasoline fire. And if he really wanted to kill her, she'd be dead." I started to protest, but Hale held up a hand. "The original plan was for Brian to fly out to Vegas, rent a car and drive to New Mexico, kill her, and then fly back out of Vegas. But it's different when you are fighting enemy combatants than when you are trying to take down a tiny lady who liked to garden, and I don't think Brian had it in him." He looked around the apartment, fixing on the stained mattress. "Brian joined the army to get away from this, but he's not a *killer,* if you get my meaning."

"It wasn't his fight," I said. "But whose was it? Because they probably set that fire. His dad? Maxim? Dan Jaleda?"

"One of them, and then they turned around and shot him to shut him up."

"But it wouldn't be his father," Hale said. "Jake is devoted to his son."

"But when push came to shove, if Jake murdered Vera—"

"And maybe his girlfriend Oksana."

"Hale, for all we know, Oksana is still alive."

"But maybe she's not. We know that Vera is the reason that there was blood all over the basement at Bernie's house, but for argument's sake, let's assume that Oksana is the reason that there was blood all over the bathroom. Who was closest to her? Jake. And who was most likely to kill her? Jake."

"We need to talk to our suspects again. Dan we can question, since he's at the hospital," I said. "But we need to find the Medved brothers now. Lucas might hunt them down . . ."

"And maybe they deserve it," Hale said. "One of them is probably our killer."

HALE AND I WALKED DOWNSTAIRS TO CUT TOMAS LOOSE. HE was even more wobbly than earlier, slumped over on the butcher block. He gripped his coffee mug with one hand; cigarette smoke rose up from beneath the table.

"No one else," he said, slurring. "I didn't see no one."

With Hale approaching Tomas's flank, I swept in from the left and grabbed his mug. I took a sniff. The contents were probably 75 percent whiskey and 25 percent coffee if I had to guess. Hale pulled a half-empty bottle of Jameson's from under the counter, waving it in front of Tomas. Tomas struggled to focus on the bottle.

"Who didn't you see, Tomas?" I asked.

"No one. Jake told me."

"Jake told you what? C'mon, Tomas."

In a way, I was glad I'd left Tomas alone. He didn't strike me as a man of moral fortitude, and Irish whiskey had crumbled his last defenses.

"I didn't see anyone hurt Brian. Not anyone was in here. But the judge, I saw him."

"Where?"

"Over around," Tomas twirled his finger in a circle. "When I went for a walk to get away from the Brian and Lucas blowout. At the grocery."

I thought of the grocery that backed onto the bar's back lot. Dave regularly cut through to save the seven seconds on his route to the bar.

"I told the judge . . . I said . . . that Brian and Lucas sounded ready to bust up the joint. 'Not to worry, young man!'" Tomas shouted, and then caught himself, switching to a loud whisper. "That's what the judge said. He said the fight would be over by the time I got back from buying cigarettes." Tomas held up two packs of American Spirits, one in each hand. "He gave me cash for these."

"How long were you gone, Tomas?"

"I bought the cigarettes. And then I went up the next block, to check in with Mikey at the newsstand. Dan Jaleda was over there, picking up a paper and I asked him like maybe he had a job for me or something? But he said no, really rude like, and rushed off." He shook his head. "He moved off the Island and forgot the people who knew him."

"And during that time, you didn't hear anything?"

Tomas looked confused. "What would I have heard?"

"A weapon discharging?" Hale asked.

"A what?"

"A shotgun blast," I said.

Look, I went to those places, and I didn't hear anything, and then I came right back and I found Brian all . . ." Tomas waved his hand as to encompass the bar and everything in it.

Tomas babbled, but nothing he said added any information. I made a note to check with Stan at the newsstand about the timing of Dan Jaleda's visit and sent Tomas over to the station so he could sober up and someone could take his statement. As he was loaded into the car, I went out front to hunt for Dave. He was gone.

"Of course he ran off," I said.

Hale and I started our trip to St. Peter's Hospital in Albany to interview Dan Jaleda. It was slow going because of the police checkpoint that cut off both lanes of the bridge, impassable even with police lights and sirens. We called Chief Donnelly, filling him in on our building search and interview with Tomas. He had his own update. Neither Maxim nor Jake had shown up, and worse, Dan Jaleda had disappeared. Bernie thought he might have gone to search for Jake, but Deirdre was frantic.

"He's gone," Chief Donnelly said.

CHAPTER 28

"Clear."

The report came from a state trooper searching Jake's house. Jake was nowhere to be found. We were almost at the checkpoint and were trying to decide whether to turn around and search the Island or head over the bridge and visit Maxim Medved's office.

"This place has been tossed. The judge's house next door, too," the trooper said. He said something else, but it was garbled. Dave had made our lives impossible. He was monitoring police radio channels, and we'd cobbled together a network of cell phones and FBI communication devices. After all the time she'd spent training us on radio protocol, Lorraine was probably weeping at her desk at having to play switchboard operator, connecting phone to phone.

"I said," the trooper repeated, "we need more manpower to search these sites as well as a third, where Batko's car was parked."

"Dave's?"

"No, Lucas's. His car was down by the Lawler place, close to the old boat landing. The information has been all over the place, but I got a report that he's armed and dangerous."

"He might be," I said. In the past I might have protested that Lucas was harmless, but not today. "Exert all deliberate caution."

"Copy," he said, using the default radio lingo despite being on his phone.

"WE'RE ALMOST AT THE BRIDGE," HALE SAID. "WHICH WAY?"

"Let's go to Maxim Medved's office."

We arrived at the judge's office to find Jake's Camaro in the lot parked right next to the side entrance. Hale parked against his back bumper, pinning Jake's car to the building, and pulled himself out of the car in one fluid motion. He didn't ask about the plan. "I'll take the side and you take the front."

The hallway to the judge's office was dark, the only light coming through the pebbled glass of his office door. I proceeded slowly, skimming the edge of the hallway, staying in shadow. Jake might very well have a rifle, and I wasn't going to give him a clear shot at me if I could help it.

Hale appeared at the far side of the door. His black suit blended into the dimness of the hallway, but his white shirt stood out in stark relief, a target if someone wanted to take a shot at him. He waved me over and we stood close, listening through the door to the judge's secretary, Marlene, speaking to someone. Her words were indecipherable, but she paused, as if waiting for a response. I pressed closer, trying to make out the voice of Jake, the judge, anybody. Nothing.

"Showtime," Hale said. He twisted the doorknob sharply.

"Shit," he said. "Locked."

"Is someone there?" I heard Marlene call.

"Police, Marlene," I called. "June Lyons."

A fuzzy-haired shadow appeared on the other side of the door. She flipped three locks and we were faced with Marlene, her eyes red, Kleenex wadded in her hand.

"You're here about Brian," she said.

I poked my head into the reception area, but there was no sign of Jake or the judge. "Is the judge available?"

The question set off fresh tears. "No. And I can't reach him."

Marlene went back to her chair, her desk rattling as she opened the drawer for another Kleenex. "Such terrible news! The judge was so proud of Brian, both his nephew's service to our country and his resilience! He bought Brian a truck, outfitted for the handicapped and last month the judge signed over the deed to the bar. More than anything, he wanted Brian to have a future."

"Wait," I said, "I thought Jake owned the bar."

"He did, up to a few years ago." Hale went to the judge's door, head tilted, listening for motion inside, as Marlene chattered away. "But finances were tough after Brian came back, and Judge Medved, he wanted to be sure his nephew was taken care of. He bought the bar, and then two weeks ago gave—gave!—the bar back to Brian. It was practically a ceremony—Brian signing, the judge signing, and Jake and Brian's Uncle Dan acting as witnesses."

I tried to signal Hale, see if he picked up what I picked up—Brian was given the deed to the bar right after Luisa was kidnapped and burned—but Hale's attention was fixed on the judge's office.

"The judge considered Brian a son," Marlene continued. "After Brian's mother passed, the whole family rallied around Brian. His Uncle Dan—"

Hale rammed the judge's door, sending it bouncing against the wall, before flipping on the light switch.

"I said he's not here!" Marlene cried.

I tried to calm her. "Jake's the person we're trying to find, really."

"By smashing in doors?!"

"I'm sorry, ma'am," Hale said. "A shooting like this has us all on edge. We saw his car out front and thought he might be here."

"Jake asked me to swap cars. He stopped by to find his brother and discovered his car was low on gas. He didn't want to run out on the way to the hospital." The anger seemed to have snapped her out of her grief, tears stopping and voice calming. She reached under her desk and threw away the wad of tissues. "He didn't need to worry. He had enough gas to make it to the hospital twice over."

Hale pulled out his phone. "What kind of car do you drive, ma'am?"

"A Chevy Impala. Silver."

"And the plate number?"

Marlene hesitated but gave Hale the number. Hale dialed his phone, reciting the make, model, and license number to his agents.

I let her collect herself before asking the next question. "When was he here?"

"Thirty minutes ago, right when I got back from the post office," she said. "Jake was desperate to find the judge. Who could blame him?"

"And where is the judge?" In the corner, Hale paused, listening to Marlene's answer.

"He was supposed to be at the Capital Club, having his weekly lunch for former judges. That's what I told Jake."

Hale walked over to the typewriter, finger in his ear, giving the agents the address where they could find the judge.

"But the judges didn't go to the lunch today."

"Hold on," I heard Hale say, pulling the phone away from his ear. Marlene had our full attention.

"Where is the judge?" I asked.

"He's at Natalya Batko's."

This was either the worst news or the best news I'd heard all day. We finally knew where he was—someplace Lucas would trip over him.

"I only found out after I got back from the post office . . . I can't believe I sent Jake on a wild goose chase." Marlene teared up again. "He was so desperate to find his brother, tell him about Brian, and I got in the way. I called over to Natalya's to track down the judge there, but no answer." She picked up the phone, "I should try over there again. What if Brian dies before the judge can say good-bye?"

"Hold on, Marlene," I said. "We can go over and tell him ourselves in just a minute."

"But I can try Jake again," she said. "I called his cell when I got the message from the judge, but what if he didn't get my voicemail? He could be desperate."

"We'll find him, too," I said. "Now that we know what kind of car we're looking for, we can give him a police escort to the hospital."

Hale ended his call. "Officer Lyons. A moment."

I walked over to where Hale stood next to the typewriter and said in a whisper, "Should we take this into the hall?"

Hale shook his head and pulled out a piece of letterhead, heavy stock with a "BP" imprinted on the center. It was the same paper as the one with the map to Luisa's house. I lifted up the box it came from, checking the labels. "Brouillette Paper Executive Elite Fine Bond."

"Can we take a few sheets of this?" I asked. I wanted to take the whole box, but I didn't have a warrant, something that would change in the next sixty minutes.

Marlene hesitated. "One sheet would be OK. It's the judge's favorite."

"Brouillette Paper stopped making paper ten years ago," I said. I knew someone who could give me the exact date they stopped producing this particular stock.

"That's the last of it," Marlene said. "We're half-day now, and the judge says we'll be closed within the year. No need to find a replacement between now and then," she said, her pink lipstick cracking on her dry lips. "We're all too old for this now."

WE PUT ON OUR FLASHERS AS WE MADE OUR WAY TOWARD THE bridge onto the Island. Even with the lights it was slow going—people wanted to get out of the way, but the cars were packed so tightly we were locked in. Hale and I worked the phone and the radio, alerting people to Jake's possible whereabouts and vehicle, and trying to arrange for officers and agents to go to Natalya's. It was tough to line people up—with law enforcement at the river's edge, running traffic control, holding the scene at Jake's, and keeping watch at the hospital, we lacked manpower, and with traffic backed up, it was hard to get more bodies onto the Island. We were accelerating away from the last blockade onto the Island when my phone rang. It was Dave.

"June," Dave said. He was panting. "I found Lucas and he's safe and kinda sane, considering everything."

"What do you mean?"

"Well, if I found out the man I called Dad my whole life wasn't my father, I'd be destroyed. But Lucas, he says it's the one thing that makes the rest of his life make sense, helped him figure out why Mom hated him from the moment she set eyes on him."

I felt sad for Lucas that finding out why his mother never loved him gave him comfort. "What did Lucas say about the confrontation at the bar?"

"He didn't shoot Brian, if that's what you're asking, and he's coming into the station to go on record with everything he knows."

I paused. "Your brother is in a lot of trouble right now."

"You heard about the argument?" Dave asked.

"Sounded a bit more heated than an argument, Dave," Hale said.

"Lucas never touched him. But listen, here's what Brian said. He said that Jake was in prison when Vera got pregnant."

I thought of the judge's words. *Jake was unable to attend the wedding that day and I offered to attend in his place. Someone needed to stand up for Vera. My brother took a special interest in her.* Jake didn't miss the wedding because he was at the dentist. He missed it because he was in prison. He couldn't have been Lucas's father.

"Dave, this is all well and good, but this nice information doesn't mean anything unless you take some action. Bring Lucas to the station right now."

"Lucas is upstairs, changing clothes, trying to slip in and out before Natalya catches him—she's in the backyard and he doesn't want to have a conversation with her about this now."

"You're at Natalya's?" I asked. Hale sped up the car, bouncing through the potholes.

"He's still mad at her," Dave said. "I was angry, but for him . . . hold on a second, Lyons. Something's up."

I made the turn onto Natalya's street too fast, Hale gripping the dashboard as he was shoved against the door. In the distance, I could see Dave's car parked in front of his aunt's house.

"Lucas is shouting, June, something about Jake," Dave said. Over the phone I heard a car door open and in the distance I saw Dave get out of the car. "June, I can see Jake Medved at the edge of the property. He's running and . . . Jesus! He's got a gun!"

"Stay with the car!" I yelled, even as I watched Dave run toward the backyard.

We pulled to a stop before Dave was around the building, and I radioed it in, having no reason to work off-channel. I went to the right side of the house and Hale went left, arriving in the backyard at the same time.

The lawn and garden beyond were beautiful, the late afternoon sun soft through the sunflowers, sentinels guarding the edge of the property. The yard was empty, but from the porch above I heard Natalya's voice. "Jacob, you show disrespect to me and my home by pointing weapon at me. Put it away! Away, I tell you!"

I unhooked my glock and Hale drew his Sig Sauer. I held up my hand where he could see, and counted off. "One, two, three." The two of us circled the porch and ran up the steps, guns drawn, ready for Jake to open fire.

None came. Jake's back was to me, the sawed-off shotgun we had been searching for trained on a lunch table where an ashen Maxim Medved sat along with Natalya.

Dave, in turn, had his glock pointed directly at Jake.

"Weapons down!" Hale yelled.

Dave and Jake held firm. I shuddered, the shaded porch blocking out the sun.

"Batko," I said.

"If Aunt Natalya's harmed, Jake, so help me God, I will send you to hell," Dave said. Jake didn't flinch; in fact, he smiled.

"Hell?" Jake asked. "I deserve it. And after today, it will be crowded. Right, brother? Are you looking forward to spending eternity with me?"

Maxim Medved was sweating, his face ashen, the remains of a lunch in front of him, marinated asparagus spears, pickled cabbage, and lamb chops. "My dear brother, you know I would lay down my life for my family."

"No, you wouldn't. But we're free to lay down our lives for you, brother. First Natalya, giving herself to the Nazis."

"I did willingly," Natalya said. "I would fight to death for you, small boys."

"You are a good woman, Natalya," Jake said, lip quivering. "A better person than me. I was so weak minded that my brother convinced me that beating that man who got in the way of his political goals would save the family's honor."

The judge strained for words. "It did."

"Not mine, it didn't. No one would look me in the eye after that, waiting for the murderer to come out. Even Oksana, so gentle, she disappeared without a trace because she thought I was a monster."

That was interesting. Even as we pursued the possibility that Oksana's blood was in the bathroom at Bernie's house, Jake still thought of her as missing. Perhaps she was. Or perhaps he didn't kill her.

"And then my son," Jake said. "My boy, who wanted nothing more than to live a life of honor, giving his life for his fellow soldiers, his country. You tried to make him kill Luisa. For what reason?" The judge opened and closed his mouth, but no words came out. "Don't tell me it was to get justice for your family, for Bernie. You would have killed her and left our brother to rot in prison for the rest of his life."

Jake's hand began to shake, an old man's quaver, the muscles worn. "You tried to get my son to do something dishonorable, and he couldn't do it. I wouldn't let him do it. And when you began to think that he might tell the truth to the police, you shot him. You shot my boy."

Dave raised his gun, pressing it to Jake's neck. "Drop the gun, Jake."

"You have no idea what you're doing." Jake craned his neck, trying to look at Dave, who forced the barrel of the gun harder into Jake's jaw. "You stupid child."

As Jake twisted around, Hale's hand shot out as quickly as a snake's tongue and grabbed the gun. He opened the barrel, let the cartridges fall to the floor, and then threw the shotgun over the porch onto the lawn. "Stupid child," Lucas said as he pushed the screen door open. "Is that what you thought of me, Jake, when you killed my mother to keep her quiet? Stupid child?"

I holstered my gun and confronted Lucas, chest to chest. He had showered and changed clothes, and his fine hair dripped water onto the collar of his green flannel shirt. He shoved me hard, unaware of me except as an object that stood between him and the person he thought had killed his mother, until I shoved him back.

"That monster," Lucas said, "deserves to die."

I watched as Hale slid around Dave, a head tilt letting me know he was going to subdue Lucas.

"Lucas, let me do this," Dave said, pressing the gun into Jake's side. "I'll make sure Mom's killer gets what's coming to him."

"David," Natalya talked over me, her voice calm. "David, *ne vbyty yoho*."

"What do you mean I don't need to kill my mother's murderer?" Dave's hands shook. "*Teta*, I thought you, more than anyone, would understand."

"Dave," I said gently, "listen to your aunt. This isn't justice. This is revenge. Let me arrest your mother's killer, send him to prison." I glanced over at the judge to see if he responded, but he sat silent and open-mouthed. "I'll make sure your mother's killer dies there."

Dave dropped his weapon, handing it to me grip first, and took a deep hitching breath, half sigh and half sob. "You're right. I don't need to do this."

"No," Natalya said, looking across the table to her lunch companion. "You do not need to kill your mother's killer. I already did."

CHAPTER 29

A KNIFE DROPPED OUT OF THE JUDGE'S HAND AND ONTO THE floor, clattering across the tile.

"Hemlock," she said. "I stop planting whole field of fruits and vegetables, and my landfills with hemlock." She waved to the open field. "Crop of poison."

Jake's eyes widened. "He's shaking. Is he in pain?"

"Some, I believe. I hope." She smiled. "Do not feign sorrow, Jacob, unless you grieve because I killed him first."

Maxim Medved slumped, his breath shallow, his fingertips blue. As Hale spoke quickly into his phone requesting an ambulance, I went to the dying man, grabbing his shoulders, trying to lower him gently to the ground. He smelled of Old Spice cologne and the faintest hint of gunpowder, and I found myself pinned under his bulk as his useless legs folded. Jake grabbed his brother's shoulders and together we laid him on his back, his feet elevated on his folded trench coat, trying to make sure any oxygen Maxim took in got to his brain.

His brother crouched next to him, slapping Maxim's cheeks to get the blood flowing, soft and then hard. The imprints of Jake's fingers on the judge's face didn't disappear, however, and his skin remained white. His circulatory system was shutting down. I reached across and stilled Jake's hands.

"What form did you use, Natalya?" I demanded. "For the hemlock?"

She pointed to the asparagus spears. "Green leaves? You see?"

"The stuff that looks like parsley?" Hale asked.

"Looks like, but is not," Natalya said. "Fronds from hemlock. Also, shredded root is in cabbage salad, and the lamb, it also has hemlock."

"He couldn't taste it?" Dave asked. "You always said growing up that we should never eat the plants that looked like wild carrots if they were bitter."

"But it takes single frond, barely anything, to kill. And Maxim had appetites. He was greedy, even as a child. Sour apples picked from tree or chocolate bars from American soldiers, he could never get enough." She looked as if she wanted to spit on him. "Food, power, women . . . never enough."

"Aunt Natalya," Dave's voice broke. "Judge Medved couldn't have children. It had to have been Jake, and when Mom tried to blackmail him, he—"

"Jake's violence, it was not in his nature. Maxim nurtured it, directing Jake which men to beat—Maxim was head and Jake was fist. And Jake took punishment. He went to prison—"

"You are proving my point, Aunt Natalya," Dave said. "Jake was capable of—"

Natalya held up her hand. "Jake was in prison during the time that Lucas was conceived. Maxim was not. Because of mumps, Maxim's wife Sonya was unable to have children. Maxim, he could. There were stories . . ." she moved closer to where I sat next to Maxim, her orthopedic shoe inches from Maxim's ear and pointed down at him with two twisted fingers, "of his proclivities."

I looked up at Natalya. "Proclivities?"

"Young women, they said, little more than children. A girl from

Odessa, who killed herself in shame when she discovered she was pregnant. A woman who worked at his brother Bernard's factory who had
a child out of wedlock, mother and child moving to Utica, and with
her stories she told of Maxim's perversions. Vera. These women . . .
these girls . . . were called liars, even by me." She stared down at
Maxim like a god at the day of reckoning. "Maxim, he said he owed
me his life because I helped him escape Nazis. I decided he should pay."

"But why not bring him to the police?" Dave said. "Things aren't
the same here, *teta*. We would have made sure justice was served."

"No, you would not!" Natalya shouted, coughing at the last
words and limping toward the rail of the porch, again an old woman.
"This morning you said you could not, David. You said I ruined all
hope of getting justice for Vera. You said I hid purse for too long
and if police had found note in 1983 instead of now . . ." Her hands
shook as she gripped the porch rail. "But I did not know of note,
and Taras . . . even when Vera was pregnant, he said Lucas was his,
and I knew no different. He treated Lucas like they shared blood. He
would have put down his life for both of you." Dave nodded along
with his aunt, but Lucas only stared down at the Judge, hand clenching and unclenching.

"That day," Natalya said, "when Luisa and I found purse in Bernard's house . . . and I saw all that blood, I knew Vera had died there,
and I thought it was at Bernard's hand and he must be brought low.
But I punished an innocent man, wronging him in worst way, rob-
bing him of life. I sent Luisa into exile and condemned you boys and
your father to a life of yearning always for a dead woman." Her hands
shook as she gripped the porch. "I had to make it right."

"By killing him?" Dave yelled. "*Teta*, you are not a murderer!"

"David, Stalin and Nazis stripped away our humanity, rotting our best parts with starvation, murder. Maxim, Jacob, me—"
Natalya said.

"You aren't like them," Lucas said. "You fed the hungry, you
protected the weak."

"I should have let Red Army capture Maxim, let him die in unmarked grave, like millions before him." Natalya dragged herself back to her chair. "Like Vera, in barrel of basement. Alone. Unmourned."

Shadows spread across the lawn as the last light faded and in the distance I heard approaching sirens. Dave brushed his shoulder against his brother, but Lucas pushed away, his eyes darting from his aunt to his brother to Maxim, helpless on the ground.

"Anything to say, my boys?" Natalya was panting. "To me or to him. He looks gone, but he can hear you."

"When you told me to build that wall," Lucas said, his voice expressionless, "was it some sort of joke to you? Having me bury my mother?"

"He can't answer, Lucas," I said. "You are never going to know."

"No. I was talking to Jake. Did you have me brick her in?"

Jake knelt, resting his hand on the seat of the chair his brother had been in, and slowly stood, facing Lucas.

"My brother didn't tell me Vera was in one of those barrels—I didn't even know she was dead until they found her after the fire. It seems that for once, my brother did his own dirty work. But I wouldn't have stopped him. I never did, not even when he asked my son to commit murder." Lucas pulled his fist back, but Dave grabbed Lucas's hand, pulling his brother away. Jake didn't notice.

"Has there been word on my boy?" Jake asked Hale, who guided him to the far end of the porch.

Sirens whined to a halt in front of the house, and I heard the clatter of paramedic equipment out front.

"There's not much time now, my boys," Natalya said, reaching out her hand. Dave let himself be pulled close, but Lucas stayed still and watchful.

"Anything to say, Lucas?" Natalya said. "The old man will soon be beyond our reach."

"Hi, Dad," Lucas said conversationally. He bared his teeth like an animal, a mockery of a smile, and I moved closer to him, ready for what I didn't know. Natalya had already done enough damage.

"You thought it was worth it to deny me." Lucas knelt, and I dropped beside him. "To deny who I was . . ." He took both hands and covered Medved's mouth and nose and pressed down. "To take my mother."

I tried to grab Lucas under his arms, but he clenched them to his sides, and I was peeling his fingers away one by one when Dave reached around and grabbed Lucas in a bear hug, pulling him free as he thrashed wildly.

"Lucas. Lucas," Dave said. "Please don't do this. Please don't. You're the only family I have left. If you kill a dying man . . ."

The emergency responders pulled the gurney up the steps, and Dave dragged his brother free.

"Do you have your mouth guard?" I asked the first paramedic. "It's hemlock, and even a blade—"

"We always have our mouth guards," he said. "Now give us room."

They strapped Judge Medved to the gurney and asked Hale to force air into the judge's lungs in steady intervals, manually pumping oxygen until they could get him on the ventilator. The metal wheels clattered against the brick steps as the group crashing down to the grass, covering the sound of Natalya's gentle fall.

"*Teta*," Dave said, his voice hoarse.

"The judge would not eat unless I joined him in meal," she said. "We always shared food." Crumpled on the ground, she looked scared. "I had to make it right."

CHAPTER 30

We MADE A DEAL: JAKE COULD STAY AT THE HOSPITAL UNTIL Brian woke up, but he had to tell Hale and me everything that happened to Luisa. Unfortunately, he was lying.

"My brother promised my son the bar if I killed Luisa."

The waiting room was packed with people hoping Brian and Natalya would live. Hale and I were the only people who were pulling for the judge to survive because we wanted to question him, although maybe Dave had his fingers crossed: He wanted to keep Natalya out of jail.

Hale, Jake, and I were camped in an empty patient room, propped up on a pair of beds. Could I leave a tip for housekeeping in the hospital? I felt guilty for messing up the sharp hospital corners, but I was too tired to stay standing.

"And you agreed," I said to Jake, "to cross state lines to conduct kidnapping and murder—"

"A federal offense," Hale added.

"Over a bar?"

"Sure," Jake said.

"That's not what you said earlier today." I stood up and started pacing. After Kevin's illness, the smell of hospital rooms left me ready to crawl out of my skin. In addition to calming me, I got to throw Jake off balance. He couldn't act nonchalant when he had to crane his neck to see me. "At Natalya's you said your brother coerced your son into committing the crime."

"You must have misheard. Maxim asked Brian to do it, and my son refused."

"And you agreed?" I asked. "Aren't you past your head-busting days?"

Jake flexed his arm, although I saw no visible difference in muscle tone. "I can still throw a case of beer around and Luisa didn't weigh much more than that. I knew I could do the job."

Hale raised one eyebrow at Jake. "But why?"

"When Brian came home from Afghanistan, all . . . broken," Jake clenched his fists, "I made a deal with the devil: I'd sign over the bar to Maxim, and he'd give me the property and cash for a house." Jake's eyes darted to the side, and I was beginning to think Jake had a reverse tell: He only made eye contact when he was lying. "My boy was not going to get better trapped on the second floor of a bar."

"So if the deal gave you what you wanted," I asked, "why'd you try to reverse the terms?"

"Brian needed a future. And that would only happen if he owned the bar."

"I don't understand what your brother got out of the deal," Hale said. "If he'd kept his mouth shut . . ."

"He was running scared. I was the first to spot her—just a flash across the screen. Didn't think anything of it at first, and showed it to Maxim as a laugh." He shook his head. "Seeing her . . . he turned to stone."

"Afraid of a new investigation?"

"I didn't think of that at the time, but now . . . yeah, he was worried. When he asked me to go, I signed right up because that bitch? She deserved to die. I was always the one that took care of people who stepped out of line."

"So walk me through it. Tell me the story of what happened in New Mexico."

Jake took a deep breath. "I lined up a fake ID, the van, the works, stuff I'd need to kill her and hide the body. But for the first time in my life, I panicked. I grabbed her, threw her in the back and drove back across country. But then I had second thoughts."

"About killing her?" Hale asked.

"About letting her live. I'd had to listen to her pissing and moaning across 2000 miles, and no way would Maxim trade for the bar if she was alive. So when I got back, I took her and the van over to Sleep-Tite and torched the whole thing."

"But killing Luisa wouldn't help Bernie get out of jail," I said.

"It would if I let the cops know who she was." He jutted out his chin. "And you would have received a call from the Albany Bus Station the day after she died."

"It's interesting," I said, "Because if I were going to arrange a hit on someone, I'd probably ask a person who'd been trained to kill. Like Brian."

Jake smiled meanly. "That's where you're wrong. The army didn't spend a whole lot of time on turning him into some kind of weapon. Him? He's such an honorable kid, they spent time training him to save lives." Jake smiled to himself. "He defused bombs and . . . he still gets letters. Men who wouldn't be around if it wasn't for him."

"Something I've made note of," Hale said, "You haven't once asked if your brother is alive or dead."

"Because I figure it might hurt my case if I talk about how much I hope he rots in hell. I never got away from my brother, and Brian was going to stay free and clear of him."

Chief Donnelly pushed open the door, and Jake jumped up. "Brian?"

"Your son is out of surgery," Donnelly said. "The doctor says—"

Jake sidestepped me, stopping only when the chief threw his arm across the doorway and grabbed the frame, blocking Jake's way.

"No visitors while he's in recovery," Donnelly said. "But Jake, your son, he has a good prognosis. They got the whole bullet, and he kept both his spleen and his kidney." He looked from me to Hale to Jake. "How's it going in here?"

"We made a deal he could stay until Brian woke up, but Jake isn't keeping up his end of the bargain."

"Mr. Medved here," Hale said, "is being less than honest."

Jake took offense. "Donnelly, couldn't it be you and me? You know I'd be straight."

"You know I can't do that, Medved. Look, you've had enough experience with this—you make a deal, even just over a handshake, and you have to live up to your side of things." Donnelly guided Jake back to the bed. "You're a man of your word, aren't you?"

Jake was not. He spent another fifteen minutes throwing out lie after lie. Finally, I gave up, reaching over and handcuffing Jake to the bed. "We'll let you stay here until we find out for sure how your son is. Then you'll be transported to jail." I turned to Hale. "I have some questions for the Lawlers and Dave, if he's up to it. Can you watch him?"

"Absolutely," Hale said, grabbing a pillow and lying down. "And since talking to Jake is going to just be a waste of time, I'm going to use my time wisely and nap."

The news about Brian had lifted the mood in the waiting room. When I'd left, Dave and Lucas had been on one side of the room, and the Medveds and the Lawlers had been on the other. Now the groups had mixed. I found Bernie, Dan, and Deirdre telling stories about Vera to Lucas. They didn't even notice me when I slipped inside and grabbed a chair in the corner.

"I was a little thing," Deirdre said. "And quiet as a mouse."

Dan laughed.

"Shut up," Deirdre said, but her husband's laughter lit her up.

"You know I was. With all the troubles at home and Bernie in high school, I made an easy target for bullies. They would corner me on the bus, so I'd walk, cutting through backyards to avoid the worst. They still caught me. One day Vera arrived when I was getting the crap kicked out of me—"

"Dee! I'm shocked!" Bernie said in mock horror. I watched as he gauged Lucas's response, upping his gestures to make Lucas smile. "Such language."

"Shut up, Bern," Deirdre said. "Anyway, Vera threw rocks at them until they ran away. Then she taught me a great trick. When the bullies are on your tail, and are about to catch you, turn around, stick your arm out straight, form a fist, and let the assholes run smack into you."

"A passive fistfight?" Lucas's lip quirked up.

Deirdre pointed at Bernie. "He's the Zen master, not me. But here's the thing, after I punched one guy in the nose, word got out, and no one messed with me again. I tried to thank your mother, but she wouldn't have it. Just told me to keep up the good fight."

Dave gave me a brief wave as he walked in, before going to Lucas and resting his hand on his brother's shoulder. "Who said that?"

"Mom." Lucas stood. "How's Natalya?"

"It's hard to say," Dave said. "She didn't get dosed the same way the judge did, but . . . she needs the ventilator."

"Can I go in now?" Lucas asked.

"Sure thing," Dave said. "But a warning. There are wires and tubes everywhere. If you were expecting the same bossy *teta*, you are not going to get it." He shoved both hands in his pockets. "She's weak."

Lucas touched Dave's shoulder on his way out the door.

"I should go visit the patient, too," Bernie said, standing.

"Brian's not . . . oh. You mean Maxim," Deirdre said.

"He's still our brother, Dee."

"He wasn't acting too brotherly when he set you up to go to

prison," Deirdre said. She stood, gathering her jacket and gesturing for her husband to follow.

Bernie shrugged. "I barely said hello to him. I should at least say good-bye."

"Say good-bye for me, too," she said. "I won't be making a visit." She walked up to Bernie, placing one hand on his cheek while kissing the other. "You were really the best of all of us."

"IS IT WRONG THAT I FEEL HAPPY?" DAVE ASKED ONCE WE WERE alone. "Lucas is a basket case, and Aunt Natalya might not make it. If she does, she's probably going to jail. But I feel at peace. For the first time in a long time. Maybe the first time in my life."

There was a low hum of activity in the hallway—a doctor being paged by the oncology department, the wheels of a gurney bouncing off the wall, a cry silenced. Normally I wouldn't have brought Natalya's crimes up at a time like this, but he had mentioned it first. "You know, prison is a very real possibility for your aunt."

"She wouldn't have it any other way," he said. "Not that we don't already have Deirdre on retainer. Natalya's sense of responsibility, well she is also going to want to face the firing squad." He looked down at his hands, twisted together in his lap. "Me, too. I did some not-so-great stuff. I hope I don't lose my job, Lyons. My dad and Natalya did right by me, but the best part of myself? Comes from the work we do." His chin softened, and I thought he might cry. Instead he winked. "Plus Annie needs someone to yell at."

I ignored his joke. "I hope you get to keep your job, too. But as your friend? Please, please go talk to someone. Get some help." He laughed, but I kept my face serious. "I mean it, Dave."

There were whispers from the corridor. I turned around to find Theo being pushed backward through the door by Nate.

"Just talk to him," Nate said, stepping left and then right to prevent his brother from leaving the room. "You don't have to be best friends."

Theo tripped back and Nate grabbed his arm, steadying him. Theo turned around, looking past us, his eyes scanning the room. Finally, he spoke.

"Is my father here?"

THE NEXT TWO WEEKS SWUNG BETWEEN NO MOVEMENT AND rapid progress on the cases. Brian Medved looked like he'd make a full recovery, at least physically. He awoke, calling for his father, but went silent after hearing that Jake was in jail for the kidnapping of Luisa. The Judge remained unconscious. His brain waves read active but his blood oxygen remained low. The doctors couldn't figure out if he was in a coma, or just pretending to be unconscious, their pokes and prods met with absolute stillness.

Natalya was a different story. Her brain waves and heartbeat remained weak, and the ventilator periodically stopped, as if she was holding her breath.

"The doctor's said she's got a 50 percent shot," I said.

"My aunt is making up her mind, trying to figure out whether she wants to live," Dave said. "You, me, the doctors—none of us will get a vote if she decides she's done."

And then there was Oksana. Despite running DMV, Social Security, and tax record searches on the missing woman, it seemed as if Oksana had disappeared off the face of the earth in 1986. We even checked with the Association of Legal Secretaries, but there wasn't a single Oksana on their list. I was ready to take a crack at Jake, currently out on bail, when I arrived at my desk to find a pink slip with Lorraine's perfect Palmer penmanship.

"Tomas Wolschowicz was here. All day." The words "all day" were underlined three times. I tried his number, but he didn't answer, and I promised myself to call him in the morning.

When I showed up at work the next day at 7:30, Tomas was waiting for me, sitting on a bench in the reception area, quiet and very, very sober.

"My sister," he said. "Do you have word on the DNA?"

"Let me make a call," I said. He sat in the chair next to my desk, hands folded, waiting as I dialed Hale's number.

"What can I do for you this fine morning?" Hale said, alarmingly chipper.

"Agent Bascom, I'm looking to see if the DNA results came in."

"From the basement wall?" Hale asked. "Didn't we get positive ID that it was Vera's?"

"No, not the basement. I'm sitting here with Tomas Wolscho- wicz and am looking for results from," Tomas sat straighter, listening in, and I kept my question vague. Asking about the blood in the tub and drain at Bernie's house seemed like a cruel thing to do in front of him. "Do we have the results from the other location?"

"Oh, of course," Hale said. "Let me call the labs."

I hung up, explaining that we hoped to have an answer soon.

"I can wait," he said. I offered him coffee, but he declined, and as I typed up reports, he sat quietly.

I got up to retrieve my first document from the printer. Tomas was looking at the far wall, where "missing" posters were tacked up, sometimes overlapping.

"Would Oksana have had one of those?"

"Oksana did. Jake reported her missing three years after she dis- appeared, and it's standard to create one."

Tomas was now standing. "Is Oksana's poster over there now?"

I looked over the wall of smiling faces, mostly teenagers. "Usu- ally those are just the current cases, but give me a second." I opened up my computer, clicking through until I arrived at the National Missing and Unidentified Persons Systems. I typed in her name, and her face popped up. It was hard to see any resemblance between Tomas and his sister other than their blue eyes, hers bright and alert, his hidden under heavy lids.

"See," I said. "She's in the system."

Tomas leaned close to the screen and then sat back. He needed bifocals. I offered to print him a copy.

"Good idea," he said, nodding. "That way if we need to still look for her, I can make copies and hang 'em up."

I had a feeling that there wouldn't be a hunt for Oksana after the DNA tests came in. When we compared the typewriter in the judge's office to Oksana's letters to her brother, they were an exact match— Maxim Medved had been sending those birthday presents to Tomas. When I asked Jake Medved about her during one of our interrogation sessions, he wasn't surprised.

"Those letters didn't start coming until after I reported Oksana missing," he said. "Before that, all quiet. I thought she'd run away from me, and I hoped maybe if someone found her they'd make her come home." Jake dropped the belligerent attitude he'd held for all our interviews. "But now I know. Maxim killed her."

I asked him why.

"You heard all those stories from Natalya, about the girls he ruined." Jake stared up at the corner of the interrogation room. I was happy to let him do it, since it meant he was being honest. "I don't think it was their age that attracted him. Well, not only their age. My brother, if you told him something was off limits, he grabbed for it. Oksana was mine, the first person to see me as me and not Maxim's brother, the first woman to love me. My brother could not let that stand. Not when she was so very, very lovely." Jake traced the vein on his left arm from the wrist up, a gentle soothing movement. "He had killed Vera. He knew where to do it, and he knew he was smart enough to pull it off." His face was grim. "If you don't find Oksana living in Arizona? Look under the rosebushes at his house."

I gave Tomas a copy of the poster, and he read her details closely— height, weight, and age—and ran his finger over her picture.

"She was so pretty," he said. "I'm really going to work to find her this time."

He jumped when my phone rang. Hale. Tomas held his breath as I picked up the phone.

"June?" Hale said. "That blood in the bathroom was a match, or close enough to it. We did a check . . ."

As Hale talked, Tomas watched me, his grip on the poster tightening.

"Let me call you back, Hale."

I hung up and leaned forward on my knees, making eye contact with Tomas, who stared at the floor. "I have some bad news about Oksana."

Two days later, Oksana's remains were found under the rosebushes. We added those murder charges to the ones the judge was already facing.

LUISA WOKE UP.

She didn't stay awake for long, the pain medications sending her slipping in and out of consciousness. By the time we arrived the first day, she was sleeping deeply—not in a coma, but unreachable. On the second we arrived to find a crowd clustered around her, Nate and Darius each holding a hand and Elda perched on the bed, petting the soft gray hair that had grown on Luisa's scalp, almost an inch in length at this point. When we asked Luisa to identify her attacker, she looked at Theo before answering.

"My memories of that time are lost," she said. "Before, I remember my house, the sun in my backyard in New Mexico. But how I got here? It's gone." She closed her eyes, drifting off, then woke with a start. "All that's in the past now, right? It doesn't matter."

It would be quite some time before she could stand up to a questioning. Theo and Nate had nothing to add, and spent much of their time holed up in the first floor lounge talking with Bernie about the new business they were going to start.

"June!" Nate said. "Nana's going to build us a factory."

So Elda was "Nana" now. Bernie's grin was just as wide, but his comments were more measured. "Possibly."

Dan Jaleda had offered to swap the Sleep-Tite land for a factory downtown, and Theo and Bernie debated rebuilding versus gutting, taping huge sheets of paper with to-do lists and graphs charted out, as if they planned to move in.

"The retail space would be hard without a more visible storefront," Theo said, pointing to a place where the graph dipped.

"Retail would be a small part of what we are doing," Bernie said. "We need super-clean indoors."

"Going into biotech?" I asked.

"No, no," Nate said. Outdoor wear."

"I kept up on all the trade journals while I was away," Bernie said, pulling out a stack of magazines that had been heavily flagged. "The advances in fabrics are amazing, and I have a few ideas . . . and Nate and Theo will know what our customers will want."

"I love it already," Nate said. "We'll be in the perfect location to catch people heading up north to fish or heading to Vermont to ski or climb."

"Plus we're close to the New York City weekend places," Theo said. "Those folks who kit out in full gear for a walk around the block. You'll have a huge market."

"Good luck with your venture," I said. "I think it would be wonderful to have a new business down here, one with real jobs, not service jobs."

"Me, too," Bernie said, and the men returned to their plans.

I WAS ALMOST SORRY TO SEE MY MOTHER GO. I WATCHED HER pack, her suitcase was only half full. Her cotton shifts didn't take up much room and her crystal collection had been coopted by Lucy, who asked to keep Grandma's "jewels" in Hopewell Falls for safekeeping until she visited again.

Mom held up a sage stick in a plastic bag. "Do you want to keep this? It will help you purify spaces."

"No thank you, Mom," I said.

"Perhaps David would like it," Mom said. "He seems so proud of the house he's rehabilitating and the dark spirits in his life . . . he's probably ready to clean them out."

"Probably," I said. The doorbell rang. "That's probably him, coming to say his good-byes."

Dave had practically moved into my house. He and my father dumped all their case files related to Vera and Luisa in the shredder, carefully recycling them under my mother's watchful eye. My mother stuffed him with vegetarian dishes whose recipes he wrote down, promising to re-create them later. I'd leave my father and Dave talking as I went to bed at night and wake up to my mother making him coffee.

"Is he living here?" I asked.

"He needs family," my mother said. "We all do."

I opened the door. "I don't know why you rang the bell. You know the side door is always unlocked."

Dave stepped inside, grabbing me into a hug. "Aunt Natalya made her decision." His breath was hot on my shoulder as he huddled closer. "She's gone."

We talked about how hard she'd fought to live, always on her own terms, right and wrong clear in her mind, unbreakable laws she applied to herself and everyone around her.

"It made her so strong," Dave said. "But with what she did to Bernie and even the Judge . . . she was brutal, too. She deserved to go to trial, even go to prison for what she did . . . and she agreed."

"Does Lucas know?" Mom asked.

The first week, Lucas had stayed by Natalya's bedside nonstop. After that he'd started to go to the bar, keeping it open while Brian was in the hospital. When Dave nagged him about why, he shrugged.

When I asked him, Lucas was more honest. "I can't be around Dave right now. I don't know where I belong."

"He knows," Dave said. "Refused to close the bar."

Mom asked me for my computer, wanting to cancel her flight and stay with Dave, but he refused, telling her to keep her reservation. He'd taken a huge liking to my mother. Oddly, so had I. I found myself sorry that she was leaving and made promises to bring my father, Lucy, and even Dave down once school ended.

"I'd like that," she said. "I'd like that a lot. Or you could come on your own, June, for a few days. We could have a girls' weekend."

We burst out laughing. Neither of us were spa day types of people, me because I was too busy, and my mother because she considered nail polish remover an environmental crime.

"Maybe a weekend in the sunshine," I said. "That would be nice."

"You, too." Mom grabbed Dave's hand. "I'm planning to come up more often. Larry's mother is still in a nursing home up here, and it would be nice to see my granddaughter." She pushed my hair away from my forehead. "And my daughter."

My father and Dave drove her to the airport. Dad returned alone. I was sitting at the dining room table coming up with a pro and con list.

"What's that you got there?" he asked tentatively. Since our blow up, he had been trying not to pry into my professional life, but it was reaching absurd proportions, with him barely acknowledging I was a cop.

"This column," I said, pointing to the one on the left, "is all the reasons to not rejoin the FBI." I listed off the reasons, which included "Lucy," "danger," and "not enough black suits."

He frowned—the "Lucy" item was upsetting him. I moved to the pro column.

"I also have good reasons to rejoin. I could do challenging work, stuff I spent years training for. I could make Kevin proud, since he always wanted me to be the best—Lucy, too." I skimmed down the list. "Donnelly has offered to hold my job for six months, which means I have some job security." Dad moved closer, trying to peek at the list, and I pulled it close. "And I know you will be there for Lucy the same way you were there for me when I was little. The same way you're there for me now."

Dad smiled. "Sounds like you have a tough decision to make. Maybe you should give Hale a call, hash it through with him."

"I know what I want," I said. "I've made up my mind."

I dialed Hale's number. The phone rang three then four times. I was ready to leave a message when Hale picked up.

"Bascom here," he said.

"I'm in."

ACKNOWLEDGMENTS

MANY PEOPLE HELPED ME CREATE THIS NOVEL. THANKS TO everyone at William Morrow: Rachel Kahan, my editor, for her instincts on story, editorial guidance, and expertise in botanicals; Trish Daly, for her attention to detail and unfailing support; and the entire team, including Ashley Marudas, Camille Collins, David Palmer, and Mandy Kain.

Thanks to all the people that lent their expertise in police procedure, legal defense, and the medical treatment of burn victims, including Amy Phillips and Stephen Frum. Any mistakes are all mine.

My writing group continues to challenge me to improve my writing, giving me critiques that are both incisive and kind. Special thanks to Kate Curry, Nita Gill, Tambi Harwood, Maggie King, and Lou Moore.

In addition to my readers, I received so much love and support from friends and family during this whole process: my mother, Maureen, and my sisters, Bridget and Mary; Michelle Ginthner, Kathy Riggins, Deane Shokes, Vicky Baron, and Rik Nicholson.

Finally, special thanks go to my agent, Lisa Gallagher. Her tireless advocacy for the books at every stage has been unmatched, and I really, truly couldn't have done it without her.